a tale of enduring love

tashi

PAUL BREER

ISBN
978-1-958690-34-5 (Paperback)
978-1-958690-35-2 (eBook)

TABLE OF CONTENTS

Preface

While several people have glanced at one version or another of Tashi, there is one person in particular to whom I am especially indebted. Her name is Sheryl Bailey, a good friend and herself a writer-in-the-making. Her unerring instincts for a good story have led to several changes and/or additions, each a pivotal contribution to the unfolding narrative. If the events described in the text come together in a meaningful way, it is due in no small measure to her efforts.

1   First Meeting

It is early afternoon as she makes her way up the trail that links her parent's summer house with the cottage just ahead, these two being the only dwellings for miles around. She is aware, although she has never gone the whole way, that the trail circumambulates the lake, dipping to the shore on one occasion where a small mountain brook passes beneath a wooden bridge. As all hikers here know, the path tends to narrow in summertime as thistles, scrub oaks and wild raspberries flourish along the edge and compete for the open, sun-filled space. With this in mind, she moves cautiously, raising her bare arms whenever the overhanging shoots and branches threaten to touch her body.

This is her first hike of the summer. After nine months of school in Back Bay, Boston, she is eager to exchange her blue and white school uniform for the tank top and shorts of life in the woods where the grit of the city gives way to a quiet broken only by the wind, rain, birds and frogs. "Yes, it is lonely here," she murmurs, "but I can use e-mail to stay in touch with my friends. Anyway, I can fill my notebook with stuff for the poems and essays I'll have to write for English class next fall." Any doubts she has are quickly forgotten as the path makes a sharp right turn to reveal a white-tailed doe and her two fawns, one of which is nursing. She stops in her tracks, not daring to breathe lest she violate the sanctity of the scene. It is only after the deer move on that she exhales and continues up the path. All thoughts are banished as she is once again enveloped in the sounds and smells of the forest.

A few steps on, she is startled to hear someone playing the piano. The music appears to be coming from the modified A-frame just ahead, the cottage which her mother said has been bought recently by someone from Boston who, hard as it is to believe given the severity of Adirondack winters, intends to live there all year around. Unlike her parent's house which is only a stone's throw from the dirt road linking both houses to the town, this cedar-shingled cottage with its massive flagstone chimney sits secure in its privacy within the embrace of a dense copse of white pines sprinkled with smooth, gray-barked beeches. Still curious, she leaves the main trail and follows a smaller path up to the porch where a screen door stands guard against a host of winged intruders. She stops to listen.

Her first thought is that someone is practicing. But it quickly becomes clear from the way the pianist keeps trying out new phrases that he is not practicing but composing. And how do I know that it is a man, she asks herself. The answer comes quickly. Who else but a man, a very unusual man at that, would buy a house out here with the intention of staying throughout the numbing rigors of a Northern winter? But it is the music itself that captures her attention. It has a romantic spirit, uplifting perhaps but nevertheless plaintive in its searching, the kind of music that stirs one's deepest longings, but ends without offering any kind of resolution. As she moves to look inside, hoping for a glimpse of the composer, the music stops.

"Who's there?" the man queries, rising from his piano bench and coming to the door.

"It's just me," she answers shyly, conscious that she is intruding. "I'm sorry that I disturbed you. I really like your music."

"Well, in that case, you might as well come inside." Then, in a voice at once curious and welcoming, he asks, "What's a young girl like you doing out here in the woods?"

"I'm your neighbor," she replies softly, looking around the living room. "We have the other house down the road, the one you pass on your way here from town. We come up from Boston every summer . . . as soon as school is over."

"So, you're no stranger to these parts. You probably know the woods better than I do (*motioning for her to sit down*). What's your name?"

"Eleanor. Kids at school call me Ellie, but I don't like it. It sounds so, well, kinda preppy I guess."

"What do your parents call you?"

"Eleanor. That's even worse . . . (*pause*) . . . What's your name?"

"Richard."

"Do you live here all by yourself (*still standing*)?"

"Not entirely. I have a cat. If we're quiet, he may come and introduce himself . . . but he's pretty shy with strangers . . . (*pause*) . . . Why don't you sit down . . . I can get you a Coke or something."

"But you're working on some music, aren't you? I don't want to get in the way . . . (*pause*) . . . Is it O.K. if I watch?"

"Well . . . (*pause*) . . . why not? You can sit there on the couch if you want to."

"Can I sit next to you on the bench? I've never seen anyone compose before."

"Alright . . . but keep in mind that listening to someone write music can be hard on the ears . . . lots of stopping and starting . . . playing the same notes over and over until they sound right. It's not like listening to a finished piece."

"That's O.K. I do a lot of stopping and starting when I practice my cello . . . and that can be hard on the ears too. Just ask my father."

"You play the cello? That's great. It's one of my favorite instruments. How long have you been playing?"

"I started when I was 9. I'm 14 now . . . so five years. I traded in my learner's cello for an adult one a while ago. I'm still getting used to it . . . but I like the sound a lot better. Trouble is, it's a lot harder to lug back and forth to school. But my mom usually comes and gets me."

"I'd like to hear you play sometime. Maybe we can try our hand at a cello-piano duet."

"That would be cool, Richard . . . (*pause*) . . . Is it O.K. if I call you Richard?"

"Sure (*smiling*) . . . But I guess I'll have to call you Ellie even though you don't like it too much."

As he returns to the piano bench and begins playing, she sits down next to him . . . at the far end of the bench. He quickly becomes absorbed in his piece which gives her a chance to look at him without his knowing it. His nose has an aquiline character, she notices, suggesting a seriousness of purpose, an impatience with all things smacking of the trivial. As he lifts his head to scan the watercolor on the wall, his eyes sparkle with the clarity of a raptor scrutinizing the heavens from its cliff-side aerie. By turning her head slightly she can see where his curly brown hair hangs low on his neck, obscuring the tops of his ears. Her eyes are drawn now to the stubble on his chin, clear evidence that he didn't shave this morning, maybe yesterday as well. When you live alone, she reflects, you really don't have to worry about those things. Turning finally to his fingers as they move up and down the keyboard, infusing each note with a power and mystery beyond the reach of words, she concludes that he is very much a man, but not one she has to be afraid of. As he draws the piano into a wordless dialogue between upper and lower voices, one questioning, the other answering, she inches closer. Against her will, the drama swiftly becomes her own, a thinly-concealed bid for oneness, a hunger for love, a hunger of which she is only dimly aware. She leans over the keys, head down, eyes closed, her whole body twisting and turning with the music, relaxing only when the last chord has faded into silence.

"Well . . . what do you think?" he asks finally, turning to his guest as his hands drop into his lap.

"It's really beautiful Richard. It gets to me the same way Tchaikovsky's Piano Concerto does or one of those by Rachmaninov. But it seems to end without getting anywhere . . . I mean, it leaves you feeling up in the air . . . neither happy nor sad (*pause*) . . . but maybe that's the way you want it to be. Is it?"

"I'm not sure . . . (*pause*) . . . I didn't have a plan in mind when I started the piece . . . just followed my feelings . . . which is not always a good idea in composing. If it lacks a good ending, I can always use it as the slow movement of a longer piece. That might give it more structure. Now . . . how about that drink I promised?"

"I should probably head back home. Mom will be wondering where I am . . . (*pause*) . . . Can I come back sometime . . . and bring my cello?"

"Of course. But how are you going to get it up here?"

"The case has wheels on it; I can roll it up the trail. I'm stronger than I look (*flexing her arm*)."

"I see."

As she gets up to leave, Richard's cat comes out from behind a chair and rubs against her leg. She kneels to pet him. "Oh, he's beautiful. What's his name?"

"Kwatz. It's a Japanese name I heard when I was studying Buddhism. Zen masters shout 'Kwatz' at their novices when they fall asleep during meditation. Apparently it wakes them up . . . it certainly worked on me when I attended retreats, but I've never had occasion to try it on my little friend here. He is unusually sensitive to sounds, so much so that I have to be careful about sneezing or coughing. With any loud sound he gets scared and jumps off my lap. He's pretty paranoid in general . . . but that's the main reason he's still alive today . . . unlike his brother whose recklessness proved to be his undoing."

"What do you mean?"

"Tashi was the bravest cat you could imagine . . . in addition to being one of the most handsome. I remember the day when I looked out the window . . . this was when I was living in Vermont . . . and saw him facing off against 23 wild turkeys. He was three months old at the time. Not too many weeks later I watched in disbelief as he chased an adult raccoon into the woods."

"So, you're saying his courage got him into trouble?"

"One late afternoon, right after I had been playing with both cats on the lawn in front of the house, he disappeared into the woods . . . and never returned. I looked for him everywhere . . . even inquired at my nearest neighbor's home which was almost a mile away. Nobody had seen him."

"What do you think happened to him?"

"The woods in rural Vermont are full of predators . . . bobcats, bears, owls, even mountain lions . . . but the most likely killer is what the locals call the fisher-cat . . . a mink-like animal with prodigious strength and a ferocious appetite, especially for domestic cats who wander too far from home. Unlike his brother, Tashi had no respect for danger . . . and he paid the ultimate price for his insouciance."

"That's really sad. Was he completely black like Kwatz?"

"No . . . even more handsome . . . a striking combination of black and white . . . tuxedo-like . . . with white face, bib and paws . . . and a pink nose . . . everything else black."

"You called him Tashi? That's a beautiful name."

"It's a Tibetan boy's name I got from a book on Buddhist philosophy."

"I wish I had a name like that. It's a lot more interesting than Eleanor."

"Eleanor is a bit stiff . . . but Ellie sounds pretty good."

"You're being nice . . . but that's O.K . . . (*pause*). . .now it's really time for me to go. I may have stayed too long already . . . (*pause*) . . . have I?"

"Not at all. I enjoyed the company. Come back whenever you want. I'm here most of the time . . . and yes, bring your cello. I have a few short pieces that I can arrange for duet if you want. It should be fun."

"Is it O.K. if I come tomorrow afternoon?"

"Well . . . (*pause*) . . . why not?"

"I'm glad you're the one who bought this house and not some creepy old guy who shoos intruders off with a shotgun. There are people like that up in the mountains I hear."

"Yes. I know. I'm glad you don't see me as one of them. I probably qualify as old, at least in your eyes, but I hope not creepy. And I don't own a gun. So, maybe I'm pretty safe."

"You don't look very old."

"I'm 32."

"Eighteen years older than me. That's not all that much. I know of a family where the husband is 30 years older than his wife."

"Are you planning on marrying me (*chuckling*)? I thought we just met."

"Who knows? It might happen. I think we're pretty compatible, don't you?"

"It's a little early to know for sure . . . but at any rate, I'm glad you dropped over. It's nice to know that I have a neighbor who loves music. See you tomorrow."

2   A Duet

Rising from the breakfast table, Richard heads to the piano to work on the piece he played for Ellie the day before. The desire to complete the piano sketch and get it orchestrated is as strong as ever . . . but something has changed. He is aware of doubts infecting his mind, robbing him of easy access to his muse. Perhaps he is more than a little troubled by her remark that the piece lacks any kind of definitive ending, leaving the listener's emotions unresolved. He can't be sure. All he knows is that there is a new tightness around his chest . . . a constriction of muscle that is holding any new ideas at bay. He sits at the bench, staring at the score before him, imprisoned in his unknowing . . . so much so that he doesn't hear the knock at the door.

"Richard, it's me, Ellie. Can I come in?"

The voice is familiar, even if faintly disturbing. "Oh, Ellie, sure. C'mon in. How long have you been standing there?"

"Just a minute or two. You must really be into your piece. Is it going well?"

"Not exactly. I seem to be stuck with this ending. Maybe you can help me."

"Can I bring my cello in? It's out on the porch."

"By all means. So, you managed to cart it all the way up here by yourself . . . strong girl."

"I think the wind was behind me (*giggling*). Or maybe God did it."

"You believe in God?"

"Well, yes . . . I think so. Don't you?"

"No. But that's a topic for another day. Why don't you set up over here (*pointing to the area to his right*). I arranged an old piano piece for

"

cello-piano duet last night after dinner. It should be easy for you to sight-read. You do sight-read, don't you?"

"I'm pretty good at it, at least my teacher, Mr. Putnam, says so . . . By the way, what did you have for dinner last night?"

"Hmm . . . some frozen chicken dish, I think. Why do you ask?"

"Well, it's just that I'm a pretty good cook . . . or at least becoming one. My Dad is teaching me some awesome Palestinian dishes. If you want me to, I could cook something for you at home and bring it over . . . or I could cook it here . . . whatever you like."

"That's really nice of you, Ellie. Maybe I'll take you up on it someday. I didn't know you were Palestinian."

"My father is. My Mom is just plain American . . . you know, a little of this, a little of that . . . (*pause*) . . . By the way I've changed my name. My new name is Tashi . . . as long as that's O.K. with you."

"Are you serious? Sure it's O.K . . . but that's a big step . . . to change your name suddenly like that, even if it's only a nickname. Did you tell your parents about it?"

"Yeah. They think I'm being silly. As far as they're concerned, I'm Eleanor and always will be. But that's O.K. I'll tell my friends at school in the fall and they'll go along."

"So, what's your last name?"

"Said. It's spelled S-A-I-D even though it's pronounced Sa-EEED."

"Tashi Said. It does have a nice ring to it. Are you related to Edward Said, the author?""

"I don't know. I don't think so . . . What's your name?"

"Dunwoody. Scotch."

"Dunwoody sounds like some kind of tree . . . or bush maybe (*giggling*)."

"I think my ancestors were Druids . . . you know, those folks in medieval Britain who worshipped white oaks. Some people say they were cannibals too."

"You're kidding (*eyes and mouth open wide*)."

"Maybe (*smiling*). Anyhow, I had a big breakfast, so you don't have to worry."

"Whew! My lucky day (*laughing*)."

Richard: "Shall we try the piece I arranged? (*placing the score on her music stand*)."

"Sure. Give me a minute or two to look the score over . . . (*pause*) . . . Is this a low E or a C . . . (*pointing*) . . . ?"

Richard: "E . . . sorry. My writing can get a little sloppy at times."

Tashi: (*turning the page*) . . . "O.K . . . . I think I'm ready."

Richard: "Let's see if we can get ourselves in tune first" (*strikes an A below middle C*) . . . (*listens to her A*) . . . Can you come up a hair? . . . (*she tightens a string and plays another A*) . . . That's better. O.K. the piece starts pretty slow . . . andante . . . and then picks up half-way through. You come in at the fifth measure. During the slow part the dynamic is pretty soft . . . say pp . . . ready?"

Tashi: "Yes."

The piano opens softly with broad, arpeggiated chords, setting the stage for the cello to enter with its wordless song, rising in eighth-notes to join the piano in a soaring celebration of oneness, only to turn and descend the scale short of its quest, content ultimately to settle for the quiet of surrender.

Tashi: "Richard, that's gorgeous. I missed a few notes there in the middle, but the part you wrote for me is awesome. Are you going to give the piece a name?"

Richard: "Glad you liked it. You sight-read really well. I'm impressed. As far as the name is concerned, I haven't given it any thought. Do you have any suggestions?"

Tashi: "Well, it's really romantic . . . but like the piece you were working on yesterday, it seems to be working toward something . . . like a goal . . . but never gets there."

Richard: "Like Sisyphus?"

Tashi: "Who's that?"

Richard: "A character from a novel by Camus . . . someone he borrowed from Greek mythology. It's about a man in Hades who is condemned to carry a heavy stone up a mountainside; he tries over and over, but is never allowed to reach the top."

Tashi: "How sad . . . (*pause*) . . . Is that the way you feel?"

Richard: "On my good days (*grinning*)."

Tashi: "You want to call it Sisyphus then?"

Richard: "Why not? But let's try it again. I think if you play a little louder, especially in the slow section, you can make the main theme even clearer. Maybe the piano was a tad too strong at that point; that's easily remedied. But I really like the rich tone you get in the low and middle registers. I can tell that you put your heart into it. The higher notes, those on your A string, are still a bit weak, but that should improve with practice."

Tashi: "Thanks. You say I put my heart into my playing. That's easy when the music is beautiful. The orchestra leader at school, Mr. Putnam, says that music is a window on the composer's soul. What he meant I guess was that you can tell certain things about a composer from the music he writes . . . things he might not want to tell you in everyday conversation . . . (*pause*) . . . Do you think that's true of you?"

Richard: "Probably. But I can't be sure. I just write what bubbles up from some place inside me. I never stop to analyze it. If I did, it might stop bubbling."

Tashi: "That makes sense. As for me, I just find this whole thing exciting . . . you know, playing a duet with you . . . especially when you've written the piece just for me . . . well, I should say *arranged* the piece for me . . . (*pause*). Do you have any more pieces we could play together?"

Richard: "Not right now, but if you want, I can arrange more of my old piano pieces for cello-piano duet. There's a bunch of them tucked away in my file drawer. At least some of them should lend themselves to transcription. From time to time I use the more lyrical ones when I'm improvising at the restaurant."

Tashi: "You play at the restaurant (*excitedly*) . . . you mean the Saranac Inn down in the village?

Richard: "Yup. Every Saturday night . . . in the busy seasons . . . meaning summer and winter. It's a lot of fun. I make a few bucks and it gives me a chance to try out some new pieces."

Tashi: "That's awesome. Do people actually listen to you when they're eating and talking?"

Richard: "A few definitely listen. Some of them even come up to me and make requests . . . usually popular songs that I don't know. And then, of course, there is the occasional loudmouth who drinks too much and makes a fool of himself. But, in general, it's a nice gig."

Tashi: "Do you think they might like to hear us play your Sisyphus piece?"

Richard: "I hadn't thought of it . . . but they might. It's the kind of music most of them seem to enjoy. When I started, the manager asked me to refrain from playing anything too raucous . . . so I stick to slow, romantic numbers. Our Sisyphus piece is all of that."

Tashi: "That sounds so nice Richard . . . to hear you say *our* Sisyphus piece. I know that *you* wrote it . . . but it already feels like something we created together."

Richard: "I would never have arranged it for cello and piano if you hadn't come along. Now, if you want, I'll give Tim a call, he's the manager, and see if it's O.K.to bring you along. But we'll probably need a few more pieces before going live."

Tashi: "I'm free just about every day this summer. Just tell me when to come over . . . (*pause*) . . . Is tomorrow a good time?"

Richard: "Better give me a couple of days to put the arrangements together. Let's say next Monday or Tuesday."

Tashi (*softly*): That seems like a long way off. Can I come and listen while you do the arrangements. I might have some ideas about what works best on the cello . . . (*pause*) . . . I promise not to get in the way."

Richard: "O.K. But I work best when there's no talking."

Tashi: "I'll just sit and listen . . . unless you ask me something. Now I better go . . . (*pause*) . . . When do you think we'll be ready to play at the Inn?"

Richard: "Maybe a week from Saturday. I don't know . . . it depends on how fast I can do the arranging. My guess is that we'll need at least three or four duets to fill out the evening. Of course, I'll be playing some pieces for piano solo in between."

Tashi: "I'll ask my parents if it's O.K. at dinner. They better say yes."

Richard: "Or what?"

Tashi: "Or I'll leave home and come live with you."

Richard: "I think you better get their permission (*smiling*)."

Tashi: "To come live with you (*eyes sparkling*)?"

Richard: "No silly . . . to play at the Inn."

Tashi: "I was only kidding."

Richard: "Hmmm."

Tashi: "Oops. I almost forgot . . . (*opening the cello case and taking out a dish wrapped in aluminum foil*) . . . I made you some hummus, with a special recipe that my dad taught me. You do like hummus, don't you?"

Richard: "That's really thoughtful of you, Ellie. It just so happens that I . . . "

Tashi (*interrupting*): "Tashi . . . please."

Richard: "Excuse me . . . Tashi . . . hummus is one of my favorites. I've tried lots of kinds but I've never had the Palestinian version . . . (*taking the dish and placing it in the refrigerator*). I'll try it with chips tonight. Thank you."

Tashi: "It's good on potato skins and stuff like that . . . just be sure to think of me as you're eating it. I was thinking of you all the time I was making it."

Richard: "I promise . . . (*pause*) . . . Now, can you get that cello down the trail without any trouble?"

Tashi: "Of course. But if I run into any problems, can I scream for help?"

Richard: "Count on me. I'll bring my first-aid kit just in case."

Tashi: "I may need to be carried home (*giggling*)."

Richard: "Don't worry. I have a wheelbarrow."

Tashi: "Ugh . . . Bye."

3   At the Restaurant

By the morning of the gig the two musicians have practiced each piece several times . . . enough to satisfy Richard's critical ear. "We're probably not good enough for Carnegie Hall yet," he tells his new friend, "but we're more than O.K. for a restaurant. We have four short pieces we can spread out over the time we're there. In between I can do my usual solo stuff with Chopin, Brahms, Schubert and the like."

"They sound really good to me too, Richard, so good that people may stop talking just to listen. I know I would."

Richard: "That would be nice . . . just as long as they don't stop eating and drinking (*chuckling*). Tim wouldn't like it if they just sat there, taking in the music. Now . . . shall I pick you up at your house about 6:00? Tim wants us ready to go by 6:30."

Tashi: "That's fine with me."

Richard: "Another thing . . . don't eat before I pick you up. We get dinner on the house at the end of the evening; that means around 9:30 . . . so nibble on some appetizers, but don't go all out on cheeseburgers and French fries."

Tashi: "No problem . . . (*pause*) . . . My parents may come to watch us; they're eager to see me play."

Richard: "Are you O.K. with that?"

Tashi: "I had to say O.K. to get their consent. They want to make sure that it's a proper environment for their little daughter. And they especially want to find out what you're like. I've raved about you for two weeks now."

Richard: "I'm eager to meet them as well . . . to make sure they're suitable parents for my new friend (*laughing*)."

Tashi (*eyes softening*): I like the way you said that. I know you were joking, but it sounds like you want to protect me . . . (*pause*) . . . do you?"

Richard: "Ask me later. I've got some stuff to do before we meet. It's time for you to be getting home."

Tashi: "O.K. I'll see you at 6:00. Just don't be late."

Richard: "Don't worry. I'll be there."

Later that afternoon, an hour before Richard is due to arrive, Tashi goes into the bathroom adjoining her bedroom. Standing naked before the full-length mirror, she appraises her body as if Richard were watching. "A pretty face, yes," she murmurs. . . "but those pimples are really ugly . . . especially this one (*fingering the large one on her right cheek*) . . . unless I can cover it up with powder. Fortunately, it will be dark at the restaurant. Oh how I wish I had bigger breasts . . . well, any breasts at all. Mom says they should grow fast now that I've started having periods. She was flat-chested at this age, but has a full bosom now . . . so I guess there's hope."

She pinches her buds . . . tugging gently . . . massaging the tiny mounds surrounding them, then sighs, "When will I be a woman? So many of the girls at school are ahead of me. Joanne threw away her trainer bra months ago. And she's not the only one. I'm ashamed to wear mine in the locker room. But won't it look worse if I don't wear any bra at all?"

Looking further down her body . . . she fingers the three or four black hairs on either side of her vagina. "Hardly visible," she mutters. Moving back a few feet from the mirror, she finds that she can't see them at all. "Why do I have to be the last one in class to get pubic hair? It's so embarrassing. I've thought of telling everybody I shaved it off . . . but they could probably tell that I never had any to begin with. Well, Richard will never know. He won't get to see me nude until I have something more to show him."

Going to the closet, she pulls out the black party dress previously chosen for the evening and lays it on her bed. Her eyes still on the dress, she steps into her pantyhose, reaches into her dresser for a bra, puts her arms through the straps, snaps the clasp behind her, then lifts a white slip from the adjoining drawer and pulls it down over her head, pausing to relish the coolness of the satin on her shoulders. Sitting now at the edge of the bed, she stretches out one leg then the other, running her hand down her thigh then back up again, her whole body tingling with the erotic feel and look of the tight-fitting nylon. Taking the dress in her hands, she rises from the bed and slides it over her head, tugging it firmly until it feels tight at the hips. She looks up at her chest again, then fingers the ruffles around the neckline. Lifting the ruffle, she looks to see if her nipples show through underneath. Disappointed to find they don't, she turns sideways and takes a deep breath. There's still nothing to see. "So what," she murmurs. "With this dress you can't see how flat my chest is, that's the important thing." The satisfaction is fleeting, however, as memories arise of her first meeting with Richard when she was wearing shorts and a pink tank top. "Why did I have to wear such a tight-fitting top that day? He's sure to remember."

When they arrive at the restaurant, the parking lot is still mostly empty. "Peak hour on Saturday night is usually around 8:00," Richard whispers. As he unloads the cello from the back of the car, Tashi takes a moment to survey the building. From this perspective it is even larger than she remembers, its girth accentuated by long white clapboards punctuated with black-trimmed windows, each with its own green awning. The patio at the far end, so inviting for dinner alfresco in summertime, stands empty now except for a young couple chatting over cocktails. Richard holds the door open as Tashi wheels her cello into the restaurant.

The subdued light heightens her senses, the way darkening clouds do when warning of a coming storm. Before they even reach the bandstand in the corner, her eyes are drawn to the white linen tablecloths and the individual candles set in pewter holders. Wherever people are seated, the candles are already lit, their specks of light creating a wall of privacy, sealing each couple off from the intrusions of unwanted company. In her girlish imagination she places herself and Richard at one of the tables; she sees them laughing now, arms touching, raising their wine glasses to celebrate something good in their lives, an anniversary perhaps. Her fantasy is broken only when she hears Richard's voice, "You can put your cello case over there behind the piano." She does what she has been told as Richard sets out a chair and music stand for her.

Richard: "I'm going to open with a selection from Schumann's Papillons . . . so you can either take a chair against the wall behind me or sit at one of the tables out front."

Tashi: "I'll take a chair behind you. "Do you need me to turn pages for you? I can do that, you know."

Richard: "I usually turn my own . . . but it can get tricky in the fast passages. So . . . why not? . . . (*pause*) . . . You're sure you can read piano music?"

Tashi: "I took lessons for two years before switching to cello."

She sits down on the piano bench next to him, their arms almost touching.

"I'm going to need a little more room than that, Tashi. Why don't you bring up that chair over there . . . (*watching*) . . . there . . . that's better."

He looks out over the restaurant, then begins. The piece he has chosen from Schumann's 'Butterflies' starts by ascending the scale with dotted triplets, mimicking the flight of a butterfly, only to fall again as the creature seeks repose. The piece ends without applause from the early diners, presumably because no one knows the piece well enough to realize it has ended. Having anticipated this, Richard continues playing without a break, improvising on the main theme while retaining the same underlying harmony, this time taking the melody to ever sweeter heights. He stops only after returning to Schumann's original theme for a final exposition.

Richard (*turning to Tashi on his left*): "Thanks for the page turning. You were right with me. Were you surprised when the score ended but I kept playing? I probably should have warned you."

Tashi: "At first, I thought I had lost you, that's before I realized what you were doing. I got scared, but when I saw you playing without looking at the music I figured you must be making stuff up . . . (*pause*). . . I really liked what you did with Schumann. You should use that in one of your big pieces for orchestra."

Richard: "Thanks. O.K. Are you ready for a duet? People are still coming in, so don't be disturbed if we have to put up with a little noise. It'll quiet down after we start."

For their first duet, Richard has chosen the one he transcribed from a lively tune originally written for his mother's birthday some years ago. "Are you nervous?" he asks, turning to his young partner.

Tashi: "A little I guess."

Richard: "Just pretend that we're back in my living room. Kwatz is the only one who can hear us . . . and he's promised to like it . . . (*pause*) . . . as long as it's not too loud."

Tashi muffles a laugh, then straightens herself out on the chair. With a nod from Richard, they begin. The piano leaps ahead with a romping motion, followed by an echoing canter from the cello. A noise in the kitchen, apparently a broken plate, breaks the somber mood of the middle section. Richard smiles and shakes his head. The piece continues without mishap, ending on a high-spirited remake of the original theme.

Once the applause has died down, Tim comes over to offer his congratulations. "That was terrific . . . but I wonder if our patrons would enjoy it even more if you introduced your pieces first . . . not the solo piano pieces; everyone here is familiar with Richard's playing . . . but the duets. They're really new. I think people would appreciate hearing a little about Tashi's role in all this. You know . . . how did the two of you get started . . . how long has she been playing cello . . . that kind of thing . . . What do you think?"

"That's fine with me," says Richard. "Tashi?"

(*Turning to Richard*) . . . I'm willing . . . unless you'd rather do it yourself. It's up to you."

Richard: "No . . . go ahead. Tell them whatever you want them to know . . . especially about you. Just leave me out of it."

Tashi: "O.K. I'll keep it short. (*rising and taking the microphone in her hand*) Hello. Tim wants me to tell you a little about myself . . . (*waiting for applause to end*) . . . My name is Tashi Said. I'm 14 and in 9th grade at the middle school in Back Bay, Boston. I met Richard two weeks ago and we've been working on these duets ever since. The themes are from works that Richard had in his file drawer . . . "

As she talks, Richard has a chance to look at her without fear of staring. He measures her objectively. Standing with bow in hand, cello on the floor next to her, she is not quite five feet tall, slender, almost skinny. Her black dress, falling effortlessly to below her knees, matches her black hair. The hair, the dress, even her full brown eyes contrast with a white skin made pale by the long New England winter. He allows himself the luxury of wondering what she will look like as an adult. While the raw pimples on her forehead and cheek serve as painful reminders of her adolescence, they mask an unstated beauty that pleases without exciting him. If she puts on a little weight, he ponders, she could probably be attractive, never sexy but certainly acceptable to any man who relishes strength in a woman. "Could I ever be drawn to her?" he asks himself. Without answering, he turns his attention back to the present. He scans the restaurant. Everyone is listening . . . many smiling as they respond to her enthusiasm. She speaks with a clear, confident voice nurtured in an environment that has known more praise than disapproval. A hint of pride rises from deep in his psyche. He turns back to watch her as she finishes.

". . . my teacher at school, Mr.Putnam, says that if I practice hard enough I could play professionally someday . . . in a symphony orchestra or maybe a chamber group. I don't know. All I'm sure of is that I love being here tonight and playing Richard's music for you. Thank you."

The applause is startling . . . far louder than anything Richard has ever heard at the restaurant. She waits for it to die down . . . then announces the next piece. "The duet we're going to play for you next is called Sisyphus. I never heard of him before, but Richard says he's a mythological king who was sent to Hades where he had to push this rock up a mountain, but it kept rolling back down so he never got to the top . . . I hope you like the music."

Just as she finishes, Tashi looks up to see her parents entering the restaurant. Because it is almost full, they have to settle for a table along the wall farthest from the band stand. As Richard opens the piece with a few background chords, she responds to her dad's wave with a nod of her own. "They've never heard me play with anyone else," she muses as she waits for Richard to finish, "except as part of the school orchestra. And they've never heard me play anything this romantic. What will they think when they hear their 14-year-old daughter, only recently graduated from a child-sized cello, putting her heart into a piece that's all about love and longing?"

At the fifth measure she lowers her head and enters with the confidence of one already steeped in the language of romance, the rich tones of her instrument giving voice to an instinctive knowing not yet realized in flesh or confession. It is only when the piece reaches its ambivalent conclusion that she looks up and is reminded of the world of faces and things. The restaurant is now full, all eyes turned to her own, many of them unblinking as if in disbelief that such sounds could come from one so young. The prolonged silence is broken when applause erupts from a table against the wall. She smiles, then waves to her father who is standing, hands clapping furiously as he sends "bravos" flying across the room.

"I think they want you to take a bow, Tashi," Richard whispers.

"But it's your piece, Richard...come" (*reaching over and taking his hand as they both stand up*).

With the fading of applause, Tashi retires to a seat to the left of the piano where she prepares to turn pages for the Schubert Impromptu Richard has chosen for the next piece. The choice is an apt one, faster and more energetic than the previous duet, yet not so lively as to shatter the somber mood left by Sisyphus. The piece weaves its way through a maze of ingenious harmonic shifts, concluding with a recapitulation of the falling arpeggios with which it began.

"Time for a little break, I think," Richard says, turning to his partner as the applause trickles into silence.

"That was terrific Richard. I hope I wasn't too late on some of the pages, especially the ones near the end."

Richard: "You did just fine. How about something to drink?"

Tashi: "Sure. I'll get it. Just tell me where."

Moments after Tashi departs, a young woman, blonde, tall and stunning in her tight-fitting sequined dress, approaches the piano and introduces herself as Vera, a would-be songwriter spending the summer in a cottage on the lake. Reaching out to shake hands, she compliments Richard on the Schubert Impromptu, even citing the date and key signature of the piece.

"You know your Schubert," Richard responds, still sitting at the piano. "Do you play?"

"Only well enough to write songs," she answers, inching closer. "I could never do what you just did. That was marvelous. But I didn't come over just to compliment you . . . I have a favor to ask."

Richard: "Fire away."

Vera: "I've been trying my luck at writing songs for a year now . . . and I think I'm getting better . . . but it's become increasingly obvious to me lately that I need some help."

Richard: "Such as?"

Vera: "Well, I've had a little training in music theory at college, but I still don't how to harmonize a tune so that it moves the song along. I'm pretty good with thinking up melodies and fitting them to lyrics . . . but . . . and several friends have told me this . . . the harmony lacks interest. One friend went so far as to call it boring."

Richard: "Yes. I understand . . . a common problem among songwriters."

Vera: "So . . . would you be willing to give me some lessons . . . in harmonizing melodies?"

Richard: "Well . . . I'm pretty busy this . . . "

Vera (*interrupting*): "I pay well. Money is not a problem. And I live not too far from here. We could do it at either my house or yours. Whatever is best for you."

It is at this point that Tashi comes around the corner with the sodas. She stops as she approaches the band stand, unseen by Vera who is leaning over the piano, her full bosom tight against her dress, her ample cleavage evident even from a distance. Richard seems unaware of Tashi's presence, his eyes fixed instead on the woman before him.

To Tashi, the woman is bending over so far that she appears to be offering her breasts to Richard. "What in the world is she doing?" she murmurs. As the question swirls in her head, sweeping aside the lingering joy of the duet, a darker feeling begins to stir, a bestial, instinctive feeling never before felt. Without forethought, she moves brusquely to the piano, blurting out, "Here are the sodas, Richard. Which one do you want?"

Richard (*taking the orange soda*): "Thank you . . . ah Tashi . . . this is Vera. She's a songwriter . . . wants me to help her with some harmony."

Tashi (*still standing*): "So . . . are you going to do it? (*waiting for Richard's answer*) . . . I thought we were going to work on some more duets this summer."

Vera (*interjecting*): "I think there's room for both, Tashi (*her voice at once conciliatory and condescending*). You can't expect to have Richard all to yourself, can you?"

"Well, why can't you take a music course somewhere?" Tashi replies hastily. "There's a community college at Lake Placid that has a lot of summer courses."

"Because I learn faster when I work closely with my own teacher," Vera snaps back. "That may not be obvious when you're still in middle school, Tashi."

"Let me think about it, Vera," Richard says, painfully tearing his eyes from her breasts.

Vera: "I'm in the phone book; the last name is Emerson. In the meantime, thanks for a lovely complement to dinner (*offering her cheek*).

Your Sisyphus piece was divine . . . (*turning to Tashi*) Your little friend was very good too."

As Vera leaves, Richard puts the score for their next duet up on the piano. "Are you ready for . . . let's see . . . what did we call this one, oh yes, Primavera . . . hmm . . . something of a coincidence (*looking across the room as Vera reaches her table*) . . . Strange," he continues, turning towards Tashi, "I don't hear any laughter."

Tashi: "I don't think it's funny," she rejoins, her voice barely audible. "How could you do that?"

Richard: "Do what?"

Tashi: "You know . . . let her talk you into giving her lessons."

Richard: "I didn't agree to anything. I said I would think about it."

Tashi: "You're going to say yes, I know it . . . *(pause)* . . . then you'll probably end up marrying her."

Richard: "Don't you think you're getting a little ahead of yourself, Tashi. I just met the woman. What makes you think I might want to marry her?"

Tashi: "The way you looked at her. You couldn't take your eyes off her breasts."

Richard: "Well, I'm a man. Men are drawn to women's breasts. It's instinctive."

With those last words, Tashi bends over, clutching her stomach, her eyes wide, teeth clenched in obvious pain. Her long-drawn-out sigh turns into a soft moan as she squeezes her eyes shut. Alone in a world devoid of sight or sound, she begins trembling as fear claws its way into her entrails, tearing at her bowels.

"What's the matter?" Richard asks with growing alarm. "Is it your stomach? Did you grab something to eat at home before coming here . . . (*pause*) . . . no? . . . then of course you're famished. Let me get you some appetizers from the kitchen. You need something right now. O.K.?"

His words have a soothing effect. Tashi senses his concern and luxuriates in it. As he rises from the piano and heads for the kitchen, her eyes follow each step until he disappears behind the swinging doors. Once alone, her mood reverts quickly. The dark feelings return, unbidden, forcing their way into consciousness, staining her innocent love with the ink of despair. She backs into the corner out of sight. Slowly, from the depths of her psyche, a fantasy makes its way to the surface, insistent in its demands, lurid in its detail, unraveling its hideous shape beyond the reach of sanity.

In her mind's eye she sees herself walking up the path to Richard's home. At the door she knocks; the music stops. Vera appears at the door . . . naked. "Oh, it's you Tashi. What do you want?"

Tashi: "I was just wondering if Richard wanted to chat . . . you know, talk about things."

Vera: "Well, we're having a lesson . . . but come in if you must. You can sit in the living room."

(*still fantasizing*) She enters and takes a seat as Vera resumes her place close to Richard at the piano. Richard too is naked.

"Hello Tashi," he says jovially. "You can stay if you want but you have to take your clothes off. We're trying an experiment . . . you know, to see if the music sounds better without clothes."

"I'd rather not," she replies, averting his gaze.

"Well then, you'd better leave right now," Vera interjects.

"Don't you want me to stay, Richard?" Tashi asks, her pleading tone obvious to all.

"Of course, Tashi, but try to get into the spirit of things. Take everything off. Vera will help you."

(*Sullenly*) "I can do it myelf." Turning away from Richard and Vera, she steps out of her cut-offs and pushes her cotton panties to the floor.

"The blouse too," Vera says, turning to watch.

Slowly, with eyes down, Tashi unbuttons her blouse and lays it on the chair.

"Come over here," Richard calls. "Let's see what you look like."

When Tashi hesitates, Vera comes to her, takes her by the arm and pulls her to the piano where Richard is sitting. He looks up and smiles as the two females present themselves side by side for his inspection.

In desperation Tashi covers the two tiny buds on her bony chest with her right arm while using the left hand to hide her hairless crotch. Vera takes a deep breath, thrusting her matronly bosom toward Richard, grinning in the knowledge that he would like nothing better than to suckle on her large raspberry nipples. "Don't cover yourself up, Tashi," she demands. "We want to see what you really look like."

With head down and eyes closed, she puts both hands behind her back as Richard and Vera take turns inspecting her naked body. Vera, whose own mound sprouts a flourishing golden bush, looks down at Tashi's smooth crotch, exclaiming with mock surprise, "Oh, my God . . . I thought you were a boy."

As Tashi shrinks back into the living room, Richard rises from the piano bench and embraces Vera. Fully aware they are being observed, they kiss noisily while rubbing their naked bodies against each other. Hastily, Tashi dresses and bolts for the door, pausing only long enough to hear Richard say to Vera, "I love you darling. Will you marry me?"

She's about to faint and fall from her corner sanctuary when Richard tugs on her arm, breaking the fantasy. "Come on, let's sit down. The chef prepared some nice hors d'oeuvres for you. Do you like . . . "

(*Interrupting*) "Oh Richard," she gasps, grabbing his arm. "How could you?"

"How could I what?" he responds, tilting his head quizzically.

"You know . . . what you did with Vera at your house. Even before finishing, she senses her confusion . . . (*pause*) . . . I don't know, Richard (*shaking her head*) . . . please . . . could you hold me . . . just for a minute?"

Richard (*taking her in his arms*): "Of course."

Tashi (*not moving, eyes closed as she leans against his chest*): "Thank you for the food. I don't know if I can eat anything but I'll try."

Richard (*softly*): "You don't have to play anymore tonight if you don't want to. I have a lot of solo pieces I can play . . . and then there are the improvisations."

Tashi: "But I want to play with you. I've been waiting all week for this."

Richard: "It's up to you. We can do two more duets and then eat dinner."

Tashi: "Oh yes. But could we go over and see my parents before they leave. I want to introduce you."

Richard: "That's fine. How about after our next piece?"

Tashi: "Yes. That would be fine."

The next duet comes off without mishap although Richard is aware of a drop-off in intensity. To his sensitive ear, Tashi's playing, while technically correct, lacks the passion of her earlier efforts. The audience too senses a withdrawal of emotion and responds with muted applause. Because the bandstand is yards from the nearest diner, Richard is the only one close enough to see the change in Tashi's face . . . her smile of youth, flush with anticipation, giving way now to the pallid stare of one shocked by life's unsentimental capacity to inflict pain.

The duet ends softly. She says nothing as she sets the cello on the floor, then looks up, the bow still in her lap.

Richard: "Are you sure you're alright, Tashi?" he asks with obvious concern.

Tashi (*slowly*): "I'm fine. Can we go and meet my parents now?"

Richard: "Of course . . . (*rising from the piano bench*) . . . Why don't you lead the way?"

As they make their way past through the maze of tables, some patrons nod, others clap briefly. Tashi's father is already standing by the time they reach the far wall. From behind Tashi, Richard watches as a short, bald man with a protruding paunch opens his arms in enthusiastic welcome. His smile is at once broad and handsome. Tashi is the first to speak.

Tashi: "Daddy, this is Richard; Richard this is my father, Asadour (*gesturing*) . . . and this is my mother, Esther."

Richard shakes hands with the father; he then bends to take the hand of the mother who remains seated. She is quite thin, a bean-pole in contrast to her toad-shaped husband, her lank, mouse-brown hair plummeting from head to shoulders without the slightest deviation. Her 'hello' is as soft as his is loud.

"Eleanor . . . you were terrific," Father intones in a rich bass voice heard throughout half of the restaurant. "This new cello sounds so much better than the old one. Your technique is improving too. And the music was good . . . very romantic, almost Italian, which, as you know, I prefer to the Germans and Russians . . . (*sitting*) . . . So, Richard (*waving him to a seat*) . . . sit down and tell us about yourself."

Richard: "Well . . . (*pause*) . . . that's a pretty big question. What would you like to know?"

Father: "Anything . . . everything . . . (*pause*) . . . how do you feel about Verdi? Did Eleanor tell you that her mother and I visited Verdi's birthplace in Italy years ago . . . and heard a concert in the town where he served as a councilman? I have some pictures I can show you . . . and a video biography spanning his whole life . . . not some Hollywood prettied up version for the masses but the real thing . . . eight hours-worth of on-site filming. You'll have to come over and watch it sometime."

Richard: "Thanks . . . I'd like that . . . although my tastes run more to the Germans . . . you know, Mozart, Beethoven, Brahms, Wagner . . . that sort of thing. I think their harmony is more . . . "

Father *(interrupting)*: "Of course Verdi's harmony went way beyond that of Bellini, Donizetti and Rossini . . . the *bel canto* composers. They were capable of writing beautiful melodies, but they didn't know how to dramatize their arias with rich harmony. Verdi showed them how to do it."

Tashi: "Daddy . . . you just went and did it again."

Mother: "Eleanor, be careful. Don't make your father mad."

(*Squinting*) "Did what?" Father asks, incredulously.

Tashi: "You asked Richard about his life, then went and talked about something else."

Father: "Well, he didn't speak up (*voice getting louder)* . . . I remember when I got my first teaching job after graduate school, the students kept interrupting me with questions to the point where I finally got . . . "

"Are you married, Richard?" Esther asks quietly.

Richard: "No . . . divorced . . . two years ago."

"Any children?" she continues, turning away from Father whose finger drumming is drawing stares from the next table.

Richard (*hesitantly*): "Not living, no." . . . (*rising*) . . . Now, Tim will be complaining if we don't play some more music . . . (*pause*) . . . Tashi, are you ready?"

"You're leaving so soon?" Father bellows, reaching to shake hands.

Richard: "Yes. It was nice meeting you folks . . . maybe we can get together again sometime."

Father: "Well, yes . . . come over for the Verdi tapes. I can point out the places where Esther and I visited."

"When will you be home, Eleanor?" Mother asks anxiously.

Tashi: "I'm not sure. What do you think, Richard?"

Richard: "We'll get to eat dinner in about a half an hour . . . so you should be home by 10:30 at the latest."

"That seems awfully late for a 14-year-old, don't you think, Richard?" Esther rejoins.

Richard: "Perhaps. I hadn't really thought about it. If you want, I can bring her home as soon as we finish playing . . . just skip the meal altogether."

"No," Tashi protests, in a voice taut with anxiety. "I want to have dinner with you. I've been looking forward to it all evening."

"She didn't have dinner at home, did she?" asks Asadour. "After all this playing, she deserves a special treat. Let her stay."

That proves to be the final word as Richard and Tashi make their farewells and head back to the bandstand for their next piece. Once Tashi has retuned her instrument, they launch into their fourth and final duet of the evening. The audience is smaller now, mainly younger couples too absorbed in their private conversations to care about the music coming from the bandstand. Their disinterest finds its way into the back and forth of Tashi's bow as her mind drifts to questions raised but never answered at her parents' table.

By the time the two musicians have finished for the evening and are comfortably seated at their own table in the corner, the audience has dwindled to a dozen people. Tashi smiles as she looks around the restaurant, secretly relishing the coziness of the tiny crowd.

"Could we ask to have our candle lit, Richard?" she asks, unaware of how much the word 'our' reveals about the feelings stirring inside her. She knows only how intoxicating it feels to be sitting across the table from Richard, unencumbered by musical instruments, free of parents and Vera, alone, just like any dating couple with nothing to distract them from the joy of being together. Unconsciously she runs her hand through her black hair, making sure it sits attractively on her shoulders. With eyes sparkling she asks, "What shall we have?"

"We don't have to have the same thing," Richard answers bluntly. "Have anything you want. It's all on the house. I usually get some kind of fish dish, but I'm ready for something new tonight . . . hmmm . . . maybe the veal medallions."

Tashi: "At the risk of being a copycat, that sounds good to me too. Will it bother you if I order the same thing?"

Richard: "Not at all."

As they wait for the waiter to bring their order, Tashi ruminates for a moment then takes the plunge. "I didn't know you were divorced. Why didn't you tell me?"

Richard (*placing his drink on the table*): "You never asked."

Tashi: "And children. You told Mother you had two children. How old were they?"

Richard (*with eyes averted*): "I'd rather not talk about it, Tashi. Maybe some other time."

Tashi: "I'm sorry. I should have known."

Richard: "That's O.K. Tell me about school. You said you play in the orchestra. What's that like for you?"

As she fills in the details of her school life, her mind is besieged with thoughts of Richard's family, the woman who was once his wife, the children who mysteriously died along the way. Somewhere between school orchestra and plans after college, she gives in to her curiosity and asks, "Do you think you will ever get married again?"

Richard (*with a faint smile*): "Perhaps. Haven't really given it much thought."

Tashi (*setting her fork on the tablecloth as she rehearses her next question):* "Well, what kind of person would you like?"

Richard (*grinning*): "You ask pretty big questions for someone still in middle school . . . (*pause*) . . . I suppose someone with a good sense of humor, smart, interested in the arts, confident but not cocky, a good listener and open about her own feelings."

Tashi: "And?"

Richard: "And . . . (*pause*) . . . let's see . . . able to make fun of herself . . . you know, doesn't take herself too seriously . . . (*pause*) . . . and, of course, nice to look at."

Extended silence follows, punctuated by the clatter of dishes in the kitchen. As the meal draws to a close Tashi ponders the wisdom of going further . . . then takes the plunge.

Tashi (*wiping her lips with the napkin): "*I know I'm only 14, but I think I can be that kind of person."

Richard: "I'm sure you will make a lovely partner for someone when you grow up, Tashi. But right now, I think we better get you home before your parents become alarmed . . . (*rising and taking Tashi by the arm*) . . . I'd say that was a pretty nice evening all in all, wouldn't you?"

Tashi: "Oh yes . . . I hope we can do it next week. Can we?"

Richard: "I don't know why not," he answers, guiding her to the car. "Tim seemed pleased and . . . "

Tashi (*interrupting*): ". . . and the customers liked us, didn't they?"

Richard: "I think so. They were very moved by your playing . . . especially the first two duets."

Tashi: "I know . . . I kind of petered out after that. I think Vera threw me off a little. I should be O.K. next Saturday."

At the house Richard leaves the car running and escorts her to the door. They chat some more about the evening, being careful to keep their voices down as footsteps can be heard inside. As Richard turns to leave, Tashi sets the cello down and in a voice at once playful and seductive, whispers, "Aren't you going to kiss me goodnight?"

Richard: "Well, I . . . (*pause*) . . . I don't think that would be appropriate, do you?"

Tashi: "Why not? My Dad says people in Europe do it all the time . . . even the men kiss each other."

Richard: "You mean on the cheek. O.K., that's different." Relieved, he leans over, his hand on her shoulder. As he approaches her cheek, she abruptly turns her head so that their lips meet. With her hands around his neck, she pulls him toward her. He pauses, trapped momentarily in a web of contradictory desires, then yanks himself free and steps back.

Richard: "Tashi, that's not a good thing to be doing. You're not old enough to kiss like that."

Tashi: "I'm sorry . . . I guess I got carried away . . . being with you at the restaurant and all. It won't happen again, I promise."

Richard: "O.K. I'll be going now."

Tashi: "Goodnight Richard. I really loved what we did tonight ... see you tomorrow?"

Richard: "I've got to do some grocery shopping in town. Better make it Wednesday."

Tashi *(barely audible):* "O.K."

4   Bapu

Weeks pass, weeks of listless wandering broken only by the restaurant gig on Saturday nights and occasional practice sessions at Richard's house. Despite pleadings from both parents, Tashi's life revolves almost exclusively around those meetings. There are girls her own age in town, friendships waiting to be made . . . but they hold no interest. Even her classmates back in Boston, all of whom have internet access and e-mail her regularly, fail to draw her attention from the sole object of her desiring, the composer up on the hill, the one who once had a wife and children but is now alone.

The days drag by, Sunday mornings weighing especially heavy as the onset of a six-day fast during which she must find ways to amuse herself without seeing Richard. She has little interest in the handicraft classes offered at the local school or in signing up for wilderness hikes in the Northern Adirondacks, a popular diversion for kids who are eager to get away from home. No, she hikes and reads. Her greatest solace is the set of books sent to her each summer by her grandfather, the one she calls Bapu. They come ostensibly as a reward for doing well in school, but they are really designed to introduce her to the world's great literature, or at least to the books Bapu thinks are great. This summer she has Anna Karenina and The Return of the Native to comfort her, neither of which her parents judged suitable for a 14-year-old girl when they arrived in the mail.

In their exploration of love between adults, love both found and lost, the books have in fact turned out to be far more than suitable. By inviting her into the private lives of Anna, the Count, Clym, Thomasin, and Eustacia they have allowed her to experience the darker side of romance, in that way universalizing the pain of her own adolescent longings. Through the alchemy of identification, she has come to share in the feelings of the story's lovers . . . and thus to feel less alone, less unique in her own suffering. And, given the chill of recent events, it couldn't have come at a better time.

When she sits down to write to Bapu, what begins as a thank you note unconsciously morphs into an outpouring of all the thoughts and feelings she cannot bring herself to share with anyone else, most notably her parents. She goes so far as to tell him of Vera's appearance at the bandstand when the woman "practically undressed" as she bent over to ask Richard for composing lessons. She alludes to, but cannot bring herself to say openly, how much she envies Vera's fully-developed body and her fear that Richard will be aroused by it. As she writes, she runs her hand across her chest, still hopeful of new growth, a swelling of breasts, an extension of nipples . . . anything noticeable that will attract Richard's attention before the summer is over and she has to return to Boston. No, there is nothing, nothing but bones covered with tightly-stretched flesh punctuated by two slightly protruding red pimples. "I feel so ugly," she writes, "a bony, pimply brat who happens to play the cello well. How can I compete with Vera who can offer him the pleasures of a woman's body?"

Leaving the unfinished letter on her desk, she wanders up the street towards the woods. Although she would swear that she had no intention of eavesdropping on their conversation, it would be legitimate to ask why she chose this particular afternoon, Wednesdays being the day of Vera's lesson, to drop by Richard's house unannounced. Just to chat about music, she might say, or perhaps to take a walk around the lake together. After all, she could argue, he must get lonely living there with no one but his cat.

She stands noiselessly at the door now, hand raised in readiness to knock, when the music stops. Frightened at being discovered, she backs away . . . but no one comes. Her adolescent heart, newly awakened from the sleep of childhood, shrinks at what she hears next. The sound of kissing, wet and hideous in its bestiality, emanates from the piano bench, striking her ears with the force of a thunderclap. She cringes . . . then bends at the waist, hands pressed against her ears. She wants to leave, to flee into the woods, to hide her head in the tall grasses, but her legs refuse to obey. At the mercy of her instincts now, she moves closer, pressing her forehead to the screen door. She can see the two of them at the piano. Vera is wearing sandals and an orange bikini covered loosely with an unbuttoned white blouse hanging down to her hips. The bra covers her nipples but not much more, her tanned breasts protruding provocatively from behind the tiny swatch of material. "And this is supposed to be a lesson?" Tashi murmurs. Vera might claim that she had come right from the beach and had no choice, but the beach in question is down at the far end of the lake. So she must have driven right past her own house on the way here . . . with ample opportunity to change into something appropriate. But no, she obviously had other things in mind.

Still dazed by the scene unfolding before her, Tashi watches as Richard places his right hand behind Vera's neck and pulls her toward him. Their lips meet amidst reciprocal moans as Richard, using his free hand on the keyboard, accompanies their kiss with a love song. It is the theme from the Sisyphus duet. Upon hearing the music, Tashi slumps to the porch floor retching, then tumbles down the stairs to the path where she breaks into a run, heedless of the mosquitoes in her ear or the trailside thistles lacerating her legs, stopping only when she has reached the safety of her bedroom door.

The following Saturday night at the restaurant, midway through the evening, Richard drives the final knife into her heart. The announcement is short . . . even casual. "Vera will be coming to pick me up at 9:30 . . . so I won't be eating dinner with you."

"Aren't you going to eat?" Tashi asks incredulously, struggling to keep her tears back.

"At her house," Richard answers. "It's an invitation. She wants to try out a new dish on me."

As Tashi falls back into her chair, the thought races unbridled through her mind, "Doesn't he know what these late-night dinners mean to me . . . the chance to be alone, the candle lights, to be the sole object of each other's attention? Oh no, he can't wait to be in her kitchen, by her side as she whips up a huge bowl of smelly goulash using a recipe she found in some fancy magazine. How could he settle for such silly things when we could be discussing music or a Russian novel."

All this information she adds painstakingly to her Bapu letter before including the newspaper clipping about the restaurant concerts in which she is cited by name. By the time she is finished, there are spots on the page where tears have wrinkled the paper to the point where it is difficult to make out the writing. She reads it over, dismayed by all the smudges, but decides to send it anyway. "He will understand; I know he will understand," she mutters to herself. "He's not your typical grandfather."

His response arrives a week later.

Hey Ellie,

Sounds like you're in love, sweetheart. That's terrific. Glad to see that you're not afraid to let your feelings take you where they want to go. Most people, including your parents, don't understand that. They hold back, afraid of getting hurt, and so they never experience life to its fullest. You've got guts, not to mention more than your share of brains. Take the pain now; the good stuff is bound to come later.

In the meantime, don't worry about your tits. They'll come. Your mother and both grandmothers all have nice ones . . . although I can't say that I've seen them up close. When I was your age, I had the smallest pecker in the class and gym was a horror story. But that only lasted a few years. By the time I graduated, mine was as big as anyone else's.

About this guy Richard. Is he hiding something? What do you think happened to his wife and kids? There are some pretty weird folks out there . . . so be careful . . . at least until you get to know more about him. And this Vera dame . . . her days may be numbered. Women who throw themselves at men lose their attractiveness pretty quickly. I wouldn't be surprised to see him ditch her by the end of the summer.

Keep me posted,

Love, Bapu

P.S. Are you on the pill . . . you know, just in case?

Within hours of reading his letter, Tashi is up in her bedroom penning an e-mail.

Dear Bapu,

Thank you so much for saying what you did . . . no, not about the pill . . . it's a little early for that . . . I mean about Vera and how Richard is going to drop her because she's so pushy. I wish he'd drop her off a cliff . . . there's a big one near his house . . . and let the wild animals eat her flesh, especially those elephant-size breasts she's so proud of. About my own . . . I think I saw a little progress this morning. Who knows, maybe by next summer I'll have something of my own to show.

By the way, I've changed my name.

Love you,

Tashi (formerly Ellie)

P.S. I hope you know that you're my favorite grandfather; O.K., so Daddy's father died years ago . . . but still, you're special . . . and you're the only one I can write to.

The days pass slowly and uneventfully with Tashi spending long hours alone in bed reading or out in the woods hiking. Hard as she tries to lose herself in books or the quiet beauty of the forest, she can't get Richard and Vera out of her head. With each passing day the obsession exacts its toxic toll on her slender body, raising the specter of anorexia as her parents watch fitfully from a distance.

All this changes on a Saturday night in late summer when Richard, resuming his seat at the piano after acknowledging the applause for a Chopin sonata, whispers to Tashi, "You want to have dinner at 9:30 . . . like we used to?"

Tashi (*leaning forward, not breathing*): "What? Well . . . sure. But what happened to Vera? You've been going to her house for dinner every Saturday for the past month."

Richard: "Vera and I are no longer seeing each other."

Tashi (*suppressing her excitement*): "You broke up. Why?"

Richard: "I don't want to talk about it now . . . we can talk about it at dinner later if you want. You can stay?"

Tashi: "I'll have to call my parents and tell them I'll be home late. But that's O.K."

As they begin the next duet, thoughts about Vera swirl out of control in Tashi's head, threatening to obscure her place in the music. Fortunately, it is a piece they have played several times and the notes come easily. With each passing movement her playing becomes more expressive, more intensely romantic. Richard turns to watch. He sees that her eyes are closed, her head slightly uplifted. She is no longer looking at the score . . . playing completely from memory . . . using the cello as a voice for her deepest longings, a voice more honest, more poignant than any words she could have uttered.

A new tenderness stirs inside him when he considers how deeply she has been affected by the news about Vera. Gradually the joy and abandon of her playing find their way from her instrument to his. In wordless communion, cello and piano soar into an empyrean world of ecstatic oneness where all the foibles of everyday existence are sacrificed at the altar of beauty. With the fading of the last note, the audience, enthralled by what it has just heard and up to now reverently mute, erupts into thunderous applause.

"Wow," Richard whispers before the tumult has died down. "You really put your heart into that one, Tashi."

(*Impishly*) "I did?" she responds, feigning innocence. "I was just trying to avoid making mistakes. You were the one who got me going. At one point I thought the piano was going to sprout wings and start flying around the room (*giggling*)."

Their playing continues throughout the evening with the same elevated level of energy. Many of the patrons remain seated long after they have finished eating. It is only after the last piece has been played and the musicians are seated at their favorite corner table that their conversation resumes.

"Well?" she asks, as if a whole sentence were implied by that single word.

"Well, what?" Richard replies, looking up from the menu.

Tashi: "You said you would tell me about Vera at dinner. So, how come you broke up with her? You seemed to like her a lot."

Richard: "Well . . . (*pause*) . . . it's pretty simple. I found out she was dating another man at the same time she was dating me."

Tashi: "That's terrible. How did you find out?"

Richard: "Tim, the manager, told me he saw Vera and this other man at a restaurant in Lake Placid. I guess Tim was checking out their new menu. According to Tim, they were . . . well . . . let's say pretty close."

Tashi: "And you asked Vera about it?"

Richard: "Yes."

Tashi: "What did she say?"

Richard: "She said she had known Norman for some time . . . really liked him . . . and didn't want to give him up completely until she was sure I wanted to marry her."

Tashi: "My God . . . how could she be in love with the two of you at the same time? . . . (*pause*) . . . That sounds so greedy. So, what did you say . . . that you weren't sure?"

Richard: "Pretty much. I had considered the idea, but couldn't seem to make up my mind."

Tashi: "And that's why she was hanging onto the other man?"

Richard: "I guess so."

Tashi: "Tell me . . . was Vera the kind of person you mentioned once, you know, the kind of woman you might like to marry? You said you wanted someone with a good sense of humor, interested in the arts, smart, and stuff like that."

Richard: "Not really. She had some interest in music . . . although no real talent . . . and not much else. I was disappointed."

Tashi (*wrinkled brow):* "But you seemed to like her a lot. What was it about her that you liked so much?"

Richard: "She was quite attractive . . . so I guess you could say it was mainly physical. She had a very pretty face and . . . "

Tashi (*testily)* : "It was her breasts, wasn't it?"

Richard: "Well . . . (*pause*) . . . I wouldn't go that far. There were other things that . . . "

Tashi (*interrupting*): "My mom says I could have breasts like that in a few years."

Richard: "Yes . . . I'm sure she's right . . . (*pause*) . . . who knows . . . but look, why don't we order some dessert and then I can take you home. It's already pretty late."

Tashi: "Can I ask one more question?"

Richard (*soft but audible sigh*): "Go ahead."

Tashi: "Do you miss her?"

Richard: "In a way I guess I do . . . although there's some anger mixed up in it too."

Tashi: "Are you sad now?"

Richard: "Maybe . . . but I have ways of dealing with it."

Tashi: "Can I ask what?"

Richard (*taking a deep breath*): "Well . . . it's meditation mainly. I try to do a little every morning and I think it helps."

Tashi: "I've heard about yoga and TM, things like that. But I don't get it. How can meditating get rid of sad or angry feelings?"

Richard: "The Buddhists say that if you meditate long and hard enough you can get rid of all desires, the assumption being that it is your desires that make you suffer. I'm no way near that goal now, but I think the basic idea is right."

Tashi (*leaning forward*): "You don't want to have any desires? . . . (*pause*) . . . That sounds so weird . . . even creepy. What kind of marriage would it be if you had no desire for your wife? What if she wanted you to make love to her in bed at night? If you love someone, wouldn't you want to . . . "

Richard (*interrupting*): "Look Tashi, this is really not something a 14-year-old should be worrying about. They'll be plenty of time for that when you grow up. Finish your pudding so I can get you home before your parents start worrying. It's already past 10.00."

5   Out on the Lake

And so, the summer passes. As petals wilt and songbirds prepare for their southward journey, Tashi is filled with a growing dread . . . only one more Saturday night with Richard before it's time to pack for the trip back to Boston. That means nine whole months before seeing him again. How is that possible? Since the time she first knocked on his door, he has moved into the center of her universe, pushing aside all interest in other relationships, either old or new. Not a day goes by without her reliving the events of their last meeting or musing over the possibilities of what might still come. To her unscathed heart, trapped now between the naïve longing of childhood and the ripened passion of womanhood, life without some kind of contact with the object of her affection is simply beyond comprehension.

There will be e-mails, of course, she reflects . . . or better yet, hand-written letters which are more personal. And perhaps phone calls . . . although they wouldn't be really private if she had to use the phone in the living room or kitchen. One way or another, she concludes, I won't be totally cut off.

It helps too when she recalls that her parents often come up to the lake for Thanksgiving weekend. She might even get to play at the restaurant since the town tends to be pretty full over the holidays. Maybe she can talk her parents into coming for Christmas as well . . . and Easter.

Right now, her more immediate concern is to find a way to spend time with Richard outside the restaurant. The thought of simply waving farewell to him at the end of Saturday night's gig is unacceptable. Two ideas present themselves one morning as she pulls up a porch chair to read. "I can propose a walk around the lake . . . with a picnic lunch along the way . . . or, better yet, an early morning canoe trip where we would get to watch deer and perhaps other animals feeding along the shore." The canoe trip strikes her as more intimate and thus preferable . . . with the exception that as they paddle around the lake, they will both be looking in the same direction rather than at each other as they do at the late-night restaurant dinners she enjoys so much.

Once she decides that the advantages of the canoe trip outweigh the disadvantages, she calls Richard and proposes an outing for later in the week . . . a few days before their last gig. She is relieved when he accepts without hesitation. "It's something I have been thinking about all summer," he says, "but have kept putting off for one reason or another. Can I make up some sandwiches for us?" he adds.

"Oh no, let me do it," she is quick to reply. "I can think of lots of yummy things to make."

(*Laughing*) "How many is a lot?" he asks without waiting for an answer. "I read somewhere that when the Tibetans celebrate something really special, they go all out . . . with a 23-course meal, if you can believe that."

"Well, maybe it's not so crazy," she replies. "Just think, if you count radishes as one course, pickles as another . . . then deviled eggs, stuffed celery and chips as one course each, then you're up to five before you even get to chicken or beef or things like that."

Richard: "It would have to be pretty small amounts of each if we're going to eat it all. But Tashi, I was only joking. Please don't take me seriously. I don't want you spending the next three days in the kitchen preparing lunch."

Tashi: "My mom wouldn't like it either. That's where she spends most of her time and she doesn't like it when I get in the way. My dad likes to teach me Palestinian dishes . . . so he's more O.K. about me being there."

Richard: "Now, about the time. I have to finish this arrangement of a piano piece I'm doing for a movie studio in New York . . . but I should be done by Tuesday or Wednesday. Is Thursday good for you?"

Tashi: "Sure. Do you want to come by the house and pick me up?"

Richard: "Fine. Early morning . . . like 8:00?"

Tashi: "If we want to be there when the sun comes up, we better make it earlier . . . like 6:00. No one else will be out on the lake then . . . except a few fishermen. But it's up to you."

Richard: "Whew. I'm usually not an early riser, but the idea of being on the water when the sun comes up over the mountains is pretty appealing. I might even think of a way to capture it in music."

Tashi: "You mean like Grieg?"

Richard: "Exactly."

Tashi: "So. It's all set? I'll see you at my house at 6:00 next Thursday morning . . . unless, of course, you want me to come over for a practice session before that."

Richard: "I think we're O.K with the pieces we now have, Tash. They sounded pretty good last Saturday . . . not perfect maybe, but good enough for a restaurant."

Tashi (*smiling*): "You called me Tash . . . that's cute."

Richard: "Just popped out."

Tashi: "I like it. Does that mean I should start calling you…"

Richard (*interrupting*): …. "No! 'Rich' is an adjective . . . which in my case would be entirely misleading."

Tashi (*laughing*): "O.K. Rich**ARD**. See you on Thursday morning. Don't be late. The sun won't wait for us."

Richard: "I'll be there."

Thursday's weather morning turns out to be ideal for canoeing, although Richard manages to be 15 minutes late. Apologizing as he gets out of the car, he heads for the porch where Tashi stands shivering in her short pants. She points to the picnic cooler at her side with the warning that "it's rather heavy," then to the brightening sky, adding, "I guess I should have said 5:00 instead of 6:00 if we wanted to see the sun come up. Sorry."

Richard: "That's O.K. with me. I enjoyed the extra hour of sleep . . . (*opening the back of the SUV*) . . . Whew, you're right about the cooler. How many courses did you manage to get in there?"

Tashi (*still shivering*): "All 23 . . . counted twice to make sure."

Richard: "Really? . . . that's incredible . . . (*pause*) . . . C'mon . . . hop in the car, the heater is on."

Tashi (*settling into the passenger's seat):* "It was really fun."

Richard (*behind the wheel, turning to speak*): "Honey, did you really find 23 things to put in there?"

Tashi: "You called me honey. You never did that before. Last time it was Tash; today's it's honey. What have I done to deserve all this?"

Richard: "Ah . . . well . . . I just got thinking how thoughtful you are. You must have put in a lot of work getting this lunch together. That's all."

Tashi: "I just wanted to do something special for our last outing together. We're leaving for Boston early on Sunday . . . so we'll have to say goodbye after our gig Saturday night. Unless we come up for Thanksgiving weekend, we won't see each other until next summer. That seems like such a long time . . . (*pause*) . . . Does it to you, Richard?"

Richard: "I hadn't thought about it 'til now . . . but yes, nine months is a long time."

They pass the two miles to the boathouse in silence, both wrapped in the cocoon of their separate thoughts. As Tashi predicted, there are two fishermen already out on the water. "Other than those two," she reflects, "we'll have the lake to ourselves."

Once the cooler is lifted into the canoe, Tashi positions herself at the bow with paddle in hand while Richard pushes off from the shore. He quickly steps in and takes up his seat at the stern. The scraping sound of canoe bottom on sand gives way to the splash of paddles as they head for the center of the lake. When Richard stops paddling, she follows suit, placing hers on her lap. They pass the next few minutes wordlessly as the lake envelopes them in the quiet of the morning.

She turns to speak, the sun now breaking over the surrounding trees to illuminate her head and shoulders, centering her in a portrait framed by water, sky and distant shore. "Look, the fish are really jumping," she says softly, careful not to disturb the tranquility of the moment. He leans forward to study her more carefully, the paddle dripping onto his leg, his eyes shimmering with surprise at the beauty of the picture before him. "Yes," he whispers.

She smiles, acknowledging his unspoken compliment.

A new gladness, all the more poignant in its secrecy, bubbles up inside her as they drift back toward shore. Turning again, she studies his face. There can be no doubt. It is as if each eye contained letters written in bold caps, saying, 'I had no idea you were so lovely.' "Let him hide his feelings," she murmurs, "even from himself if need be . . . I know better." She turns back to paddle, breathing deeply now, her mind freed from the nagging doubts of recent months and newly graced with the peace that requited love brings in its wake.

As they make their way around the lake, taking turns pointing to the deer, bear, and birds they see along the shore, they gradually slip into a trance-like state in which nothing exists but the other. For her, the fixation is not only conscious but intentional; for him, it remains below awareness, hidden behind a curtain of confusion. As they move silently through the water, he is conscious only that she is more beautiful than he had thought . . . pleasing, yes . . . but a child nevertheless. And so the morning passes.

By noon Tashi is feeling the pangs not of love but of hunger. Turning, she asks, "Do you think we could stop over there, Richard *(pointing to an open area at the far end of the lake)*? Are you getting hungry? I know I am."

"It looks good to me," he answers. "It looks like there's some kind of trail there . . . above the beach."

"There's some sand and grass right by the water," she adds . . . "a perfect place to picnic I think."

Using his paddle adroitly, he steers the canoe to the open area. It takes every bit of Tashi's strength to pull the canoe, including Richard and the cooler, up onto the sand. Once they have everything in place . . . the blanket she has brought, the cooler, and Richard's knapsack . . . Tashi announces with a playful whoop that she has to pee. "O.K. I'll hold the fort while you do your business," he replies with a smile. "If you meet up with any bears or mountain lions, give a holler. I'll come running with my jackknife."

(*Laughing*) "I feel so safe with you, Richard," she mutters . . . and off she goes, up the trail they had seen earlier from out on the lake.

The trail is a wide one, probably cut through the woods to make way for power lines in the past. Right now, there is nothing to see but grass and pine needles and tall conifers on either side. It is comfortable walking as she makes her way up the path to a knoll a hundred yards or so above where the canoe rests on the beach. At the top she turns to face the lake, assures herself that Richard is not watching, then pushes her shorts and panties to her knees. Squatting on the grass, she breathes deeply, opens her legs and pees.

As the urine trickles down the slope and disappears into the grass, she reaches into her blouse pocket for a tissue. First daubing the outer lips of her labia, she continues under the hood and in between the pink folds of her slit, all the while looking down at Richard and the canoe. The sensation is more pleasurable than she can remember, pleasurable enough to make her back up a few inches onto dry ground and continue to daub. By pressing a little harder on the flesh inside her vagina, she discovers that she can increase the sensation. Excited by her discovery, she tosses the tissue to the side and continues her exploration with bare fingers.

By now the noon-day sun is almost directly overhead with its rays caressing the lower half of her body. She lifts her head to get a better look at the lake. Richard has taken off his t-shirt, his broad shoulders and furry chest now observable from the knoll. With eyes fixed on his every move, she sinks her warm fingers deeper into her moistening sex, drawn by the firm ball of flesh just inside her folds. She is aware of a tension, an unnamable and never-before-felt throbbing centered on this mound of flesh. She is startled to find it hardening as she massages it. As Richard gets up to move the picnic cooler into the shade, she pushes her shorts and panties down to her ankles, then kicks them off onto the grass, allowing her legs to open fully. With legs apart and open to the sun's embrace, she cups her vulva with her right hand and inserts a single finger into her girlish slit.

There is no thought in any of this; it is instinct alone that guides her finger to that fleshy epicenter of desire. As she raises her head to watch his movements, she begins circling her clit, first clockwise, then counterclockwise, unaware of what is about to happen. Then, as if woken abruptly from a deep sleep, she senses a tightening in her loins, a stirring that spreads to her thighs, her abdomen, even the tiny nipples on her chest. Richard raises his arms, stretching to welcome the overhead sun, the hair in his armpits visible even from the knoll. Her lips twitch with an unspoken message, "If only he would look this way." He turns toward the path. She strains to see his face, seeking contact, but unable to wait. At the mercy of her need now and oblivious to shame, she yields to the flame within, throws her head back, and with a spasm that sets her whole body trembling, reaches out to the heavens, trumpets her ecstasy to the world and in a violent thrust of will, tears herself free from childhood's embrace.

"Are you O.K up there?" Richard shouts in response to her cry.

Rising quickly and running down the path, "Yes . . . yes," she shouts, unable to slow her descent as she comes onto the beach. Richard is directly in her path. Sensing that she has lost control, he opens his arms to catch her as she crashes into his body. "Oh, thank you," she whispers, gasping for breath, her arms wrapped tightly around his neck. "I'm sorry . . . I couldn't stop." "That's alright, Tash," he answers.

His words, so simple in themselves, carry a message of caring, acceptance . . . even love . . . to her newly-awakened heart. At least that's what she hears. As the two embrace on the sand, at the edge of a windless lake empty of all but a few fishermen patrolling the opposite shore, she presses against him, unwilling to surrender her prize. The feelings swirling inside her signal that something has changed. The love is still there, the same wanting, the same need for closeness she has known for months . . . but they are no longer centered in her chest. This is a darker, less easily-contained craving, more consuming, more menacing in its willfulness, radiating out now from her groin. Her breathing stops. All thoughts are swept from her mind by the tightening just above her pubic bone. As the pain penetrates her viscera, twisting the sinuous fibers of her flesh into a pulsating knot, she raises her lips for a kiss.

Richard anticipates the move and backs away, announcing simultaneously that he is ready for lunch. Moving quickly to hide her disappointment, Tashi drops her arms and heads for the picnic cooler where the fruits of a week's thought and labor lie waiting. Richard, fearing that his skinny friend might try to move it herself, rushes to help. "Let me do that," he calls. "No need, Richard," she answers. "It's O.K. where it is. We can eat right here if you don't mind a few rocks. I brought a blanket we can sit on."

Richard: "I'm impressed with how carefully you've thought this all out, Tashi."

Tashi: "It was fun, really."

Richard (*smiling*): "Maybe you have a career waiting for you in catering."

Tashi: "I don't think I would enjoy it very much if it weren't for a special person."

Richard: "I'm flattered. Thank you."

As he watches, Tashi opens the cooler and checks to see that everything survived the trip intact. Each item has been packed in a separate container, mostly small plastic bowls left over from purchases at the local deli. When Richard asks how she knows what's in each, she points to tiny penciled markings on the covers. "So, where do we start," he asks, rubbing his stomach in anticipation. "Over here on the left," she answers. "We start here and move to the right, like reading a book."

Richard: "You mean you've arranged it all in a certain order?"

Tashi: "Sort of. First come the appetizers, then two kinds of soup, crackers, breadsticks, lots of veggies, several meat courses, rice, pasta, four kinds of fruit, a chocolate dessert, a raspberry dessert . . . ah, let's see . . . oh, (*pulling out two small bottles of lemonade*) and something to drink."

Richard: "This is incredible Tash."

Tashi: "You better be hungry . . . I'd rather not take any of it back home where Mom will see how much food I've used up."

One by one she reaches into the cooler and brings out a small plastic bowl with mysterious markings on the cover. Each is introduced with a word of explanation, then dished out to Richard who holds a small plate in his lap. First come the radishes, then the stuffed celery followed by a series of crackers, each topped with a tiny square of cheese. Unfettered by dining room protocol, the feast continues through an array of veggies . . . green, red, white, and yellow, accompanied by a bowl of peppered sour cream for dipping. Mushrooms stuffed with spinach follow, then fettuccini surrounded by tiny chunks of salmon. As the sun slides toward the horizon, the meal reaches its peak with three successive meat entrees, wafered prosciutto in a bed of wild rice, barbecued chicken, and diminutive pizzas topped with a single slice of pepperoni.

Through it all Richard receives each gift with a nod, followed by a sigh of appreciation. Somewhere between the little pizzas and the fruit to follow, he stops eating, looks over at Tashi, and begins waving his arms like a baby bird. She is confused at first but then breaks into laughter when she fathoms the meaning of his pantomime.

Tashi (*shaking her head*): "So my little bird wants more food, does he?"

Richard (*opening his mouth like a beak*): "Mmm."

To their mutual delight, she then leans over and places a small chunk of pineapple in his mouth which he swallows only to start flapping his arms all over again. She pretends to be awed at his prodigious appetite, but immediately reaches into the cooler for the melon slices which are next on the list. With intermittent flapping, they make their way through the cherries, the mandarin oranges, mangoes and blueberries . . . and then on finally to the tiny dessert cakes, cookies, and chocolate-covered almonds, each lovingly transferred from her fingers to his mouth.

"Ah, Tashi, that was great," he exclaims as she shuts the cooler. "But I think I only counted 22. Did I miss one?"

"No," she answers demurely, preparing for her little surprise. "There's one more . . . but you have to shut your eyes. It's a secret."

He does as he is told . . . but not without an inkling of what is coming. "Perhaps this once is alright," he muses, "especially since she has gone to such trouble to please me." He waits with eyes closed, his head tilted slightly backwards as she kneels in front of him. The first thing he is aware of is her hand on his shoulder; the next is of her lips on his. He can feel himself tightening but does not move away. She smiles inwardly, delighting in his acquiescence, then pulls away only to kiss him again and again.

"I think we're up around 28 or 29," he jokes, finally drawing back onto the grass.

"But they're only little ones," she protests, still kneeling.

Richard: "Do you think the Tibetans wind up all their big celebrations like this?"

Tashi (*giggling*): "I think it's traditional . . . if not, it should be."

Richard (*rising*): "I'll check my anthropology book when I get home."

The sun is again behind Richard as they paddle back across the lake to the boathouse. Fully conscious of its rich, late afternoon hues, Tashi turns often to let Richard admire her profile. "Someday soon," she whispers to herself, "his eyes will be drawn to my breasts when I turn like that. If he's starting to find me attractive now, just think how excited he will be then." The warming in her heart finds its way to her lips as a contented sigh slips out.

"What was that all about?" Richard asks, lifting his paddle.

"Just thinking," she answers softly. "It's been such a beautiful day."

Richard: "I'm glad you liked it. I know I did. And thanks again for your heroic effort in preparing all that food. I won't be forgetting that for a long time."

Tashi: "I enjoyed doing it . . . (*pause*) . . . but maybe next time we can settle for ten courses . . . or even five. I'm going to have some explaining to do when I get home. My mom is probably wondering what happened to all those plastic bowls she's been hoarding for years."

Richard: "Not to mention all the food that disappeared from the refrigerator."

Tashi (*laughing*): "I could try blaming it on the bears, but they don't like plastic bowls, do they?"

Richard: "Only if they have something edible inside, I would guess."

Tashi: "I think I'll just fess up to the truth. It's less complicated that way."

Richard: "As a last resort you can blame it on a bad case of bulimia . . . you know, that eating disorder where you eat everything in the house and then throw it up to avoid gaining weight."

Tashi: "Might explain why I'm so skinny . . . yes?"

Richard: "Why not?"

Tashi: "But they might send me to a psychiatrist for help. And then I'd have to spill the beans about my real addiction."

Richard: "Which is . . . ?"

Tashi (*smiling*): "Silly."

The long day ends when Richard leaves Tashi off at her house and returns to the quiet of his cottage in the woods. Kwatz is waiting at the front door as he enters. "Are you hungry little fella?" he asks, picking him up and carrying him to the kitchen. A predictable amount of nuzzling and rubbing follows. Once he has dished out the usual bowl of whitefish and salmon (diversity not being high on Kwatz's list of priorities), he settles into his favorite living room chair and reflects on the day's events.

Interesting and pleasant as the outing has been, he is relieved to be back in his familiar haunts. Living alone has its advantages. Unlike the first two years after the divorce when loneliness cast a pall over even his most personal activities, the last few months here in the Adirondacks have brought out a part of his personality he never knew existed. He is honestly starting to feel happy again. As if on cue, Kwatz jumps down from the kitchen counter, races into the living room and leaps up into his lap, stretching his back in readiness for the stroking he considers his due after being left alone all day. Richard is quick to give him what he expects.

"Yes, it is a contented household with just the two of us," he concludes as he looks around the room, shifting his ministrations to Kwatz's neck and ears. "It is a bit strange, then," he adds, "that this young girl seems eager to spend time with me when she could be out shopping, playing games, dating or whatever it is that kids that age do. Instead, here she is at my doorstep, unneeded and unsought, bubbling over with adolescent enthusiasm, asking to hang out with a man more than twice her age. I don't know that many 14-year-old girls, but my guess is that she is an unusual child . . . emotionally more mature than her peers and not obsessed with the narcissistic concerns that motivate most adolescents. So, what would make her that way? Would growing up in a home with two adults and no other children have that effect? Is she simply lonely because she has no siblings? Maybe she's so much smarter than her peers that they bore her . . . or is it just that she has aged quickly and already has the interests and desires of a young adult?"

"Saturday will be her last day in town," he muses, "and I know that she would like to stay longer. Perhaps I should do a little something extra at the end of the evening, especially in light of all the work she put into our trip today." When no ideas come, he decides to sleep on it and try again in the morning. With Kwatz still purring contentedly on his lap, he reaches for the remote and flicks on the TV. Within seconds, thoughts of Tashi disappear into the vortex of a thousand voices shouting as grown men in colored shorts race up and down the court bouncing a large brown ball. Kwatz, clearly annoyed, jumps down and retreats to the safety of his pad under the coffee table.

(*Saturday*). At the restaurant no one other than Richard and Tim is aware that this is Tashi's last night. Many of the diners have deliberately come early to get as close to the performers as possible. For the few who are listening carefully, however, a change can be heard the minute the musicians begin playing. Tashi's bowing is deeper, the sound richer. In the slow passages she plays with her eyes closed, her body rising and falling as if she were dancing and playing at the same time. If one listens closely enough one can almost hear her singing . . . there being no need for words when her feelings are so obvious.

Richard is aware of the difference. How could he not be aware when she is sitting so close? Without looking in her direction he brings the piano into synch with her playing, foot on the sustain pedal, watching her bow for a signal before moving on. The effect is electric. Diners find themselves holding their breath as she lingers on every half or whole note . . . waiting, pausing, grasping for timelessness . . . unwilling to let the piece end.

Hidden from view, visions of a cold, desolate nine-month Boston winter haunt her every stroke. How is she going to get through it? How can she survive so far removed from everything she has come to love . . . the woods, the lake, the restaurant, the duets . . . and at the center of it all, a man called Richard? Algebra, history, biology, gym classes, field hockey, homework, exams, grades, gossip . . . what do any of them have to do with love? "I will freeze; I will starve. I will stop breathing . . . (*pause*) . . . If only there were some way to make next summer begin tomorrow."

She cannot talk to Richard this way. She certainly can't talk to her parents. Yet the feelings are too intense to remain locked up inside . . . voiceless, unheard, left to perish in the buried, sound-proof chambers of her psyche. The only way to give them expression is to let the cello speak for her, to open that hidden vault of desire and pour her love out into the world through music. "It's so strange," she muses, taking up the bow once again, "to give vent to something so lofty, so uniquely human . . . by drawing horsehair across cat gut. But I want to. I must."

And this is what the diners hear . . . at least those still young enough at heart to recall their own early loves. For these sensitive souls, the lament reaching them from the girl with the cello stirs up dormant longings, longings still alive, but long ago buried beneath the burdens of marriage and parenthood, longings resurrected now in the form of remembered loves . . . loves embraced, loves foregone. The applause is muted as listeners defer to their hearts, many shielding themselves from the candle light to conceal their secret anguish.

At the end of the second duet, Richard leans over and whispers: "I've never heard you play so beautifully. You've got most of the diners crying . . . I've even felt a few tears myself."

Tashi: "Thank you."

Richard: "Is this all because you're leaving tomorrow?"

Tashi: "Perhaps."

Richard: "Let's talk about it at dinner . . . (*pause*) . . . if you're willing."

Tashi (*softly*): "If you want to."

With the last duet concluded and the cello back in its case, the two musicians seat themselves at their favorite corner table. Neither speaks. As the waiter arrives to light the candles and take their order, Tashi breaks the silence. "Will you be playing again when the ski season opens in December?"

Richard: "Probably. I've played each of the last two years."

Tashi (*with playful smile*): "Will you miss me when you have to play alone?"

Richard: "Of course. It's not as much fun that way. But maybe someone else will come along like you did . . . you know, a violinist or perhaps a female vocalist. I haven't tried my hand at song-writing yet, but the idea has always intrigued me. Something simple, of course . . . maybe using some of my favorite poems."

Tashi (*wry smile*): "A singer? Not too pretty, I hope. I know how you fell for Vera."

Richard (*scoffing*): "In a setting like this, it's the voice that counts, not the looks."

Tashi: "I hope she's so ugly you have to put a bag over her head."

Richard (*laughing*): "I'll keep that in mind when I interview her . . . (*pause*) . . . In the meantime, I have a little something for you . . . sort of a send-off present." At this point Richard reaches into his equipment bag and pulls out a CD. "As you know, I recorded each of our duets during the practice sessions at my place. I've brought all five of them together on this disk so you can listen to them or share them with your friends and family when you get back to Boston. I'm sure they will enjoy hearing you . . . and it might even give you a new perspective on your playing." He slides the CD across the table to Tashi.

Tashi: "What a wonderful present, Richard. I like the title you've given it, too . . . 'Rhapsodies for cello and piano' . . . but you should have made it clear that you wrote all the music . . . (*pause*) . . . Nobody is ever going to accuse you of having a big ego." The word 'darling' comes to her lips as she reaches to take Richard's hand, but better judgment prevails and she settles for a soft and tearful 'Thank you.'

Later in the evening, standing at her doorstep, she reaches out for a final hug. Aching to be kissed, but not daring to offend, she presses her cheek to his and whispers, "I love you." He says nothing, but continues holding her. "Someday," she muses silently, "he will come to me on his own. I can wait." And with that she turns and goes into the house.

6   Thanksgiving

Dear Bapu,

Mom is taking up painting again. I think she can be really good if she puts her mind to it. Dad is busy writing his memoirs . . . I think he likes to write about himself . . . you know, his achievements and all. Are you going to write yours someday? I want to read about the things you did when you were my age . . . especially your first love. And other stuff too. Be sure to mention me somewhere along the way.

Love, Tashi

◆

An answering e-mail comes a few days later.

Yo Tashi,

Glad to hear that Richard ditched Vera . . . looks like you've got a clear field in front of you now . . . but don't rush it . . . you can't expect a grown man to get all that excited about a 14-year-old girl. You're growing up fast . . . in a few years things could be very different.

Your Dad is a little young to be writing his memoirs, isn't he? Maybe he's got a lot to talk about . . . or maybe he doesn't expect to be around much longer. I don't know. From here the whole thing sounds a bit narcissistic. I don't have any plans to write any of my own . . . who the heck would be interested anyhow?

On a more important matter, have you started to masturbate yet? I got into it around your age and once started could hardly stop. It was so exciting I ended up doing it four or five times a day . . . sometimes excusing myself to go to the bathroom right in the middle of class. In 9th grade we had a really cute science teacher who liked to sit on my desk at the front of the room when she was talking to the class. And yes, I played with myself under the desk as she was lecturing to us. One time . . . and I really didn't mean to do this . . . I let out a huge fart when she was sitting there. You can imagine how the kids howled when she almost fell off the desk trying to escape.

Sex is one of the greatest delights life has to offer . . . at least it has been for me. I hope it turns out that way for you too. Your mother sees it differently . . . more as a means for making children . . . work of a sort . . . to be carried out with minimal fooling around. She must have gotten that prudish attitude from your grandmother . . . or someone else . . . certainly not from me. We Americans have come a long way but we're still pretty uptight about sex. That's not true of all societies. In grad school I remember reading about this custom among primitive tribes in Australia whereby grandfathers were expected to introduce their granddaughters to sex . . . O.K. maybe it was uncles and their nieces. I'm not sure, but the idea is the same. What better way for a young girl to learn about sex than in the context of a loving relationship with an older relative? But can you imagine what would happen if someone tried that in our world?

So long for now,

BaPU (*hold your nose*)

———◆———

As soon as she gets home from school on Friday, Tashi rushes upstairs to her bedroom, turns on her laptop and types her answer.

Dear Bapu,

About the M word, the answer is yes *(blush)*. It startled me at first . . . was even painful in a way . . . but I now see it as the most exciting thing that has ever happened to me. And it happened out in the open where I love to be. Richard was really a big part of it although he didn't have any idea what was going on. You're the only one I am telling about it. Well . . . you and God . . . Do you think He listens to things like this?

Love, Tashi

And so the Fall passes, punctuated by her dialogue with Bapu as well as occasional e-mails to Richard in which she inquires about new compositions and the changing scenery in Saranac. Richard is good about answering although his own writing tends to be briefer and less personal. Back in Boston Tashi is hard at work trying to convince her parents to spend Thanksgiving at the cottage. The unbridled intensity of her petition proves counterproductive as mom and dad grow increasingly worried about her interest in the reclusive composer. Their decision comes late one night after Tashi has gone to bed.

"She's too young to be chasing after a man 18 years her senior," Esther whispers, "especially someone who has already been married and has two children who died mysteriously."

"He seems nice enough," Asadour replies, but you can never tell. I don't understand why she isn't dating boys her own age. What's going on with her anyhow?"

Esther (*leaning forward*): "I don't understand it either. But I think going to Saranac for Thanksgiving would be a big mistake. We'd just be asking for trouble. The less she sees of him the better."

(*Softly*) "How will we explain it to her," asks Asadour. "She's bound to be disappointed."

Esther (*whispering*): "We come out and tell her the truth . . . that we don't want her spending a lot of time with Richard."

Asadour: "So what do we do next summer when the same issue comes up? You want to spend a hot, humid summer here in Back Bay?"

Esther (*feeling more sure of herself then usual*): "We can deal with that when the time comes. Right now, I think we should say no to Thanksgiving at the cottage."

Asadour: "O.K. Let's tell her in the morning. By the way, what's going on between Eleanor and your father? I have the feeling that he may be working at cross purposes with us on this issue. As you know, he is capable of saying some pretty nutty things."

Esther (*bristling*): "He's different for sure . . . but I wouldn't consider him any nuttier than your father."

Asadour (*pushing his chair away from the table*): "Oh, really? Maybe we should ask Eleanor if we can read his most recent e-mails. I'll bet he's been saying some pretty weird things."

Esther (*squinting*): "Are you serious? I can't think of a better way to make her mad at us. Is that what you want? Really Asi. Sometimes you sound like you don't know the first thing about people. She's growing up . . . and needs a little independence of her own now. She's not a woman yet, but she's no longer a child either. I say we leave it with a firm 'no' on Thanksgiving at the cottage . . . and say nothing about the e-mails."

Asadour (*rising and heading for the kitchen*): "As you wish . . . I bow to your superior judgment."

When the decision is announced at breakfast, Tashi complains bitterly, offers every argument she can think of . . . then sinks back into her chair when both parents remain resolute. All efforts to get her ready for the school bus yield nothing but frustration. Long after the bus has left, Father ushers her into the car and takes her there himself only to have her return a few hours later with a note from the school nurse diagnosing her as 'depressed with no obvious cause.'

Back in her room Tashi shuts the door and turns to the only person she can trust. Opening her e-mail folder, she writes:

Dear Bapu,

We're not going to Saranac for Thanksgiving like we usually do. They don't want me to see Richard anymore . . . at least for now. What am I supposed to do? I just want to see him . . . and talk about things. What's wrong with that? Please write. I don't have anybody else to turn to. Nothing feels good anymore.

Love, Tashi

An answer comes almost immediately.

Hey my little one,

It hurts me so see you depressed like this. I would call your mother right now and see if I could change her mind if I thought it would do any good. But as you know, my advice on matters like this doesn't carry much weight in your family.

Are you having trouble sleeping? How about eating? Here's an idea: going without food for several days could really get the alarm bells ringing (hint, hint). Just don't carry it too far; you're already skinny enough as it is. Be careful and things may still turn out alright.

Know that I love you,

Bapu

After a third day of watching their only child shrink before their very eyes, not to mention countless frantic calls to a child psychologist, the Saids are ready to throw in the towel. "Maybe we've been a little too strict," Father whispers during dinner, his eyes wandering to the empty seat next to his own. "I trusted you to come up with the right answer, but it looks like you've gone too far."

Esther (*softly*): "I never realized how much she cared for this man. But Asi, she's only 14. I was only doing what most mothers would do. Please don't be mad at me."

When the change of plans is announced in the morning, Tashi breaks into tears, then rushes to give each parent a hug and kiss. "What is it I smell in the kitchen?" she asks, eyes wide open and sparkling with unconcealed joy. "Waffles and sausage," Mom replies, eyes now wet with tears of her own. "One of your favorites," Dad adds. "Come and join us. We've missed you these past few days."

That afternoon, as soon as she gets home from school, Tashi sits down to write two e-mails, one to her grandfather, the other to Richard.

Dear Bapu,

You are so smart! Everything worked out fine. We're going to Saranac for Thanksgiving after all. I want to invite Richard for Thanksgiving dinner . . . but maybe that's going too far. What do you think my wise and loving friend?

Love,

Your grateful g-daughter

Hello Richard,

Just wanted to let you know that we're coming to the lake for Thanksgiving . . . so, if you're playing at the restaurant on Saturday night, I can join you . . . assuming you want me. If you have any new pieces arranged for duet, we could practice them on Friday. I'll bring my cello just in case.

Hoping we can get together, one way or the other,

Tashi

Once dinner is finished and Tashi is in her bedroom doing homework, Esther turns to her husband and whispers, "Do you know what Eleanor asked me this morning?"

Asadour (*brusquely*): "Hardly, I was at work."

Esther: "She wants us to invite Richard to our cottage for Thanksgiving dinner."

Asadour: "So, what did you say?"

Esther: "That we'd think about it. I assumed that was O.K. with you."

Asadour: "Boy, you give that kid an inch and she takes a mile. I wonder . . . is she going on another hunger strike if we say no."

Esther: "I don't think so. We'll be at the cottage for Thanksgiving whether we invite him for dinner or not . . . so she probably won't be that upset if we say no."

Asadour: "Hmm. Inviting him over would give us a chance to learn more about him . . . you know, if you're worried about a fox hanging around the chicken pen, it might be better to bring him in where you can keep an eye on him."

Esther (*scowling*): "That's really crude, Asi . . . but maybe you're right. I want to ask him about his marriage . . . and those children of his who died. We'd have to be careful about it, though. We don't want to offend him in front of Eleanor."

Asadour: "Well, he did say that he wanted to hear my Verdi tapes. I'm sure he's aware that even though he's a composer, I know a lot more about Verdi than he does . . . so maybe he's eager to learn a little something."

Esther: "Maybe. But don't overdo it. You have a tendency to . . . "

Asadour (*reddening*): "Don't start that again Esther, please. It's perfectly normal. If I have some special knowledge about something, I want to share it. Just because you're tired of hearing it doesn't mean that everyone else is."

When the decision has finally been made, it is relayed promptly to Tashi who responds with an enthusiasm one might expect if she had just been invited to solo with the Boston Symphony. Within minutes she is at her computer writing to Richard.

———◆———

Dear Richard,

Guess what? My Mom and Dad want you to spend Thanksgiving with us at our cottage. Can you come? We don't want you to be alone on such an important day. Please say yes. I promise to make you the best dessert you've ever had.

Tashi

An answer arrives later that day.

Tashi . . . tell your parents thanks for the invitation. I had planned to spend the day at home with Kwatz, but this sounds much nicer. And about the restaurant . . . yes . . . Tim has asked me to play on Saturday, so sure . . . we can do a few duets, some old ones and a couple of news ones that we can practice on Friday. Give me a ring when you get here . . . Richard

Tashi (*shouting*): "Oh . . . such good news. Thanksgiving dinner at our house and a practice session at his house . . . and then Saturday night together, just like last summer." Reading the e-mail again, her troubled heart swells with a joy more typically reserved for an avowal of requited love and the promise of eternal bliss. She runs downstairs and collapses into her mother's arms, gasping the news, "He's coming. He's coming." Esther holds her close, her eyes moistening, more aware now than ever of the depth of her daughter's caring.

7   Verdi, etc.

Esther: "There's the doorbell, Eleanor. Go let Richard in. And tell your father to offer him a glass of wine . . . the fancy bottles we bought yesterday. We have both red and white."

"Come in and take a seat," Asi says, shaking Richard's hand. Hope you're hungry . . . we've got tons of food. Can I get you a glass of wine? Red or white? Let me guess . . . white."

"So, you have psychic abilities as well as professorial ones," Richard answers as they enter the cottage.

Asadour: "No. You composers are all alike . . . Verdi was a big white wine drinker . . . liked to grow his own grapes. You know he bought this huge farm in Busseto once the money from his operas started rolling in. Some years back Esther and I visited the house where he and Despina eventually settled down. Everything had been preserved . . . even the piano he used when . . . "

Esther (*from the kitchen*): "Asi . . . tell Eleanor to come fetch the appetizers. Richard must be starving."

Tashi winks at Richard then rushes to the kitchen. Moments later she emerges with a large platter of popcorn chicken, scallions, hummus, crackers and cut-up veggies. Setting it down in front of Richard, she points to the hummus, giggling: "With my own hands."

" . . . when he was working on Nabucco," Asi continues, undisturbed by the interruption. He was more at home there than in Milan which boasted a much more sophisticated culture. Of course, Despina never felt comfortable in Busseto where Verdi's first wife grew up . . . but that improved when Verdi offered to marry her and . . . "

"I like your sweater, Richard," Tashi whispers beneath the drone of her father's lecture. It's really handsome . . . goes well with the color of your hair and eyes."

Richard: "Thanks (*looking at her carefully now*). That's a really pretty dress. Have you grown a bit since I saw you in August?"

"A half an inch," she exclaims, clapping her hands in mock applause. "Better watch out. I may end up bigger than you."

"Not too likely," intones mother from the kitchen. "No woman in either my family or your father's has ever been more than 5'6."

"Verdi was quite tall . . . probably a foot taller than Despina," Asadour adds, co-opting the subject to his own agenda. "But the German soprano he admired so much and used in many of his late operas was close to 5'8' if I remember correctly. There were rumors of an affair but . . . "

"Are your mother and father still living, Richard?" asks mother, again from the kitchen.

"Yes. They divorced seven years ago; my mother remarried but my dad lives alone in L.A."

"Do you ever spend holidays with either of them?" she continues, inserting the thermometer into the turkey.

"Not lately, no," he replies. "They seem to be busy with other things . . . travelling abroad or going to friends' homes for the holidays."

"So, you're alone for Christmas?" Tashi inquires. "I mean you and Kwatz."

Richard: "Usually, yes."

Asadour: "I spent a lot of holidays away from home when I was a student in Cairo," adds Father. "It sounds bad but you get used to it."

"You studied in Cairo?" asks Richard. "Where were your parents living?"

"In Jerusalem . . . too far away to go back and forth just for vacations. It forces you to grow up . . . unlike most kids in America today. I feel fortunate that . . . "

Esther (*from the kitchen*): "I think we're about ready. Eleanor, would you pour the gravy into that bowl over there . . . the one with the spout. And the glaze for the sweet potatoes . . . use the smaller bowl on the second shelf."

Tashi takes a chair on Richard's left, Esther on his right. Once everyone is seated, Asadour turns to Richard, saying, "We're not very religious in this family . . . how about you? Are you the grace-saying type?"

Tashi: "Richard doesn't believe in God, Daddy; isn't that right, Richard?"

Richard: "Well, I haven't been in a foxhole lately . . . so maybe my opinion doesn't mean a whole lot. As of now though, I feel more comfortable with a naturalistic outlook. That doesn't mean I don't feel grateful for this lovely meal, Esther. Thank you."

Tashi (*laughing*): "Better taste it first, Richard. You might not like it."

"Did you like the hummus, Richard?" asks Father, referring to one of the appetizers. I taught Eleanor how to make it using a traditional Palestinian recipe. The kind you get in the supermarket these days just doesn't compare."

Richard: "Very much. Tashi . . . Eleanor that is . . . was kind enough to bring me some when we first started practicing together at my house. I agree. It has more character than the store-bought kind."

The tiny group grows silent as the pleasure of eating takes precedence over communicating. Outside, an autumn wind tugs at the last few oak leaves, stripping away the lingering signs of summer's abundance. Under the crisp air, the earth seems to huddle in readiness for the chill of winter. All the songbirds and butterflies have left; only the crows remain, calling to each other now with exaggerated alarm. It is too late to leave, they seem to say; the snow is already falling. Through the window, the sun begins a wistful descent, spreading its munificent rays across the table, illuminating both food and company. No one speaks, yet all are touched by its blessing.

"When we finish, can I show Richard my room?" Tashi asks finally, looking at Mother.

Esther: "Well . . . I guess there's no . . . "

"Why would a grown man want to see a girl's bedroom?" booms Father from across the table. "Let me show him my study. You like books don't you Richard? I've got a whole roomful, seven of which I've written myself."

"Maybe I can see both," Richard replies, stepping carefully.

Esther (*rising*): "There's plenty more turkey. Anyone ready for seconds?"

Richard (*holding out his empty plate*): "It's so good, Esther. Thank you."

Tashi (*anxiously*): "Richard, be sure to save room for dessert. I made something especially for you. You do like chocolate, don't you?"

Richard (*nodding*): "I can't imagine turning down a chocolate dessert."

The table is finally cleared and coffee served. From the kitchen Tashi shouts, "How hungry are you, Richard?"

Richard (*smiling to Esther, but talking to Tashi*): "I think I still have a little room left."

With that, Tashi marches into the dining room, dessert in hand, grinning with unconcealed pride. She sets a small bowl in front of Richard and waits at his side. At the bottom of the bowl is a moist chocolate pudding cake, still warm from the oven. Splashed over the cake is a layer of fudge sauce sprinkled with whipped cream. Lodged in the cream are flakes of chocolate, artistically arranged around a cherry center.

Richard leans over to breathe in the aroma. "This is so beautiful Tash . . . I hate to disturb it."

"Go ahead," she insists, still standing by his side. "You've got to taste it to see how good it is."

As Richard spoons his way down through the cream and sauce to scoop up a mouthful of pudding cake, he closes his eyes and sighs contentedly. Tashi beams as she follows his every move.

"What about your mother and me?" bellows Father. "Don't we count anymore?"

"Oh, sorry Dad. Yours is coming right up." With that she scoots back into the kitchen to get the remaining bowls. Alone at the counter, she covers her face with her hands and replays the scene in her imagination. She sees a man at peace, a man whose physical wants are satisfied, a husband being cared for by a loving wife. "I know I can make him happy," she muses. "If he will just wait for me."

When no one opts for seconds on dessert, Asadour rises and motions for Richard to follow him into his study. "Take a seat," he says, pointing to the black leather chair at the side of the desk. Each wall of the tiny room has its own book case . . . most being empty of everything but dust.

Asadour: "Most of my books are back in Boston where I do my serious work. I just brought a few for summer reading."

Richard: "You teach somewhere in the Boston area?"

Asadour: "Yes . . . at Emerson College. It's not in a league with Harvard or MIT, but we get our share of bright kids . . . mostly girls."

Richard: "I spent six years at Harvard, including two for my Masters."

Asadour: (*surprised*) "Really? In music I assume."

Richard: "Yes . . . although as an undergraduate I took almost as many courses in economics and sociology."

Asadour: "Strange combination . . . .music and economics."

Richard: "Well . . . the ec classes have helped me to maneuver my way around the stock market which is where I make most of my money these days."

Asadour (*moving to one of the book cases and picking up a book*): "Do you have any interest in the Middle East? That's my specialty. For example, this one focuses on the history of Armenia between the genocide of the early 20th Century and the fall of the Soviet Empire in the late 1980's. If you're interested, I'll give you a copy. I brought several with me just in case."

Richard: "Sure. I've often wondered what happened during that period . . . the fall of the Ottoman Empire and what it meant for the people who lived there."

Asadour opens the book and writes a brief inscription on the title page. Handing the book to Richard he says, "I wish Eleanor thought more of her Middle Eastern heritage. It can be a real anchor when you're growing up. I know it has been for me."

Richard: "That may come from having a mixed ethnic background. From what she has told me, I think she sees herself as simply American . . . not much more. I don't think you have to worry about her losing her direction in life. She strikes me as more certain about who she is than most kids I've met."

Asadour (*softening his voice*): "By the way, just exactly what are your intentions toward Eleanor?"

Richard (*quizzically*): "Intentions? I don't have any? You mean like marriage? . . . (*pause*) . . . I hope you're not serious."

Asadour: "Well. I realize it's early . . . but I don't want anyone giving her false hopes. She's pretty impressionable. And she's obviously very fond of you."

Richard (*uneasily*): "But she's only a girl, exceptionally mature perhaps, but still a girl. Does she have a crush on me? I can't be sure . . . but if she does, it won't last long. If I know kids, by next summer she'll have a hard time remembering my name."

Asadour's response is interrupted by a knock on the study door. Tashi enters smiling.

Tashi: "I think you've had Richard long enough, Daddy. It's my turn now." Taking her guest by the hand, she leads him upstairs to her bedroom where little has been done to tidy things up. "I hope you're not turned off. I wanted you to see me the way I really am."

The cello is leaning up against a book case filled with books and music scores. On the bed is an open copy of Les Miserables, on the floor a laptop displaying a half-written e-mail. In the corner next to the bed, a single large teddy bear leans against the wall, its fur frayed from years of cuddling.

As Richard scans the room from the doorway, his eyes slip from cello to books to laptop . . . coming to rest on the teddy bear.

"Well," she asks, "what do you think?"

When he does not answer, she turns to face him, then quickly looks away when she sees his eyes beginning to moisten. Moments pass without a sound.

Tashi (*softly, taking his hand*): "How old were they when they died, Richard?"

He shakes his head, unable to speak.

"I'm so sorry," she whispers, squeezing his hand.

He stands there for another minute, then turns to leave, reaching into his back pocket for a handkerchief as he descends the stairs.

A final thank you at the door and he heads for his car. As he turns the ignition key, there is a frantic rapping on the window. It's Tashi.

Tashi: "Aren't you going to say goodbye? . . . (*pause*) . . . I won't see you again until next summer."

Richard (*face down*): "I'm sorry . . . (*pause*) . . . It was the bedroom . . . I shouldn't have gone in."

Not to be denied, Tashi opens the door and reaches for his hand. "I need a hug, please."

Slowly he gets out of the car and embraces her. Still silent, he pulls her close.

Tashi (*whispering*): "I want you to know that you aren't alone in this world, Richard . . . (*pause*) . . . I will be loving you even though I'm far away in Boston . . . (*pause*) . . . Will you remember that . . . please?"

Without a word he brushes his cheek against hers and gets back in the car.

From the porch, Esther and Asadour watch nervously as he exits the driveway and disappears down the road.

Tashi remains standing in the driveway until she sees her parents coming toward her. Before they can say a word, she reaches up to touch her cheek. It is still moist. "His tears," she muses, "his and mine together . . . does he have any idea what I feel . . . any idea at all?"

8   Winter Chill

Dear Bapu,

How am I supposed to get through six more months of Boston? School seems stupid after last summer. I've already missed three days. Mom and Dad won't even let me call Richard . . . they thought I was all over him on Thanksgiving. Oh yes . . . I'm allowed one e-mail a month plus a call on Christmas day . . . one measly call. He might not even remember me by then. O.K., that's an exaggeration . . . but he could find someone else any day now. What would you do if you were me?

Love, Tashi

Mi carina nieta,

(I'm working on my Espanol . . . hope to take a trip to Mexico soon . . . want to find out more about the Indians down there and how they're getting screwed by the government).

So, what would I do if I were you? Well, I'm not nearly as smart as you . . . and certainly not as pretty . . . so what I say might not be too relevant. But let me give it a try.

I guess the first thing you have to do is accept the situation. Stop protesting. Tell yourself that this is the way things have to be right now . . . and stop fighting reality. Events may not be unfolding the way you want them to, but life is like that . . . at least some of the time. So, take a deep breath and relax.

Now, once you have stopped protesting, you're in a position to do something positive . . . for example, you can take those tormented feelings of yours and turn them into a poem. My guess is that you could be quite good at it. But start by reading some of the great love poems of the past . . . you know, Shakespeare, Donne, Burns, Byron, Keats, Wordsworth,

Dylan Thomas . . . people like that. Then try some of your own. I'd be happy to read them if you want some feedback. But don't send them to Richard . . . not yet anyway. Besides pissing your folks off, you might drive him away with all that emotion. Someday . . . after he wakes up to what a prize you are . . . you can show him what you wrote when you were 14 (or are you 15 now?).

Con mucho amor,

Bapu

◆

Dear Bapu,

Fifteen this month (you don't have it written down . . . how are you going to remember a present?) Don't worry . . . just kidding.

It's been a struggle to get started, but I like your idea. I've been reading some of Shakespeare's sonnets and poems by Richard Herrick, Thomas Gray and Keats . . . old stuff mainly.

It would be nice to find a woman poet I liked but the ones I've tried so far . . . modern writers like Sylvia Plath are too far out for me. I seem to respond to the simple stuff better. Wordsworth's love poems to the peasant girl Lucy are more my speed. You know that one where he refers to her as

"A violet by a mossy stone, half hidden from the eye,

fair as a star, when only one is shining in the sky."

That is so beautiful . . . and so sad when you find out later in the poem that she was dead when he finally reached her cottage after riding there by moonlight. I think reading a poem like that does relieve some of the pain of not seeing Richard. It reminds me that other people have suffered too. But like you said, dear abuelo (I looked it up in Daddy's Spanish dictionary), writing the poem instead of just reading it would probably make me feel even better. With that in mind, I'm going to give it a try. Please feel free to comment. I want the poems I write to be the best ones you've ever read.

Un abrazo afectuoso de su nieta (*two can play this game*),

Tashi

———————◆———————

Dear Tashi,

Happy Birthday . . . I think. . . at least it's sometime this month you told me. Have you received my package yet? No? Maybe it's because I haven't sent it (Ho!). Actually I haven't even picked out a present . . . but I *have* thought about it. Any day now something should happen.

Any poems emerge yet? Your (unpaid) editor stands ready to get to work.

Mit vielen liebe,

Bapu

———————◆———————

Dear Bapu,

German now? What's next, Latin?

It's nice to hear that that you've put so much time into thinking about my birthday present. But please don't go overboard about it. Just keep in mind that I'm not quite 16 so there's no point in getting me a car. Maybe next year though?

O.K. Here's my first go at a poem. Don't laugh. It took me three days.

Lost in the woods, I turn this way, then that. I call but there is no answer. Where are you? The sky is darkening and I am far from home.

Why don't you answer? I miss you so much. I stop to sit under a tree, my cheeks wet with tears. The forest can be frightening at night. Please don't leave me alone like this. I call again, but there is still no answer.

Too emotional? Probably. I was never very good at hiding my feelings. Let me know what you think. Be honest. I can take it.

Love, Tashi

Dear Tashi,

I like the idea of the poem . . . potentially very touching. The *idea* has the power to move readers, but at present the words sound too much like prose . . . too much like ordinary speech. It needs more metaphors . . . fewer statements about *what* you feel and more *demonstration* of someone having those feelings. For example, instead of saying "I miss you so much," try "I keep looking behind me, but no one is there." Or instead of "the forest can be frightening at night," try "the sound of unseen paws on dried leaves quickens my heart."

It might help to recall the poem you quoted earlier. If he wanted to write prose, Wordsworth could have said that Lucy was beautiful, shy and one of a kind . . . but instead he referred to her as "a violet by a mossy stone, half hidden from the eye, fair as a star when only one is shining in the sky." A lot more powerful, don't you think?

And pay attention to the rhythm . . . read the poem out loud . . . see if it moves. Does it carry you forward, rising and falling, now fast, now slow . . . heading toward some resolution? For someone who loves music, you should be able to write something more musical . . . yes?

x0*m% @3d *

(4^*<?#fT

P.S. O.K. so my Latin is a bit rusty.

Dear Bapoo,

Thanks for your thoughts. I'm sure you're right about my poem being too prosy . . . but I really don't how to think in metaphors. Maybe you can give me more examples of how to do it. But guess what . . . I made a few corrections then submitted the thing to a regional poem contest at school . . . and won third prize. It's going to be published in the superintendent's quarterly newsletter. Looks like I'm on my way! Thanks for the help.

On another subject, cooking really helps me to forget about Richard . . . at least while I'm doing it. Next time you come (assuming you ever get invited) you can try my basil pesto pasta (courtesy of Dad). And there's bell pepper soup too . . . . (courtesy of Mom) . . . goes great with jamba juice and crackers.

I'm also learning how to throw pots. Be nice and I might make you a vase or bowl or something.

Love, Tashi

P.S. I wish you could come and live with us.

Hey Tasherino,

Thanks for the invite . . . but I still fart and burp a lot . . . not sure your mother could handle that.

Glad to hear you're throwing pots instead of smoking it. And it sounds like you're really getting into cooking. Your basil pesto dish has my mouth watering already (ok . . . so I drool anyway). I would say without hesitation that basil pesto is the most delicious culinary creation I've ever experienced. The bell pepper soup sounds terrific too. Your Mom is fortunate to have you around (at a rather stiff price to be sure).

Congratulations on the coming publication of your poem. It's clear that you're on your way (where I don't know). Never heard of jamba juice . . . but I'll look it up next time I go to the supermarket (or should I try a pet store?).

By the way I'm sending you a copy of the book I wrote on philosophy (no, this is not your birthday present). I'm sending it because you asked about it a while back. Feel free to use it as a door jamb if you don't like it.

Love, Baaaaaaaaaaaaaaaaaaaaaaaaaaaaaa pu!

✦

Dear Bapurino,

I started reading your philosophy book. Must admit I stopped after about 50 pages, but what you said draws you in and makes you wonder. It was difficult to read partly because the language and concepts were difficult, and because I really tried to understand it, not just read it, but wonder about it and contemplate it, and it was weird because you wrote it. To the readers you're this unknown entity, "the author," but you're my grandpa, and it's odd because I can see you, hunched over a computer screen, writing about this serious stuff, but then I also see you sending me fake puke and dog poop for my birthday when I was younger, and the person reading this book has no idea that the person who he's reading about is you. And to me, the author and the person who sends me these things are totally unrelated. As the author, you seem incredibly smart, but a totally different person than the one who ambushed my poor parents with a squirt gun. Remember that day? It kind of makes you wonder about what other authors are like as people. Sorry, this turned into a whole long thing. It wasn't supposed to, but I apparently have more going on in my head than anticipated.

Richard hasn't answered my latest e-mail yet . . . hope he's not turned off by something I said.

Looooooooooooooooovin' u

Tashi

◆

raeD ihsaT,

Don't fret if my head seems screwed on backwards. I tend to get this way around Groundhog's Day. Something to do with the sun I think. I can feel myself getting itchy for spring. Tired of all this snow.

It's nice to know that you took my book seriously. O.K., so you only got through 50 pages. Don't sweat it. If you had raced through it, you might have missed the whole point. Let's see, the book runs 300 pages . . . so if you do 50 a year you should finish in about six years . . . unless you get sick or have a lobotomy, then it could take a tad longer. So . . . assuming all goes well, call me in 2015 and let me know if you liked it.

Regarding Richard, he might be suffering cabin fever by now, seeing as he's been cooped up in that cottage for months. How about sending him some cookies or home-made bread . . . something to remind him he's got a friend in Boston. If your folks object, tell them you're just feeling charitable. You may have to prove your sincerity by making cookies for all the homeless Bostonians camped out under the Longfellow bridge . . . but hey, it should do wonders for your reputation.

Speaking of values (we were?), what kinds of things are most important to you . . . excluding Richard for the moment? To put it another way, what do you want to do with the rest of your life? Big question I know. Don't be bashful.

Yikes!

B.

◆

Dear Bapu,

You've really got me thinking now . . . which is good because it takes my mind off of Richard.

I guess, most of all, I want to do something to benefit mankind. By the time I'm your age I want to have affected my generation and made a mark on the world. And if I can't do that, I would like to be remembered and celebrated by the people I love. This is really more important to me. It would mean that I've become the person I want to be, that I'm a pillar of my family, a trusted friend, someone that people honor and respect, not just the aloof relative who nobody got to know. I want to give part of myself to the people I love, and have them know that and be proud to know me.

So, there you have it. Do you still love me?

Tashi

Querida Tashi,

I do. And I'm impressed with what you say. Aside from a slight excess of ego, you appear to have the wisdom and maturity of a woman three times your age. It may be genetic . . . if so, I want some of the credit. But be forewarned: recent research suggests that when you mature too fast, the maturing process begins to reverse itself in middle age. In other words, once you turn that corner you become increasingly infantile and eventually end up where you began. The moral: hang on to your diapers.

Seriously, do you really want to affect a whole generation and make a mark on the world? Sounds like a tall order. Hitler probably had a similar aspiration and achieved all of it. But you don't want to be another Hitler do you? So maybe you have to spell out HOW you want to affect your generation . . . and what KIND of mark you want to make on the world. Trivial concerns I'm sure . . . but hey . . . as you know, my mind runs along petty channels.

Yes, I still love you . . . well, maybe . . .

Bapu

Dear Bapu,

I think I did spell out the HOW and what KIND when I said I wanted to be remembered and celebrated by the people I love. That's benefitting the world, isn't it . . . although you will probably argue that Hitler thought he was benefitting the world by starting WWII and killing millions of Jews.

Now that you've got me thinking about all this stuff, I'm getting clearer about what I really believe. My #1 ideal is that I want to be absolutely happy with myself, #2 is that I want to be respected and admired by my peers and make a good mark on my generation. Hopefully, being happy with myself will make other people respect me and allow me to have an impact on my generation because I won't be hung up on lots of personal issues.

Then again maybe I'll be like Van Gogh and be utterly weird for a time, but after I die, they'll all decide that I'm a genius. Just don't tell Richard, O.K.?

Love, Tashi

Dear Tashi,

Please don't go cutting off your ears or other critical parts of your anatomy. I mean, who is going to feel like celebrating you if you're lying there in a coffin without a nose or a chin? And keep this in mind: if you're dead, how much will other people's admiration and respect mean to you?

All kidding aside, I think your ideals are just great. Of course, it's highly unlikely that you will ever live up to them . . . but what the heck . . . it's better to have something to believe in than nothing at all. Yes?

Now that the subject of admiration has come up, consider this nasty little thought: Is your desire to be approved of going to make you a prisoner of other people's opinions? Will your need to be admired put your freedom to be yourself in jeopardy? After all, you're not going to get people to admire you unless you do things which *they* value . . . and that could interfere with your freedom to "march to your own drummer."

Just a thought (*hmmm*),

El Burpo

--------◆--------

Dear Senor Burpo,

I don't ever want to give up my freedom to be myself . . . even if means having people turn against me. But I don't think that will happen. So far anyway, people seem to respect me for standing up for my own opinions even when they're different.

I like your humor. Maybe you should write for Saturday Night Live . . . or Mad Magazine. That way you could get rich . . . then you'd have enough money to buy me a car for my birthday next year.

Still laughing,

Tash

--------◆--------

Dear Tashi,

Following up on the "being yourself" theme, what would you do if Richard insisted that you convert to Buddhism or some other religion as a condition for getting married? Would you do it . . . if refusing to convert meant you could never marry him? Just wondering.

I like your suggestion about writing funny stuff. Actually, I've been thinking of doing a little book of skits based on characters from the old Steve Allen comedy hour. He was great. Borrowing from that program, the main figures would be Robb Storrs, Sandy Beach, and Park Carrs. Early on I would introduce a new character by the name of Sheik Hans. The whole thing is a play on words. First episode might go like this (abbreviated version):

(Everyone sitting around a table . . . Sheik has just been introduced to the others . . . lots of kidding about terrorists; after a while Robb gets up and heads for the men's room . . . several minutes pass)

Sheik (*anxiously*): "Robb has been gone for a long time. What's he doing?"

Sandy (*impatiently*): "He's going to the bathroom, what do you think? Don't you terrorists ever have to go?"

Sheik (*with irritation*): "I know that, stupid. I'm asking what he's doing in there that's taking so long."

Park (*quickly*): "Like Sandy just said, he's going to the bathroom."

Sheik (*rising from his chair*): "I'm not a moron. I know *where* he is. I want to know what he's doing in there."

Sandy (*shouting*): "What the hell do you think he's doing in there, dummy? He's going to the bathroom."

Sheik: "Jesus Christ!"

Park: "Hey, watch your language!"

Love,

Your Grossvater (*accent on the first syllable*)

Dear Bapu,

I agree. Your story is definitely gross. I think you're going to have a hard time getting it performed on television. But don't let me discourage you. It's just that our ideas about what's funny happen to be a bit different. Sorry.

About Richard and converting to Buddhism, I'd have to wait and see. Maybe I'd like to become a Buddhist some day. I don't know enough about it right now, but I want to learn. The real test would be if he wanted me to become a born-again Christian or something else I couldn't stomach. But I guess if he believed in all that, I probably wouldn't love him as much in the first place.

Did I answer your question?

Tashi

Dear Tash,

I'm a little surprised by your negative reaction to my skit. Do I detect a hint of Puritanism still buried deep in your adolescent psyche? Thought you had gotten beyond all that uptight stuff . . . but maybe you're not alone . . . maybe the whole damn culture is moving backwards. Look out John Calvin, here we come. I can see it all now. Another generation of this and we'll be spooking our kids anew with tales of hell-fire and brimstone. With nothing better to do, we'll huddle in church and listen to pious toads rant about the evils of sex, then picnic in the park while watching heretics, adulterers and sexual deviants getting burned at the stake in an orgy of self-righteous purification. Scholars will re-interpret the Dark Ages as a model for social harmony; laws will be passed banning the holding of hands in public; kids caught masturbating in the garage will have their dorks removed . . . I don't want to be around when all this comes to pass. Do you?

Having fun with my Jeremiads,

Bapu

Dear Gloomy One,

I like it when you pretend to know something that the rest of us don't. You may not be very convincing, but you can still be funny . . . sort of.

Right now all I can think of is getting back to Saranac. School ends this week and we're heading for the cottage on Wednesday. Richard said in his last e-mail that Tim wants us to start playing at the restaurant on the 20th. That will give us a couple of weeks to practice the new duets he's arranged for cello and piano. He also mentioned a new wrinkle: this year I am to get paid. Last year it was a free dinner . . . now it's going to be dinner plus $50 each Saturday. So, stop worrying about how to survive in your golden years. I'll be there to support you.

Love, Tashi

P.S. I hope you know how much your e-mails have meant to me these past six months. Not sure I could have made it through the winter without you. Hope you liked mine too.

9   A Hot Day in June

The knock on the door is familiar. Without rising from the piano, Richard shouts, "Come on in, Tash."

Tashi, dressed in saffron tank top and khaki shorts, enters wiping the sweat from her forehead. "How can you write music when it's this hot and humid?"

Richard: "The fan helps. Want something to drink? There's soda in the fridge . . . help yourself."

Tashi (*going to the fridge and taking out an orange soda*): "I think people really liked the new duet we played last night. I was thinking that you could use it as the slow movement of a cello sonata if you wanted to . . . maybe even a cello concerto. But that would be a lot of work I know."

Richard (*turning to face her*): A ton of work. So, what are you up to today? You're not exactly dressed for church."

Tashi: "It's so hot Richard. I was thinking of going up to the brook and lying in the water. I've done it before on hot days. There's a place where the rocks form a little pool. You can't really swim in it . . . but if you squat, the water comes up to your shoulders. I like it better than the public beach because no one ever comes there. It's private enough so that you can even take your clothes off."

Richard (*hesitantly*): "Hmmm . . . interesting. But I suppose you could go in with your top and shorts on, couldn't you? It would be pretty much like wearing a bathing suit."

Tashi: "Not really. Clothes get in the way. You don't feel the water as much. Besides, they're heavy . . . they weigh you down."

Richard: "I can see I'm old-fashioned about this. Why don't you go on up to the brook and join me back here for lunch later. All that cold water should make you pretty hungry. I can whip up a tuna fish sandwich . . . I'll even throw in some pickles and chips."

Tashi: "I like the idea . . . I'll even make the sandwiches myself . . . but it's not as much fun going to the brook by myself. I was hoping you would join me. You look pretty hot right now . . . and it's going to get even hotter as the day does on. Wouldn't you like to cool off?"

Richard: "Well . . . yes . . . . .but . . . "

Tashi (*sensing some hesitation*): "Up at the brook the water is a perfect temperature . . . neither hot nor cold. And the little pool is shaded by this huge maple. It's like having our own private spa."

Richard: "You make it sound pretty enticing."

Tashi (*taking him by the arm and leading him to the door*): "C'mon, don't be an old stick-in-the-mud."

Richard (*stopping at the door*): "But I should change clothes."

Tashi: "Into what? Once we get to the pool, you won't need any clothes. Or if you want, you can go in the water with those shorts on. It's up to you. But there's no point in changing."

Richard: "Maybe we should take something to drink. Want me to throw a couple of sodas in my backpack?"

Tashi: "Mmm. Do you have any munchies to go with it? Maybe some nuts or chips?"

As Tashi looks on with growing excitement, Richard goes into the kitchen where he stuffs a can of mixed nuts, a bag of potato chips and two granola bars into his backpack. "O.K. I think we're ready."

Once they are off the porch and onto the trail, Tashi takes the lead. "It's a little uphill for the first half mile," she says without turning, so it will be better to take it kinda slow. When we get up higher, we should start getting a little breeze . . . and that will help with the bugs."

Richard (*laughing as he slaps his neck*): "Bugs, bugs? I haven't seen any yet, have you?"

Tashi (*giggling):* "Just one . . . on my wrist. But he was so cute I didn't want to hurt him, so I let him go."

Richard (*with mock concern*): "Oh, that must be the one I just whacked. Sorry."

Tashi (*turning to smile*): "I think you should apologize to his mother."

Richard: "O.K. But shouldn't we stop for a burial?"

Tashi (*shaking her head*): "It's too hot. We can get to it on the way back."

As they make their way up the hill, Tashi is aware of a new warmth in her chest, a rare sensation known only when all worries have been banished from her mind. This is what I've always wanted," she murmurs, "to be alone with him . . . just the two of us . . . enjoying the outdoors together, saying funny things back and forth to each other." Her secret joy is quickened by the knowledge that behind her tank top something of considerable interest has been stirring since their canoe trip last summer. With half-closed eyes she recalls what she saw in the mirror this morning as she was dressing. "These are no longer the breasts of a little girl," she told herself then, cupping both breasts with her hands and running her thumbs around her areolas. "Not the full breasts of a woman like Vera perhaps, but ample enough to make a man notice."

Further up the trail she tries to imagine what she looks like to Richard now. Still walking, she runs her hand across her chest, reassured by the soft bumps that something marvelous has indeed happened. "I can feel the difference," she whispers, "but can he see it? When he looks at me now, do I seem more grown up compared to last year? I want to ask him, but that would make me look needy and he doesn't like that in women."

Unaware of his hiking partner's preoccupation with physiology, Richard lets his mind drift back to the music he was working on when she arrived this morning. "Her idea of a cello sonata or even a cello concerto is a striking one," he reflects, "but that might take up to six months and how could I pull it off without ever having played the instrument myself?

Writing little pieces for the restaurant is one thing; composing for a symphony orchestra is quite another." He is distracted from his reverie when a mosquito finds his bare arm and drives a needle into his skin. The violent slap of his hand resounds through the forest.

Tashi turns her head, smiles and makes a "V" with her fingers, then quickly falls back into her reverie. Once again she sees herself as she appeared before the mirror . . . still slender but no longer skinny, a woman in the making, an attractive, desirable woman with something to offer the opposite sex . . . a flower ready to bloom. In the shadows of her imagination she sees herself magically transformed from child to adult . . . from a formless, gray larva to a multi-colored, radiant butterfly, springing free from its chrysalis, its moist wings unfolded to the sun as it prepares for its maiden flight. The fantasy draws her ever more deeply into its imagery, pushing aside the reality of mosquitoes, thistles and footsteps on the trail behind her. Luxuriating in her metamorphosis, she drops her guard and gives voice to the realization welling up inside her. "I can have babies," she shouts to the forest. "I'm a woman now and can have babies."

"What did you just say?" shouts Richard from a few yards behind, not bothering to conceal his alarm.

Tashi: "Sorry. I didn't mean to shout. I was just . . . well . . . I guess I was daydreaming about butterflies and things and it suddenly hit me that I can now have babies. I started having periods two months ago and Mom says . . . "

Richard (*interrupting*): "Hmmm. I hope you're not planning on starting a family any time soon."

Tashi: "Of course not, silly. It's just that I'm growing up and I want to be treated like a young woman . . . that's all."

No words are exchanged as they climb higher, keeping pace with the sun as it reaches for its noon apex, each lost in a separate world yet joined in the common goal of getting to the pool and escaping the heat. At the crest of the hill where the brook makes its sharpest descent, Tashi stops, wipes the sweat from her face and announces that the sought-after pool is only yards away. With that, she dashes ahead and slips behind a cluster of gooseberry bushes. By the time Richard reaches the pool, she is standing next to the water, completely naked.

To escape his unwanted gaze, she could have jumped into the pool, squatted and thus covered everything below her shoulders. At the very least she could have retreated into the obscuring shade of the huge maple. But she does neither. So great is her need to share these harbingers of womanliness with the man she adores . . . and so unequivocal her conviction that he will be aroused by his discovery . . . that she allows her normal instincts of modesty and coyness to be pushed to the edge of consciousness where they can observe but no longer interfere.

She stands at the edge of the pool, her slender body fully exposed to the sun's caresses. Her breasts are lovely, yes . . . but hardly more than a fraction of what they are destined to become. Unlike her mother's which now lie flat on her chest like tired, jelly-filled donuts, Tashi's leap from her frame with a sense of purpose, soft yet erect, tense at the nipple, pointing, eager to show themselves to the world.

As Richard approaches, her body, still white from a long, New England winter, trembles from the volcanic energy bubbling within. She turns to face him. Noticeable even from the trail are the soft black hairs adorning her slit. She makes no attempt to hide them. The slit itself, still girlish in its innocence yet already moist with unarticulated desire, glistens under the sun's furtive glances.

"So what are you waiting for?" she shouts triumphantly. "Leave your clothes by the tree and let's get in the water."

Richard (*from under the big maple*): "You go ahead. I'll join you in a minute."

Tashi steps into the pool and wets her whole body, even her hair whose curls fall deliciously to her neck as she shakes the water from her shoulders. From the center of the pool, her modest bush just visible above the surface, she cries (*pointing*), "Look at the oriole nest up in the maple, Richard." As Richard emerges from the shade to look, her eyes are riveted to his naked body. Had she been guided more by convention than by impulse, she might have looked down or away but she does neither, surrendering instead to a curiosity nurtured in the heat of countless dreams. "Oh my god," she exclaims, "it's so big and fat !"

Richard smiles awkwardly, using his right hand to cover his crotch, then steps down into the water. Given the diminutive size of the pool, they are forced into a closeness that makes escape from her scrutiny impossible. "I never realized it was so big," she says, unable to avert her eyes. Then, with a suddenness uncensored by good judgment, she asks, "Can I touch it?"

Richard *(abruptly)*: "No you cannot."

Tashi *(giggling uncontrollably)*: "How do you walk around with that between your legs all day?"

Richard *(backing up against the embankment)*: "You get used to it."

By now the sun has risen over the maple and captured her face and torso in all their youthful loveliness. The sight of her infectious smile, wet hair, and hardening nipples threatens to bring hitherto buried instincts to the surface. His cheeks redden.

"Oh my god," she bursts out. "It's getting bigger. Look, it's pointing upwards like a rocket. That's so weird. Are you making it do that Richard?"

Richard *(locking his knees)*: "No . . . well . . . not exactly . . . sometimes it acts on its own."

Tashi: "Why is it sticking up in the air like that?"

Richard: "I don't know. Probably the air . . . or water. Being outdoors can make that happen."

Tashi: "It looks hard . . . does it have a bone inside like a finger?"

Richard: "No."

Tashi: "Why can't I touch it?"

Richard: "I'm the only one who can do that."

Tashi: "The way you talk, you'd think it has a life of its own. Maybe you should give it a name."

Richard: "Like what?"

Tashi: "Oh, I don't know . . . maybe Junior . . . or Little Richie . . . *pause*) . . . Oh look . . . it's going back down. What happened?"

Richard *(lowering himself in the water)*: "It's not used to all this attention."

Tashi (*squatting*): "I hope I didn't embarrass you. It's just that I've never seen one that big before."

Richard: "I'm O.K."

Tashi *(spreading her arms on the water):* "It's really cool here, isn't it, Richard. And the shade makes it even nicer. I hope you're glad you came."

Richard: "Definitely."

As she squats in the water, nude, face-to-face with a partner whose self-consciousness is evident from his silence, her legs are open, her knees only a few feet from his.

Tashi (*softly*): "Can we talk about love a little bit," she says. "I think about it a lot. Do you?"

Richard: "Occasionally."

Tashi: "I want to give myself completely to a man. To tell that person I love him, and to hear him say 'I love you too' is the most wonderful thing I can imagine."

Richard: "Well yes. I say that a lot to Kwatz. He still hasn't reciprocated . . . but there could be a language problem there."

As they talk, her hand goes underwater to her crotch where she begins to stroke her labia, running her fingers up into the folds that enclose her sex. A throbbing arises around her clitoris similar to what she felt that day at the lake when she had her first climax. Just inches from Richard's knees now but hidden from his gaze, she searches out that same hardening flesh and begs for its secret release.

Tashi (*with breath coming faster*): "I think the most beautiful thing imaginable is to hear someone say, 'I am in love with you'. Don't you agree, Richard?"

By now her face is contorted by the fires raging within. The change is obvious to Richard who leans backward against the rocks. From the edge of the pool, he scrutinizes her body, searching for an explanation but finds none. Not to be denied, she slides forward, her knees grazing his.

"Do you think you will ever love again?" she gasps, hand pressed to her vulva while two fingers massage her clit, her whole body in the throes of an uncontainable longing.

Richard: "Perhaps, but I'm in no rush."

Breathless and at the mercy of her need now, she yields to the throbbing in her crotch, tantalizing in its promise of bliss, and presses hard on her sex. With head thrown back, no longer guided by reason, she thrusts her pelvis toward her bathing partner. Her groin tightens, then relaxes, then explodes into ecstasy as waves of healing warmth ripple through her slender frame. With eyes still closed, she falls forward into his arms, sobbing.

Richard (*wrapping his arms around her*): "Are you alright, Tash. What's the matter?"

"Oh darling Richard," she cries out. "Love me, please tell me you love me."

Richard (*startled*): "Of course I love you. What makes you think I don't?"

Tashi: "No . . . I mean . . . oh God . . . that's alright Richard (*pulling away slowly and leaning against the opposite bank*). I just got carried away . . . (*pause*) . . . I'm sorry. Let's just enjoy the water."

On the way down the hill, the two hikers, now fully clothed, remain closeted in their separate thoughts. The silence is finally broken when Tashi asks, "Can we get together Wednesday for a practice session; my pottery class was shifted to Friday."

Richard: "I can't make it Wednesday because that's the day I have my class at the Correction Center."

Tashi (*stopping on the trail*): "What class is that? I never heard you mention the Correction Center before?"

Richard: "I give a composition class there . . . you know . . . teaching kids how to write their own music using a synthesizer and laptop. No one's interested in classical so we stick pretty much to pop and jazz. It's a small class, usually five or six kids, but it's fun because they're really motivated to learn. And a couple of them have real talent."

Tashi: "How come you never told me about this before? In all the time we've known each other you've never said a word about it . . . (*pause*) . . . If we get married someday, I hope that . . . "

Richard (*interrupting*): "What in the world makes you think we're going to get married? You're still a girl . . . just barely out of middle school."

Tashi (*hand on her hips*): "But shouldn't we be practicing things like sharing now . . . before we commit ourselves to each other?"

Richard (*taking a deep breath*): "To be honest Tashi, I have other things on my mind right now . . . like how to get my music performed in concert. Marriage is the last thing I'm thinking about."

Tashi (*wincing*): "Don't you find me attractive?"

Richard (*sighing*): "Yes I do. I'm sure you're one of the prettiest girls in your class."

Tashi: "So you still see me as a girl rather than a young woman; that's not what I hoped to hear. Haven't you noticed any changes since last summer?"

Richard: "Yes . . . you're obviously filling out a little . . . and maybe an inch or two taller."

Tashi: "But when you saw me naked, weren't you a little bit excited?"

Richard (*looking down at the ground*): "I think that was the water . . . it often happens when I first step into a lake or stream."

Tashi (*softly*): "But you were still on the bank when it happened . . . weren't you?"

Richard (*head shaking*): "I don't remember . . . but look Tash . . . this is not something your parents would want you to be talking about. Let's save it for another time."

Tashi (*biting her lip*): "O.K. but before we drop it I need to know how you really feel toward me. I don't want to be guessing all the time . . . (*pause*) . . . Do you love me?"

Richard (*sighing again*): "Like I said before, of course I love you. Why else would I be spending all this time with you?"

Tashi (*squinting*): "But *how* do you love me?"

Richard: "I love you like I love Kwatz and my friends in town. You're all special to me. I enjoy being with you . . . I'm glad to have you in my life . . . (*pause*) . . . What more do you want me to say?"

Tashi (*eyebrows raised*): "You love me the way you love your cat? Richard, that's cruel. In case you haven't noticed, I'm a human being . . . and a female one at that. Can Kwatz play the cello with you at the restaurant? Can he talk to you about personal things? Can he make you hummus? Can he excite you when he takes his clothes off?"

Richard: "Well O.K., that wasn't a very good way of putting it. I'm sorry. I should have been more sensitive . . . "

Tashi: "So?"

Richard: "So . . . I love you as a friend, as one of my dearest friends, as someone whose companionship I have come to treasure. . . (*pause*) . . . Is that better?"

Tashi: "A little."

Richard: "Only a little? And I thought I was being magnanimous. Oh well, I never was any good with relationships. Just ask my ex-wife."

Tashi: "And what would she say, Richard?"

Richard: "I'd rather not go into that Tashi, at least not right now. Let's get home. Kwatz will be hungry and my feet need a rest."

At home that night, Tashi makes her way through dinner with a minimum of discussion about the day's activities. As soon as the dishes are done, she withdraws to her bedroom and sits down at her computer. There is no question about where this e-mail is going.

Dear Bapu,

I just had an exciting day with Richard . . . but I'm not sure what to make of it. Hoping you can help. Here's what happened. It was a really hot humid day so we decided (my suggestion) to follow the brook up to the pool that sits on top of the hill and cool off there. Each time I've gone there before I've taken my clothes off (nobody ever comes by so it's real private) . . . so I did it again. Richard was a little hesitant at first but he finally gave in and got naked too.

When he saw me without any clothes on, his penis got real hard and stuck straight out. I pretended not to know what that meant and kidded him about it. He said it often happened when he went swimming . . . but he wasn't even in the water yet! Now, here's what I want to know: could he have been telling the truth . . . or was he just trying to hide the fact that he liked seeing me without any clothes on?

I know it sounds silly but it makes a big difference to me. When I ask him if he loves me, he says yes but it sounds like someone talking about a friend. He also said that he loves me the way he loves his cat . . . yes, he actually said that! What gets me the most of all is that even though I've developed a lot from last year, he still sees me as a little girl. And yet he gets excited when he sees me naked. I just don't get it.

What does it all mean to you? I need a man's opinion . . . especially a wise, old man who I can count on to tell me the truth. Please don't take too long to answer.

Love, Tashi

------------◆------------

Dear Tashi,

I've had a chance now to think about your e-mail and would venture the opinion that your friend Richard is hiding something, certainly from you but possibly from himself as well. Men don't get erections from looking at water, but they do get them from looking at people (either male or female) they find attractive. It's pretty clear from what you said that he sees you as something more than a little girl. It's equally clear, though, that he doesn't want you to know this. And it's my guess that he doesn't even want to admit it to himself. Why? It's probably got something to do with his ex-wife . . . like not wanting to get involved again. Perhaps he was hurt earlier and is unwilling to try again with someone else.

But let's not forget that you are still very young for this kind of thing. You may be turning into an adult but you're still only 15 (do I have that right?). And when he looks at you, that's what he sees, not a little girl perhaps but someone not yet his equal. It's my guess that he's not going to fall in love with you until you become his confidant . . . that is, someone he can talk to about the painful things still bottled up inside him. I'll even go so far as to make a prediction: the day he tells you about how his kids died is the day he's going to fall in love with you.

See you later, Bapu

———————◆———————

Dearest Bapu,

How your e-mail thrills me. I don't dare tell you how many times I have read it. Everything you said sounds so right on. Oh, I do want to become his confidant . . . more than anything I can think of. But how do I do it? I've asked about his family several times but he always puts me off. I'm afraid if I ask again, he'll get mad and pull away altogether. We're going to practice on Thursday and then play at the restaurant Saturday night. Should I bring the subject up either of those times?

Hurry!

———————◆———————

Dear Tashi,

What's the big rush? You've got your whole life ahead of you. You're going to blow this whole thing to Kingdomcome if you don't keep your knickers on. Don't ask him again . . . about either his wife or his kids. Wait until he comes to you on his own which he will . . . given enough time. It won't happen this summer; it may not even happen next year. But, if you stand at his side day after day, week after week, he will eventually trust you enough to open up. And when he does, he'll be yours . . . all yours.

Love, Bapissimo

———————◆———————

Dear Bapu,

Thanks for all the advice. I feel so good talking to you about this. I'm off to our practice session now. Will write later.

I love you so much . . .

Tashi

10   At the Restaurant II

As the car comes to a rest in the restaurant parking lot, Asadour turns to Esther, "This could be a little awkward, seeing how he left the house at Thanksgiving without even a thank you."

"Well, he did voice his appreciation at the dinner table," she replies softly.

Asadour (*louder*): "That's hardly enough after all the preparation it took to put on a meal like that. I don't know about this guy. There's something strange about him."

Esther: "But she seems to care a lot for him, so we have to . . . "

Asadour (*interrupting*): She's only 15 for Christ's sake. What the hell is she doing getting involved with a man old enough to be her uncle?"

Esther: "He's not that old, Asi. And he's done some nice things for her . . . like inviting her to play here at the restaurant. It has really made the summer for her. Remember how lonely she used to be."

Asadour (*gruffly*): "Better lonely than preyed upon by some older man who has already gone through one marriage and lost his kids in the process. I'm going to keep my eye on him if he comes over to the table tonight."

Esther: "Try to be nice. We don't want her angry at us."

Asadour: "Another thing: we still don't know what kinds of nonsense that father of yours is pouring into her ears."

Esther (*at the restaurant door*): "I think he means well . . . and it's obvious she loves him."

Tashi spots them entering and comes to the table soon after they are seated. "Got your favorite table again, I see," she says, pulling up a chair.

"How come you're not turning pages for Richard?" Father asks. "Did you lose your job already?"

"No Daddy, the piece he's playing right now is something he composed a long time ago. He knows it by heart, so he doesn't need my help."

"Are we going to hear any duets this evening?" Mother asks, "I loved the ones you played last summer."

Tashi: "Oh yes. Some old ones and two new ones that Richard wrote over the winter."

Asadour (*shaking his head*): "So he survived the whole winter up there in that little cottage?", making no attempt to conceal his disdain for anyone who would eschew the comforts of urban life for a primitive existence in the middle of the forest.

"He likes the privacy," Tashi answers. "He says he can compose better when there's nothing going on around him. It makes sense to me."

When the waiter appears for their order, Tashi returns to the bandstand and waits in the corner until Richard has finished his solo piece. As soon as he is done, she comes to the piano and asks if he would like to join her parents during their next break. "They are anxious to see you again." When he doesn't respond immediately, she adds, "We don't have to spend more than a few minutes."

Later, with the conclusion of the new duet and the dying away of applause, Tashi leads Richard to her parents' table over near the wall.

"Nice to see you again Richard," Asadour says, rising. "Come, sit with us and tell us how you made it through the winter up there in the woods. By the way, your new duet was quite beautiful. Did you have the Italians in mind, perhaps, when you were writing it?"

"Nobody in particular," Richard responds. "I just write whatever comes to mind at the time."

"Richard told me that he's been teaching composition to kids at the Correctional Center," Tashi interjects. "And that some of them have real talent."

"Isn't that dangerous though, Richard," Esther suggests (*frowning*). "I mean, associating with young criminals. Who knows what they have done to get put in there?"

"Well Esther, I actually do know what they have done," Richard says. "The warden gave me all the facts before I started the course last winter."

"So, what kinds of crimes have they committed?" grumbles Father. "Stealing autos for one . . . maybe selling or using drugs for another?"

Richard: "Yes. Both of those plus rape and assault. The most promising student, Raul, is in for raping a 13-year-old classmate. He would have been sent to Attica if he hadn't been so young himself. He's presently 17. And Juan, another Hispanic, was sent there for using a gun (it turned out to be a toy gun) to hold up a convenience store. Both are also on the basketball team I coach."

Tashi (*surprised*): "You never told me you coach basketball at the Center too. How did you get involved in all this in the first place?"

Richard: "I love basketball and so it was only natural to go to some of the games at the local high school. One night . . . that was two winters ago . . . I attended a game between Saranac High and the Correctional Center. Quite without any forethought, I found myself cheering the kids from the Center."

Asadour (*scowling*) "And why would you do something like that? You probably made your fellow townspeople angry."

Richard: "It just happened. The Center kids were the clear underdogs. They didn't even have uniforms like the home team. They wore t-shirts and whatever colored shorts they could muster. What really got me, though, was that there were only five kids on the team . . . which meant that there could be no substitutions. Each boy had to play the whole game . . . all 40 minutes . . . whether he was up to it or not."

"But how'd you get to be their coach?" Tashi asks. "Didn't they have someone from the center to do it?"

Richard: "They had a prison guard with them . . . but I soon learned that he had no interest in basketball and used the game as an opportunity to visit his girlfriend in town. So, I just came over to the bench and started cheering for the Center kids. Nobody else was cheering for them. Pretty soon they began talking to me and asking questions about strategy. Now, I'm no expert on basketball. I played in high school myself, but I was never very good at it. But I guess I know more than they do . . . so they listened to me. By the end of the first game, we were bonded. They even made a place for me on the bench. Unofficially I was their new coach."

"But weren't they suspicious of a white coach?" asks Asadour. "I'm assuming that most of them were black kids from the big city . . . black or Hispanic."

Richard: "Yes. Two or three of them were wary of me at first. What really turned things around was an incident off the court. But I don't want to bore you with a lot of details while you're eating."

"Oh no, Richard," cries Tashi. "We really want to know (*looking around the table*) . . . at least I do."

(*Softly*) "Yes, of course, Richard," sighs Esther, with a stern glance at Tashi. "Please continue with your story."

Richard: "Well, alright. Not too long after I met the team, I put in a request at the Center to have the boys paint my cottage. At that time the Center was experimenting with a new policy whereby the kids were allowed to make a little money by doing work outside the Center under the supervision of a guard. I wanted to support the program so I put in my own request. The kids were not told whose cottage it was they were going to paint. They just showed up with their guard and went to work.

"That's kind of risky, isn't it?" advances Father. "I mean, think of the trouble they could cause outside the prison. Yes, they have a guard supervising them . . . but as you said earlier, these guards aren't too reliable."

"I wasn't told which day they were coming," Richard continues, "so I went ahead with plans to meet with friends in Lake Placid that morning. When I got home that evening, I was more than a little surprised to see the cottage completely painted. And even more . . . "

Asadour (*interrupting*): "What kind of job did they do? Pretty lousy I would expect."

Richard: "Since I got home so late, I didn't get to evaluate their work until the next morning. But I did notice some things out of place that evening . . . especially in the utility room where I store projects I'm working on, things like the chair I was repairing as well as the uniforms I had bought for the team. I was attempting to sew their names onto the back of their jerseys . . . you know, like the other teams they play."

Tashi (*eyes sparkling*): "You bought them uniforms? What a beautiful idea, Richard. Did they know about it?"

Richard: "No. It was meant to be a surprise. I was going to . . . "

Asadour (*leaning forward*): "So they broke into your house while they were painting it, saw the uniforms and . . . what . . . what did they do?"

Richard: "Of course I wasn't there so I can only guess what happened. When they saw the uniforms, they must have known immediately that it was my cottage they were painting."

Asadour: "So they felt terrible about robbing you . . . and put everything back in place"

Richard: "Yes, mostly . . . and then pretended to be surprised when I showed up at the next practice with the uniforms."

"Weren't you angry?" Esther asks. "I know I would have been. And what happened to the guard who was supposed to be watching over them?"

Richard: "I assume he did his usual thing and went to visit his girlfriend in town. But no, I wasn't angry. The kids were all over me at practice. It was clear that no one had ever done anything like that for them in the past. I felt very appreciated . . . well . . . maybe it was more than that . . . more like being accepted or even loved. We were all pretty close after that."

At that point Tim appears. "Excuse me. Richard . . . we've got some patrons who have to leave pretty soon . . . and they haven't heard one of your duets yet. Could you . . . ."

"Of course," says Richard, getting up. "Sorry. We got involved in a discussion here and I completely forgot about the music. We'll get right to it. Ready Tash?"

Once they are safely out of hearing range, Asadour turns to his wife and asks, "What is it that he's calling her now? Did he say Tash? Where in hell did he get that name?"

Esther (*softly*): "I think she thought it up. She seems to like it."

Asadour (*lowering his voice*): "You know, this guy is starting to worry me. First there's this mystery about his kids' death and his divorce and now he's gotten involved with a bunch of delinquent kids who broke into his house . . . but he likes them in spite of it. Do you think it's safe for Eleanor to be spending so much time with him?"

Esther: "She seems to think very highly of him."

Asadour (*slamming fist to the tabl*e): "What the hell's that got to do with it? I'm talking about her safety. Are you tuning me out? You do that a lot I notice . . . and now our daughter might be in danger and you're still not listening. Remember how wrong you were about not coming here for Thanksgiving. She got so depressed she almost starved to death. So much for your superior wisdom about feelings. I say it's time to put some limits on how often she sees this guy."

Esther: "Such as?"

Asadour: "Well, how often does she see him now? I know they have a practice session before Saturday and then meet again for their restaurant concert. Is that it?"

Esther: "Sometimes they get together for a picnic or a chat at his cottage. And then there are the e-mails . . . and phone calls. I don't know how often they communicate over the computer, but I know she calls him at least once a week."

Asadour: "What? You never told me all that was going on."

Esther: "You never asked."

Asadour: "What do they talk about? Have you overheard any of her conversations?"

Esther: "I don't want to be a spy."

Asadour: "Well, maybe it's time to get off your high moral horse and listen to what's going on. I'm too busy with my writing to do it. If something bad happens here, you're going to be indirectly responsible."

Esther: "I don't think it's all up to me. You're her father after all."

Asadour: "Are you saying I should give up work on my book to eavesdrop on my daughter? For Christ's sake, Esther. I haven't spent years reading and thinking and building a reputation in my field in order to sit around listening to a 15-year-old girl's chit chat . . . (*pause*) . . . You do it!"

From her place at the bandstand Tashi can see her parents arguing. "You seem preoccupied," Richard asks as he adjusts his piano score for their next piece. "What's going on?"

"I don't know. My parents seem upset about something. I hope it's not about me."

Richard: "Why would they be upset about you? . . . (*pause*) . . . Maybe it's about me."

Tashi: "We can talk more later during dinner. I'm ready to play if you are."

Richard: "O.K."

Not long after they start the next duet, it becomes clear to Richard that Tashi's playing is more tentative than before. Gone are the rich, sweeping phrases, the arching melodic curves in which she typically loses herself when she's relaxed. Even her bodily movements are more constrained now, suggesting a heightened caution in the face of potential danger. When the piece ends, the applause is more polite than enthusiastic. As Richard rises in acknowledgement, it is clear that the diners are too engaged with their table conversations to pay much attention to the music.

With a new, unnamed tension hanging over them, the musicians labor through two more duets and a solo piano interlude with minimal emotional investment. By then Tashi's parents and most of the patrons have left. It is with noticeable relief that they finally put away their music for the evening and head for their own dinner table. Once they are comfortably seated, with candles lit and orders taken, Tashi is the first to speak.

Tashi (*eyes fixed on his*): "Now that we're alone, I'd like to hear more about your work with the boys at the Correctional Center. You give a class in composition . . . and you coach a basketball team. And it's all voluntary, yes? . . . (*pause*) . . . So, what are the boys like?"

Richard: "Well, they're all different . . . just like the rest of us. As I said earlier, Raul and Juan are the most serious about song-writing. The others . . . Sam, Khalique and Rajon are in class because they have nothing better to do."

Tashi: "Do you have to lug your synthesizer over there every week? That's a chore, isn't it?""

Richard: "I did at first . . . both the keyboard and my laptop . . . but I finally convinced the warden to get us a couple of used electronic keyboards and some beat up old computers. So now the kids can practice during the week when I'm not there."

Tashi: "What kinds of music do Raul and Juan like? It's probably not classical, right?"

Richard: "Raul is into blues, Juan more into jazz. Raul's stuff is so good that I'm trying to find a group in New York to perform it. It could turn his life around."

Tashi: "What a gift that would be, Richard. Such a beautiful gift. Too bad the other three aren't as interested."

Richard: "Yes. But when it comes to basketball, the roles are reversed. Sam is by far the best, so good in fact that if we can get him accepted at some college, he could end up being their star player. Trouble is, he never finished high school and doesn't seem all that interested in getting his GED at the Center. Actually, Juan doesn't play on the team. I had to dig around to come up with a fifth player . . . finally got Myron, that is Myron Komarzanski, to come to our practices He's 6'5" so he can play center. The problem is that he's never played basketball before and isn't all that much help. He commits so many fouls that he often gets thrown out of the game, leaving the other four players to go on without him."

Tashi: "How can they play with only four people. Don't you have to have five?"

Richard: "You don't have to have five . . . but it's pretty difficult when the other team has all five and you're playing with only four. And the other team has the luxury of inserting substitutes every now and then to give the starters a breather . . . (*pause*) . . . Myron's problem is his anger (he's in for aggravated assault). When he gets frustrated, he begins throwing his elbows around and that's a no-no in basketball. On one occasion he got so mad at the opposing center he took a swing at him and broke his jaw. Needless to say, the referee chucked him."

Tashi: "Do they ever win a game? It sounds like they don't have much of a chance."

Richard: "Not since anyone can remember. They lose every time . . . but now and then they come close. They do best when Sam and Khalique are hot. Both are really good three-point shooters; they're also good with the intermediate jump shot. But the team has no inside game to speak of, that is, no one who can post-up an opposing player. So, unless Sam and Khalique score a lot of points, the final score tends to be pretty lop-sided."

Tashi: "I hope I can come to see them play some time."

Richard: "Well, if you come out for Thanksgiving in November, you can probably catch a game then. They usually play here at Saranac or somewhere nearby on that weekend."

Tashi: "I'd love to sit in on one of your composition classes at the Center too. That would really be awesome . . . but it's probably against the rules."

Richard: "They won't let you in unless you're a relative or a friend on somebody's visitors list . . . or a lawyer. The best you can hope for is that we make a CD of their music and you can listen to it at home."

Tashi: "Could you play one of their CD's at the restaurant . . . you know, while we're taking a break."

Richard (*nodding*): "I never thought of that. Great idea, Tash. As soon as we have something recorded, I'll ask Tim about it."

Tashi: "Of course, even better would be to have Raul or Juan play something live at the restaurant but I . . . "

Richard (*interrupting*): "I'm pretty sure they wouldn't be allowed to do that . . . after all, they're in prison."

Tashi: "But they're allowed out to work on people's houses . . . like the time they painted your cottage. Playing at a restaurant is just another kind of job, isn't it?"

Richard: "That's true . . . and they do occasional work in the forest clearing brush from the trails and cutting down beetle-infested trees.

I can always ask the warden. But let's remember who typically comes to the restaurant. Most patrons seem to prefer the soft romantic stuff . . . classical or semi-classical. I don't think they're going to appreciate rock and roll while downing their lobster Newburg . . . or rap lyrics that glorify rape and violence."

Tashi: "But Raul writes blues, you said. That could fit in here, couldn't it? And perhaps jazz as well."

Richard: "Maybe. It's too early to make any plans. Let's see what the boys come up with after a little more training. They're still beginners . . . although beginners with promise."

Tashi: "Yes."

Richard: "Oh, I almost forgot. I can't make it Thursday . . . have a dentist appointment in town . . . would Friday be alright instead?"

Tashi: "Fine. As you know, any day of the week is really O.K. with me. Why don't I call you Monday to see what works best for you."

With that, they rise from the table and head for Tashi's house where Richard drops her off in the driveway. "I'll give you a call Monday," she says, waving goodbye.

Richard: "Goodnight Tashi."

(*Monday morning*). With breakfast dishes done, Tashi picks up the kitchen phone and calls Richard's number. Father is in his study at the rear of the house; meanwhile, Mother has disappeared upstairs with plans to clean out her bedroom closet.

While waiting for a response, Tashi looks around to make sure both Mother and Father have left. Reassured, she readies herself to talk.

(*Excited*) "Hello Richard. Good morning. This is your adorable, sweet, brilliant, witty companion . . . (*pause*) . . . " (*Richard, answering*) "Hmmm. Let's see . . . adorable . . . you must be Christine . . . no? . . . O.K...

sweet . . . that can only be Samantha. No again? Hmmm. O.K . . . .brilliant, that's obviously Sarah . . . "

Tashi: "Stop teasing me. You know very well who it is. It's your one and only T . . . t . . . t . . . "

Richard: "Oh yes . . . t . . . t . . . t . . . Tammy?"

As the conversation unfolds, Tashi is oblivious to the fact that her mother has not yet gone upstairs, but is still standing quietly on the other side of the living room wall. In her eagerness to get as close as possible, however, Esther is unaware that her left foot is sticking out a few inches into the doorway. With her back to the living room door, Tashi cannot see it and proceeds with the call.

Tashi (*giggling*): "You devil, Richard. How could you be so cruel to someone who loves you as much as I do. Next time we go to the pool, I'm going to grab your clothes and run off into the woods. Maybe I'll bury them in some secret place so you have to walk around naked for days looking for them. And some old lady in long skirt and umbrella will come along and see you. I can hear her now, 'Just what are you doing here in the woods without any clothes on, Mr. Dunwoody?'"

Esther clutches her blouse as the toxic words reach her ears.

Richard (*laughing*): "Having recently buried an extra pair of shorts and a t-shirt near the pool in case you get nasty, I feel prepared for the worst."

Tashi: "You are too cute Richard. I love talking to you."

Richard: "But now, about our practice session . . . is Friday still O.K. for you?"

Tashi: "Yes, it is. And what if it's another hot day . . . would you like to try the pool again . . . say, before our session. We'd get nice and cool and that should make it easier to get into the music."

Richard: "I don't know. I think maybe once a year is enough for me."

Tashi: "You're starting to sound like an old man."

Richard: "Well, I could hike up there with you if that's what you want . . . and then you could cool off in the pool while I eat my lunch on the bank."

Tashi: "Doesn't sound like as much fun that way. Was I too bold last time . . . you know . . . taking my clothes off and all?"

Richard: "You surprised me a little . . . that's all . . . but I'm O.K. with it."

Tashi: "Well, if you want to do it again, we should do it on Friday since my baby-making days start again on Sunday or Monday. It'll be more fun for me if I don't have to worry about that."

Richard: "I see. But there's no need to hurry as far as I'm concerned. Why don't we just wait for another hot, humid day and make our plans then?"

Tashi (*softly*): "Alright. I'll come by at the usual time on Friday. Bye Richard. See you then."

Putting the phone down, she turns and heads for the stairs to her bedroom. As she passes the door to the living room, she catches a sudden movement out of the corner of her eye. Turning to look more closely, she sees a shoe being pulled back from the opening. It is her mother's shoe.

"Mom, is that you?" she whispers, her voice taut with fear. When there is no answer, she steps into the living room and looks down where the shoe was. There's no one there.

Later in the day Esther knocks on her husband's study door. "Is this a good time to talk, Asi? I have some disturbing news."

Asadour (*putting down his glasses and swiveling his chair to face her*): "What is it?"

Esther: "I heard everything. You won't believe this. She apparently went to the brook . . . you know, the one that empties into the lake over by Richard's cottage . . . well, I guess there's a pool up there where you can go swimming. It sounds like they took their clothes off and got into the pool together. And now she wants to do it again, but she's telling him when her period starts so they can plan around that."

Asadour (*rising from his chair*): "Oh my God . . . (*pause*) . . . Did you confront her? Did you tell her what you heard?"

Esther: "No. I thought I'd wait and tell you first. You're better at these things than I am."

Asadour: "God dammit Esther. This is too much. Why do you keep harassing me with these domestic crises? Things like this shouldn't be happening to us. They certainly don't happen in normal families and they wouldn't be happening here if you were doing your job. I told you to bear down on her but no, you were too squeamish to spy on her . . . better to let her to go swimming in the nude with a divorced man 18 years older than her . . . a man who lives like a hermit and whose closest friends are a bunch of juvenile delinquents. I can tell you right now that if you had kept an eye on her all along, we wouldn't be in this mess . . . (*pause*) . . . So, what am I supposed to do? Tell me."

Esther: "I don't know. Maybe we should stop coming to Saranac . . ."

Asadour: "And have her go on another hunger strike? She's already too skinny. You want her to become anorexic? For Christ's sake Esther, use your head. From what you say, it's obvious that she's obsessed with this guy. There's no way to put an end to that without sending her into an emotional tailspin. The only hope we have of controlling the situation is to bring him into the family . . . find out more about him . . . guide him . . . make sure he realizes how vulnerable she is. Maybe, if we can get him to trust us, we can talk some sense into him . . . make him see that this is just an infatuation . . . the kind that adolescent kids have all the time . . . bring him around to seeing that it will soon be forgotten and that he should keep her at arm's length until she gets tired of the whole thing."

Esther (*nodding*): "That makes sense to me Asi. We could start by inviting him over for Sunday dinner."

Asadour: "Let's go to the restaurant on Saturday and we can invite him then."

Esther: "Well, a day in advance is rather short notice. He might already have other plans."

Asadour: "Jesus Christ, Esther. So, what if he does? We'll just invite him for the following Sunday. Don't be so goddamn picky."

Esther (*rising from her chair*): "I don't think I deserve to be called names . . . besides . . . you needn't be so . . . ponkey."

Asadour: "Ponkey? . . . and just what the hell does that mean?"

Esther (*softly*): "I don't know. I couldn't think of anything else, so I made it up."

Asadour: "God, Esther . . . you're getting more and more weird like your father. Maybe Tashi has inherited some of the same genes. If so, we're in deep doo here."

Esther (*wrinkling her nose*): "You never used to talk like that. I hope Eleanor doesn't hear you . . . it might encourage her to start using coarse language."

Asadour (*shaking his head*): "So I'm not supposed to say 'deep doo' for fear of corrupting my daughter? Save me, please. You're turning out to be more of a Puritan than I thought . . . but maybe that's good because the whole thing is starting to make more sense. Eleanor is probably asserting her sexual feelings with this guy Richard as a way of rebelling against your prudery. If you weren't so uptight about sex, she might not be chasing him and we wouldn't be having all this trouble . . . and I wouldn't have to waste a lot of time thinking about other women . . . "

Esther (*sternly*): "Have you ever . . . ?"

Asadour (*quickly*): "That's a subject for another day. Right now, we need to focus our attention on seeing her safely through adolescence. Once she's off to college, we can relax. She'll be on her own. Whatever she does from that point on . . . whether we approve or not . . . is her own business. We will have fulfilled our obligations as parents."

11   The Correctional Center

After parking his SUV in the visitors' lot, Richard enters the main door, making his way down a long neatly-scrubbed hall still redolent with the morning's application of pine oil soap. He has his wallet open when stopped at two successive checkpoints and asked to show his temporary teacher's permit. With a guard at his side, he is finally ushered into the storeroom that now serves as his classroom. Despite his repeated request for more space, the walls remain lined with plumbing supplies left over from a repair job in the basement. In the middle of the room two electronic keyboards have been set up, each attached to a computer. At one Raul is experimenting with a chord sequence to go with a rap poem he's been working. Juan is at the other, with headphones, dancing in place as he adds drums to a piece featuring guitar and strings. Sam is leaning against the pile of CVP over on the left.

"So, where's Khalique?" Richard says, looking around.

Sam (*laughing*): "He's got the trots."

"Yeah, too much of that Mex shit they keep givin' us," adds Juan, dropping the headphones. Maybe he'll come later . . . maybe he won't. If he comes, he'll probly be wearing diapers."

"Yeah," responds Raul, "and if he lets loose we might have to hose him down."

The laughter is raucous. Not wanting to be left out, Richard adds, "Too many refried beans?"

"Nah," cries Sam, doubling over, "it's the fuckin' chili peppers. They put 'em in everything so you can't taste the rest of the shit they throw at you."

Richard: "Hmm. I'll keep that in mind if they ever ask me to stay for lunch. Now, how about some music. Anybody got something they want me to hear? . . . (*silence*) . . . Raul, how's that rap piece of yours coming?"

Raul: "I've got some words . . . still working out the harmony."

Sam: "Yeah, you otta hear the words . . . how's it go Raulie? . . . ass is yours anywhere you find it. . . just walk the streets and come up behind it. Somethin' like that, right?"

Raul: "Yeah . . . I'm still workin' on it. Can't seem to make the harmony move. Like Richard says, you can't keep playin' the same notes over and over."

At this point Richard moves to the keyboard and takes Raul's place. After hearing the words several times, he switches the keyboard from piano to bass and begins experimenting with a sequence of beats. When the notes seem to fall into place with the lyrics, he turns to Raul and asks, "Well, what do you think? Does that work any better?"

Raul (*smiling*): "Yeah, I like it. Let me try it . . . (*taking Richard's place at the keyboard . . . playing and singing*) . . . Jeez . . . this is cool. Fuck yes . . . "

Applause erupts from the others. "You're good, dude," shouts Sam, turning to Richard, . . . "real good."

"Yeah, maybe he otta be a composer," cries Juan, adding to the hilarity.

"Hey, keep it down in there," barks the guard from the hall. "This ain't no birthday party."

"Asshole," whispers Sam, fist clenched. "When I get outta here and see him on the street, I'm gonna whip his black ass."

"Come on, Juan, you're next," says Richard. "What've you got to show me? Did you finish that jazz piece you were working on?"

Juan: "Shit no. Got stuck half way through. It starts good but when it hits the end of the second theme, it jis' hangs there like some kid with a stiff rod who don't know how to make it cum. I can't think of no way to get back to the beginnin'."

Fighting his way through the laughter, Richard says, "Let's look at the harmony. Do you remember what I told you about modulating?"

Juan: "Yeah, I tried this shit you told us about . . . you know, dominant sevenths and augmented sixths . . . movin' down by thirds . . . but I still got fucked. Maybe you told me wrong."

Sam (*laughing*): "Maybe it's over your head, you dumb Spic."

Juan (*coming closer*): "You want your jaw broke or somethin'?"

Sam: "Kiss my ass."

Richard (*getting in between*): "O.K. guys, break it up. Let me see if I can help Juan with his harmony. The rest of you can look over my shoulder . . . you might learn something."

By the time the allotted hour and half is up, everyone who wanted help has gotten it. As the boys head for the door, Raul lingers behind, not speaking until Sam and Juan have both left. Turning to Richard, he says softly "I got somethin' I wanna talk to you about. Can I stay a little longer?"

Richard: "Let me ask the guard if it's O.K. It's fine with me, Raul." The guard says, "O.K. but keep it short. He's due for rehab in a half an hour."

Raul continues. "My old lady drove all the way up here from Albany to see me yesterday. I knew when they told me she was comin' that somethin' had to be up. She wouldn'a come all that way in the shit box she drives unless somethin' serious-like happened . . . "

Richard: "She doesn't come to see you too often?"

Raul: "Nah. Albany's too far away. So far she come on my birthday . . . that's it . . . once."

Richard: "So, what did she have to say?"

Raul: "My old man got shot in a street fight . . . something to do with drugs. He died last week in the hospital."

Richard (*softly*): "I'm sorry Raul. Were the two of you close?"

Raul: "Nah. He left the apartment three years ago . . . before we moved to Albany . . . never came back, never sent us any money. I got a brother and a sister. Since I was the oldest, I had to get a job so we could buy food and stuff. That's when I dropped out of school and got this job carryin' tiles and shakes for a roofer.

Richard: "You were 14 at the time?"

Raul: "Almost 15. Mom was working at the post office . . . so together we made enough to get by . . . barely. Then she met this guy who worked there in the shippin' department. He moved in after a couple of months. For a while it was ok . . . then I found out he was stickin' it to Angela, my 13- year-old sister. That's when things blew up."

Richard: "Did you mother know about it?"

Raul: "Worse than that. Sis said Ben . . . the boyfriend . . . would wait until I was out of the house and then sniff some coke and get shit-faced with my Mom. And then . . . this is the sick part . . . together they'd force some dope into Angela and drag her into bed so they could fuck her. Yeah . . . my mother. Can you believe that? I was hopin' my father would come back someday and beat the shit outta this guy Ben. But he never showed . . . so I had to take care of things myself."

Richard: "What did you do?"

Raul: "I borrowed some heat from a friend and waited 'til Ben was sittin' at the table drinkin' with my mother. I came up behind him and held the gun to his head and told him I was goin' to kill him unless he took off right then. When he said, "What's the problem?" I told him what Angie told me. I guess he knew I was serious because he went upstairs, got his things and disappeared into the street. He never come back."

Richard: "Sounds like you haven't had many good experiences with men so far."

Raul: "I don't know . . . you seem different, Richard."

Richard (*smiling*): "I fool a lot of people. You know, Raul, I've been thinking of ways we could get you started in the music world. You certainly have enough raw talent to make a name for yourself. It was a friend of mine who suggested that we might be able to play your music at the restaurant where I have a Saturday night gig. Probably not the rap pieces . . . they're a little raunchy for the people who come to eat there. But your blues could go over nicely."

Raul: "But I can't get outta here to play at a restaurant, can I?"

Richard: "As my friend said, it's a job and they let you out to paint houses and cut down trees . . . so why not?"

Raul: "Yeah, but there's a guard with us on those jobs . . . or at least he's supposed to be there."

Richard: "Well, if the warden says no, we could go with a backup plan. Burn a CD of your pieces and we'll play it when I'm not at the piano. Just don't make it too loud . . . (*pause*) . . . and we can even pay you for using your music."

Raul: "Really? How much?"

Richard: "I don't know . . . maybe $25 a night."

Raul: "Wow! Would you just slip me the cash when you come to class? I know how to use that kinda dough."

Richard: "That probably wouldn't be good for either of us. Better that I get the warden's permission and give the money to him for safe keeping in your personal account . . . you know, an account where they put the money you've earned for doing jobs outside the Center. No one will take it away . . . and it will all be there when you leave the Center. That's only a year away now . . . right?"

Raul: "Yeah, if I can just stay outta trouble from here on in."

Richard: "What do you think you'll do when you get out?"

Raul: "Part of me wants to go after the guy who killed my father . . . and slit his throat. The other part says why stick my neck out for somebody who never did shit for me . . . except for sticking his dick in my Mom 17 years ago."

Richard: "I understand . . . but if you give into that impulse you'll spend the rest of your life in prison . . . not here either but in Attica which isn't exactly hospitable to young, good-looking kids. That can't be a pleasant thought . . . (*pause*) . . . How about learning some more about music? It's obvious you've got plenty of talent, but you're not going to get very far until you get some more training."

Raul: "You're teaching me a lot. I didn't know shit about harmony when I came here. I just wish you could come in more than once a week."

Richard: "You need to be in a music school . . . a place like Berklee School of Music in Boston where you can hone your performance skills at the same time you're learning about harmony, orchestration, arranging, counterpoint . . . stuff like that. They have scholarships that cover most expenses. If you run a little short, I can make up the difference."

Raul (*shaking his head*): "You'd pay out of your own pocket? That's crazy, man. Who knows if I could ever pay you back."

Richard: "There's no need to pay me anything . . . no matter what happens. It's simply something I want to do . . . (*pause*) . . . Now, we better get out of here before they send out an APB on you."

Raul: "One other thing, Rich. In a few months I have to appear before the parole board and they'll want to know if I'm ready to get outta here. If they say yes, I can get a couple of months chopped off my sentence. I haven't fucked up so far . . . so that looks good . . . but it will help if someone who knows me . . . someone like you . . . says I'm good to go. My rehab counselor will be asked for his two cents too . . . but the guy strikes me as a phony. He says I still have a problem controlling my feelings. How the fuck he knows that just sitting on his ass across the table, I don't know.

But he's got power here and I need someone like you to say something good about me. Would you do that for me?"

Richard: "Of course . . . but it would help if I knew what you did to get sent here in the first place."

Raul: "I told you. I went bicycle riding with this fat girl and screwed her up in a barn. When I had her down in the hay, she acted like she liked it . . . but afterwards she went to the police and they got me arrested. Her parents musta talked her into it. At the station she said I raped her . . . and they took her word for it. That's how I ended up here."

Richard: "And how old was she at the time?"

Raul: "Twelve or thirteen; I can't remember."

Richard: "So definitely underage . . . which means statutory rape whether she consented or not."

Raul: "I guess so."

Richard: "You're lucky you were under 18 yourself, so you got sent here instead of Attica."

Raul: "Yeah."

Richard: "Were you aware at the time that she was underage and could get you into trouble?"

Raul: "Not really . . . I mean, yeah, I knew how old she was but she acted like she liked me . . . and so when I asked her to go riding with me and she said yes, I got really turned on. She's fat . . . so fat that everybody at school called her Hippo . . . but she was a good looker with nice little baby tits. I just got carried away. When she let me kiss her in the barn, I figured that was a green light. I mean, a girl lets you kiss her when nobody's around . . . doesn't that mean she wants to be fucked?"

Richard: "Not necessarily. Maybe she liked you and enjoyed kissing you, but had no wish to go beyond that. Not too many 12-or-13 year-olds think of going all the way with a guy."

Raul (*voice rising*): "This one did. I could tell from the way she kissed me. And when I began rubbing my hand against her shorts, she just kissed me harder. By that time my whole body was screaming for her ass. How the fuck could I stop when I could already smell her cunt?"

Richard: "Did she make a move to stop you?"

Raul: "Yeah . . . but not until I started pulling her shorts down. Then what I am I supposed to do . . . say sorry and cover my dick up? No way. I was burning up inside. My cock was on fire. The only way to put the flames out was to get inside her hole. I just had to get inside her."

Richard: "Were you having any thoughts of what might happen if you went ahead . . . you know, the consequences?"

Raul: "Are you crazy, Rich? Thoughts? The only thought I had was to shove my cock in her hole and give her my jizz . . . (*pause*) . . . there wasn't no choice. I was like a wild animal . . . all feelings . . . no sittin' back and wonderin' about the future. You know what I mean? You're a guy . . . you must know."

Richard: "It sure sounds like your desire for this girl took you beyond the point where you still had a choice. And that's not good. We all have feelings . . . sometimes very strong feelings . . . but it is our thoughts that keep us from getting into trouble. What you're saying is that your feelings got so strong that they just overwhelmed you. You were at their mercy . . . and ended up doing something you shouldn't have done."

Raul: "Yeah. So?"

Richard: "It means you have some serious work to do before you get out of here. Some way or another, you've got to learn how to . . . "

Raul (*interrupting*): "Yir sayin' I'm not ready for parole? But I thought you was on my side. For Christ's sake Rich, why'd you make me tell you all this shit? . . . (*pause*) . . . Look it, forget that I ever asked you to testify for me. Just forget it (*knocking the chair over, heading for the door*). And you might as well forget me too. Don't look for me in your class no more."

Richard (*standing*): "Raul. Come back here. We need to talk some more . . . Raul . . ."

12 Tempest in a Teapot

Dear Bapu,

I'm in real trouble. Mother overheard a conversation I was having with Richard and she got all upset because I mentioned swimming together in the nude. She told everything to Dad so now I can only see him at practice and at our gig on Saturday night. That means no more hikes or picnics on the lake or anything. I can't even stop by his cottage and chat. How am I ever going to get to know him? Could you come and talk to them about it? Please. I promise to love you forever if you come (I might even if you don't).

Your adoring granddaughter,

Tashi

P.S. We can always have a family barbecue on the 4th . . . yes?

Dear Tashi,

I would definitely like to come . . . haven't seen you in the flesh for two years now. But your mother probably won't like the idea of me inviting myself . . . so let's leave it like this. I'll come if she calls to invite me. But not if she doesn't.

Tough love from the Adored One

Dear Toughie,

I've talked to Mom about it and she says you can come as long as you promise to do your burping and farting outdoors. Fair enough?

Please, Tashi

Dear Tashi,

Since we're going to have an outdoor barbecue, I think I can handle it. To be on the safe side, I'll lay off the garbanzos and beans. That should help. In case that's not enough, I'll sit downwind from your mother.

Jhrrrrt,

Bapu

The Fourth turns out to be a perfect day for a barbecue . . . warm but not hot, clear skies and a gentle breeze from the West. Esther is at the grill; Asadour, Tashi and Bapu are sipping drinks on the deck. Once the last of the burgers has been grilled, Esther calls everyone to the table.

It is Tashi's first chance to see Bapu up close since his last visit two years ago. Unlike most men his age he is as slender as ever, his stomach flat and his beard neatly trimmed. His hair, nearly white now, has receded more, but still manages to cover most of his handsome head. When he turns to his left, she is reminded how large and pointed his nose is, hinting at residues of a raptorial ancestry. There are wrinkles on his cheeks but fewer than one might expect for someone in his 70's. When he talks, he looks directly at you with eyes as blue and clear as those of a much younger man. He laughs easily and often.

Across the table Asadour scoops up some potato salad, adds a tomato, a scallion or two, a radish . . . chews, swallows, then reaches for a burger which he covers with ketchup before jamming it into his mouth. He is surprised when his first few bites fail to soften the meat enough for swallowing. As he struggles, his smile gradually turns to a scowl. Anxious to discover the problem, he puts the burger down and opens it up. "Esther," he shouts, holding the meat up for all to see. "This thing is black. And it tastes like rubber. What the hell did you do with it?"

Esther (*cowering*): "I told you I wasn't very good with the grill and that you should do the cooking. You wouldn't listen."

Asadour (*eyes bulging*): "Do you really expect me to spend my time flipping hamburgers when I'm in the middle of an article on America's future role in the Middle East?"

Tashi *(nodding)*: "Mine is fine, Mom. Maybe Daddy got a burnt one."

Asadour *(anxiously, turning to Bapu)*: "You haven't tried any of my tomatoes yet. I raised them from seedlings . . . in pots . . . right in the kitchen. Go ahead . . . take one . . . I guarantee you they're the best-tasting tomatoes you've ever had."

Bapu (*softly*): "I don't like tomatoes."

Asadour (*voice rising*): "You don't like tomatoes? What's wrong with you?"

Bapu (*picking his words carefully*): "Let me introduce you to a radical concept, one which I'm sure you have never heard of before . . . (*pause*) . . . People are different . . . they look different, they talk different, they have different values, they have different tastes."

Asadour: "So?"

Bapu *(sighing)*: "So, just because you like tomatoes doesn't mean that everyone else has to like them too."

Asadour (*nonplussed, turning to Esther*): "You like tomatoes, don't you?"

Esther: "Oh yes. I've already had two."

Asadour (*dumping a tomato onto her plate*): "Well, here, have another."

Meanwhile Bapu can be seen attacking the salad bowl with obscene relish. In his haste to shovel in the spinach, carrots, broccoli, cauliflower and cucumbers, he manages to leave an assortment of flora dangling from his beard.

Tashi: "Don't you want a burger, Bapu? They're quite good."

Bapu (*with mouth full*): "Didn't I tell you, I've become a vegetarian?"

Tashi: "I didn't know that. When did you stop eating meat?"

Bapu (*checking his wrist watch*): "It's been about five minutes now."

Asadour (*sighing*): "Don't mind him, Esther. He left his manners at home. By the way . . . (*pointing at Bapu*) . . . you have a baby carrot and a piece of broccoli stuck in your beard. It's rather disgusting."

Bapu *(curling his lip)*: "Then stop looking at me. Get back to chewing on that burger. Another ten minutes should do the trick."

Esther *(turning to Bapu)*: "It would be nice if you could be appropriate . . . just this once."

Bapu: "Of course." He then plucks the carrots and broccoli from his beard, tosses them into the air and catches them with his open mouth.

Esther (*exasperated*): "I wish Mother were here. She'd know how to handle you."

Bapu: "She tried for years . . . but fortunately never succeeded. As you might have surmised, your mother was a pretty uptight lady . . . in all kinds of ways."

Asadour (*staring*): "Then why did you marry her?"

Bapu: "She was smart, attractive . . . and saw me as the white knight she had been waiting for. We got along just fine during the engagement; she was a little reticent sexually, but otherwise pretty normal. It was only after the wedding that she began to clam up. And when I say 'clam up', I mean closed tight like a wall safe . . . (*smiling*) . . . Without that bottle of Chardonnay I brought home one night, Esther might never have made it into this world."

Esther: "I really don't think it's appropriate to talk about these things in front of Eleanor."

Asadour (*quickly changing the subject*): "How's that book of yours coming . . . the one on . . . psycho-philosophy if I remember correctly?"

Bapu: "About half finished . . . I'm having a little trouble with the part where I . . . "

Asadour (*interrupting*): "I just got back the proofs of my latest journal article . . . I'm surprised by how many errors they made. Instead of putting the maps in the middle, they . . . "

Bapu (*interrupting*): "I thought you were asking about *my* book."

Asadour (*scowling*): "I was . . . you said you were having trouble. Weren't you finished?"

Bapu : "Maybe you should have your ears checked."

Asadour (*leaning forward*): Maybe you should *yours* boxed."

Esther: "Please . . . not in front of Eleanor."

Asadour (*turning to his wife, shaking his head*): "I don't see why he bothers coming if he just wants to stir up trouble."

Bapu: "I came because Tashi asked me to."

Asadour (*biting his lip*): "Her name is Eleanor, not Toni or Tabby or Tashi. What kind of grandfather are you if you can't even remember her name?"

Bapu (*calmly*): "Apparently, I remember a lot more than you do. She changed her name months ago, but you're so wrapped up in your own solipsistic little world that you didn't even know it."

Esther (*turning to her father*): "I wish you wouldn't use such foul language in front of Eleanor. You've gotten much worse since mother died."

Bapu (*shaking his head*): "Esther, solipsistic is not a dirty word . . . look it up . . . it refers to someone who sees the whole word as an extension of himself . . . (*whispering*) . . . Remind you of anyone you know?"

At this point Tashi excuses herself and heads for the bathroom.

Asadour (*waiting for Tashi to leave*): "So, you think I have a big ego."

Bapu: "'Big' is an understatement. 'Colossal' is more like it. All the signs are there. You can't stop talking about yourself; you brag constantly; you get impatient when other people talk about themselves instead of listening to you; you're opinionated, dogmatic, intolerant, and totally blind to how irritating your behavior is to others. Shall I go on?"

Asadour (*frowning*): "Esther, do I brag a lot?"

Esther (*softly*): "Yes." As soon as she says it, she shudders at the realization that in 18 years of marriage this is the first time she has ever contradicted her husband.

Asadour: "Two against one. Maybe you're right . . . I don't know. . . but have you considered that all the great men of history have had big egos. How can you achieve something extraordinary unless you have faith in yourself? Look at people in the music field . . . men like Beethoven and Wagner. You wouldn't call them humble, would you?"

Bapu (*amused*): "You're confusing confidence and ego. It's possible to be very confident of your ability without trumpeting that fact to the rest of the world. For every Beethoven or Wagner, we have a Bach, Mozart, Schubert, Schumann and Brahms, none of whom had big egos . . . In fact, if there is any consistent relationship between confidence and ego, it may be the very opposite of what you propose. People who are very confident have no need to brag. Because they are secure in themselves, they don't need others to tell them how good they are. They know it down deep . . . (*pause*) . . . Whenever I hear someone bragging about his achievements, I immediately suspect self-doubt. Here is someone, I say to myself, who needs to be reassured that he is indeed a worthy person. A confident individual is, by contrast, a humble person. He is at peace with himself. And because of that, he is a better listener . . . (*pause*) . . . Amen."

Asadour *(smiling)*: Maybe you should have been a preacher."

Bapu: "It's a little late now. Besides I would have to give up my free-wheeling ways . . . and that's asking a lot of an old codger like me."

Asadour: "I like my freedom too; that's one of the reasons I came to this country in the first place. But you take it too far; maybe you should tone it down a little, especially around Eleanor. From what I've seen, American kids have too much freedom, especially regarding sex. Look at all the lives ruined by unwanted pregnancies. We contribute to that, don't we, when we're permissive with our children?"

Bapu: "Maybe . . . it really depends on the individual . . . how mature he or she is. Kids mature physically at a pretty young age these days . . . and they need to be educated about the consequences of becoming sexually active. We can do a lot more with that than we're doing right now."

Asadour: "Coming from the Middle East, I have a different perspective on all this. . . more objective perhaps than someone like you who grew up in the middle of this culture."

Bapu: "I don't have much truck for a society that treats its women like slaves, insists that they wear bags over their heads and then punishes them unmercifully for adultery while letting their seducers off the hook."

Asadour: (*reddening*) "I'm not a Muslim. I was brought up in the Eastern Orthodox Church."

Bapu: "So, maybe you don't know what it's like to grow up here in America."

Asadour (*defiantly*): "Tell me something I don't know."

Bapu: "O.K. You don't your own daughter. You don't realize how mature she is. She's not your run of the mill pubescent female who goes gaga over Hollywood hunks and rock stars. She's not the kind to . . . "

Asadour (*interrupting*): I know her hellluva lot better than you do. I see her every day . . . you know her mainly from e-mails."

Unnoticed in the exchange of barbs, Tashi returns to her seat in time to hear the latest exchange. "I feel that Bapu knows me real well. Maybe he's the only one who does."

Asadour (*turning to face her*): "So what does he know about you that your mother and I don't know?"

Tashi: "Maybe Bapu should answer that."

Bapu (*quietly*): "I know that she has an enormous capacity for love. And that she's not afraid of her own sexuality . . . like some people I know."

Asadour: "Ah yes. I agree. But at her age that could get her into trouble."

Bapu: "Depends on her judgment. Here's the question. Does she know men? Can she tell the difference between someone who is a worthy object of her affection and somebody who's simply out to use her?"

Asadour: "Well put. Now, keep in mind that this guy Richard is much older, divorced, lives like a hermit and has two kids who died mysteriously. And he teaches music to a bunch of rapists and automobile thieves. Sounds a little flaky to me. Wouldn't you agree?"

Bapu: "Can't say until I've met him."

Tashi: "Oh yes. It's going to happen tomorrow morning; he's invited Bapu and me over to his cottage. Bapu can see for himself."

Asadour: "All I ask is that you keep an open mind. Don't let your desire to please Eleanor get in the way. Agreed?"

Bapu: "Agreed. And Esther, thanks for a great meal. Don't worry about the burgers . . . you can always use them as coasters."

13   **The Visit**

The two guests arrive promptly at 10:00. Tashi knocks.

Tashi: "Richard, this is my grandfather . . . his name is Robert but I call him Bapu."

Richard (*shaking hands*): "Nice to meet you, sir. I remember that Ghandi's followers used to call him Bapu. Come in, please."

Bapu (*entering cottage*): Yes. Right now I have but one follower (*putting his arm around Tashi*) . . . but we hope to have a mass movement someday. If you get in now as an original member, we could give you a discount."

Richard (*laughing*): "How about an honorary membership. Sounds cheaper . . . (*pause*) . . . Could I get you folks a drink? I've got tea, lemonade or orange soda."

Tashi: "I'll take the soda. I know where it is."

Bapu (*smiling*): "The lemonade sounds fine . . . unless you happen to have a little dope."

Richard (*chuckling):* "Sorry. Kwatz and I used up the last of it this morning . . . a belated July 4th celebration."

Tashi (*from the kitchen*): "Kwatz is Richard's cat."

Bapu: "Japanese?"

Richard: "Good guess."

Bapu: "The name is familiar. As a young man, I spent several months in Kyoto trying to learn something about Zen Buddhism. By then there were some teachers here in the states, but I wanted to get it straight from the horse's mouth."

Richard: "So, did you attain satori?"

Bapu: "No. In fact I'm still working on it some 40 years later . . . but it could happen any day now . . . (*pause*) . . . How about you? Ever get interested in Zen?"

Richard: "Yes. I got into it in college through Alan Watt's The Way of Zen. Like you, I thought of going to Japan to study, but practical obligations got in the way . . . (*pause*) . . . I still do zazen every day . . . well, most days. Enlightenment seems a long way off, but I find it relaxing and it's a pleasant break from writing music."

Tashi: "Is there any chance you could play something for Bapu. He knows a lot about music. Besides I've told him that you're going to be a great composer someday."

Richard: "Well, I don't know about the 'great composer' business, but I could play you a short piece I finished yesterday. I'll probably arrange it for cello and piano later so we can play it at the restaurant."

Tashi: (*clapping her hands*) "That sounds wonderful. Oh Bapu, I wish you could stay and hear us play Saturday night. Do you really have to leave tomorrow?"

Bapu: "Your mother was kind enough to let me stay for three days. I wouldn't want to overstay my welcome. But I appreciate the offer."

Tashi (*getting up):* "I could run down and get my cello now and we could play one of our duets here in the cottage."

Bapu: "That sounds like a lot of work. Why don't we listen to Richard's piece and save the duets for a later time. I'll make it a point to include a Saturday night in my next visit . . . if I ever get invited again."

Richard goes to the piano and takes out the score for his new piece, placing it carefully on the music stand. As the music unfolds, Bapu follows each note with an attention sharpened by years of meditation. Tashi is careful not to move. When the piece ends, no one says anything while Richard remains at the piano. Finally, Bapu speaks:

"Rondo form, right? I love that recurring theme. Each time it appears it's slightly different . . . either melodically or with a change of harmony."

Richard: "Yes. Thank you."

Bapu: "If I were going to change anything, it would be the ending. It doesn't feel final enough. Maybe a repeat of the original theme, but with some counterpoint in the left hand."

Richard: "Hmmm. You mean like this (*plays a few bars*)?"

Bapu: "Yes. Much better that way."

Tashi: "Oh Richard. That's wonderful . . . it *is* better. It brings everything together. Now you really know the piece has ended."

Richard (*picking up his pencil*): "Let me get that down (*makes changes in the score*) . . . Well, Bapu . . . thanks for the suggestion. Maybe I should send you all my compositions."

Bapu (*chuckling*): "You couldn't afford it."

When Richard resumes his chair in the living room, the discussion of music continues, centering on the reasons why contemporary classical music is still so unpopular among listening audiences.

Bapu: "The whole genre is dying. People can't stomach all this fart and squeak atonal stuff. If composers don't give up their obsession with experimentation, they're going to lose their audiences completely. More and more people are already turning to pop music, things like rock, country, and rap. Even the government is pulling back on its financial support for fine art music."

Tashi: "But why do composers go on writing things that people don't like? How do they make any money if nobody comes to their concerts or buys their CD's?"

Bapu: "They don't even bother to present their stuff at concerts. They know damn well that no one would come. If they had to rely on public performances of their work like Mozart, Beethoven, and Brahms did, they'd starve. They only way they survive is by getting cushy sinecures at universities where they get paid to teach young people how to write the same kind of trash they write themselves . . . (*pause*) . . . but Richard seems to have resisted that pressure. Of course, Richard, your style is going to be seen as dated, old-fashioned, out-of-keeping with the times . . . which means that you're going to have difficulty getting any of your pieces played by the well-known orchestras."

Richard (*nodding*): "Yes. I know the pressure is there, but so far it hasn't affected what I do. There are some advantages to 'marching to one's own drummer,' like living out here in the woods far from Carnegie Hall, the New York Times, and the Pulitzer Prize committee."

Bapu: "But, if you go your own way, how do you make any money when the music establishment insists that you write the same kind of crap as everybody else?"

Richard: "I do some arranging . . . that brings in a few bucks . . . but I live mainly on what I earn in the stock market. So far I've been lucky enough to keep my head above water."

Bapu: "That's a hazardous occupation these days, isn't it? I mean, how the hell do you know what to buy or sell when the market is up one day and down the next . . . and when there's so much lying going on? Can you trust anybody to tell you the truth about what is happening? The company CEO's twist, distort and fudge their reports to make their profits look good when they are actually losing millions if not billions. And Washington? The Feds keep telling everyone that we'll be out of this recession in a few more months when the fundamentals indicate that we're actually heading for the toilet."

Richard: "It does make investing difficult when you don't know whom to trust . . . if anybody. What got me last year in particular was what the rating agencies were saying. These are the firms that are supposed to tell us which companies are in good shape and which ones to avoid. And up to the very moment the economy went over the cliff they were saying 'Trust us. If we give somebody an AAA rating, it means they're in good shape. No need to worry. You can take our word for it."

Bapu: "And then we discover that they are being paid for their ratings by the very companies they are supposed to be evaluating. It's really disgusting . . . (*pause*) . . . I think it says a lot about where this country is going. The lust for money is undermining our values. We used to care about the truth; officials who lied to us were promptly removed from office. Today putting a 'spin' on the facts is accepted as the norm. Everyone does it; we know it and take it for granted, not realizing that our tolerance is pulling down the very foundations of society."

Richard: "I agree. Greed has trumped morals. That's another reason I prefer to live apart from the centers of money and power."

The discussion continues until Tashi announces that they are due for lunch with her parents at a restaurant in town. At the door, Bapu shakes Richard's hand vigorously, adding that he has not enjoyed a chat this much in years. "It's nice to know we agree on what's happening to American culture. And your music is beautiful, Richard . . . keep it coming. I live just outside New York, surrounded by the very pressures you have resisted. It takes guts to do what you are doing. I hope you never give in." With that, he hops into the car with Tashi and heads for town.

As Bapu eases the car down the dirt road toward town, Tashi turns and asks, "Well, what did you think? You seemed to like him. Or am I imagining things?"

Bapu: "Not at all. It's easy to see why you are so attracted to him. He's good looking, smart, articulate . . . there's a lot there to like. But what I like most is his courage . . . the courage to write the kind of music he loves in spite of the fact that his peers . . . composers, conductors, critics . . . are demanding something very different. That is a strength you don't see too often these days. And I respect him for it."

Reaching over and taking his arm, Tashi says, "Oh, thank you for saying that. It means so much to me that someone else thinks as highly of him as I do . . . (*pause*) . . . I hope you are going to tell Mom and Dad what you saw today. That could make a big difference in how they feel about him."

Bapu: "I'll do what I can, sweetheart . . . but I must admit that I do have some doubts. Well, maybe I shouldn't call them doubts . . . questions might be a better way of saying it."

Tashi: "Really. What kinds of questions do you mean?"

Bapu: "Well, when I look at Richard, I see a man whose physical features . . . his height, broad shoulders, sharply defined features . . . suggest strength and resolve. Yet his movements say something quite different. Have you noticed a certain tentativeness in the way he walks . . . and again in his speech? He stoops slightly when he crosses the room and his voice is unusually soft . . . as if he were afraid to assert himself. I can't help feeling that deep inside, he questions his right to project the strength that is his birthright."

Tashi: "I think I know what you're talking about. Up to now I just thought of him as kind of gentle, maybe even shy. But maybe you're right, maybe he's holding back in some way . . . (*pause*) . . . What in the world would make him that way?"

Bapu: "I'm not sure. The basic sense I get is that he feels he doesn't deserve to show his true strength, that because of something that happened in the past . . . perhaps the distant past . . . he has forfeited the right to follow his natural instincts. So he's hunkering down, keeping a low profile . . . "

Tashi: "You think he feels ashamed of something?"

Bapu: "I'd call it guilt."

Tashi: "I hate to think that's true. He really is a strong person. I see it every time we're together . . . and that's one of the reasons I love him so much."

Bapu: "And that's what's so special about you Tashi . . . that despite your youth, you can see beyond the externals, behind all the self-doubt and tentativeness, to the strength inside . . . and to love him for what you see. At some level he's got to be aware that you see him for who he really is . . . and that's a gift he's not likely to find elsewhere."

Tashi (*taking his arm again*): "Thank you for saying that, Bapu. It feels so good when you talk that way. But what should I do right now? How should I act when I'm with him?"

Bapu: "I wouldn't change anything. You're exactly what he needs, whether he knows it or not. The only way he's going to get beyond this self-doubt is to find someone who loves him for who he is regardless of the past . . . (*pause*) . . . and that someone has to be willing to stick with him until he feels accepted, no matter how long it takes."

By Saturday night, Bapu has left for home and Tashi and Richard find themselves playing for a large holiday weekend crowd at the restaurant. To the observant listener Tashi's playing appears listless, reserved; gone are the sweeping movements of the bow that spring from a heart at peace.

Between pieces Richard leans over to speak to her, "You seem disturbed. Is anything wrong?"

Her face is wan, her eyes drained of their usual sparkle. "Can we talk about it at dinner?" she replies softly.

Tashi: "Of course. There's no hurry."

Once they are seated at their favorite table and the candles lit, Tashi lowers her head and speaks. "The reason I haven't called you this week . . . or sent an e-mail . . . is that my parents think I'm seeing too much of you. So, no more phone calls, e-mails or getting together except for when we have to practice or perform at the restaurant. Bapu did his best to convince them to lift the restrictions, but they wouldn't listen . . . especially Dad. They say they're protecting me, but it feels more like being squashed."

Richard: "I'm sorry, Tash, but it's not hard to understand their motives. You're still only 15 and, like good parents anywhere, they feel responsible for your safety."

Tashi: "But doesn't it upset you . . . .that I'm not allowed to see you when we want to get together?"

Richard: "Not really. . . the way I see it, they're just being protective. It shows they love you. Most of the kids at the Correctional Center have parents who are either missing or don't care. Maybe you should be grateful that your Mom and Dad are concerned enough to place limits on your behavior."

Tashi: "But love can be suffocating . . . even if it's not meant to be. It feels like they don't trust me . . . but I trust myself. And Bapu trusts me. He knows who I am. He told my parents that I have an unusual capacity for loving . . . and that I know enough not to let anyone use me."

Richard: "But grandparents don't have the same responsibility as parents. It's easier for them to be permissive. They don't have to pick up the pieces if something goes wrong."

Tashi: "You mean if I don't act sensibly. Do you think I act sensibly?"

Richard: "You're very bold. You take chances. But I trust your judgment. You strike me as very mature for 15 . . . but still not completely wise to the ways of the world. So, you could still get hurt."

Tashi: "But isn't that true of adults too? If you give your heart to someone . . . at any age . . . aren't you taking a chance you'll get hurt?"

Richard: "Of course."

Tashi: "Do you think I care too much for you, Richard?"

Richard: "Perhaps. I would hate to see you get hurt because of something I did or did not do . . . (*pause*) . . . now, it's almost 10:30 . . . time to be getting you home. Ready to go?"

Outside her door, Tashi lingers long enough to ask, "One tiny kiss? I won't be seeing you until next Thursday."

Richard: "O.K. Just this once." A brief kiss and he leaves.

What to do between the restaurant on Saturday nights and the practice sessions at Richard's place on Thursdays? That is the question that haunts Tashi now. At her parents' insistence she has agreed that there will be no phone calls to Richard, no e-mails, no visits. But what about a chance meeting, something unplanned and thus not in violation of the agreement? The thought, pregnant with possibility, is followed quickly by the recollection that Richard likes to go walking in the meadow near the pool where they bathed together. "I like to take a break from composing right after lunch," she remembers him saying. "Going to the meadow clears my head; it gets me out of the house and away from the piano."

The decision is made. As she packs her lunch, her mind overflows with images of a surprise meeting in the meadow. She sees him coming out of the woods onto the grassy slope. A desire to throw her arms around him bursts into consciousness, but is quickly clouded by doubt. Will he welcome her presence . . . or resent the intrusion? How can she know?

With a shake of her head, she closes the lunch bag and places it in her knapsack. It doesn't matter. She looks up at the wall clock and hoists the knapsack onto her shoulders. Not knowing when he will come, she will go early and eat her lunch in the meadow, thereby maximizing the chance of an encounter. With lips drawn tight and a final nod of the head, she slams the door behind her and heads for the woods.

The trail leads out of town and past Richard's cottage. As she approaches the place where a small path veers off to his cottage, she slows down, hoping either to catch a glimpse of him or to have him see her passing. As she anticipated, there are too many trees in the way to make either possible. She hurries on, eager to get settled in the meadow before he arrives.

The spot she chooses is a favorite one, an open, grassy place surrounded by bluets and flax where the meadow begins sloping down into the woods. From here the view leads all the way across the valley to the five-thousand-foot peaks in the distance. It is a view that on any day stirs her heart. Today she is too anxious to enjoy the scenery. As she pulls her lunch from the knapsack, she keeps looking toward the opening where the trail emerges out of the woods onto the meadow. Her eating is fitful, the sandwich tasteless. When her neck begins to hurt from all the twisting, she shifts her position so that she is looking directly at the opening. Minutes pass with nothing happening.

Just as she is about to return the unfinished sandwich to her backpack, she spots someone in blue jeans and a white tee shirt coming out onto the grass. It's Richard. As he approaches, she stands to greet him with a hug.

"Fancy meeting you here," he offers.

"Yes. It's such a lovely day," she replies, resuming her place on the grass. "I guess we both had the same idea. Would you like to sit down? There's plenty of room."

Richard: "I'm just taking a break from the music . . . can't stay long (*sitting next to her*) . . . I hope this doesn't get you in trouble with your parents . . . you know . . . "

Tashi (*cheerfully*): "It wasn't planned so they can't say I'm breaking the law. . . (*pause*) . . . How's your new piece coming?"

Richard: "O.K. I can't say I'm thrilled with the opening bars but once the main theme kicks in it moves right along. As usual I'll struggle when I get to the ending . . . but that's not for a while yet."

With their sides touching, they sit quietly, looking out over the valley as two red-tailed hawks ride the thermals up the distant mountain-side until they become no more than gyrating specks in a cloudless, blue sky.

Tashi (*turning to face him*): "Ok if I put my head in your lap?"

Richard (*chuckling*): "You sure we're not being watched . . . by satellite or something?"

Tashi (*nestling into his lap*): "I'm sure."

Once she is comfortable, Richard resumes talking about his music while at the same time stroking her hair with his fingers. His breathing slows to match the rise and fall of her breasts. As he scans the mountains in the distance, he lapses into a quiet, unguarded state. Out of the blue he brings up the subject of Margot, his ex-wife . . . a smart, professional woman, he says, attorney by trade . . . quick to accuse . . . often defensive . . . not someone to blame herself for anything. Too ambitious, he adds, to be supportive of anyone but herself.

Tashi (*running her fingers across his wrist*): "How supportive of her were you?"

Richard: "Not too. I retaliated by denying her the encouragement she refused to give me."

Tashi (*turning, looking up at his face*): "What did she accuse you of?"

Richard (*selecting his words carefully*): "Small things . . . not doing my share around the house . . . spending too much time alone . . . not being with the kids enough."

By now the sun has fallen far from its peak, bathing the two visitors in the glow of its golden light. From the West a freshening breeze ripples across the grass, whisking away all awareness of time and place, drawing all who would listen into a space where only the moment exists. Neither speaks; all doubts fall from their shoulders as they surrender to the enveloping silence. She sighs then trembles with inexpressible joy. He bends over, using his outstretched fingers to comb her hair; tremors echo throughout his body.

Sinking now into fantasy, Tashi imagines Richard leaning to kiss her. Through the veil of her longing, she holds him tight, brushes her lips back and forth across his, and whispers, "Do you promise to love me forever?" "Of course," he replies, with an intensity bordering on desperation.

"You are my whole life. Kiss me again," she insists. "Tell me you want to marry me."

As she waits for an answer, Richard's knee suddenly jolts upward catapulting her onto the grass. He reaches for his leg and rubs it vigorously. "Oops, I didn't mean to do that. Something just bit me on the leg. Are you O.K.?"

From the grass, eyes flickering, still wrapped in the cocoon of her dreaming, she replies, "I'm fine. How about you? How's your leg?"

Richard (*rising*): "It's nothing . . . just a beetle mistaking me for a juicy caterpillar . . . Why don't we head back. My muse is calling. I don't want to disappoint her."

With that they leave the meadow.

That night she dreams. In the subterranean haunts of her desire, a scene takes shape and presents itself for viewing. Fuzzy at first, it slowly comes into focus, stunning now in its palpability. The morning air crackles with laughter as she and Richard frolic in the mountain pool, their clothes tossed casually on the bank. With the sweet freshness of youth on her lips and wet hair falling in ringlets to her shoulders, she delights in the knowledge that he finds her beautiful. Just inches away, he remains squatting, the water level with his chest, his back against the embankment, eyes fixed on the loveliness before him. On pretext of pointing to a bird in the oak tree, she rises from her squatting position and stands before him while the water runs off her exposed breasts. "I think it's a Baltimore oriole. Look!"

He turns to look without rising. "Yes . . . lovely, isn't it?" he responds, fully aware of her deception.

The dream continues. Disappointed, she sinks back into the water while plotting her next move. When she fixes her eyes on his, he averts her stare, tilting his head downward instead. It takes a moment or two before she realizes that he is looking beneath the surface of the water. A gladness fills her heart as she follows his gaze to the fur-lined slit between her own legs. In response she opens her knees, giving him an unobstructed view of her girlish crotch. As her curiosity mounts, she directs her own eyes below the surface to Richard's knees, then his thighs. Her young heart begins to race when she sees that his member has swollen to twice its normal size and is pointed like an arrow at her maidenhood.

It is instinct, not learning, that takes the dream deeper. Smiling nervously and fumbling for words, she scootches forward until their knees touch, then reaches under the water to take his sex in her hand, guiding it deftly toward her puffy, outer lips. When it doesn't quite reach, she leans forward and throws one arm around his neck. Using her free hand, she massages her labia with the head of his penis and is surprised by how smoothly it moves inside her flesh. As he brings his lips up to meet her own, she feels him entering her, stretching her pink folds with massive thrusts, finally bursting through her girlish membrane to claim his prize. A new and unexpected warmth fills her inner cavity as his lips remain locked to hers.

"I am yours, Richard, darling," she murmurs as the dreaming nears its end, her voice quivering with both joy and apprehension. "Yours and only yours," she adds softly without moving. "I adore you, Tashi," he whispers, still hard inside her. "Will you love me forever?" he asks. "I promise to be yours," she answers, "until death do us part."

At the breakfast table, Esther asks, "Are you alright, Eleanor? You don't seem like yourself this morning . . . (*pause*) . . . Did you have a bad dream?"

Tashi: "I'll be alright Mom . . . it's just a little stomach upset."

Esther: "I hope you've started your packing. Remember, we're leaving for Boston early next Sunday."

The words fall on Tashi's head with the fury of hail stones. "Sunday . . . why so early?"

Esther: "It's hardly early when your school starts on Thursday. That'll give us just enough time to get you registered for classes and buy you a new outfit or two at Filenes. You'd like that, wouldn't you?"

By this time, Tashi is on the stairs heading for her bedroom.

"Tashi?" Esther calls, looking into the empty hallway. When there is no answer, she turns back to the kitchen, murmuring, "Oh God, that child. What is going to become of her? I fear the worst."

At the restaurant Tashi struggles to stay focused on her playing while thoughts of separation gnaw at her attention. The promise of a candle-light dinner at the end of the evening keeps her spirits from sagging altogether. Richard is aware of her mood and attempts overtly to lighten the occasion with tidbits of humor while secretly rehearsing how to handle what promises to be a painful goodbye.

Once the playing has ended and they are seated at their favorite corner table, Tashi is the first to speak. "The candles seem softer tonight, don't you think? . . . (*when there is no response*) . . . I don't know; maybe it's just my imagination."

Richard looks at the candles, then back at Tashi. "Perhaps. It's hard to say . . . (*pause*) . . . Are you at all excited about going back to school . . . seeing old friends?"

Tashi: "Not really."

As he looks at her, he feels a tightening in his chest. It bothers him to see so much distress on her face, especially when it is obvious that he is the cause of it. What could he have done differently, he asks silently. Should he have pushed her away, made it clear from the outset that he had no interest in her other than as a playing partner? To be fair, he did communicate his lack of interest in marrying again soon, but she couldn't have been thinking about marriage anyway . . . not at that age. So, what is the nature of her interest? It's got to be that she's simply in love. But is it any more than an adolescent infatuation, the kind of puppy love that most kids go through in high school? Maybe, but he has to admit that this has been going on for so long now and with such intensity that it's hard to dismiss it as a mere crush.

When the waiter comes to take their order, Tashi has trouble making up her mind. "What are you going to have, Richard?" she asks listlessly.

Without answering, Richard returns to his internal probing, this time raising the question of his own feelings. "I do find her attractive," he continues, "both physically and intellectually, as much as you can say that about one who is no longer a girl, but not yet a woman. And there's no question I look forward to seeing her each week . . . even holding her like I did in the meadow . . . but. . . romance . . . obsession . . . you can hardly say that I'm in love with her."

"Are you having trouble making up your mind too?" Tashi asks. "Or maybe you're just not hungry . . . like me."

Richard (*shaking off his reverie*): "Sorry. No . . . that's not it . . . (*pause*) . . . I think I'll get the pesto chicken."

"You got the same thing last week," she retorts.

"You're right," he says, sitting back in his chair, uninterested in defending himself.

Neither speaks for a minute or two.

Tashi (*softly*): "Are you as upset as I am?" she asks, breaking the silence.

Richard: "I'm not sure. I know I'll miss you while you're gone, but beyond that I don't know . . . (*pause*) . . . You're better at saying what you're feeling. I'm not even sure what's going on inside me. It's confusing."

Tashi: "I understand . . . after all, you're a man . . . (*rising*) . . . I think I'll let you work on it while I go to the ladies room. By the time I get back, you can tell me everything."

As soon as she leaves, he falls back into self-examination. Without forethought, an image of Margot rises into consciousness. He sees her standing before him in the doorway, getting ready to leave. Her eyes are dark, her lips pressed together, her gray business suit jacket drawn tightly across a white starched blouse. She picks her briefcase up from the floor and stares at him without uttering a word. The sneer on her handsome face looms before him as an unchallenged accusation, oppressive in its righteousness. It doesn't matter that what happened was an act of omission rather than commission. The children are gone now, her face seems to say, dead before their first day in school, taken from us before we had a chance to find out who they really were. She turns the door handle and looks back a final time. I can't bear to live with you any longer, her eyes declare. And with that she is gone.

His eyes drift back to the empty seat across from him. Where Tashi was sitting he now sees Margot, her eyes fixed in a merciless stare, mouth twisted in unconcealed loathing. All the sting of rejection, the withdrawal of affection, the silent accusations, the scorn and blatant disgust he endured at the time come back to him now. "What is love," he asks silently, "that it lasts only on condition that you never make mistakes? What of the promise to 'love until death do us part'? It all depends, does it not? It all depends."

Tashi returns to her chair. As Richard looks on helplessly, she assumes the shape of Margot's body. Taller now, older, her hair blonde and cut straight around the neck . . . she looks at him without blinking. He recoils in disbelief, then rubs his eyes and leans forward. Behind her frozen stare he sees the outline of an adolescent face. Yes, yes it *is* Tashi. Gradually the images of the two women morph into one as her hair turns a motley gray and her lips grow pale. He watches in horror as the smile of a young girl, new to love, metamorphoses into the curled lips of disgust. Where once he saw the sparkling eyes of desire, he now sees the lidded glare of hate. The assembled figure, unrelenting in its spitefulness and oppressive in its proximity, holds him fast in its grasp. Unconsciously he pulls back from the table, frightened by what he has seen.

"Richard," Tashi calls out, a rising terror evident in her voice. "Where are you? Talk to me, please."

He pretends not to hear. Secretly, far from anyone's knowing, he begins putting the pieces together. As the waiter places the entrées on the table, he refocuses his gaze and pulls up his chair. His mind is clear now. Looking across the table, he sees his friend in a new, objective light. Pretty, yes, and smart he concludes . . . even precocious in some ways, but a female nevertheless, thus an object of concern. As she matures, she is bound to develop the power that others of her gender possess, the power to pierce a man's armor and eviscerate his most sacred possession . . . his independence. Once a man lets that happen, once he yields his ultimate prize, he remains forever at her mercy . . . to be nurtured or abandoned according to her whims. The odds are not favorable. Be smart, he tells himself. Remember, it is the wise man who looks ahead, resists her charms, holds his desire in check and keeps her at arm's length.

He looks up at Tashi now, ready to resume their dialogue. Behind his broad smile he is aware of a new resolve, the resolve never to make himself vulnerable again. I can be your friend, he reflects as their eyes meet, but I will never let myself love you, not the way I loved Margot. A new and welcome peace radiates throughout his body as the last of his doubts vanish.

"I'm right here, Tash," he responds with renewed enthusiasm. "You haven't touched your chicken yet. C'mon. Let's dig in."

As the evening progresses, they go through the rituals of eating, driving home and saying goodbye at the door. Most of their conversation revolves around duets for next year and praise for her cello playing. He is calm and reassuring on the surface, but her instincts tell her something has changed. What is going on, she asks, withdrawing into the privacy of her thoughts. Is he pulling back out of some newly-awakened fear, pretending not to care? Over and over, she looks into his face in search of an answer. She sees nothing. Where are the misting eyes, she asks, eyes like my own that threaten to spill into tears at any moment? Where is that shortness of breath born of a fear that unforeseen twists of fate will keep us from ever meeting again? She sees nothing but smiles and a countenance at peace. No, this is not the way she expected the summer to end. It is not at all what she wanted. It is hardly an ending to reassure an anxious heart during the long winter ahead. It is an ending fraught with fear and uncertainty, one that can only sow the seeds of doubt.

In the driveway he leaves the car running, then accompanies her to the house. At the door she hesitates, desperate for a kiss but unwilling to risk rejection . . . then waves goodbye and goes in.

Two days later she writes to her grandfather.

Dear Bapu,

Back in dreary old Boston, out shopping for new clothes . . . school starts Thursday. I just can't get into it. How am I going to survive nine months of this?

I can't stop thinking about my last night with Richard. He acted like he didn't care that we wouldn't see each other until Thanksgiving or maybe even until next summer. There I was, on the verge of tears, and he was as calm as ever. I don't get it.

Well, actually he wasn't that way all the time. When we first sat down to eat, he was off somewhere in his mind, thinking about something he didn't want to share with me. And then when I came back from the ladies room, he looked at me funny, like he was in a trance or something. He didn't even hear me when I talked to him. When he finally came out of his trance, he smiled like he had just discovered some great secret. From that point on he sat there like a Buddha . . . enjoying his meal and content to make pleasant conversation. He wasn't any better on the way home. I knew better than to ask for a goodbye kiss.

I'm stumped . . . and really disappointed at the way the summer ended. Can you make any sense out of it? Please write soon.

Anxiously,

Tashi

Dear Tashi,

This relationship seems to be giving you a lot of heartache. I hope it's worth it.

You say that Richard's behavior was different on Saturday night . . . less communicative than usual, more withdrawn. That leads me to wonder if there was anything special about that night. The answer, of course, is that it was your last night together for the summer. On the surface, it might appear that he was glad to be done with you and lost in thoughts about the future . . . his music presumably, maybe even the stock market. So, maybe having dinner with you was a boring affair that he couldn't wait to be done with.

On the other hand, it could mean the very opposite of that. Maybe he looked across the table at you, got thinking how much he was going to miss you and that realization frightened him. We need only assume that he'd been suppressing his feelings of affection all along and got alarmed when they began to surface. If that's true, he was probably pulling away from you not out of boredom or indifference, but because he was afraid of getting too deeply involved.

So, how do you know which is true . . . that he was glad to be rid of you or frightened by the possibility of falling in love with you? It's impossible to say without more evidence. I would look for clues in his most recent behavior . . . that is, prior to Saturday night. Have you had a chance to be alone with him outside the restaurant . . . if so, how did he act toward you? Maybe your parents put the kibosh on that, so the question is irrelevant.

I can't say much more without some new facts. So . . . give me some more facts.

Loving you, El Bapo

Dearest Bapu,

I love the way you're thinking. Here are some facts that might help.

Fact #1: We had a chance meeting (still not known by Mom and Dad . . . so shhhhh) in the meadow by his cottage not too long ago. He stayed with me while I ate my lunch.

Fact #2: He let me sprawl out on the grass with my head in his lap.

Fact #3: He stroked my hair while I was lying there. It felt very romantic . . . at least to me. But he didn't say anything.

Fact #4: It all ended when a beetle bit him on the leg.

Hope this helps. Please write as soon as possible.

Love, La Tashita

P.S. Oops. I forgot fact#5: while we were there on the grass, he brought up the subject of his ex-wife for the first time. He sees her as a very unforgiving kind of person . . . and not very supportive. I guess he didn't support her much either.

Liebe Grosstochter,

Glad you remembered fact #5 . . . it tells me he's starting to trust you enough to open up about his past . . . at least a little. The lap business and hair stroking both point to a growing affection for you . . . certainly not the kind of thing a man would do if he's looking forward to getting rid of you when the summer is over. From what you say, it looks like things ended badly with his wife and he's afraid to get involved romantically with anyone else . . . and that includes you. All this would suggest that on your last night together he started to get in touch with how much he cares for you and this frightened him into withdrawing. He may have tried to suppress his affection for you . . . and even feigned a certain indifference . . . but the opposite is probably true. I think the fish has seen the bait, bitten on it and is fighting with all its might to avoid getting pulled in. What I'm saying is: I think he's falling for you, but don't yank too hard or you'll lose him.

My bill is in the mail,

Herr Bapu

Dear Herr Bapu,

I love the way your mind works. What you said . . . your guess about Richard's feelings for me . . . is so reassuring . . . even if it's only a guess. I want to believe with my whole heart that you're right. But don't worry about the "yanking" . . . it's going to be months before I see him again, so there's no way for me to force myself on him even if I wanted to, which I don't.

Your e-mails are so important to me. I don't know if I could have made it this far on hope alone.

When you make out your bill, please be generous to yourself. I'm sure Daddy will be happy to pay.

Your patient patient,

Tashi

14   A New Neighbor

This is not a good morning for Richard. For the last half-hour he has been sitting at the piano waiting for his creative juices to start flowing. Perhaps it's the stock market . . . four days now in a row of losses. He has been counting on an annual gain of 12-15% just to pay his mortgage, food, car expenses and healthcare. So far this year his portfolio has failed to gain a cent. This morning's news of another drop simply adds to his worry. But there's something else disrupting his peace of mind . . . something stealthy, even ominous, a subcutaneous ache hidden beyond the reach of consciousness. He feels it not as a concrete worry but as an undefined discomfort . . . something he can't see directly but senses as a remote throbbing.

If he were to relax and let a mixture of unselected images and thoughts arise, he might see what is going on internally and thus experience some clarity . . . but this is not his wont. He is a fighter. When things trouble him but remain outside the reach of awareness, he either drops the issue altogether or goes after the answer with the tenacity of a bloodhound. Neither works very well in the long run. Today is a bloodhound day and like all the others of that sort, it's getting him nowhere. He sits at the piano with closed eyes and clenched teeth as if he were challenging the intruder to come forth and present himself for battle. If he could just relax and stop straining to get at the problem, he might get a clue as to what is going on below the surface. For example, he might see that many of the images and thoughts that continue to dart in and out of consciousness have something to do with Tashi. He might see that despite the fact that she has been back in Boston for a month now, she continues to occupy a central place in his everyday world. If he were to go even deeper, he might even wake up to the fact that he misses her . . . so much so that her absence has become a source of pain . . . a simmering, unarticulated pain to be sure, but one with the power to hold his muse at bay. Unable to relax, he sits at the piano now, horns locked in mortal combat with an internal demon that refuses to show itself. His breathing is quick and shallow.

Adding to his petulance is an irritating new sound . . . the sound of loud rock music coming from somewhere outside the cottage. For a second or two he assumes that it must be a passing car or truck, although not too many vehicles have reason to come this far up the county road. When it persists for seconds and then minutes, he rises from his piano bench and goes outside to listen. Standing in the middle of the road, he quickly determines that the music is coming from an area about 100 yards east of the cottage . . . .that is, down the road as you head back into town. He stands there listening for a few minutes, then goes back into the house where he waits for the noise to stop. He takes a seat in the living room and tries to relax. There is no point in even trying to compose so long as the offending sound continues to assail his ears. Sitting there, sipping a lemonade, he tries to visualize the kind of person who would be thoughtless enough to play his music that loud. It's got to be someone working in the area where they recently cut down the white pines, he concludes. He knew when he drove past the place last week that someone was preparing the land for a new house. Sure enough, the next time he passed, he saw a truck there pouring cement for a foundation. It follows, then, that it's probably some workers with a boom box who are finishing off the foundation or perhaps laying a floor.

With that new understanding, he rises, goes out onto the road and heads down to the work site. His intention is to introduce himself . . . and politely make it clear that he can't do any composing with someone else's music blaring in his ears. He has done much the same thing many times back in Boston when as an apartment dweller he had neighbors on all sides, at least some of whom insisted on playing their stereos at high volume, especially when they had guests. For the most part his experience has been a positive one. When he has gone to knock on someone's door or call on the phone, almost everyone has apologized and quickly corrected the problem.

So, it is with a confidence based on real-life experience that he heads down the road toward the source of today's problem. He remembers the clearing to be about 100 yards down the road but his ears are sufficient in themselves to tell him where the sound is coming from. By the time he reaches the new driveway the music is so loud that it is hurting his ears. As he turns into the clearing, he gets his first up-close look at the beginnings of a new house . . . or, judging from the size of the foundation and floor, more aptly a new cabin. Quite oblivious to his presence is a man nailing together the studs that will make up the first of four walls. Richard's greeting is lost in the blare of bass guitars and drums. It is only when he gets close enough to tap the stranger on the shoulder that the man turns around and acknowledges his unexpected guest with a scowl. As Richard extends his hand and shouts an introduction, the man spits a wad of dark brown tobacco juice onto the ground, barely missing Richard's foot. With hands still at his side, he shouts, "What d'ya want?"

Richard answers with a combination of lip movements and a hand pointing to the boom box at one end of the floor. With his fingers and thumb he makes a rotating movement, leaving no doubt that he wants the man to turn the radio down. Adding to this, he lip-synchs the words, "I'm your neighbor. Name is Richard. Nice to meet you." The introduction he has carefully rehearsed on the way down is considerably more elegant . . . but is rendered useless now by the voices and instruments screaming their incantations from the radio.

The stranger smiles and nods his head, pauses, then shouts, "Arnie," the foulness of his breath evident even from five feet away. He makes no movement toward the radio, instead smiling vacantly. Each time he smiles some of the tobacco juice in his mouth spills out onto his lips and down into his beard, adding to its wet, stringy appearance. It is obvious that he hasn't bothered to cut either his beard or his moustache in weeks if not months. The latter hangs unevenly over his upper lip like the kind of moss that falls from cypress trees in southern swamps, leaving an observer to wonder how he manages to get food into his mouth without ingesting a mass of hair along with it. His mouth is particularly disgusting. The sneer into which he twists it when talking reveals one missing tooth on the side of his curled lip along with a few stunted teeth yellowed with nicotine. He has a habit of tugging on his beard whenever he talks, giving the impression that he either wants to pull it off or unconsciously to make it more pointed, perhaps in honor of some Mephistophelean idol.

His age seems something of a mystery until he takes his baseball cap off and wipes the sweat from a completely bald head. Somewhere in his late forties, maybe early fifties, Richard surmises, assessing the evidence before him. So, he wonders, where did a man of this ilk find the money to buy such an expensive piece of land . . . and to build a cabin on it? Perhaps he doesn't own the land, but a squatter wouldn't dare to build a cabin on someone else's property . . . would he?

By now Arnie has moved to the cabin floor and turned the radio down to the point where the two men can hear each other. "So ya don't like ma music," he snickers, wetting his forehead with a dirty red kerchief drawn from his back pocket. Ya got somethin' against rock and roll?"

"Thank you," Richard responds, acknowledging the lower but still uncomfortably loud sound. "I'm a composer . . . make my living writing music . . . classical music . . . you know, stuff for piano, cello . . . sometimes a whole orchestra. Right now I'm trying to do a . . . "

Arnie (*interrupting*): "Classical, eh? Better than the crap I listen to, right?"

Richard (*hesitating*): "Different, not better. The thing is that I can't write my own music if I'm forced to listen to someone else's at the same time. It really doesn't matter whether the other music is rock or classical or anything else . . . (*pause*) . . . For me to write a piece, I need silence. It's from that silence that the music emerges . . . although wind, rain and even bird songs don't seem to pose a problem . . . (*pause*) . . . I've even written pieces with car traffic in the street outside . . . it's not as easy but still doable. It only becomes non-doable when I have to listen to someone else's music."

Throughout this little soliloquy, Arnie has been busily arranging the studs for the first wall. Whether he heard any of what Richard said about composing is not clear. What is clear is that he has done what he is willing to do . . . and no more. Without looking at Richard, he picks up his hammer and pounds another nail into the frame.

Richard is aware that at this volume he will still be able to hear the radio back at his cottage. Not wanting to return, he approaches Arnie, points to the boom box and motions for him to turn it down more. "It's still too loud," he shouts.

"For Christ's sake, that kind of music has gotta be loud," Arnie shouts back. "Maybe you high-brow types like your music soft so you can keep on talkin' . . . not me . . . I can't work without music and it's gotta be loud enough to drown out all the other shit goin' on in my head. Comprendo?"

Richard considers his options as he wrestles to keep his anger in check. After sorting through a variety of alternatives, he makes his decision. Calmly but with barely restrained force he says, "I'm going back to my house and call the police. Let's see what they do."

Arnie: "Go ahead. You think the cops are going to waste time comin' out here to investigate your petty little complaint when they got their hands full keepin' the drug dealers and hookers from takin' over the town . . . (*pause*) . . . You think they give a rat's ass about somebody playin' music too loud here in the woods with all these birds chirpin', owls hootin' and frogs bellyachin' to get laid. They're goin' to laugh in your face . . . I'll bet on it. They ain't even gonna come out here to look. Some fat-ass sergeant is gonna lean back in his swivel chair, take a puff on his cheap cigar and tell ya to stay home and close your fuckin' windows. And that's all they're gonna do."

With those chilling words ringing in his ears, Richard turns and heads back to the road. When he has taken no more than five or six steps toward his house, he hears Arnie turning the volume back up on the boom box. He stops in mid-step, unwilling to accept what his ears are telling him. "That fucking creep! How could he?" Within seconds his whole body fills with a loathing that threatens to tear his flesh apart. Whirling, he runs back into the driveway and toward the foundation. Arnie can't hear his footsteps over the music coming from the boom box.

As Richard approaches the area where Arnie is nailing studs, his body bursts into flames, devouring all thoughts in an inferno of hate. His heart is racing so fast his chest is about to burst. Where thought once reigned supreme, instinct now shouts in his ears: "Take him by the throat . . . smash his head against the foundation . . . kill him." It is too late for thinking about consequences . . . too late for an appeal to reason. This is the same fury that has lain dormant for years, imprisoned behind impenetrable bars of guilt and shame. All the scorn he has for so long heaped on himself cries out now for relief . . . for a new target, a new outlet, a new villain. Once again, he feels the raw power of loathing, the same power that has held him hostage since his wife walked out . . . the overweening power to destroy, perhaps even to kill . . . it is all there . . . still unsatisfied . . . but no longer aimed at himself. Now, it's directed toward the figure crouching in front of him.

Without hesitation he races forward and hurls himself at Arnie. Just seconds before their bodies collide, Arnie turns, sees Richard coming and swings his hammer with all the force he can muster. As Arnie's head is slammed against the foundation, his hammer buries itself in Richard's upper arm. A single scream fills the clearing.

Richard rolls off his adversary and grabs his upper arm, rubbing it vigorously. To avoid fainting, he kneels, breathes deeply, then turns to see Arnie on his back with eyes closed and mouth spurting blood. His immediate reaction is one of horror. "Have I killed him?" he murmurs as his own breathing accelerates. "Oh God, no," he gasps as he crawls over to the prone body. By the time he gets there Arnie's chest is rising and falling and his eyes have opened; cloudy at first, they slowly come into focus.

"You cocksucker," he mumbles through his blood-drenched moustache. "I'll get you for this." With his wrist he wipes away some of the blood, then sits up, fixing Richard in a glare so odious as to make his knees tremble.

As distasteful as the sight is, it comforts Richard to the point where he mounts a smile, adding, "If I had known I was going to do some tackling today, I would have worn my shoulder pads." With that, he heads up the driveway . . . then stops, turns back and goes over to the boom box. With considerably more force than is required, he turns it down sharply and then all the way off. "You bastard," Arnie cries out, as he struggles to get to his feet. At the road Richard looks back to see him sitting up, dabbing blood from his forehead with his dirty red kerchief. "Keep the goddamn sound down Arnie," he shouts, "or next time I'll finish the job." He then heads for his cottage, rubbing his shoulder as he walks.

By morning the flesh just below his shoulder has turned blue at the edges and a dark purple bordering on black at the center. The mere sight of the wound tightens his stomach, robbing him of any appetite for breakfast. He goes into the kitchen and pours a small glass of orange juice. From his seat at the table, he begins counting the number of hummingbirds at his feeder. Just as the first sip of juice reaches his tongue, the morning's silence is suddenly shattered by the sound of loud rock music. The glass falls from his hand and breaks on the kitchen floor. Rather than picking it up, he runs to the door and steps out into the yard. There can be no question; it's Arnie's boom box, loud as ever.

His first thought is to grab an axe and head down the road. He goes so far as to open the garage door, grasp the wooden handle and point it in Arnie's direction. After three steps up the driveway he stops and looks down at the axe. The head of polished steel glistens in the morning's light; the cutting edge, newly sharpened, is fine enough for shaving. In his fevered mind's eye, he pictures Arnie with eyes closed, his head resting against the foundation sill, the axe raised high, poised to sever head from body. He sees the axe descending, just inches now from his neck, a torrent of blood about to spurt from his carotid artery. "Oh God no," he cries out, falling backwards in horror and dropping the axe to the driveway. "What am I doing?" He stumbles back into the house as the music continues to blare, louder than ever.

In the kitchen he picks up the broken glass and pours himself another juice. Still dazed by the scene he has imagined, he struggles to recover his bearings. Shaking his head in disbelief, "How could I have contemplated such a barbarous act? It is insane to sacrifice my career and freedom to a momentary lust for revenge, however sweet that might be." Gradually his equilibrium returns. So concentrated is he now that he can scarcely hear the music outside. With sanity restored, he calls on his core principles and sets his priorities back in order. As thinking resumes its control over feeling, all desire for revenge recedes to the outer edges of consciousness. He is calmer now, reassured of his ability to manage his emotions, an ability that has sustained him through years of inner turmoil. Rising from the table, he heads to the front door, grabs a jacket and wanders out onto the trail.

"It's best this way," he murmurs to himself, a few yards to the West up the path. "Just get away from trouble, don't allow yourself to be tempted by vengeance again." So eager is he to escape his emotions that he fails to consider the prospect of having to listen to the sound every day until the cabin is finished . . . or even beyond. Worse yet, what would that mean for his future as a composer?

Further up the trail, past the pool where he and Tashi bathed earlier, he hears familiar voices. He recognizes the voices of Sam and Raul, but can't see them. Suddenly they appear up ahead on the trail, leaning on their hoes and shovels. "Hey Rich," Sam shouts. "Whatcha doin' up here? How come your not home whippin' up some new tunes?"

"Hello," comes the response. "Just out for a walk. You guys repairing the trail . . . or shouldn't I ask?" (*looking around*) "I don't see Pug, your babysitter. A new girlfriend?"

"Nope, the same old one," Sam answers. As the two banter, Raul remains behind, eyes averting Richard's glance. Quickly guessing what's up, Richard approaches, then extends his hand, first to Sam and then to Raul. "Hope I'm going to see you two in class next week," he offers. "I'm especially anxious to hear what Raul has done with that blues piece he was working on. How's it coming, Raul?"

Raul (*softly*): "I'm not sure I can make it next week . . . lots of stuff happening . . . new work detail and other shit."

"That's a bunch of crapola, Raulie," says Sam. "You're just pissed 'cuz Richard didn't promise to paint you pretty for the clowns on the probation board. Lookit, he's sayin' he wants you to come back. What the fuck more do you want?"

Richard (*looking at Raul*): "I did get a chance to talk to the restaurant manager about playing a CD of your music during intermissions and he says he'll think it over. My guess is that he's going to be O.K. with it."

Sam (*excited*): "For Christ sake, Raulie, thank the guy. He's tryin' to help ya."

Raul (*head down*): "Maybe I can make it . . . all depends."

Sam (*voice rising*): "Depends my ass. Be there (*turning to Richard*). He'll be there if I have to drag him . . . (*pause*) . . . So, how's your own stuff goin, Rich? Any big hits lately?"

Richard: "Afraid not. I don't know. I'm not even sure I'll be able to keep on writing."

Sam (*startled*): "Why not? That's your job ain't it? You're a composer."

Richard (hesitantly): "Well, yes . . . but . . . I've had some trouble lately and . . . "

"Hey," says Raul, "if he ain't goin' to compose, maybe he can help us with these here trails."

"Why not," answers Sam, "Great idea. How about it Rich . . . want to give us a hand (*pushing a shovel toward him*)?"

As Richard extends his left arm to take it, he winces, dropping the shovel to the ground.

"What's up?" Sam asks. "Somethin' wrong with your arm?"

"It's a bit sore," Richard offers, rubbing it hard. "I ran into a hammer the other day . . . this guy who's building a cabin next door was on the other end of it. He was playing his boom box so loud I couldn't concentrate on my own music, so I went over and asked him to turn it down. He obviously didn't like the idea but went along with it . . . for about two minutes. As soon as I left, he turned it right back up . . . so we had a fight."

Sam (*leaning forward*): "Did you lay him out?"

Richard: "Yeah, I did . . . right against the foundation he's working on . . . but at the last minute he got me with his hammer . . . right here (*rubbing his arm*). It looks like it was all wasted effort because he's got the music back on this morning. Even if I shut the windows, I can still hear it; I don't see how I can do any composing when his radio is blasting away.

I've thought about calling the police, but they're probably busy doing other things."

Sam: "You mean that cocksucker wouldn't turn the fuckin' box down even when you asked him polite and everything?"

Richard: "Yup. First time anyone has ever responded like that. He strikes me as a pretty ornery kind of guy . . . a real chip on his shoulder. He's also one of the ugliest people I've ever come across."

Sam (*laughing*): "Maybe he needs a lesson in good manners. *(turning to his companion)* Whad'ya think, Raulie? Should we round up the other guys and pay 'im a little visit?"

"Definitely," says Raul. "He needs his ass kicked . . . anyone can see that."

"Wait a minute guys," interjects Richard, making no attempt to hide his anxiety. "I don't want you doing anything that's going to get you into trouble back at the Center."

"Like what?" asks Sam, feigning innocence.

"You know damn well what I mean," retorts Richard. "No violence . . . nothing illegal."

Sam: "Yeah, but you weren't too neighbor-like when you knocked his ass against the foundation . . . were ya?"

Richard: "True . . . but I'm not in the hoosegow waiting for a parole hearing. I appreciate your support, but be sensible. Don't go looking for trouble. I'll figure out a way to deal with this guy on my own . . . (*pause*) . . . And don't forget we've got a basketball game this Friday . . . that means a practice session Thursday morning. We'll need everybody there if we're going to beat Saranac High. Who knows, with a good practice we might even win a game."

Sam: "Yeah . . . and maybe they'll tear the Correction Center down and put us up in the Ritz Carlton instead. I don't know. Myron may not be up for the game . . . the motherfucker's got some kind of cold, I think. Or maybe it's jist his herpes actin' up. We'll know Wednesday. Hope we don't hafta to go with jist four . . . last time we did that, I ended up on my back for two days."

Richard (*laughing*): "O.K. Try getting someone else to take his place . . . preferably somebody 6'10" or taller."

Sam: "Very funny Rich. I'll work on it."

Richard: "See you guys . . . I'm off to the meadow."

Before disappearing over the hill he looks back to wave. Sam and Raul have already left. Unknown to Richard they are now hurrying down the trail toward Arnie's place. A third member from the work detail has joined them. All three carry clubs fashioned from dead pine branches found along the way.

Not long after they pass Richard's cottage, Raul shouts, "I can hear some music comin' from over there in the woods (*pointing*). That's gotta be the place."

"Yeah, I can hear it," grunts Sam. "We're gonna hafta bushwhack our way through all these bushes. What we need is a fuckin' machete."

After ten minutes of fighting mosquito bites, scratched legs and fallen logs, they come to a clearing and stop. "This is it," whispers Sam, looking out over the empty field. "Over there . . . that's the cabin he's workin' on."

Raul (*pointing*): "There's the asshole himself . . . he's kneelin' on the ground; I think he's nailin' up some studs."

"Yeah . . . he's already got the floor in and two walls put up," adds Raja, the third member of the group . . . "and the fuckin' music is loud enough to reach New York (*covering his ears*). Is this guy deaf or what?"

"I think he's tryin' to stick it to Rich," adds Sam. "Nobody in his right gourd hasta play music that loud. This mother-fucker is askin' for trouble."

"So, what are we gonna do?" asks Raul.

Sam (*motioning with his hand*): "C'mon, it's time to learn 'im some manners. Let's put some fear in this prick . . . make him shit his pants. But like Rich says, nothin' too serious. We don't want the fuckin' cops all over us when we get back to the Center."

Side by side, with make-shift clubs gripped firmly, they advance toward the cabin. When they get within a few yards of the foundation, Arnie sees their shadows on the grass and rises to confront them.

"So, whad'ya want?" he barks, hammer in hand. "Yir on my property."

Like young lions surrounding an isolated wildebeest, but not yet adept at making a kill, the three boys circle their prey.

"Yir music is kinda loud, ain't it?" says Sam.

"Yeah," adds Raul, "we wuz takin' a nice walk through the woods and we couldn't hear the birds 'cuz yir music was so loud."

Arnie (*snickering*): "I thought rock was your kinda music. You sayin' you don't like rock and roll?"

Sam: "Whatd'ya mean *our* kinda music?"

Arnie *(nervously)*: "You know . . . city kid stuff."

"You mean ghetto shit, don't ya, asshole," says Raja who is several shades blacker than Sam. "Who the fuck do you . . . "

(*Interrupting*) "We like classical," says Sam quietly, unable to conceal a smile. "You know . . . Beathoven and those guys. Stuff that's over yir honky pinhead."

"Classical my ass," Arnie rejoins, sneering. "You wouldn't know a violin from a G-string. Let me guess. You met a guy named Richard and he's too chicken to come back and fight it out so he's sent you thugs to do his dirty work. Well, you can kiss my ass . . . because that radio stays right where it is."

Raul: "Ya mean that boom box over there (*pointing to the cabin floor and walking in that direction*)?"

"Keep your hands off that fuckin' thing," Arnie shouts as he rushes to head Raul off.

Raul is the first to get there. As he raises his club over the radio, Arnie lunges at him, knocking the smaller man to the ground. In grasping Raul by the throat, he drops the hammer to his side. Sam, who is only a few steps behind, picks it up and wields it over Arnie's head.

"Let him go," he shouts, "or I'm gonna turn that ugly dome of yirs into squash meat."

Arnie takes his hands off Raul's throat, rising slowly. Once free, Raul jumps to his feet and grabs a loose 2 x 4 stud lying on the ground. Brandishing his new weapon like a javelin, he pokes it at Arnie, prodding him away from the boom box. "Use the hammer," he shouts to Sam, nodding toward the radio. Sam shakes his head in disagreement, assuming the target to be Arnie. "No, the fuckin' radio," Raul bellows.

With a cry of "Oh yeah," Sam moves quickly onto the cabin floor where the radio is still screaming its shrill beat. As he raises the hammer to strike, Arnie pushes Raul's stud away and leaps to grab the hammer. Using both hands, Raul swings the stud at the lunging figure, catching his right leg just as it leaves the ground. The sound of wood on bone, sickening in its clarity, is loud enough to be heard above the music.

The hammer smashes through the plastic casing of the boom box just as Arnie falls to the ground, grasping his right leg. "You cocksuckers," he yells through his soup-strainer moustache. "You broke my leg . . . I can feel the bone stickin' out. You fuckin' apes. Animals . . . that's what you are. Get me to a fuckin' doctor . . . NOW . . . before it's too late . . . (*pause*) . . . The truck is over there (*pointing*)."

A minute or two passes. The music has stopped. No one says anything. Finally, Sam breaks the silence, "My driver's license expired last year . . . haven't bothered to renew it."

"Yeah, mine too," adds Raul.

"Same here," says Raja.

"Hmmm. Guess we'll just hafta leave ya here," continues Sam. I wouldn't sweat it. Somebody's bound to come along sooner or later and give ya a ride . . . (*pause*) . . . But I'm a little worried about these here two stud walls you got up . . . could blow over in a storm and fall on yir head. Better let us take 'em down. Raulie, you see any rope anywhere?"

"Over there by the truck," Raulie answers gleefullly, dropping the 2 x 4 and running to the pickup.

Still clutching his leg, Arnie turns toward Sam and spits in his direction. A glob of viscous brown tobacco juice falls at his target's feet. "You leave those fuckin' walls alone," he cries. "It took me a whole day to get 'em up there. You touch 'em and I'll see that your black ass spends the rest of its sorry life behind bars."

By now Richard's earlier call for restraint has completely disappeared behind the thrill of wreaking vengeance upon a villain so undeniably evil. With a gusto hitherto reserved for toddlers aching to kick over a tower of wooden blocks, Raul loops the rope around the overhead crossbar of the easternmost wall and pulls it taut, eyes sparkling in anticipation.

"Let 'er rip Raulie," comes Sam's exultant command.

Down comes the wall as Raulie backpedals onto the grass. Arnie's cry is lost in the impact as the studs are ripped from their sills and fall to the ground. Crawling toward the truck, one hand still on his leg, he shouts a string of obscenities, then pulls the cab door open and makes his way into the driver's seat. A quick examination of his leg reveals a badly swollen calf muscle, but no broken bones as he had feared. His relief is short-lived as he turns to witness the unfolding scene.

"Nice work, you crazy Spic," shouts a jubilant Sam from just beyond the cabin floor. "Let's go for two. Raja, give 'em a hand with that rope." With Raja's help, Raul loosens the rope from the first wall and attaches it to the crossbar of the second. Within minutes, the second wall crashes to the ground amid a chorus of euphoric wolf howls. Arnie turns on the ignition, grits his teeth and presses his swollen leg to the accelerator. The engine fails to turn over. Before he can try again, Sam runs over to the truck and sticks his head in the window. "I wouldn't complain about any of this if I wuz you . . . 'cuz if you do, we'll be back to finish the job . . . (*pause*) . . . and that includes you . . . (*turning around*) . . . right guys?" Raul and Raja trumpet their enthusiastic assent. With the jeers of all three ringing in his ears, Arnie twists the ignition key again, hears the motor catch this time, gives his aching leg a final massage and heads for the motel and the promise of a hot bath. The boys watch as he leaves, then turn to survey their handiwork. Lingering long enough for a victory dance on the cabin floor, they start back through the woods to the trail just in time to meet Pug, the baby-sitting guard coming from his weekly tryst in town. No questions are asked. In silence the troupe makes its way back to the work-site where they join the rest of the detail, pick up their tools and head back to the Correctional Center.

15   **The Theft**

Back at the motel Arnie's first act is to get in the tub and soak his aching leg. As he sits chest-high in the hot water, massaging his rapidly-swelling calf, all thoughts devolve around Richard. He's got to be responsible for this . . . somehow. Why would three teen-aged hoods make their way to his cabin site, smash his boom box and pull down the two walls he had just erected if they hadn't been put up to it by someone else? Did they really object to the music because they couldn't hear the birds? That's absurd. It's the kind of music they play themselves . . . and when they play it, they like it loud. One of them said he preferred classical. Can you imagine anything more ridiculous? Beathoven? They don't even know how to say his name. No, someone put them up to this and that someone must be Richard. They obviously know him from somewhere . . . or maybe he just paid them to do the job . . . like hired hit men. It's Richard I have to thank for this leg and my wrecked cabin.

As his thoughts become clearer, his whole body tenses. He can feel his breath quickening . . . as if in readiness for combat. He rests his hands on his knees, his eyes no longer focused as his mind is flooded with images of destruction. A fire . . . yes . . . Richard's house in flames . . . some day when the owner is gone . . . gasoline around the foundation . . . a single match . . . then racing back along the trail. But no . . . the deed, so satisfying in its execution, would be too easily traced, too easily linked to the neighbor with the offending music.

He searches further . . . for an act equally malevolent, equally painful but of less certain provenance. Perhaps something about his music . . . he said he was a composer . . . probably uses a piano in his writing . . . a few cut strings or bent hammers . . . that could slow him down. But no, he'd just get them fixed . . . a few days lost . . . nothing more. The situation calls for something more permanent, a trauma befitting the violence that preceded it, a calamity profound enough to sink his spirits for months if not years to come.

While waiting for a concrete plan to emerge, his thoughts drift to Richard himself . . . a professional artist, good-looking, well-dressed, articulate, probably something of a snob . . . classical music he said . . . most likely sees himself a cut above the rest of us. "I could have had all that," he muses, his mind drifting back to his own childhood. "They gave it to me on a silver platter . . . nice clothes, music lessons, a weekly allowance, summer camp vacations, and later an expensive education at prep school . . . but I didn't want it." He was referring, of course, to those years he had spent in Gloversville, New York with his Aunt Margaret and her husband William. His own mother had died when she was 36, leaving a husband and two kids, Arnie aged 7 and his sister Phyllis two years younger. Up to that time life in Medford, an Irish Catholic, blue collar Boston suburb, had been good, simple but comfortable. True, he was skinny and not very good at sports in a town where the Red Sox and Celtics vied with the Virgin Mary as objects of veneration . . . but he more than made up for that with his mental agility. Even as a kid he was looked up to by his peers. They turned to him for all manner of things . . . solutions to riddles, puzzles and games, help with grammar and arithmetic homework, predictions on the World Series and NBA Finals, even advice on domestic problems. They sought him out for entertainment since he was such a good joke and story-teller, rather remarkable for a boy that young. He could also draw . . . so well, in fact, that one teacher, Miss Aronson, said he might become a famous artist when he grew up. All in all, Medford was a pretty satisfying place to spend one's childhood.

All that changed when his mother died. The turning point came near the end. As she lay on a bed in the living room, struggling to squeeze air from her cancerous lungs, she pleaded with her sister to take both children back to Gloversville after she died. The kids' father agreed but Aunt Margaret balked, knowing full well how intensely her own husband would resist the idea. For him, the good years were just beginning now that they had gotten both their own children off to college . . . Harvard at that . . . and he could look forward to having his wife all to himself. That's what he really wanted. As an only child brought up by a mother more interested in winning a place in North Shore society than in spending time with her only son, he longed for the comfort of a woman's love and devotion. And soon after his graduation from MIT, he found it in the form of Medford-raised Margaret Sullivan. Together they raised two sons, both bright, talented and headed for successful careers in the world of medicine and law.

But now came a development that threatened to despoil the intimate nest for which he had so patiently waited. Margaret sensed all of this and prepared her request carefully. His first response was a quiet but firm no. Gradually, by appealing to his loyalty and a steel-blue conscience forged in the smithy of strict Presbyterianism, she won his consent. Within two months of their mother's death, the children, with their meager possessions in tow, were moved from Medford, Massachusetts to Gloversville, New York. They were allowed to keep their father's last name, but in all other respects they were forcefully immersed in a radically new way of life . . . white-collar instead of blue-collar, Protestant instead of Catholic, college-oriented instead of factory-bound.

Phyllis proved to be no problem. She was sweet and affectionate and as the first girl in the family, filled a void neither Aunt Margaret nor Uncle William had foreseen. Her relationship with her uncle was especially warm and conforming, at least until she reached college and eloped, over his apocalyptic warnings, with a smooth-talking man, considerably older, who later proved to be a convicted bank robber. After a period in which all family contacts were frozen, a reconciliation was arranged and Phyllis returned to the fold.

Arnie was something else. From the day he set foot in his new home, he rebelled . . . by refusing to address his uncle as 'sir,' by clinging stubbornly to the patois of the Medford streets, and by continuing to use his fingers at the dinner table despite Aunt Margaret's repeated lessons in middle-class etiquette. Those were the small things. More significantly, he refused to buy into an ethos where everything was sacrificed to ambition. In this new family, getting good grades was compulsory; sports, recreation, dating, or just hanging out were all subordinated to the pursuit of success where the end goal was defined as getting into a good college . . . meaning Harvard, Yale or some other Ivy League school. Essentially, he was on probation . . . he knew that he must either conform or get sent back to live with a deadbeat father who, according to Uncle William, was already reneging on his promise of financial support.

Despite his longing for the more relaxed atmosphere of Medford, Arnie tried his best to conform. He applied his considerable intelligence to school work and won good grades in all subjects. Making new friends did not come so easily. Back home he had always been looked up to as the intellectual leader among his peers. As early as elementary school they were calling him The Brain, the unquestioned arbiter in arguments over matters of right and wrong, school work, the Red Sox, or Boston politics. Now, despite his best efforts, he was just another good student, nothing special, nobody you had to look up to. In the midst of his struggles, he never stopped thinking about the streets of Medford. Despite all the appurtenances of a comfortable home in Gloversville, he could never feel that he really belonged. His memory of life among Medford's three-deckers, fish on Friday, street hockey on Spring St., Red Sox radio with Curt Gowdy and the smell of Mrs. O'Malleys Irish sourdough kept pulling at him, drawing him back to the place, the culture, the people where he had started out. It was a gravitational force he felt helpless to resist.

As he matured, moving from grade school to junior high and then on to high school itself, his relationship with Uncle William grew ever more frosty. Finally, they stopped talking altogether, communicating instead through Aunt Margaret who increasingly felt the burden of her promise to her dying sister not only as a millstone threatening her ability to endure but as an axe that was cutting her off from her husband. As the atmosphere spiraled downward into a state of undeclared war, William began spending more and more time away from home. When she realized that she might in fact lose him, either to alcohol or to another woman, Margaret capitulated. Despite fears of a dead sister's wrath and God's eternal damnation, she agreed to send Arnie off to private school.

It seemed to work . . . for a while. He received mostly A's the first year amidst a chorus of kudos from his teachers. Back home, expectations soared. Finally, they thought, he would live up to his potential and become the success everyone knew he was capable of. Dinner table discussions during vacations centered on college. With several more years of top grades, he was told, he could probably get into Harvard, like his two cousins. And Harvard, of course, was the stepping stone to a brilliant career as a doctor or whatever profession he preferred.

While Arnie appeared to be listening, his thoughts were drifting elsewhere. "Yeah, I got mostly A's," he muttered to himself . . . "and now I'm supposed to keep getting A's until the cows come home. What if I fail . . . what if I don't feel like breaking my balls next term . . . what if I just want to relax and have some fun? We all know what'll happen. Panic in the streets. There goes the whole shebang down the toilet . . . Arnie the Whiz Kid . . . Arnie the future valedictorian . . . Dr. Arnie Murphy the world-famous oncologist . . . all suddenly a distant memory."

More and more often he daydreamed about life in Medford. He pictured himself surrounded by friends who liked him for what he was right then . . . not somebody he was supposed to become after breaking his ass for a hundred years. He was The Brain . . . he didn't have to get a dozen degrees to prove that he was hot shit. He was already a walking encyclopedia . . . smart, funny, artistic . . . everybody around him knew it. He didn't have to prove a goddamn thing . . . just be himself. But in this world . . . Christ . . . a day didn't go by that you didn't have to prove yourself all over again . . . you could never relax . . . never take a day off from the rat race . . . never get off the fucking treadmill.

In his second year at the prestigious prep school Uncle William and Aunt Margaret had sent him to, he gave up. His grades plummeted to the point where he was eventually asked to leave. He came back to Gloversville High for a year, then dropped out of school altogether, taking a job in one of the local glove mills. Once he had enough money, he left Aunt Margaret's house and moved into a small apartment with a buddy. He felt an immediate connection, not only with his roommate but with the other workers at the factory. This was more like Medford. The guys talked the same way, they had the same interests . . . chasing girls, making money, and buying a car. Nobody talked about becoming a big success in life, not even about going to college. He was soon accepted as the brightest of the bunch, the person you could go to for answers about money, history, labor-management relations, politics, philosophy and religion. He was home again and contented . . . despite Aunt Margaret's occasional visit to his apartment to express her disappointment with the way things were going. Each time she dropped in, he could see self-reproach written all over her face. It made sense. After all, she had promised to raise her niece and nephew as her own . . . to get them through school and off to a good college, but it wasn't working out that way. All she had done, really, was to alienate her husband . . . perhaps irretrievably. She saw herself as a failure.

Arnie read the guilt on her face and exulted in it. Hearing her admit her failure and plead for his forgiveness allowed him to suppress any thoughts he might have had about his own failure. It was her problem. She should never have given in to her sister's dying request. She and William should never have torn him from a safe, familiar environment and transplanted him to a soil where it was impossible for him to be himself. It is good that she feels bad now, he thought, good that she blames herself for what she did. Let's face it; she made a terrible mistake.

There's no question that he felt bitter . . . bitter toward Margaret and her husband, bitter toward the whole world of education, money and ambition. And yet, to any impartial observer, this umbrage, however deserved by his well-intentioned elders, could be seen as a defense against self-judgment. The strategy, though unconscious in its origin, made perfect sense. By luxuriating in his resentment, he could keep at bay any acknowledgement that he was the one who had failed . . . that he was the one who hadn't risen to the occasion and taken advantage of the opportunities he was given. But he was far from being ready to admit any of this, even to himself.

In the years to come, as he followed the factory jobs from New York and Massachusetts to Georgia and the Carolinas, his resentment of his aunt's world and its apotheosis of achievement grew increasingly virulent. It was an emotion that demanded expression. Without any conscious plan to do so, he began looking for ways to strike back.

At first his efforts were childish, even humorous. He let his appearance go . . . face unwashed, hair uncut and stringy, overalls caked with grease . . . and used his repulsiveness as a weapon. Suitably armed, he would approach a fashionable men's clothing store, spit a wad of tobacco juice onto the ground just outside the door, then enter and look around. As the alarmed salesmen rushed to confront him, he'd casually paw whole racks of suits and run his dirty fingers over the fancy underwear. He'd go so far as to try on some of the shirts and pants. Once when he was trying on an expensive Armani suit, he actually spit on the floor, just in front of the mirror. To Arnie, the look of disbelief on the clerk's face was as fulfilling as the dying gasp of a battlefield adversary and continued to bring a chuckle to his lips long after he had left the store.

He carried his resentment everywhere, the favorite target being anyone or anything representing the upper-middle class life that had rejected him. Of course, many folks would argue that it was Arnie who had rejected them . . . but it was not in his interest to see it this way. The blame was entirely theirs. They expected too much; they demanded too much. It was all that pressure . . . pressure to succeed, to achieve, to keep on achieving . . . that drove him out . . . out and down. And now that he was back in the ranks of the proletariat, he would make life as uncomfortable for them as possible.

One of his favorite thrusts was to walk down Newbury Street, Boston's elite shopping district, in his grungiest clothes, hair oily and uncombed, directing tobacco juice at the feet of the most elegantly dressed pedestrians. When people scattered to avoid him, scowling as they clutched their Gucci handbags, he would smile inwardly and record it as another skirmish won.

Toward lunch time, still looking like he had spent the night under a bridge, he would head for the French restaurant, La Rose Jaune, which was well-known to Newbury Street shoppers and charmingly tucked away just below street level. Once inside, as expected, he would be left standing while the maître d' pretended to busy himself looking after other customers. When five minutes had past and he had still not been seated, he would walk over to an empty table and sit himself down. After another long wait without a menu, he would get up, accost the nearest waiter and rip one from his grasp. If still no one came to take his order, he would yell repeatedly for service to no one in particular, frightening adjacent diners to transfer their half-finished meals to the other side of the restaurant. By the time his order was taken and delivered, much to the consternation of the maître d' and the line of people still waiting to be seated, he was surrounded by a circle of empty tables, rather like a lonely, disheveled lion guarding its kill, its fierce gaze sufficient to keep hungry jackals and hyenas at bay.

He knew that he wasn't breaking any laws, so they couldn't very well throw him out. Finally able to enjoy his meal and in full awareness of his rights, he would surrender to his most primitive wonts by picking up the entrée with his fingers, forcing it into his mouth, mixing soda with the half-chewed food, and punctuating his satisfaction with a series of guttural burps that could be heard across the restaurant. When his fellow diners turned to look with a mixture of surprise and disgust, he met their stares with a smile, as if to say "Did I ruin your lunch, oh dear." Of course, he never left a tip. Why reward the bastards, he argued, when they gave him such a hard time.

Out on the street again, he would think back on lunch and smile contentedly at his mischief. With bits of entrée still clinging to his beard, he would continue on down the sidewalk, zigzagging his way through a slalom of scowls and stares, eventually arriving at his motel on the outskirts of town.

As he sits in the tub now, massaging his calf, all these memories . . . of Medford, Gloversville, Aunt Margaret, prep school, the factory, Boston and Newbury Street . . . come racing back, both humorous and soothing in their self-justification. Amidst this tale of chaos and upheaval, he sees the making of a hero who, through sheer strength of character, finds the courage to strike back and eventually defeat his tormentors. What he can't see is what lies buried beneath the resentment, something as yet unnamable that if allowed into consciousness could threaten the conviction that he, like all the great rebels of history, has truth and justice on his side. He has no way of knowing as he sits there soaking his leg, sealed off from both the world and his own deepest feelings, that things are about to change.

Morning brings a new resolve. He will go back to the cabin site, wait for Richard to drive into town, then sneak up to his cottage along the forest trail. Once there, assuming no one else is home, he will wait for opportunity to reveal itself . . . a theft perhaps, something to do with the man's music, something that will hurt him deeply for months to come. What that something is he doesn't need to know, not now anyway. Such is his faith in the justice of his mission that he can go to the cottage and wait for events to unfold on their own.

At the cabin things happen pretty much as anticipated. Arnie is loading 2 x 4's into his pickup as Richard drives by in his SUV. Out of the corner of his eye he sees Richard surveying the scene, probably wondering if

Arnie has given up on the cabin. The truth is that he *has* decided to move on . . . but there is unfinished business to attend to before leaving. It is time for action. Dropping the studs, he races down through the woods to the trail leading up to Richard's cottage. No one sees him running. Never having been to the cottage before, he knows only that it is the first one to the West from his own place. At the small path leading to the right, he stops and looks around. Tucked in among the white pines, the cottage is barely visible. As silently as possible, he makes his way along the path and up onto the porch. He knocks softly to see if it draws a response . . . after all, Richard might be married for all he knows. No one comes to the door. He tries the handle and breathes more easily when the door gives way.

Once inside he makes his way to the living room, quickly taking in the leather chairs, walnut coffee table and paintings on the wall. Klee and Kandinsky, he whispers as he looks around, recalling the art course he took in prep school. It is all too familiar. Despite his best efforts to stay focused on the present, he is drawn back into the affluent world of his aunt and uncle . . . and the fancy prep school they sent him to. It is not a comfortable feeling. Through the lens of his half-glazed eyes he sees their smiling faces now . . . Aunt Margaret, Uncle William, Dean Atkins, the teachers, the older students . . . their voices still ringing in his ears . . . you can do it Arnie . . . keep up the good work . . . start thinking Harvard . . . medicine . . . law . . . don't let up . . . don't quit now . . . you're on your way. Unbelievably it all comes back to him . . . here in this stranger's living room . . . the voices, the suffocating pressure, the expectations clamped to his shoulders like a giant yoke, binding him to *their* dreams, unwilling to let him wriggle free and go his own way. And the anger . . . the need to rebel . . . to cast off that yoke. . . the bitterness over a childhood lost . . . all still so vivid after all these years. How could it be?

The memories are too much. He leans over and steadies himself on a chair arm, his breath coming faster now. Hints of something deeper go flashing through his mind . . . something still buried beneath layers of anger and rebellion . . . an unacceptable truth lurking behind the misconceptions he has for years foisted on both others and himself. His fear is a signal, a warning . . . but he is not ready to heed it.

As he stumbles past shelves of books on music theory, literature, history, art and philosophy, his stomach tightens. "My God," he mumbles, "this is the world they all tried to force on me. This is what they wanted me to have." At the door to the adjoining studio, he turns and looks back into the gracefully-appointed living room. "They never understood who I was," he murmurs, "never even tried to understand . . . so eager were they to rescue this poor bastard from the shame of life in the working class."

The studio is dominated by a baby grand piano. On the manuscript holder above the keyboard he sees an open score . . . written in pencil. At the top is a title: Iglesia de los Dolores, Mvt. III. His Spanish is minimal but sufficient to get the gist of it: Church of Sorrows. "Sounds sad," he reflects. To his left, on the flat panel, are two other scores. On closer inspection they turn out to be Mvt's I and II of the same piece. Returning to Mvt. III, he flips to the final page to see if it is finished. It is not. "So, this is what he's working on," he whispers, curling his lip into a wry smile. "Weeks of work, maybe months . . . and it's all in pencil, meaning there are no copies." His mind is quick to capture the significance of his discovery. Sitting down on the bench, he fondles the manuscript as if it were the still-beating heart torn from a slain Aztec warrior. He chuckles, then wets his lips. "Why not all three?" he asks innocently, reaching for Mvt's I and II. Clutching the scores in his hand, he turns and prepares to leave. Thus far, all has gone exactly as he wished. Could revenge be any sweeter? In his exultation, he can feel Richard's anguish as something real, almost palpable to the touch . . . first disbelief . . . then a frantic search that reveals nothing . . . followed by grief and despair . . . then resignation to the horror that the piece is lost forever.

It is at this point that Fate intervenes, clearly dissatisfied with the way events are unfolding. Outside it has begun to rain, masking both bird songs and the occasional car passing. Arnie stops to listen, then looks down again at the manuscript title . . . Iglesia de los Dolores. The title intrigues him: Church of Sorrows. What could it mean? He can only guess.

If the target of his vengeance had been there to explain, Arnie would have learned that Richard spent a month last winter traveling in Oaxaca, Mexico where he fell in love with an old Spanish church a few yards from the central plaza or zocalo. According to the guidebook, it is called Templo San Juan de Dios. While admiring the classical 18th Century architecture from the sidewalk, he is treated to voices inside singing a hymn. The music is captivating enough to draw him into the church where he takes a seat in the rear. Up front in the nave, next to a statue of the Savior surrounded by lilies and roses is a priest leading a small congregation in song, accompanied by an organ hidden somewhere overhead. The hymn . . . a prayer of some sort . . . is repeated three or four times. With each stanza the tiny troupe becomes more fervent in their supplication, their eyes fixed on the statue, cheeks wet with tears of regret, grief, guilt, fear, shame . . . all the torments which human life is heir to.

From his seat in the rear, Richard's attention is drawn to the young woman near the aisle, the one holding a baby. With that hauntingly melancholic song in his ears, rising and falling in wordless testimony to life's unbearable burdens, he follows her lips as she shapes her lonely prayer, then, with heart bursting, he slumps to the bench, unable to watch anymore.

Throughout his travels in Mexico that winter Richard never forgets the hymn. Once back in his Adirondack cottage, he immediately goes to work on Iglesia de los Dolores, saving the song he heard in church that day for the main theme of Mvt. III, the movement which Arnie is now looking at.

Thanks to the two years of piano lessons Uncle William paid for years ago, Arnie has a good idea of what the opening theme sounds like just from viewing the score. The melody is simple but moving. He hums it once, stops, then sits down on the bench to try it on the piano. The effect is mesmerizing. He looks around to make sure he is alone, then plays it again, this time adding the accompaniment with his other hand. Over and over again he plays the heartrending theme, unconsciously reliving the anguish Richard felt when he first heard it on the streets of Oaxaca. As he plays, he becomes dimly aware of something new stirring in his gut, a feeling that lies buried beneath layers of anger and resentment, a sensation beyond the reach of rational thought. Inchoate at first, it gradually takes form as it rises into awareness. He experiences it first as an ache spreading outward from his solar plexus, then as an unarticulated heaving in his chest, finally as bitterness on his tongue.

The music continues its hypnotic spell even after he has stopped playing. His eyes redden. Slowly, words come to his lips, giving shape to his feelings. Looking up at the wall paintings, then around to the leather chairs, the couch, the books and finally back to the piano, he murmurs, "I could have had all this. I could have had this and more. It was all handed to me on a silver platter . . . but I said no thank you . . . I don't want it." He drops his head, still clutching the manuscripts. "I could have done something useful with this brain, maybe written a book, painted some portraits, perhaps helped some people. I could have made something decent of myself . . . a home owner, a family man, a writer, an artist . . . but I've done none of it. Instead I've become . . . what . . . an object of disgust and derision, a bitter outcast, a steel trap waiting to take the head off anyone who possesses the things I turned my back on." He closes his eyes in disbelief. "I could have had it all."

By now the rain has stopped although Arnie is too immersed in his thoughts to hear a car pull up in the backyard. Carefully he puts the three movements back where he found them, wipes the tears from his eyes with his dirty kerchief, and rises from the piano bench. At the door he turns to take a last look at Richard's world . . . then pulls it open.

With his SUV safely in the garage, Richard walks to the back door and stops suddenly. "What is this?" he gasps, feet rooted in place. Someone is playing the theme from Iglesia de los Dolores. His thoughts race ahead. "Who would have the audacity to enter my house without permission . . . and the gall to sit down and play the piano? Tashi perhaps? It couldn't be; she's in school back in Boston. It's got to be a thief . . . but what kind of robber would be foolish enough to . . . ?"

From the back door he can hear the music, but can't see into the studio. He quickly decides on a plan . . . to sneak around to the front porch and peek through the storm door window, positioning himself for a blow the moment the intruder emerges. But first he must arm himself. With images of mayhem racing through his head, he sprints to the garage and grabs a hatchet, the one reserved for splitting wood. With the weapon firmly in hand, he makes his way around to the front of the house. Stepping noiselessly up the porch stairs, he leans against the cottage wall and peers in. "Oh my God, it's Arnie," he gasps, barely able to believe his eyes. Unconsciously his fingers tighten around the hatchet.

It is at this point that Arnie gets up from the piano bench and heads for the door. Seeing him coming, Richard leans back against the cottage wall. As Arnie emerges, his shabbily dressed, lean frame is bent, his shoulders drooping. To Richard, half-hidden behind the opened door, his manner suggests someone who has just been dealt an emotional blow . . . terrible news perhaps about a loved one or an adverse prognosis pertaining to himself. As the intruder stumbles out onto the porch, steadying himself with a hand on the side railing, Richard relaxes his grip on the hatchet. Arnie stops. Dimly conscious of another presence, he suddenly turns and confronts his adversary. His eyes flare with animal fear, his body taut and poised to flee.

The two men stare at each other, the one poised to run, the other confused and hesitant. In the wordless space between them a crow calls from high in the pine tree. Richard is the first to smile as he lowers his hatchet to the porch floor. The other's lips tremble in response. As Arnie's hand slips from the railing, his knees sagging, Richard lunges forward and grabs him before he falls. In silence they stand with arms locked in embrace, each man hanging onto the other, the one with eyes open, offering forgiveness, the other, head down, begging for absolution.

No words are needed, none spoken. Arnie finally pulls free, steps off the porch and starts down the path toward the main trail. Richard watches from the porch until he sees him turn left at the junction. Just a few feet onto the trail, Arnie turns his head toward the porch and lifts his hand half-way in shy farewell. It only lasts a second or two. Without waiting for a response, he pulls his hand back down, buttons up his coat and continues around the bend out of sight.

The following day on his way into town, Richard sees Arnie loading the 2 x 4's into his truck. The boom box is nowhere to be seen. The two men wave to each other in silent salute. Two days later while passing the cabin site Richard looks again, but sees no one. Nearly a week goes by without any sign of his former antagonist. It is only when he picks up the Sunday paper that the mystery is solved: the cabin property, once the source of near-lethal combat between the two men, is now on the market. Arnie is gone, never to be seen in these parts again.

16   A Hymn

Dear Richard,

I tried to get my Mom to invite you for Thanksgiving dinner this year, but she said it would set a precedent . . . you know, that you would expect to be invited every year from now on . . . and she didn't want you to be disappointed if you weren't invited in the future. But we can still play together at the restaurant on Saturday night if you want to. I know I do.

I would have written earlier, but I couldn't. My parents are trying to discourage any relationship between us so they limited me to this one e-mail . . . plus the gig on Saturday and a practice session on Friday, if that time is still good for you.

Hope the composing is going well. My playing is getting better thanks to a new teacher, Mr. Edmonds. He's very strict but really knows the cello. I showed him some of your pieces for cello and piano . . . the ones we played at the restaurant last summer and he thought they were awesome. He wants to meet you some day.

Love, Tashi

Hi Tashi,

Don't worry about Thanksgiving. Kwatz will be glad to have me stay at home. I told him he could invite some of his buddies over for a big fish dinner. As you know, he's really not into turkey or any of those barnyard delicacies like lamb or beef. His rule of thumb is simple: if it doesn't swim, he won't eat it.

Doesn't sound like your Mom and Dad will like the idea but, just in case, you are hereby invited to a basketball game between Saranac High and the Correctional Center on Friday night. I'll be there coaching. I can come by and pick you up around 7:00 if it's O.K. with everyone.

Nice to hear about your cello playing. I'm looking forward to hearing the results of all your hard work. I've got two new duets I've arranged from some old piano pieces . . . we can try them out when we practice on Friday. Is morning a good time for you? Let me know.

Richard

Hello again,

Bummers! Mom and Dad said no to the basketball game. They don't want me getting too close to the boys from the Center. I told them you'd be right there to protect me, but they didn't like that idea either . . . so, I guess I won't be seeing you until we practice on Friday . . . is 9:00 O.K. with you?

T.

At 9:05 on Friday morning Richard looks out the window to see a car coming into his driveway. He emerges from the cottage just in time to observe Tashi retrieving her cello from the rear compartment. "Got a ride this time I see," he says before waving to Esther who remains in the car.

Tashi (*coming forward with arms open*): "It's so good to see you again, Richard . . . three months is such a long time."

Richard (*hugging briefly*): "Three months? . . . I guess you're right. I hadn't counted . . . C'mon in . . . here, let me take the cello."

Tashi (*waving to Mother*): "I'll call you when we're done, Mom . . . probably a couple of hours . . . maybe a little more . . . O.K.?"

"That's fine Eleanor," nods Mother. "Just don't be too long." She waves a final goodbye and drives off to town.

Once they are inside the cottage, Richard turns to Tashi, "That was nice of your Mom to drive you up here. I know it's a bit of a struggle getting that monster up the trail."

Tashi: "Well, I would have done it the usual way, but I hurt my shoulder playing field hockey at school last week and it's not back to normal yet . . . but don't worry, I can still play the cello."

Richard: "Which shoulder?"

Tashi: "The right one . . . unfortunately. It still feels a little stiff when I move the bow back and forth so I haven't practiced as much lately . . . but it's definitely getting better."

Richard (*at the piano*): "Hmmm. We have two new duets to try but maybe we better save one of them for next summer. I'm thinking of the one where the cello has to do a lot of jumping around. We don't want to put any extra strain on that shoulder."

Tashi: "Let's try the other one first, then see how it feels."

Richard: "O.K. (*handing her the score*) Why don't you take a peek at your part while I get us something to drink . . . (*from the kitchen*) Is an orange soda O.K.?"

Tashi: "My favorite. Yes."

Richard (*back at the piano*): "Ready to give it a whirl?"

Tashi: "Mmmm yes. It looks beautiful Richard. The opening theme is so . . . kind of . . . operatic. It reminds me of Wagner . . . you know . . . one of the Siegfried themes I think."

Richard: "Could be. It's a more dramatic than my usual stuff . . . maybe brought on by a little local drama we had here a month ago . . . but I can tell you about that over dinner tomorrow."

Tashi: "A local drama? . . . sounds exciting . . . can't wait to hear about it."

As they begin the piece, Richard watches Tashi out of the corner of his eye, his attention focused on the movement of her bow. He is quick to see that it is not as fluid as usual . . . not as smooth, more labored. He stops midway through the piece and turns to face her. "You've got the notes alright . . . but you're struggling with that bow. I don't want to do anything that will make your shoulder worse."

Tashi (*eyes down, rubbing her shoulder*): "It's still a little stiff. I've been taking a prescribed ointment that seems to help . . . but I forgot to pack it when we came. I'll see if they have something at the pharmacy in town when we finish."

Richard: "I've got something in my medicine cabinet I use for muscle aches. In fact I've used quite a bit of it lately for soreness in my upper arm. It's got a lot of camphor in it and it seems to help. Would you like to try it?"

Tashi: "Of course. I'm sorry I left mine back in Boston. Thank you."

Richard (*returning from bathroom*): "Here you go (*handing her the jar*) . . . Use all you want. I can always get more."

Tashi (*smiling):* "Is there any chance I could get some help? It's a little awkward to reach around and rub with my left hand."

Richard: "Well . . . I'm no expert . . . but if you think it would help . . . What do you want me to do?"

Tashi (*undoing the top two buttons of her blouse*): "Here's where it hurts the most (*tracing the area around her shoulder with her fingers*)."

From behind her chair Richard opens the jar and scoops some cream onto his fingers. As he touches the top of her shoulder, he adds, "Hope this isn't too cold. Should warm up a bit as I rub it in." To balance himself, he places his free hand on her other shoulder, moving to her neck as he rubs harder.

Tashi sighs softly, then closes her eyes to banish everything from awareness other than the sensation of Richard's hands on her bare skin.

She follows each up and down movement of his fingers as if they were notes from a page of music she was playing for the first time. When he stops to scoop up more ointment, she casually opens another button on her blouse, pointing to her upper chest as the main source of tenderness. When, out of either fear or failure to decipher her signal, he places the new ointment on her upper arm instead, she reaches up and gently pulls his hand down to her chest. As she does so, she is reminded that the strap on her bra is getting in the way. Without looking at Richard, she slides the strap off onto her arm and lets it fall to her elbow. In doing so she lays bare the upper half of her right breast, a move that sets off an immediate alarm in her partner's brain. He drops his hands to his sides.

"Did I frighten you Richard?" she asks softly. "You were doing such a nice job. I'm feeling better already."

Silence.

From behind the chair Richard peers down her chest, his eyes drawn instinctively to that patch of bare skin where each globe of pubescent flesh, identical in size and shape but not yet ripe for nursing, goes its separate way. His fingers begin to tremble. "Am I getting the right spots?" he asks as he resumes rubbing, his fingers just inches now from her cleavage.

"I feel so relaxed," she answers. Sighing, she places her left hand on his, then squeezes gently, forcing him to squeeze her breast in response. Without a word but with his implicit consent, she pulls his hand down on her chest until it covers her nipple, then turns her head and offers him her lips. "I've missed you so much, Richard. Do you still love me?"

"Of course," he answers in a voice less passionate than she might wish. Struggling to regain his composure, he pulls back and observes her from a distance. From this perspective he notices, not without alarm, that her other bra strap is perilously close to slipping off her shoulder, an eventuality that would send both cups to her lap and leave her girlish breasts completely uncovered. "Oh, oh," he whispers as if a stranger might be watching, then leans over and pulls both straps up high on her shoulders. Reluctantly she rises and buttons up her blouse.

"Are you ready to play some more," he calls, hurrying to the piano, "or should we call it quits for the day? It's up to you."

Tashi (*walking to the piano, eyes still cloudy*): "Yes, I feel better now. Let's continue."

Together they run through both new duets, Tashi looser now but still not ready to bear down with her bow hand. "I'm sorry that I couldn't do the fast passages justice, Richard, but . . . "

Richard (*interrupting*): "You did just fine . . . the people at the restaurant won't know the difference. I just hope we didn't make things any worse for you. If your arm tightens up overnight, we can always play one of the old pieces . . . (*laughing*) . . . you know, the slow, romantic ones that make folks order more wine."

Tashi (*smiling*): "Tim would like that for sure."

Richard: "Are you going to call your mother or do you want me to drive you home?"

Tashi (*turning quickly*): "Oh, it's not time yet, is it? I told Mom two hours or more . . . we still have 30 minutes . . . at least."

Richard: "Well, I don't want to overdo the practice . . . especially since we have to play tomorrow night."

Tashi: "Couldn't I stay and listen while you work on your latest piece?"

Richard (*sighing*): "Really? . . . Well, O.K . . . if you really want to."

Tashi: "Thanks (*sitting down next to him on the piano bench*). What's the name of your new piece?"

Richard (*opening the score*): "It's in Spanish . . . Iglesia de los Dolores . . . means Church of Sorrows. It's based on a hymn I heard while traveling in Mexico last winter."

Tashi: "You were in Mexico last winter? You never told me . . . (*pause*) . . . maybe it's better that you didn't . . . I found it hard enough to concentrate on algebra and history. If I had known that you were having fun visiting these new places . . . (*pause*) . . . were you alone?"

Richard: "Yup. Made some new friends along the way, but went everywhere by myself."

Tashi: "Glad to hear that . . . can I hear the hymn that inspired the piece?"

Richard: "O.K. It's only about 16 measures long but lends itself to all kinds of variation for a symphony . . . even a retrograde version that Bach would have loved. Here's the hymn itself. Just keep in mind that I heard it in a church where it was sung by a group of worshippers just off the street. Sounds better with voices . . . a lot more emotional than anything I can do here with the piano."

He plays the hymn.

"That's so beautiful Richard. Could you play it again?"

The second time through he closes his eyes and plays from memory. In his mind's eye he sees the church, the statue of the Savior up front surrounded by lilies and roses, the priest, the tiny troupe of believers, the young woman standing with her baby, her lips moving in silent prayer. He sees himself watching. From his seat in the rear, he studies their faces, some lined with the grief of loves lost, others contorted by the fear of sins still hidden, all turned now to the Savior in supplication. He listens, transfixed, as the music swells, lifted skyward on the wings of hope only to fall again, drawn back to earth by the tug of life's inexorable sorrows.

Richard's eyes open. With the sound of prayerful voices echoing in his ears, he drops his head and lets his fingers bring the hymn to a close.

"Does it have any words?" Tashi asks (*eyes moistening*).

Richard: "I never found out what they were singing but the emotional message is clear enough . . . that's what I want to bring out in the symphony."

Tashi: "It's going to be a beautiful piece, Richard, one that will move many people. How close are you to finishing?"

Richard: "I'm working on the ending to the last movement now . . . so, one more movement . . . probably another month or so. Perhaps when you come next . . . "

HONK! HONK!

"Who the hell can that be?" Richard cries, rising from the bench and racing to the back door. *(Peering out)* "Oh, for Christ's sake, it's your mother. I thought you were supposed to call her first."

Tashi (*from behind Richard*): "I was. I don't understand. Let me go talk to her."

Tashi (*at the car, scowling*): "You're early . . . how come?"

Esther (*taking a deep breath*): "Don't blame me, Eleanor. This was your father's idea. He didn't want you overstaying your welcome."

Tashi (*biting her lip*): "Don't you think that's up to me to decide? Richard was just playing his new piece for me . . . and . . . well, we're enjoying each other's company. If he wanted me to leave he would have said so . . . and he hasn't . . . (*pause*) . . . besides, he offered to drive me home when we're done."

It is at this point that Richard emerges from the house and waves. "Hello Esther. Yes, she's right. I'd be happy to drive her home if that's O.K. with you."

Esther (*leaning out the car window*): "Richard, I'm afraid her father wants her home right now . . . (*pause*) . . . Maybe you can help put her instrument in back . . . (*pause*) . . . I have to be at a Book Club meeting in half an hour, Eleanor, so please hurry."

With both Tashi and Esther gone, Richard returns to his piano and takes up the hymn once more. A single replaying of the theme is enough to transport him back to Oaxaca and a seat in the old Spanish church by the zocalo. "If this piece ever makes any money," he reflects, "I know exactly what to do with it." An image returns . . . the one of the woman with the baby, standing in the aisle as she floats her silent petition to the clay figure in the nave. "How can I give her voice," he asks. "How can I make this piece *her* piece?" He plays the hymn again. As evening shadows creep across the lawn, the muse returns, whispering in his ear. He picks up his pencil and begins to write. Notes come quickly now, rising unbidden from those unlit corridors of mind where memories, rich in meaning and portent, lie dormant, waiting, eager for new life. Hours pass without thought of food or rest. An owl calls from deep in the woods as the moon creeps across the skylight, leaving a tableau of stars in its wake. Under the piano, Kwatz's chest rises and falls in rhythmic repose as vigilance yields to dreamless sleep. Through it all the image of the woman in the church stands watch, her lips moving silently with each note set to paper as her plea for deliverance is given the voice it has never known. Slowly, night eases its grip on the land; birds signal the coming of a new day. It is only then, only when the last measure has been written that our composer rises from his bench and falls into bed, exhausted, pencil still in hand, at peace finally with the joy of a promise fulfilled.

On Saturday night, the restaurant fills early. Well aware of the duo's growing appeal, Tim has taken care to advertise the event weeks in advance. To the attentive listener, the very first piece signals something special as Tashi's excitement enlivens each movement of her bow, filling the room with a sound both radiant and voluptuous. For the young cellist, it is not simply that she finds the music beautiful. Animating each note is the knowledge that it is Richard's music, perhaps even music inspired by his not-yet-conscious love for her. With that thought dancing in her head, she plays out her fantasy. In her mind's eye, each stroke of her bow becomes the caress of her lover, the touch of his hand against her cheek, a whisper, a confession of eternal devotion. When the piano enters to support her rising, twisting melody, she feels his body pressed tightly against her own, strong, caring, unwilling to let her fall. Each paired note becomes a kiss, a melding of lips, a confession of hunger for complete union. Through phrase after phrase, movement after movement, the music voices its ecstasy as cello and piano lose themselves in a merging of separate selves.

It is possible, of course, that some of those listening to the pair see through the charade, who sense that the notes heard, while beautiful in their own right, serve to mask a hidden scenario in which two lovers act out their mutual affection. Those are the fortunate few. For them, the music is more than the simple interplay of sound; as they listen, they find themselves transported into a realm where their own yearnings for sexual oneness, long-sacrificed to the demands of child-rearing and family togetherness, are newly awakened. Their dinners go uneaten, their eyes and faces locked in wordless embrace. If you were to look now you might see hands reaching across the table, self-consciously searching, pleading, uncertain in their bid for closeness, two separate souls struggling to reconnect while at the mercy of a new, unsought tenderness, their reborn dreams still wet and shivering behind the candles' glow.

Later that evening when the concert is over and the two musicians are seated at their own table, Tashi's mood changes dramatically. She makes no attempt to conceal her despair. "Six more months now before we can play again. Summer never comes fast enough for me . . . does it for you, Richard?"

Richard (*compressing his lips*): "Time goes more quickly at my age, Tash. I'm always surprised that months slip by now like weeks did when I was a teenager . . . But I will certainly miss our duets. Playing pieces for piano solo has lost much of its appeal since we became partners."

The words have a soothing effect, particularly the word 'partners.' "If only he meant it the way I want him to mean it," she murmurs silently. She forces a smile and looks down at the menu. "While you make your decision," he says, rising from his chair, "I'm going to run out to my car and get rid of all this music (*pointing to his briefcase*). I'll be right back."

With a secret smile on his lips, he hurries to the parking lot and deposits his scores in the back seat, then picks up a package hidden under the front seat. It is carefully wrapped and addressed 'To Tashi on her 16th birthday.' Back in the restaurant, he sits down with the gift behind his back. He asks innocently, "You did say once that it was sometime in December, didn't you?"

Tashi (*a revived sparkle in her eyes*): "What do you mean?"

Without further teasing he slides the package across the table. Carefully, as if unsheathing an unexpected gift from a mysterious admirer, she strips away ribbon and paper and holds the boxed CD set up the candle. "Oh my God, Richard, Beethoven's cello and piano sonatas, all six of them. What a wonderful present. Thank you darling . . . (*hand over mouth*) . . . oops, I didn't mean to say that. Just thank you. That's such a thoughtful present. I had forgotten that I told you when my birthday was."

Richard: "Which day is it?"

Tashi: "The 14th. December the 14th . . . When's yours?"

Richard: "August 3rd."

Tashi: "I have that etched in my brain . . . now (*leaning forward*) . . . may I kiss you to show my appreciation?"

Richard (*visibly shaken*): "Not here Tash. Why don't we wait until I get you home."

Tashi (*giggling*): "That's O.K. My patience is infinite . . . as you might have noticed."

Richard (*nodding*): "Hmmm. Maybe I missed it. Remind me next time."

Tashi: "Next time . . . what?"

Richard: "You know . . . next time you show restraint."

Tashi (*smiling*): "I'm showing it right now, silly."

Richard (*head down*): "O.K. You win. Can we eat now?"

With the meal over, the cello safely on board, and the car headed for Tashi's home, she can think of nothing but the promised kiss. "I don't want it to be brief, like a hit and run peck that might be appropriate for a distant cousin. This has to last me for the next six months." She smiles at her silent resolve.

Although his eyes remain fastened to the road where patches of ice have already formed, Richard is sufficiently aware of his passenger to guess what she is thinking. He plans his strategy accordingly . . . an affectionate hug . . . then a short kiss on the mouth . . . but nothing that could be interpreted as sexual . . . followed by a few words of farewell. He brings the car to a halt in the driveway, leaves the motor running and walks her to the door, confident that his carefully laid-out course of action will bring the evening to a quick and graceful close.

At the door she lays the cello down and lifts her face to his. Suddenly, "Can we pretend that we're in love, Richard, just for fun?" she asks, throwing her head back seductively. And then, with the boldness of youth in full awareness of its charms, "Pretend that you've been chasing me all evening while I've held back."

Richard tilts his head quizzically.

Fluffing her hair, she continues: "Throughout dinner you repeatedly tried to touch me, but each time I withdrew my hands. In the car you leaned against me, silently begging for some sign of intimacy while I remained aloof. And now you want me . . . here at the door . . . you will do anything to have me . . . if only you can trust my love. I am young but pure of heart . . . you sense that my love is deep and unconditional . . . that whatever comes our way, I will never leave you . . . you know all that . . . it is only your fear that stands in the way . . . you want to let go . . . you have waited so long . . . just pretend . . . darling."

To Richard, her words, first heard as the chattering of a lovesick teenager, morph into the intuitions of an all-knowing adult, ominous in their grasp of an inner, threatening truth. She is only play-acting; this is nothing more than fantasy . . . of this he is sure . . . yet, despite a defense carefully constructed and fortified over the years, he finds himself yielding to her caprice as it circumvents reason, slipping silently into that vast, inchoate territory of mind known only dimly to himself. He feels a weakening, first in the knees, then spreading to his arms and hands. She studies his face carefully, leans forward, then follows her words into the inner reaches of his soul where she finds what she is looking for. With her eyes alone, she pulls the veil from his poorly-concealed desire, laying bare the secret conflict between love and fear that for years has held him in its grasp. Reeling from her gaze, his eyes soften, then moisten. Defenseless now, his whole body sags in vivid confirmation of the truth behind her words. He is at her mercy.

She is only a girl, not yet sixteen and still innocent of love . . . yet his surrender evokes in her unstained heart a pity that is quickly infused with desire. Guided by instinct, she reaches up and pulls his face down to hers. Absent any sign of resistance, she places her lips squarely on his and opens his mouth with her tongue. Even as footsteps can be heard inside the door, she hangs on with the ferocity of a she-wolf fighting for her first and only mate. "Tell me you love me," she gasps, the power in her voice leaving no room for dissent.

Richard (*covering his face with both hands*): "How can I know?"

Tashi (*sternly*): "Tell me. I know it is true."

Richard: "How do you know . . . when I am not sure myself?"

Tashi: "You *do* know . . . you are just afraid to say it."

Richard (*pulling her tight*): "Yes, I *am* afraid. My whole life I have been afraid."

Tashi: "You have nothing to fear now. I have loved you from the moment we met . . . you must know that. Sharing my love with you means more to me than anything else in life. I will never stop loving you, Richard."

Richard (*head down*): "I have sensed that . . . in your words, in the way you look at me. I want to believe you."

Tashi: "Trust me . . . tell me."

Richard (*trembling*): "Tashi . . . "

Tashi (*softly*): "Tell me . . . tell me, my love."

Richard (*caressing her cheek):* "I do love you . . . so very much . . . (*sobbing*) . . . forgive me . . . forgive me for being afraid."

With that sacred incantation ringing in her ears, she lets her arms fall and turns toward the door. "Goodbye, my darling," she whispers, no longer afraid to address him with a term befitting her affection. "Goodbye until next summer," she adds. With that she turns the handle, opens the door and disappears into the house.

17   Game Time

By the time Richard arrives at the gym, it is already half-full and the Saranac High players are out on the floor practicing. Over on the sidelines a bevy of cheerleaders provocatively-dressed in the home team's purple and gold colors are warming up. Richard takes his customary seat on the bench and looks around.

Sam is the first to emerge from the visitor's locker room. "Hey man . . . we gonna do it tonight?"

Richard: "Hope so . . . but the odds aren't exactly with us. By the way, did you find us a fifth man?"

Sam: "Yeah . . . we got Kato . . . he's comin' out now (*pointing*) . . . all 6'9" of 'im."

Richard: "Great."

Sam: "Trouble is, he ain't never played basketball before. Me and Khalique, we been showin' him the basics at the Center . . . but he still don't know much . . . like you're s'posed to dribble whenever you move your pivot foot."

Richard: "Well, O.K. We still can use him for rebounding. With his bulk he's going to take up a lot of space under the basket." As Khalique, Raul, and Myron join Sam on the bench, Richard motions for Kato to come and sit. Carefully he goes over the game plan . . . which consists of little more than having Sam and Khalique drive to the basket while Myron and Kato stay near the basket to rebound any missed shots. On defense each player is assigned a Saranac player to guard.

"What about Cool Dog?" Khalique asks. "I remember last year he ripped us for 20 points."

"It's up to Sam to slow him down," Richard answers. "If he proves to be too much for one guy, I want either you or Raul to rotate over and double up on him. If we can shut him down, I think we have a chance to win this game. Their 6'8" center from last year graduated, so we can control the boards if Myron and Kato can manage to stay in the game. Myron . . . that means no foolish fouls. Kato . . . remember, you're allowed four fouls; you get kicked out on the fifth one. So, be careful. Make each one count."

When the referee signals an end to practice, all five of the players come off the floor and take up seats on the bench. No one, neither Richard nor any of the players, is ready for what comes next. Five girls, all dressed in different shades of red blouses and shorts, rush over and kneel in front of the bench. One of the taller ones, an especially attractive black girl with prominent breasts, looks at Richard, then the boys. Sam elbows Raul, "What the fuck is this, man?"

"Hi, I'm Shawna. We're all from the Center like you guys only we're over on Block B where you can't see us. A while ago the warden told us . . . and this was all hush-hush . . . that he's tired of you guys losing every game . . . said it was bad for the Center's morale . . . so he asked us to join you as cheerleaders. So here we are . . . (*pointing*) the skinny one is Maria, this here is Carmen (*tapping her on the shoulder*), then next comes Lisa (*pointing*) and the gorgeous one on the end is Sugar. We're here to see that you guys win. The warden says we all get a day off from chores if that happens. We've been practicin' a few routines for time outs and the half . . . (*laughing*) . . . so we're ready to fly . . . OK?"

Khalique (*with wrinkled brow*): "We ain't won a game since I got here two years ago. What makes you think a few chicks can change all that?"

Shawna (*smiling*): "We got our ways."

Sam (*leaning forward*): "What you mean?"

Carmen (*concealing a smirk with her hand*): "If you win, we gonna give you a little something . . . you know, a reward."

Sam: "Like what?"

Shawna: "Like this (*reaching down and pulling her shorts to the side*)."

Khalique *(straining)*: "All I see is pink panties."

Shawna: "Oh yeah? What about this *(pulling panties to side, showing pussy)*?"

Khalique *(big smile)*: "Mmmm . . . now I get it."

Myron *(nodding knowingly)*: "That's nice stuff."

Khalique: "What if we ahead at halftime . . . any samples?"

Shawna: "Uh-uh. Only if you win."

Raul: "So, where we gonna do it?"

Shawna: "In the bus stupid . . . in back where Pug can't see us. Maria says she'll keep him busy if he don't go to sleep."

Sam: "If we's goin' to win, you better make a lot of noise 'cuz every one of these honkies gonna cheer for the home team. The place really gets rockin if they're ahead."

Khalique: "Yeah . . . but they ain't all honkies on the team . . . I remember Cool Dog from last year . . . he's their best player and he's a brother."

Sam: "I don't care what color the mother fucker is . . . tonight he's the enemy . . . and we gonna lose if we don't stuff his black ass."

Shawna: "Maybe we can help with that."

Sam: "What you mean?"

Shawna: *(giggling)* "You'll see."

The ref motions for all players to come out onto the court and take up their positions. By now the stands are full of law-abiding, righteous-thinking fans eager to cheer their heroes on to another lopsided victory over the car thieves, store robbers and girl-molesters from the Correctional

Center. In case anyone in town had forgotten, this morning's newspaper reminded readers of last year's score: 52 to 26, Saranac High by 2:1. A similar outcome was predicted for today's game.

Lester, Saranac's 6"5 center, controls the opening tip. Seconds later the host team scores on a drive by Cool Dog in which he swings around Sam and lays it up over Kato who doesn't get around to blocking the shot until it is falling through the hoop. "Little slow on your toes, ain't ya big boy," growls Cool Dog as he races past Kato to get back on defense.

On their next possession, after a futile three-point attempt by Sam, the home team drops in another basket when Cool Dog's fellow guard, Tiny Tim, dribbles untouched past Kato for an easy lay-up. Richard calls an immediate time-out.

"Kato," he cries, looking right at the big man. "You're letting these guys go right through you. They're going to kill us if we can't stop their penetration . . . (*pause*) . . . Here's what we do. When you see one of the guards starting to drive, get in front of him as he heads for the basket and take a charge. Be sure to move your feet fast enough so that you're stationary before he hits you. You're bigger than he is so he'll bounce right off you . . . and the ref will give him a foul. And Sam, you can slow his drive with one of Michael Jordan's tricks, you know, by grabbing his trunks as he dribbles around you . . . (*smiling*) . . . just make sure the ref can't see you do it. O.K . . . let's go."

After Khalique throws up a three-point beauty giving the Center its first points, Cool Dog comes racing back, slips past a lunging Sam and dribbles hard to the basket. Several feet from the hoop he is met by the newly awakened Kato who steps in front of him and absorbs the charge. Much to the big man's surprise, it is he, not the smaller Cool Dog, who goes crashing to the floor. He rises slowly, rubbing the back of his head. "Hurt yourself, punk?" Cool Dog croons as he brushes elbows with the still-groggy Kato on the way to the other end. Kato, with blood now surging to his temples and mindful only of revenge, follows his teammates down court where he bulls his way into a spot close to the basket. Memories of street fights, won and lost, flash through his sluggish brain as he jostles with Lester for position. When Raul's mid-range jumper clangs off the rim, he goes quickly for the rebound and pulls it down, then swings his elbows to ward off any would-be attackers. The blow to Lester's jaw can be heard throughout the gym. The ref blows a whistle, pointing to Kato as the offender. Given the seriousness of the blow, a flagrant foul is called and two foul shots awarded to the victim who is busy checking to see if his teeth are still intact.

From the sidelines Richard grows alarmed at the way events are unfolding and calls his team over for a huddle. Kato remains in the rear with head down as 'Coach Rich' cautions against getting sucked into the other team's trash talk. "They're trying to bait us into fouling, yes? They know damn well that we only have five players . . . remember last year when we lost Myron and had to go the whole second half with only four guys. We were right there with them until he started swinging elbows at anyone who taunted him. So Kato, listen up . . . you only get three more fouls before you have to leave the game. Be patient, use them wisely. Try to get to the end of this half with no more than two fouls . . . O.K.?"

Kato, of course, interprets this warning as permission to go out and foul three more times. The opportunity to use the first of these comes when Sam and Khalique tie the score with two jump shots and a lob to Myron. The crowd goes silent. All eyes are on Cool Dog as he dribbles over the half-court line and checks out the defense. Is he going to shoot or will he penetrate? He looks over Sam's shoulder to Kato, sending an unspoken challenge with a curl of his lip. Anyone can see that he intends to penetrate.

"No more easy stuff, Dog Shit," Sam mutters as he goes to block the way to the basket. "You come in here and you gonna get your ass whipped." His words fly like darts at Cool Dog's ego, swollen to Goliath proportions by years of hero-worship and acclaim in the local press . . . even talk about a scholarship to Michigan State where hopes of a national championship run high.

The crowd comes alive. Riding a new wave of energy, the Cool One looks past Sam, fakes to the left, then switches hands and dribbles sharply to the right. As the Dog shoots past, conscious of only Kato to beat, Sam lunges to his left and grabs his trunks, sending him spinning to the floor.

The victim rises quickly, yelling expletives at his foe while blood spurts from his nose. "Did ya see that ref," he screams. Did ya see that punk grab my trunks and pull me down?" The ref shakes his head. From the sidelines, Richard nods approvingly to Khalique for blocking any official view of the crime. No foul is called. Since Cool Dog fell while dribbling, the ball goes over to the visitors.

On the ensuing play the Saranac players can be heard whispering something about Kato as they prepare to defend their end of the court. "Watch yourself," Myron shouts to the intended target above the hiss of a frustrated crowd. Being new to the game of basketball and its emotional subtleties, Kato has no idea what lies ahead. He will pay for his ignorance. Within seconds of settling into position, he gives out a scream and goes crashing to the floor, clutching his thigh where Lester has kneed him from behind. The ref comes rushing over. "I saw that. I saw that, Lester. You're outta the game," jabbing his thumb toward the bench. The crowd responds with shouts of condemnation more befitting a gladiator's defeat at the Roman Coliseum. Kato is awarded two foul shots. A new center is inserted for the home team.

At the foul line Kato rubs his thigh and eyes the basket. This will be his first foul shot . . . ever. He closes one eye and looks again. To his untutored mind, there appear to be an infinite number of ways of getting the ball to the basket. From that list, he picks the one most familiar to him and places his right foot on the line. A final deep breath indicates that he is ready. With a shot-putting motion learned in high school track, he does a quick 360 and hurls the ball at the basket. The deafening thud against the backboard can be heard throughout the gym, followed by ripples of uncontrolled laughter. The ref looks up to check the backboard for signs of damage; reassured that all is still well, he motions for Kato to go ahead with his second attempt. As the jeers swell to ear-splitting proportions, he eschews the 360, choosing this time to hold the ball in his right hand and throw it, javelin-like, at the hoop. His aim is perfect. The ball hits the rim with such force that it explodes, scattering fragments of plastic among the players underneath. Nonplussed, the ref stands there for a minute, gaping at the fragments on the floor. To his knowledge, which is considerable given his 20 years of officiating, the rules book says nothing about exploding basketballs. With the crowd noise rising exponentially, he decides to call the shot a miss and give a substitute ball to the opposing team.

Looking to go up before the half ends, the Saranac players race down the court, anxious to set up a play before the limping Kato has a chance to establish himself under the basket. The strategy works. Before Kato even gets all the way to the other end, Tiny Tim launches a three-pointer, misses, but rebounds his own miss and puts it in the hoop. Raul inbounds from under the basket as Richard holds up three fingers, calling for an alley-oop between Khalique and Myron. When it misses, Cool Dog grabs the rebound and, mistaking Kato, still at the other end nursing his thigh, for one of his own teammates, hurls the ball the length of the court . . . right into Kato's hands. Bewildered by this strange and unforeseen turn of events, Kato turns around, faces the hoop, and dunks the ball. Richard covers his face with his hands as two points are added to the Saranac total. The howls of joy from the crowd are so loud that no one hears the bell signaling the end of the first half. It takes a minute or two for the ref, with help from both coaches, to escort the players off the court. The half ends with Saranac leading by a score of 28 to 26.

During the intermission it is agreed that cheerleaders from each side will take turns performing their routines. The Saranac High girls go first, alternately entertaining and exhorting the crowd with an impressive display of carefully coordinated numbers, each involving ballet-like moves in tight-fitting uniforms designed to highlight the girls' reproductive assets. They return to the sidelines to the roar of an adoring audience.

A hush falls over the crowd. Hesitantly, the five girls from the Center come out onto the floor, their multi-colored, home-spun outfits standing in unflattering contrast to the spiffy uniforms of the Saranac group. Those spectators not thirsty enough to go downstairs for a drink look on with amused interest as Shawna leads her friends through a series of casually constructed routines. A wayward move by Maria, going left when everyone else is going right, gets the crowd twittering, but it is the actual slip and fall by Sugar that brings on the biggest laugh. Soon, fans are saluting the hapless girls with boisterous applause and stomping of feet. The performers begin to lose heart. As the crowd mocks their efforts with ever-increasing mirth, their routines become so undone that the crestfallen troupe stops moving altogether. When she sees that all is lost, Shawna turns to the crowd and acknowledges their cruelty with a raised finger, then, amid a cascade of boos and catcalls, shepherds her flock back to the bench.

Back in the locker room, Richard and the boys are too busy plotting strategy for the second half to hear what is happening on the gym floor. It is only when they return for the resumption of play that they notice the girls in tears. All eyes point to the cheerleaders as Sam proceeds down the sidelines to where they remain crouching. Shawna is the only one who appears calm enough to speak. As Sam approaches, both palms up, questioning, she quickly drops the pretense of imperturbability. With eyes black and menacing, lips still trembling, she details every humiliating step of the nightmare performance. The other girls can do no more than nod their tearful agreement.

"You sayin' they laughed at you?" Sam asks, incredulously. "They done clapped when Sugar fell? Jeesuz! And they pretend to be good folks. They think that 'cuz we in the Center they can treat us like shit. Fuckin' animals . . . that's what they are. I gotta tell the boys . . . they goin' to be pissed. It ain't in our blood to let nobody treat us like that."

"Beat' em, Sam," begs Shawna, crying openly now, "beat the shit out of 'em. It's the only way we can get back."

When Sam finishes reporting to the team, no one says anything. Nothing needs to be said. Their response shows in the hardening of their eyes, the stiffening of their bodies. Richard is the only one to speak. "O.K. This is it. We're only two points behind. Let's get off to a fast start and keep going until the final bell. Kato . . . don't worry about that last shot . . . it could have happened to anybody. Maintain your composure . . . if they drive to the basket keep taking charges. Don't let them bait you into fouling. Sam and Khalique . . . keep those mid-range jump shots coming . . . assume that you're going to make more than you miss. Raul . . . keep passing, setting up plays . . . treat the ball like a hot potato . . . get rid of it to Sam or Khalique the moment you get it. Myron . . . don't let your man push you away from the basket . . . we need your rebounding . . . (*pause*) . . . O.K. guys . . . keep in mind what they did to our girls . . . yes . . . they're *our* girls . . . they came here to help us win and got humiliated . . . it's our duty to get back at the people who did it . . . and the only way to do that is to win this game."

Back alone on the bench, Richard is more than a little amazed at the intensity of his speech. He is aware that it comes not from any heightened desire on his part, but osmotically from the collective rage of a team that has been exposed to years of disrespect . . . even contempt. The fury, the despair, the need to strike back . . . are all there now . . . in spades. The question is whether that passion can be channeled into behavior sanctioned under the rules of the game. When the whistle sounds, he calls for a play in which Sam drives to the basket and passes off to Myron for a layup at the last moment. It works. The score is tied again.

For the better part of the half the score goes back and forth, each team eschewing long jump shots for the higher percentage drives to the basket. When Tiny Tim is fouled as he streaks to the hoop, Richard signals a timeout and pulls Kato over for last minute instructions. "You're too late in fronting these guys," he shouts over the buzz of the crowd. "The second you see them starting a drive, move your feet. Get in front . . . but don't throw your body at them like that . . . it's an obvious foul. You've now got four . . . one more and you're out of the game. Remember . . . we don't have any substitutes . . . (*pause*) . . . O.K. we're all tied with eight minutes to go. Show me how much you want this game. Let's go for the kill."

The game continues with little change. Every time Sam or Khalique scores with a jump shot, either Cool Dog or Tiny Tim responds with a lay in. The frustration grows. On the way up the court Sam turns to Kato, "You gotta stop these bastards; they's killin' us. Kato nods and mulls over his strategy. The next time the Dog comes driving to the hole, Kato is waiting for him. Shifting quickly to front his opponent, he stands tall, braces himself for contact, then drives his knee into his adversary's groin. The Dog falls to the floor, writhing. The gym shakes with the screams of irate fans. Both boys are forced to leave the game, one helped off by his teammates, still clutching his stomach, the other ejected for unsportsmanlike conduct. The Center is now down to four players. Richard calls his team over for adjustments at the defensive end. There is no choice but to go with zone coverage.

Less than three minutes after his collision with Kato, Cool Dog, still weak from the blow, asks to go back in. The crowd rises to its feet as they see him limping out onto the floor. Inside the huddle, he whispers a play called by the coach and waits for the inbounds pass from Tiny. Once the ball is in his hands, he swings past Sam, careful to avoid being grabbed, then flies to the hoop and dunks over Myron's outstretched arms. The building shakes with ecstatic voices and pounding feet. Saranac is back up by two points.

Sam and friends are not finished, far from it. As Shawna, Maria, Sugar, Carmen and Lisa shout themselves hoarse from the sidelines, the boys from the Center, now down to four, lift their game to a level none of them has ever known. Raul starts it off with a three-pointer from the sidelines, his very first of the season. At the other end, Tiny feeds the ball to their new center for a quick post-up over the shorter Myron. The ball never gets to the basket. With the center's back to the basket, Raul sneaks around him and rips it from his hands . . . then hurls it down court to a streaking Khalique who drops it in for a thunderous dunk. The crowd is stunned as the scoreboard shows the Center up by two points with less than 30 seconds to play.

On the ensuing possession Raul is caught slapping the Dog on the arm as he goes up for a jumper. A foul is called; two shots are awarded. While a thousand agonized fans hold their collective breath, the still-hurting Dog throws up his first attempt. It bounces teasingly from side to side before falling in. The gym explodes with relief. Richard calls time out.

It is at this point that Shawna leaves her sisters to take up a position on the floor directly under the Saranac basket. Once all the players are properly lined up on either side of the lane, the ref pitches the ball to the Cool One. From his position at the stripe, The Dog is the first to notice Shawna squatting directly in front of him. When she flashes a seductive smile and playfully fingers a blouse button, he looks away and shakes his head. Did he see what he thought he saw? While continuing to dribble . . . or at least pretending to dribble . . . he darts a second glance in her direction. In response she wets her lips with her tongue. Within seconds he is smitten. His heart begins to race. Yes, he knows . . . the game still hangs in the balance and everyone's eyes are upon him . . . but he cannot clear her from his mind. Even as his teammates clench their fists in support, the image of her fully-developed breasts and long, slender legs forces its way into consciousness, shattering his concentration.

Ten seconds pass without a shot. The ref shouts a loud "Let's go" from just off the court. Now he has no choice but to focus on the basket itself. He dribbles again.

Before he can finish his routine, Shawna reaches down between her outstretched legs and pulls her panties to the side. From this vantage point her vagina is in full view to the Dog but no one else. He gulps and tries to look away but is immediately pulled back, his mind flooded with possibilities, each more erotic than the next. His knees weaken. A deathly silence fills the gym. He looks down once more at Shawna, takes a deep breath and launches his shot. To the collective moan of a stunned and disbelieving crowd, the ball falls a foot short of the basket where it is gobbled up by Khalique. The bell sounds as he is pummeled by all five Saranac players. The ref signals the end of action; the game is over. The Center has won by a single point.

Out on the floor Richard, the players, and all five cheerleaders continue hugging and dancing even after the crowd has left the gym. "I bet you didn't think we could do it, Richie," Sam shouts as he lifts Shawna onto his shoulders. "Maybe not," Richard shouts back above the din . . . "but who could have known about our secret weapon?"

"We all knew," says Sugar, laughing. "We talked about it before the game."

"Yeah," chimes in Maria, "but we never thought it would come down to the last play of the whole fuckin' game."

"All's well that ends well . . . yes?" says Richard. "I guess your warden is going to be pleased with what you all did here tonight."

"Yeah . . . and he better not forget what he promised about lettin' us off chores for a day," adds Lisa.

"Yeah, now what about *your* promise?" shouts Kato from the back, his large brown eyes riveted to Shawna's cleavage. We held up our end, didn't we?"

"We always keep our promise, big boy," drawls Shawna as she slips her arms around his waist and heads for the exit. "C'mon all you lovers. The bus is waiting. Let's enjoy the ride."

18   Violence in the Woods

It's Monday, the first full day after the Said's drive from Boston to Saranac Lake, a trip dominated by the sound of screeching Italian sopranos on the CD player and harangues about U.S. policy in the Middle East from the driver's seat. For Tashi, it is the first chance since Thanksgiving to see Richard again. Yes, there have been a few e-mails . . . and one phone call to affirm this summer's schedule of practice sessions on Thursday and performances on Saturdays . . . but nothing personal . . . nothing that could build on or even acknowledge the new-found intimacy of their final goodbye at her house. Today, tomorrow and the next day all promise to be bleak . . . unless she just happens to meet him in the meadow above his cottage. It has happened before . . . once . . . all by chance and thus not a breach of rules laid down by her parents. So, why not again? With that reassuring thought in her mind, she packs a lunch, tosses it into her backpack and waves goodbye to her parents.

As she wanders up the trail toward the meadow, memories of last year's meeting come rushing back. She sees the two of them on the grassy slope overlooking the valley . . . her head resting peacefully in his lap, his fingers brushing back her hair while they listen to the birds in the woods and scan the mountains in the distance. With last November's doorstep farewell still fresh in her mind, she begins speculating on the possibilities before her . . . a more ardent kiss, a tearful protestation of love, even a mutual surrender of self in sexual union. She is ready for whatever the day offers.

As she walks, memories of Richard's face and hands are folded into the panoply of images and sounds offered by the forest. A cotton-tail rabbit scurries across the path and disappears under a covert of protective branches. Overhead the sun peers through the leafy canopy of maples and birches to dapple the trail with splashes of gold. Down in the lake, a female mallard protests the encroachments of her male admirers and takes to the air honking. There is a calm here, she notes, a peace unknown in a world fragmented by cars, subways and Ipods . . . a harmony missing in a world where machines disrupt the natural flow of things.

Once past the cut-off to Richard's cottage, she slows, letting the ambient forest air draw out the toxic residues of city life. It is then that she hears human voices for the first time . . . two boys calling to each other deep in the woods. And then a chain-saw . . . shouts of 'Raulie, get outta the way' . . . followed by the thud of a tree falling to the ground . . . and laughter. She continues on her way . . . more cautiously now.

As she comes up over the rise just below the pool where she and Richard bathed, she is suddenly confronted by a young, good-looking Hispanic boy who has been following her movements carefully from behind a thicket of serviceberry bushes. The boy steps in front of her, blocking her way. "Why you in such a hurry?" he asks, his eyes fixed on her breasts. Like his friend Myron who observes from a distance, he is naked to the waist, the scratches on his arms and chest clear evidence of the vengeance thorns and thistles can wreak on human skin. From the shouting heard earlier, she assumes his name to be Raul.

She clutches her blouse, saying "I'm going to meet a friend." Her breathing comes quickly now. It is not his face that frightens her; he is nice enough looking . . . and still only a boy. It is his words, "Why you in such a hurry?" and the way he stands before her, feet apart, blocking her way. As she grips her blouse, she makes a quick survey of the options open to her. There is only one that offers a reasonable chance of escape . . . that is to turn around and run as fast as she can back towards Richard's cottage, screaming as she runs. When he drops his chain saw and steps toward her, she makes her move.

At field hockey she plays defense because of her speed . . . and her voice is loud and clear. Add to that a healthy fear of being violated and you have the makings of an alert, young biped capable of evading the jaws of the hungriest predator. But this is not an even match. Where she is fast, he is even faster. Where her legs are driven by dread, his are fueled by a lust kindled in the bosom of a depraved mother-son relationship. Within five or six steps he is on her, dragging her to the ground, one hand on her mouth, the other pinning her arm to the trail. With her free hand she claws his neck with her fingernails; she feels his blood on her fingertips, but he takes no notice. To get her shorts down he must either release her arm or take his hand off her mouth. He does both. As her screams fill the forest, she begins beating wildly on his ears and temple. He raises his head to avoid her blows, then rips open her blouse, pulls down her shorts and pins his crotch against hers. Her panic reaches frenetic levels as she feels his penis ready to enter her. "No, no, not you, it mustn't be you," she shouts as her eyes open wide with terror.

With a final burst of rage known only to wild animals in the throes of death, she raises her torso and rakes his cheeks with her nails. In defense he closes his fist and strikes her hard on the cheek. She falls back . . . unconscious. When she awakes a minute later, he is inside her, his chest rising and falling rapidly in response to his ejaculation. Her mind clears quickly. With her right hand she searches the ground next to her for something she can use as a weapon. Dirt, some weeds . . . then yes, a rock. She reaches out and grasps it as he lays his head on her other shoulder, oblivious to her awakening. Sure now of his ignorance, she coils her hand around the rock and smashes it with full force into the back of his head. He cries just once . . . then slides off her onto the trail, clutching his head.

Quickly now, she wriggles out from beneath his body and pulls up her shorts. He is conscious but not moving as she gets to her feet and begins racing down the path. Just before the trail makes a sharp turn to the right, she stops to look back. He has started after her but is stumbling, still clutching the rear of his head. She turns and continues running all the way to Richard's door. In less than a minute she is there. She pounds once, pulls the door open and, without waiting for an answer, flings herself at Richard as he rises, speechless, from his piano bench.

He holds her tight as she sobs on his shoulder. "Oh Richard, Richard," she gasps. "He's out there . . . coming down the trail." "Who?" he asks, peering out the door window. "I don't see anyone." "Raul . . . . it's Raul . . . he hurt me, he hurt me . . . up near the pool." With that she collapses to his feet. As he stoops to pick her up, his heart tightens with what he sees . . . the ripped blouse . . . . and then, more menacingly, the blood on her legs. "Are you alright, Tash?" he asks, still reluctant to digest the evidence before him. "Shall I take you to a doctor?"

"The hospital," she murmurs, "Take me to the hospital."

"Of course, of course," he answers, brushing back her hair and lifting her off the floor. Once in the car, he asks, "Should we call your parents first or . . ."

"No, the hospital," she whispers without hesitation.

On the way to Saranac Lake Hospital Richard leans over and asks, "Can you tell me what happened or . . . would you rather wait?"

Silence . . . then more tears. He puts his right arm around her shoulder while steering with the other. It is obvious now that she has been assaulted . . . and raped . . . by his prize pupil, Raul, the one with all the raw talent, the same Raul whose music Tashi herself suggested playing at the restaurant.

At the hospital she is immediately rushed into a treatment room for examination. A social worker is instructed to call her parents and tell them they are needed right away. Within minutes a second call is put in to the sheriff's office with information on the offender's name and location provided by a still-shaken Tashi. The buzz at the nurse's station is palpable.

While waiting alone in the starkly furnished visitor's area, Richard lets his mind drift back to the forest . . . Tashi on the trail up by the pool . . . out for her first walk of the summer . . . a strange boy leaping from behind the bushes . . . knocking her to the ground . . . her screams, only a hundred yards away from where he sat at the piano, but obscured by his playing . . . blood on her legs. He shivers, then buries his face in his hands. A nurse passes by, asking if he is alright. He murmurs something and throws his head back against the wall.

Recoiling now from his fantasy, he goes looking for answers to what has happened. He ponders what he already knows about Raul's past . . . the confrontation with Ben who molested his younger sister . . . his father's abandonment and early death at the hands of some gunman . . . his rape of the 13-year-old fat girl and assignment to the Correctional Center. This is all Raul has told him. He suspects there may be more . . . things too personal to divulge to a man he has come to like but does not yet trust . . . but he cannot be sure.

If Raul had told him everything, Richard would have learned that after Ben was forced to leave at the end of a pistol, Raul, his mother Cheryl and the other two children were invited to move from Phoenix, Arizona to Albany, New York to live with Laura, his mother's best friend from high school. At that point Raul has just turned 16. Cheryl accepts the invitation with little or no hesitation. Over Raul's and Angie's objections, she packs everybody's belongings into an assortment of shopping bags and drives east. The atmosphere in their new home, both clean and peaceful thanks to the fastidious Laura, offers welcome relief from the tension-filled apartment she has shared with past lovers. Laura's apartment below the old capitol building is barely big enough for two people, let alone five but she is lonely and eager for the company of an old friend. Given the cramped quarters, Raul, his sister Angie and younger brother Moses have to share a single bedroom while Cheryl sleeps on the couch in the living room. This arrangement doesn't last very long. Before the month is up, Laura invites Cheryl to share her small bedroom, going so far as to remove some of her old clothes to the basement so that Cheryl might have room for her own.

Laura is several inches taller than Raul, dark haired, full-breasted, and still strikingly slender in her late-thirties. She cannot be considered beautiful thanks to an usually large nose and small mouth, but her ample breasts and shapely legs more than make up for the unaesthetic contours of her face. Never married, she has kept her bi-sexual orientation hidden from both co-workers and family, preferring to explore her needs for intimacy in private. She has always found Cheryl's plumper frame and cocoa-brown skin attractive, but never found the courage to act on it while the two were in high school. If she had, it would very likely have backfired since at that time Cheryl had no sexual interest in other women. All that began to change with years of beatings at the hands of Raul's father, beatings severe enough to warrant hospitalization and court-ordered restraining orders. A subsequent year with Ben simply confirmed her fear that men see her as little more than a receptacle for their ejaculations and will quickly resort to violence when they don't get what they want.

Once settled into her new home, with memories of her ex-husband and Ben still fresh in her mind, Cheryl begins looking at Laura in a different light . . . as a non-threatening, alternative way to satisfy her needs for physical closeness. On their very first night in the bedroom together they experiment with facial caresses and furtive kisses . . . all such gestures being initiated by Laura while Cheryl submits without protest. In subsequent days their overtures become bolder as both women yield to their long-suppressed desires. Lips and nipples become the object of mutual adoration; tongues find their way into the inner recesses of each other's sex. When, in the ensuing months, their passion reaches its zenith and threatens to recede, Laura opens a small box concealed in her dresser and pulls out a tiny packet of cocaine. During long, languorous afternoons when the children are in school, they ride the waves of its magical power across an ocean of desire in which every carnal fetish, including those hitherto unknown, is explored and exhausted.

In time even these games grow stale, predictable, lacking in imagination. Laura, for whom sex has long been the sole source of excitement in a lackluster life dominated by fears of poverty, feels the shrinking of libido more keenly than her younger companion. On this particular afternoon she is determined to try something new. When Raul arrives home from school, he is surprised to find her bedroom door wide open. When he tries to avert his gaze and head for the kitchen, Laura motions for him to come in. Hesitantly he enters the bedroom, nervous because of what he knows about their relationship, but completely unprepared for what he sees. Laura is sitting up in bed, her breasts fully exposed, the sheet pulled up to cover her knees but not far enough to conceal the black, heart-shaped bush poised demurely just above her sex. Her left hand is massaging the shoulders of his mother who lies curled up fetal-like at Laura's side.

He throws an awkward glance toward his mother who quickly looks away. "Come, sit down and tell us about your day, Raulie," Laura whispers, moving her legs to make room on the bed. It is only then that his mother turns to face him, murmuring, "It's O.K. honey." He is immediately aware of the glaze in her eyes and the redness in her nostrils. He glances over at the night table for confirmation and finds what he is looking for . . . a column of white powder and a straw. "Ma?" he asks, questioning with his eyes. Before she can answer, Laura reaches out and begins unbuttoning his shirt. With her warm hands still on his chest, she offers her lips, then pulls him down on top of her. Together the two women push his pants to his ankles, then off onto the floor. "He never did like underwear," Cheryl giggles as Raul takes Laura's head between his hands and begins kissing her hard on the mouth. Laura moves her hips until his manhood is pressing against her labia. When he feels a hand moving slowly up and down his back, he assumes it to be Laura's. It is only when she takes his head between both hands and kisses his nose that the truth reveals itself. For a moment he stops breathing, torn between disgust and an eroticism elevated beyond anything he has ever experienced. Laura is aware that the drama hangs delicately in the balance . . . and pulls him to her as she forces her tongue into his mouth. Distracted by her boldness, he is only dimly aware of a hand slipping between his body and Laura's, inching its way toward his hardening flesh. With her own breath coming quickly now, Cheryl takes his swollen manhood in hand and guides it to Laura's vagina where she moistens it with the cream covering her host's labia. Once assured of Laura's receptiveness, she inserts the head of his penis into her slit and resumes massaging his back. "Yes, darling," she croons as he slides his boyish member in and out of Laura's pink cave. When she senses he is on the verge of climax, she throws her arm across his back, whispering, "Show her you love her, darling. Show her how much you care."

In the days that follow, the scene is repeated many times, with the lingering images of Laura and Cheryl gradually conflated into a single female . . . at once alluring and comforting, both sensual and maternal . . . until the memory of his seduction becomes etched forever into his young psyche. His childhood is now behind him, his innocence torn from him by people who should have known better. He has had too much sex, too early in life. He can no longer view the girls at school with the same haughty disdain sanctioned by his male peers. Wherever he sees breasts peeking out from summer blouses or tanned thighs protruding from jean cut-offs, he pictures the girl calling to him from an open bedroom, offering herself in wanton lust. It happens as well with older women, like his teachers and waitresses and the conservatively-dressed ladies he passes on the Albany streets. Like Laura and Cheryl, they too beckon to him with their sad eyes and unloved breasts. He sees them all one-dimensionally, as fragmented, imperfect souls, not yet complete until he is lying on top of them. He thinks sexually; he dreams sexually. But it isn't until he goes bicycling with the Hippo and takes her up into the barn that he goes so far as to act upon his fantasies. And that, of course, is his undoing.

Some of this Richard knows or suspects, much of it he doesn't. But what he knows is sufficient to keep him from writing off Raul as just another rapist. Uncomfortably, his dream of rescuing him from the maw of poverty, of giving him, through music, a chance to prove himself to the world, begins to intrude upon his anguish for the girl in the exam room. On the surface he appears quiet, saddened . . . as one might expect from a close friend at a time like this. Deep within, however, far from public scrutiny, the two feelings, the two contradictory loves, wrestle for his attention, each threatening to neutralize the other.

Within minutes of the phone call, Tashi's parents arrive at the hospital, demanding to see their daughter. Both are hysterical. The head nurse does her best to calm them down, explaining that tests are still being run, samples taken, drugs administered. Still sputtering, they take their seats along the waiting room wall. A full minute passes before Asadour acknowledges Richard's presence with a jerk of his head. Not a word passes between them, the father's eyes being sufficient to suggest that in some way he holds Richard to blame for the tragedy. "After all," he whispers to his wife, "it was one of 'his boys' that did it. That's what the nurse said, didn't she?" "Yes," Esther whispers, careful to turn her back to Richard. "I don't know why they let him stay. I just wish he would leave before Eleanor comes out." The nurses at the intake station are too far away to hear what is being said, but they have no trouble making out the dynamics of the situation from the lips, eyes and seating position of the three people against the wall.

As Tashi comes out, both parents rush to comfort her. "Oh honey," Esther exclaims. "Are you alright?" "What did he do to you," adds Asadour, opening his arms for a hug. Without answering, she flies past them both into Richard's arms, sobbing, clutching. By now the rage has passed, the need to strike back that roiled her blood just hours ago is gone, replaced by another ache . . . a feeling deeper than revenge, a feeling that goes to the very heart of her being. At the core of her anguish lies a promise made to herself, a promise born of a love not yet corroded by flesh grown stale, a promise that now lies shattered. With her arms wrapped around his neck, she cries, "I wanted it to be you Richard . . . I wanted it to be you." He pulls her toward him, cheek on cheek, their tears flowing together in a synchrony of grief. The nurses standing at the desk turn away, their knowing hearts unable to endure any more.

Asadour coughs, then looks down, not sure what to do with his feet. When he can no longer bear the tension, he strides awkwardly to where Tashi is sitting, grabs her by the wrist and yanks her off Richard's lap. "C'mon," he shouts, "It's time to get you home where you belong." "Yes, honey," Mother adds, "you'll feel better when you're back in your own room." Tashi goes limp in his grasp. To the casual observer she appears to be giving in. Her surrender is an illusion. Once her parent's intention becomes clear, she pulls her wrist loose and backs away, her eyes feverish with horror. With a glance toward Richard, she starts screaming and kicking, then flailing her arms as if warding off an army of angry bees. Esther pulls her husband back, muttering, "Oh God, Asi . . . what have we done?"

At the intake desk, two nurses look at each other, then rush for medication. Gloria, the senior of the two, waves off the parents and approaches Tashi with bottle in hand. Guiding her to the bench, she strokes her arm and whispers, "What do you want, Tashi; what would make you feel better right now?" When Tashi turns quickly to face Richard, Gloria motions him to come and join them. He takes the seat on Tashi's other side, then reaches over and offers her his hand. Without hesitation she takes his hand and squeezes it forcefully between the two of her own. To Gloria that squeeze, innocent enough in itself, suggests a terrified child clutching a ship's guard rail as gale-force winds threaten to sweep her off the deck into the water below. Richard, sensing a similar desperation, responds by massaging the top of her hand.

As Tashi's breathing returns to normal, Gloria rises and draws Asadour and Esther into a huddle by the desk. "I think it's best if she spends the night here," she whispers. "We'll have our social worker talk to her . . . and then of course (*holding up the bottle*) the Valium should help. If we can get her through the night without mishap, you can take her home in the morning." "Can we come and see her after dinner tonight," Esther asks. "We needn't stay long . . . just enough to assure her that we're concerned." "Of course," Gloria answers. "Come by around 7:00."

Tashi consents to stay, but refuses the Valium. She is assigned a small room of her own in the psychiatric ward. There are two stuffed chairs facing each other; she turns one around so she can sit facing the window. Within the hour, dinner is offered but refused. When a social worker arrives, eager to help with formalized questions and reassurances, Tashi turns the chair back around to face her, but says very little, answering most questions with a nod of her head. A half hour later the social worker leaves, closing the door behind her. The chair is turned to face the window again. Finally, she is alone with her thoughts.

At first, they come quickly: simple, isolated bits and pieces of memory joined only by their common anguish. Gradually they form themselves into a coherent narrative: walking slowly along the trail, hopes of a meeting in the meadow, the sensation of cool forest air, the sound of birds in the trees and sun on the arms . . . then out of nowhere, shock, fear, screams for help, alone in the woods, horror at what might happen . . . thrown to the ground, pinned, the struggle, the fighting . . . the blow on the cheek . . . then the rock, the striking . . . finally the running.

She stops to check her feelings . . . the fear, the fury . . . all of it more painful than anything she has ever felt. But it is still not clear. "Behind the shock, beyond the horror," she asks, "what is it that hurts the most. Is it the physicality of the act, the assault, the bruises, the bodily pain? Would I have felt the same if my purse had been ripped from my shoulder? Would I be this upset if my bedroom had been ransacked, my valuables taken or scattered? They too are physical. No, this is different . . . something far more personal. A total stranger has forced his way into my body despite my screams. He has torn away my clothes to gorge on my flesh. He has treated me as if I were less than a person . . . less than himself, a mindless object without feelings, without boundaries."

She pauses, still gazing out the window, her eyes dry now. "But there is still more to it than this," she murmurs. "The brutality of it hurts, yes, but there is something that hurts even more, something that goes deeper than violation of me as a person. It is a pain that transcends anything physical." She closes her eyes to let the truth come to her. Breathing slowly, she waits for the words to form, then speaks out loud, "This man, this boy called Raulie, has robbed me of a gift that I can never replace . . . one that I was saving for someone I love . . . a unique gift . . . a gift to show that I belong to him and only him. That token of my fidelity has been torn from me, ripped from my body by a stranger . . . yes, a gift meant for the person I love most in life . . . ripped from me against my will by someone I don't even know."

For hours she remains staring out the window, watching the hummingbirds at the feeder storing up energy for the long night ahead. Soon they will fly away to the Gulf of Mexico . . . thousands of miles from Saranac Lake . . . so small . . . facing so many dangers . . . many will not make it . . . will never return to where they were born. As she watches, she begins seeing her own problems in a larger context where life itself transcends the quotidian problems that inevitably come in its wake. A hint of solace appears at the edges of consciousness. Her heart more quiet now, she leans forward to listen to the birds' gentle clicking.

At that moment the door opens abruptly and Father bursts in, smiling. "Thought you might like to know that the police have picked up the boy who did it . . . they've got him locked up at the Correctional Center." Tashi frowns as the birds scatter, then turns to face him. "We're going to get him shipped out," he continues, "to some place far from here where he can never touch you again." Without responding, she turns back to the window.

Esther is right behind her husband. "Did you eat some dinner, honey?" . . . (*pause*) . . . "Was the social worker helpful? I've been told they have some good ones here." When nothing works, Esther looks at her husband anxiously, ponders the issue for a moment, then turns back to Eleanor. "Would it help to call Bapu and tell him what happened?"

Suddenly she sits up, nodding vigorously. Without further questions, Esther hands over her cell phone, then motions Asadour to join her out in the common room. Tashi waits for the door to close then dials the number.

The conversation starts tearfully, but gathers strength as Bapu takes in every word, interjecting comments only when she falters. She tells him everything . . . the walk, the sudden attack, the rape (this is the first time she allows herself to use the word) . . . and the flight to Richard's cottage. The tears start again when she whispers, "I wanted it to be him."

Bapu (*softly*): "I do understand, Tashi, but I find myself wondering how much he values that which means so much to you? Who knows whether he values it at all? Compared to having your love, your virginity may mean very little to him, a flattering acknowledgement of his specialness in your eyes but nothing more. Turn the situation around and ask how much it would mean to you to hear that he had never slept with another woman. A big deal, a relationship maker? I doubt it . . . (*pause*) . . . but perhaps I'm wrong here. Am I?"

The response comes slowly. "I've never thought of it that way. So, I'm not sure. What seems clear is that his love for me comes first. If I'm sure he loves me, I can probably accept just about anything. Things he may have done in the past are not going to change that feeling . . . (*pause*) . . . so, you're saying . . . I guess I know what you're saying . . . maybe I . . . "

Before she can finish the sentence, Asadour pushes the door open and walks in. "Eleanor, let me talk to your grandfather; there are some things I need to say." It is her scowl alone that keeps him from grabbing the phone. She hesitates, immobilized by the suddenness of his intrusion, then reluctantly hands over the phone. "Be sure to let me say goodbye before you hang up. I'll wait outside."

"Hello Robert . . . it's Asadour. I assume that Eleanor has told you what happened today . . . (*pause*) . . . I just wanted to add that it might be a good idea if you cautioned her about getting too close to this guy Richard. You know, of course, that she has this crush on him . . . and because she respects your opinion, she might be willing to listen if you . . . "

Bapu (*interrupting*): "She's kept me informed."

Asadour: "Well then, you must realize that there's some potential for danger here. From what I see, getting attached to him can only bring trouble . . . like today for instance."

Bapu: "I thought one of the kids from the Correctional Center did it."

Asadour: "Yes, of course, but he was one of Richard's pupils . . . his prize pupil in fact. He was also on the basketball team Richard coaches. So, there's definitely a connection there."

Bapu: "What kind of connection are you talking about?"

Asadour: "Do I have to spell this all out for you, Robert?"

Bapu: "Yes . . . if you can."

Asadour (*with growing irritation*): "Look, Richard is this kid's friend . . . by now he must know all about him . . . so he should have warned Eleanor about going for a walk in that part of the woods where the kids were cutting trees."

Bapu: "I thought he was a composer, not a social worker."

Asadour: "Still, he should have known, don't you think?"

Bapu: "No I don't. They have a social worker at the Center, don't they? And this person, presumably a trained professional, saw fit to allow Raul outside the prison walls to do some work in the forest. We know now that it was wrong to do so. Despite one-on-one meetings with the boy (I'm guessing they all get a little therapy there), he still couldn't come up with the right decision. So how do you expect an outsider, a composer like Richard, to see what the social worker could not see?"

Asadour: "I don't know. But I still don't like the idea of Eleanor's spending so much time with this guy. We've tried cutting off contact but each time we do, she goes into a tizzy, stops eating or goes into a deep depression, and then we have to back off. Today, here at the hospital with everyone running around with their heads off, I wanted to put a stop to those concerts at the restaurant . . . but I was afraid she'd have a holy fit if I said anything."

Bapu: "I'm sure she would have."

Asadour: "And you would have backed her up . . . yes?"

Bapu: "Probably."

Asadour: "So you're admitting that you're part of the problem."

Bapu: "I didn't say that."

Asadour (*shaking his head*): "You know, you remind me of this guy I met in college. Hadn't seen him in 20 years, but he called me last night and . . . "

Bapu: "You went to college?"

Asadour (*reddening*): "They felt sorry for refugees back then. Anyway, I remember this guy as somebody who contradicted everything I said . . . like you. He called to say he was in town and wanted to get together. So, we met in a restaurant and talked for hours about school and our ties to the Middle East. He grew up in Palestine like me so we had a lot to talk about, especially the hard time the Israelis gave us. He had a rough time getting admitted to the U.S. so he could teach; even back then Palestinians were suspected of terrorist intentions. Once he got to Kansas University he began writing and won an international reputation for his analysis of Middle Eastern history. All three of his children were brought up in the Islamic tradition, and went on to become scholars in their own right. His wife too is a professional historian and . . . "

Bapu (*interrupting*): "Why are you telling me all this?"

Asadour: "I thought you'd be interested."

Bapu: "So, it's for my sake that you're telling this story. It's essentially an act of altruism . . . yes?"

Asadour (*surprised*): "Well, why else would I bother?"

Bapu: "What if I told you I'm not interested in your story . . . that I find it boring . . . and totally irrelevant to what happened today to your daughter?"

Asadour: "Maybe you should be interested . . . you're such a hermit back there in New York . . . I'm giving you a chance to learn something about the world."

Bapu: "Again, it's all for my sake . . . that's what you're saying?"

Asadour: "Of course. Isn't that obvious?"

Bapu: "Not to me, no. What seems obvious is that you like to tell long-winded stories for your own pleasure, whether they are relevant or not."

Asadour: "You mean I like hearing myself talk?"

Bapu: "No, if that were true, you'd go around talking to yourself all the time . . . and so far anyway, I haven't noticed that particular aberration. No, I think you do it because you need other people's attention. You go on talking incessantly because it's the only way you know to get other people to pay attention to you. Let's face it; you're a compulsive talker. This is your primary way or relating to others. You don't know how to interact, to listen, to engage your partner in a two-way exchange of ideas and experiences. Even in the privacy of a two-person conversation, you lecture. You can't stop lecturing . . . you're like a little kid who is constantly thinking of himself . . . a kid tortured by self-doubt whose major concern in life is to get people to look at him, to listen to him, to acknowledge his presence in some way . . . and that is why you're so irritating to be with. Besides . . . "

Asadour slams the phone down, too upset to remember his promise to his daughter. Together he and Esther step outside to tell Eleanor they'll be back to pick her up in the morning. When she complains about the phone, she is told that her grandfather hung up. With that they head for the car. "So, what was the conversation with my father all about," asks Esther, hurrying to keep up. "The usual crap," he replies without stopping. "He just can't stop psychologizing. It's a wonder you're as sane as you are."

At the restaurant Saturday night, a subdued Tashi announces that from now on her parents will be coming to pick her up at 9:30 . . . right after their last piece. "They're really worried," she murmurs. "It was either that or giving up the gig entirely. I'm sorry Richard. You know how much I love our dinners together . . . *(pause)* . . . Oh, and tonight they will be having dinner here themselves . . . just to 'keep an eye on things' as Daddy put it. They'll expect us to drop by and say hello."

Later in the evening, between pieces, Tashi leads her partner over to her parents' table for a quick hello. Asadour motions Richard to sit down and have a drink. When Richard remains standing, Asi rises and draws him off into the corner. "Richard," he says struggling to keep his voice down, "as you probably know by now, a week from Tuesday the district attorney is holding an evidentiary hearing to review the facts about the rape prior to turning the case over to the judge for sentencing. It is important that you be there."

Richard: "I've heard of the meeting but I'm not sure why it is important for me to be there."

Asadour: "You know this kid Raul better than most adults around here. I think they would respect your opinion. And if you say he's a menace who has to be gotten rid of, they'll believe you. For Eleanor's sake, you've got to come and testify." Richard listens carefully, then turns and heads back to the bandstand without saying a word.

Several days later Richard enters the Correctional Center for his weekly music class, more than a little apprehensive about his reception. Sam, Juan and Khalique are there but no Raul. "He's in the hospital," Sam explains, "She hit him so hard with that rock that he can't hear on one side any more . . . could have killed him. The docs are sayin' he may never get his hearin' back. And he's a musician, right?"

"I had no idea," Richard answers, shaking his head. "You're right about the music, Sam. He'll be hard put to compose with only one ear . . . but I guess it can be done. After all, Beethoven did it while totally deaf. Of course, he had already written a lot of music when he lost his hearing."

"But Raulie's jis' gettin' started," Juan objects. "He still learnin' how to do it, ain't he?"

Sam (*impatiently*): "Richie, you gotta go to that meeting they're havin' and tell them what a good kid he is. If you don't go, they're goin' to ship him out to Utica . . . and then when he turns 18 next year, on to Attica. And you know what that means Richie, especially for a young good-lookin' hunk like Raulie. It's really the end of the line . . . forget the music . . . life over . . . he'll never get outta there in one piece. Here at least, he's got a chance. With you helpin' him with his music and lots of friends, he can turn his life around easy. O.K . . . they goin' to add a year or two to his sentence . . . but he can handle that. Attica he can't . . . no way he can do that."

"I think it's best if I can see him in the hospital," Richard says. "That'll give me a chance to see where he is . . . you know, emotionally. You guys already know that I've had my reservations about giving him parole this year. This latest incident confirms my hunch that he still hasn't developed the self-control he needs for living on the outside. Attica is certainly not the best place to learn that self-control . . . but he may be too dangerous to stay here any longer."

Sam (*voice rising*): "He wouldn't done nothin' if she hadn't laid it out there for him. Raulie told me she deliberately turned him on . . . real cunt-like. What do you expect . . . out there in the woods by herself . . . hardly any clothes on . . . waggin' her ass up that trail like a bitch in heat . . . just askin' for it. Who the fuck coulda resisted that? I ask you Rich . . . if youda seen her out there, dressed in them skimpy clothes, her little girl-tits peekin' out the top . . . wouldn't you want to fuck her? Wouldn't you?"

Richard: "Maybe I'd want to, but I doubt it, Sam. And even if I wanted to, I certainly wouldn't have forced myself on her. Sex without your partner's consent violates everything I believe about respecting the rights of other people. Hell, even wild animals like tigers, elk, and rabbits wait until they have the females consent. And that's the way it should be. Both parties have to agree, if we're all going to get along together. What Raul did was totally unacceptable."

Sam: "Hey, it's O.K. if we have different opinions, Rich . . . but let's at least give Raulie a chance. Just go to the meeting and say some nice things about him . . . you know, about his music, his talent . . . maybe point out some stuff about his family . . . his old man gettin' shot and all. Let 'em tack on another year or two . . . but make sure they don't ship 'im out . . . stay with us on this one, Rich."

In the days leading up to Tuesday's meeting, Richard's thoughts are flooded with conflict. If he goes, what should he say? Should he bow to Asi's demands that he share his doubts about Raul's self-control? That would certainly tip the scales in favor of shipping the boy out to a more secure prison. Or should he go along with Sam and play up his promise as a talented composer with a great future before him . . . if he can remain in a safe, nurturing environment? Or perhaps both? After all, both are true.

What of his loyalty to Tashi? Doesn't their friendship require that he speak up in her behalf . . . which would mean recommending whatever it takes to protect her against the possibility of future assault? Given her innocence in this tragedy, not to mention her unwavering devotion, that's the least she deserves. And what would she do if the roles were reversed? The answer is clear.

But there are other actors besides Tashi, Raul, and Sam in this drama. Khalique, Juan, Myron, Kato, Rajon . . . members of both the music class and the basketball team, are all counting on him to stand up for Raul, to be his voice, his representative, to argue his case as one of the few who genuinely cares for the boys and is eager to present their side of things. Who else can they turn to . . . the warden whose main responsibility is to make sure they don't run away? Certainly not the social worker who spends his time counting the days to retirement while pretending to listen to their problems. What about Pug, the baby-sitting guard who has ample opportunity to interact, but who sees the boys as little more than a convenient cover for his in-town trysts? And finally, there are the parents. Can you really expect much help from people who are embroiled in delinquencies of their own, whose brief and infrequent visits to the Center have all the hallmarks of an unpleasant duty. So, in the end, who do the boys have? They have each other. They have each other . . . and Richard.

"What difference does it make whether I go or not?" the composer asks himself, still looking for reasons not to go. "There will be plenty of people there to testify both for and against Raul. I would just muddy the water with my remarks. And what if Tashi herself is watching? Do I have the gall to stand up and argue for clemency when her eyes are on me? On the other hand, can I share my doubts about Raul's maturity when both Sam and his friends are listening? Wouldn't it be better to stay at home and leave the testifying to others?"

Throughout the day he tries working on his current piece . . . the one called Church of Sorrows. When his mind remains frozen, he pleads with his muse for help. Despite his most ardent invitation, she will not come, kept at bay by his obsessing over Tuesday's meeting. To go or not to go, that is the question, he jokes wryly, his words muffled by the cry of a soul called to choose between friends, but paralyzed by the fear of alienating the one not chosen. It is a predicament that has plagued him for years . . . tainting his childhood, adolescence and adulthood, leading ultimately to the death of his children and the end of his marriage.

He seeks comfort in food, in an extra glass of wine, in the warmth of Kwatz's body. "Can you believe it, my little friend," he whispers, holding the cat in his lap and stroking his fur. "It's all happening again . . . despite years of therapy, despite everything I have learned about the problem." In response to loud purring, he moves his fingers to Kwatz's ears. "Why does it continue to haunt me after I have relived the same trauma over and over again? Why haven't I been able to lance the boil and rid myself once and for all of its suppurating juices? I can't believe it. Here it is again, the same problem all over, the same agonizing inability to choose when a simple choice would suffice."

He shakes his head in disbelief . . . then closes his eyes. In no particular order, memories begin flooding his mind. "You weren't there when it happened, Kwatz, but I remember the day, 15 years ago, when I was nearing the end of my freshman year at Harvard. Like the other students, I had to indicate who I would like to room with the following year. Jimmy Scovel the English major and Tom Barnes who aspired to becoming an historian like his father were my roommates at the time. Both were very bright, very funny . . . and enjoyed classical music as much as I did. They were a pleasure to be around . . . but they were constantly fighting over what seemed like trivial matters . . . you know, which great author said what, to whom, and when. In short, they couldn't stand each other, but both expressed an interest in rooming with me in one of the upperclassmen houses next year. That's when the problem kicked in. I just couldn't make up my mind, afraid as I was to offend the one not chosen. In my agony, I took the coward's way out and left the preference form blank . . . and ended up spending the next year rooming with a total stranger.

He reaches for the small bag of treats on the end table. Kwatz, whose nose can detect a mouse at 100 yards, turns quickly to investigate. He snatches first one, then a second. "Still not enough?" Richard asks, opening the bag all the way.

"There were other, similar episodes, of course," he continues, "some more trivial, others more serious . . . none as serious, however, as the one involving the kids' death. You've heard about that many times, Kwatz . . . I really don't want to talk about it now. I can't. Each time the memory comes up in a nightmare or in therapy I go spiraling down into a deep depression. No music. No sleep. No peace of mind for days on end. Of course, it is never completely out of awareness, always lurking at the edge of consciousness, like a tornado hovering over a Kansas prairie, capable at any time of unleashing its lethal power on everything below. I don't want to go there; I can't afford to."

With all the treats gone, Kwatz seeks to get closer. Not content with his berth in Richard's lap, he turns to look him in the eye, then climbs up onto his shoulder and presses his body against his host's neck where he can enjoy even greater warmth. Richard smiles, then reaches over his shoulder to scratch him under the chin. The little drama is soothing enough to allow more memories into consciousness, particularly the less threatening ones that took place earlier in life. It is clear that they form a pattern, the same pattern of paralyzed will that holds him in its grip right now. No matter how many times he has sought to negate their power through understanding, they persist in haunting him; that is especially true now with the conflict between Tashi and Raul so fresh in his mind. "But," he asks, "don't those memories hold the key to greater clarity, perhaps even relief. If I want to break free of this problem, what choice do I have but to examine them all over again?"

He sighs, then runs his fingers across Kwatz's cheek. "The first sign that something was wrong appeared back in grade school. The house we lived in was across the street from the Murphy's with their long, sloping front yard. As neighbors we had access to the yard for all kinds of sports including sledding in winter and softball in summer. During the softball months, kids from around the neighborhood would gather at the bottom of the yard and choose up sides for a game. Two players were usually picked at random to start things off; they would then take turns choosing the rest of the team . . . the best players getting chosen first. As I recall, nobody else had trouble with this simple procedure. When I was picked to do the choosing, however, it was a disaster. I would look carefully at each of the kids surrounding me, study their eager faces . . . and freeze. I couldn't choose. The thought of disappointing anyone was too much. I interpreted every choice I made as a rejection of those not chosen, even though they all got picked eventually.

"Small potatoes, you say, Kwatz. I agree . . . but the problem kept reappearing as I got older. You'd think it would go away with maturity but it didn't. If anything, it got worse. I've already told you about picking roommates in college. Well, before that, it appeared in high school near the end of our senior year when we had to vote for the person Most Likely to Succeed, the Funniest, Best Looking, etc. I was convinced that both Margaret Ferguson and Ed Walsh would make it big-time in life. Margaret was both beautiful and brilliant . . . narrowly missed being valedictorian because of a lousy 85 in Physics. Ed on the other hand was a born leader, class president, president of his fraternity, captain of the basketball team, etc. I sat there at my desk for 10 minutes trying to make my mind who was more likely to succeed. In the end, rather than choose one of them, I left that part of the questionnaire blank . . . with the result that both Margaret and Ed lost by a single vote to this jock named David Stone. It didn't help to find out later that Margaret got knocked up by an Englishman right after college and gave up a career in medicine to come home and raise her new son. Ed, meanwhile, got in with some rich kids at Yale and settled for gentlemen C's instead of the A's he could have gotten. As a result, he never went on to graduate school. Last I heard he was selling insurance in Albany."

It is about this time that one of Kwatz's well-intentioned but potentially blood-letting 'love bites' to the ear brings about an abrupt halt to Richard's soliloquy. A sudden cry of pain (on the victim's part) sends his incredulous friend leaping to the floor. But not for long. All it takes is a quick scratching of the back and a welcoming pat of the thighs to restore order. Once Kwatz is back in his lap, Richard resumes stroking and talking.

"Shall I go on? I know you've heard all this before, but let's go back to the very beginning. Here's where it all began . . . at least that's what Dr. Sachar, my therapist at the time, believed. He was a clever man . . . knew how to use the incidents I just told you about as a window into the past. His technique was simple. I would be recalling something like the incident at Harvard . . . you know, the one where I had to choose my roommate for the following year. Once I got to that point where I was actually reliving the experience, he would ask me to forget any thoughts I might be having and just focus on my feelings. That's more easily said than done . . . but with practice I got pretty good at it. The feelings I got into . . . feelings of helplessness and terror . . . could then serve as a stepping stone to earlier events when I felt something similar . . . and eventually all the back to when the problem first started. After several sessions devoted to this kind of focusing, I found myself reliving a night in Vermont when I was six or seven years old.

"I awoke from my bed to the sound of angry voices. Standing at the half-opened door, I could see my mother and father facing each other in the living room. My mother's fists were clenched, her body bent forward as if she were ready to spring at my father. Her hair was all messed up and she was clutching a small vase. My father was brandishing a poker, the kind you use in the fireplace . . . his office shirt seemed to be ripped near the top. I can't remember what they said, but the sound was deafening. Mother was screaming when she threw the vase, hitting father on the shoulder. He immediately grabbed his shoulder and shouted a kind of war hoop as he charged into her with the poker. I was terrified, helpless to stop them, so afraid they would hurt each other. Here were two people I loved more than anything in the world . . . and they were fighting like they hated each other, like they wanted to kill each other. To a six-year-old who loved them both and who, as the only child, was spoiled in turn by each, it made no sense. Didn't we all love each other? Weren't we a family, a happy family? I couldn't stand it any longer.

"That's when I yelled from the doorway. Immediately they stopped fighting and turned to look at me. Father lowered his poker and told me to go back to bed. Mother held her ground and said nothing. Unable to sleep, I lay there listening as the fighting escalated. I heard my mother scream then fall to the floor. I crept back to the door and looked through the keyhole. As my father bent over her, I saw her pick up a heavy glass ashtray and drive it into his temple. There was blood everywhere. I was terrified . . . but what could I do? I closed my eyes, then crawled into my closet and curled up in a corner. When I finally woke up in the morning, everything was quiet again. I was too afraid to go out into the living room, so I waited until our neighbor Mrs. Andreas knocked on my door and came in. I was shivering as she put her arms around me. Both mother and father were gone; it was only later that I learned they were in the hospital, both badly bruised. When I visited each one in turn, I could say nothing. The words just wouldn't come. I felt the same paralysis I had felt the night before . . . the same helplessness . . . the same inability to intervene, to make things better, to choose one over the other. They must have found it strange that I said nothing. Their expressions told me that. I found it strange too.

"Nothing was said about that night in the days that followed. For me what happened, and I can thank Dr. Sachar for this insight, was that I pushed the episode off into a corner of my mind where it retained the power to assert itself whenever I found myself in a similar situation. And that's how this whole pattern began. Now, unbelievably, some twenty-eight years later, it has returned to bedevil me again. You'd think that understanding where a problem comes from would erase the fear and anxiety that lie at its roots. Isn't knowledge supposed to set you free? That was my hope when Dr. Sachar forced me (with my permission) to relive that early experience. So far anyway, it hasn't worked out like that. Here I am in my early thirties and I can still feel it . . . can still feel the nauseous cloud that comes over me when I have to choose between two people I love."

Despite his small brain and lack of language, Kwatz has a definite feeling for despair. He can smell it the way he smells mice hiding in the grass. As the twice-told tale fades into an uneasy silence, he reaches up and places his paw on Richard's cheek. His claws are retracted, his pads warm. Richard smiles in acknowledgement and runs his hand down Kwatz's back. "Thank you for listening," he whispers. "You are indeed a good friend."

19   The Insight

Tuesday's meeting goes ahead as planned. Tashi's parents are both there, along with the warden, the social worker and Pug from the Center as well as nurses from the hospital who will testify about the severity of the assault. Raul's mother has driven up from Albany to support her son. The only one of note who is missing is Richard. When it is clear that he's not coming, Asadour turns to Esther and says, "Where the hell is he? I told him that it was important to be here." By the end of the meeting, with Richard still missing, his tone darkens. "How could he do this to us? I think it's time to cut ties with this guy altogether." Esther nods her head in agreement.

Back home, they waste no time giving Tashi the bad news: Richard has let them down by not coming to the hearing. Asadour is quick to embellish the facts. (*Turning to Eleanor, with lips trembling*) "The guy's a phony. If he really cared about you, he would've come. He knew this Raul kid better than anyone else. He knew damn well that he couldn't be trusted outside the prison. So why the hell didn't he come to the hearing and say it?"

Esther (*nervously*): "Asi. Please watch your language."

To an observer not easily taken in by all the ranting and raving, it is clear that Asadour welcomes this turn of events since it gives him license to forbid any further contact between Richard and his daughter. With an eagerness that belies his indignation, he lays out his plan carefully: from now on there will be no more practice sessions, no more Saturday concerts, no walks together, no canoe trips, no swimming nude in the brook . . . in other words, no more contact of any kind. Once assured that he has Esther's unwavering support, he prepares to lay down the law.

Tashi is still reeling from the news about Richard's absence when her parents approach her in the living room. She finds it difficult, even impossible, to believe that he would not take this small step to support her. Why not? As her parents stare, she drops to the couch and covers her face with her hands. By pressing her flesh, she manages to hold the sobbing in check. Even in the darkness, however, there is no escape. She can hear her father's footsteps as he approaches the couch, his gloating all too apparent in the rapidity of his breathing. As his towering shadow falls across her crumpled frame, she girds herself for the words to come.

Asadour (*sternly*): "I told you so. I told you what I thought of this guy, but you wouldn't listen. He's way too old for you; his wife left him and he's mixed up with the death of his children. And now he deserts you out of loyalty to what . . . to a convicted hoodlum. Why the hell didn't you listen to me? Don't you think I know anything?"

Esther: "Asi, please."

As Father stands over her, his warty shape blocking the day's last light, his eyes ravished with malicious satisfaction, Tashi withdraws into the privacy of her thoughts. "Why didn't he come? He must have known how much it meant to me. It must be his attachment to Raul . . . but why didn't he testify in Raul's behalf? None of it makes any sense. Was I wrong in guessing that he was falling in love with me? What about that tearful goodbye at the door last August when he broke down and admitted how much he cared? That can't be faked, can it? Yes, I had to pull it out of him, but isn't that because of the divorce and his fear of being rejected again? When I went to bed that night, I was convinced that time would heal everything. Now I'm not so sure. Was I being naïve? Did I misread his feelings?"

Over the next few weeks, confusion gives way to withdrawal. Without any deliberate action, indeed without her even knowing it, she begins to question her love. Up to now she has built her whole future on the expectation of being with Richard . . . as his partner, ultimately his wife. As the doubts mount, those expectations begin to shake, then crumble. Despite pleadings from both parents, pleadings to stay active, do things with friends and go places, she remains curled up in her bed reading. Even here she is drawn to romantic tales with a tragic ending. With Hardy's Tess of the D'Urbervilles fresh in mind, she reflects, "I am not alone. I am not the only one to gain and then lose a noble love," thereby affirming the psychological if paradoxical truism that there is solace to be found in the suffering of others.

It is around this time that Richard heads to the Correctional Center for his weekly music class. No one shows up, not Sam, not Juan, not Raul. The computers and synthesizers are already covered with dust. When he inquires, he is told that Raul has been transferred to the medium security facility in Utica, New York where he will stay until he turns 18 next year. He will then have a hearing and, depending on circumstances, may be transferred to a maximum-security prison, most likely Attica since it is the closest to his mother's home in Albany.

The rest of the summer passes without his seeing either Tashi or the boys in the music class. When he realizes that, as far as the boys are concerned, he is persona non grata at the Center, he gives up the idea of coaching the basketball team again. The only thing left is his Saturday night gig at the restaurant, now once again a solo affair. Back home, the Church of Sorrows becomes the centerpiece of his daily life. But there is a difference. Whereas he previously saw the piece as a way of capturing the pain of others, he now sees it as a vehicle for the expression of his own. Day after day as he sits at the piano, playing and replaying the hymn, he is reminded that he has a problem that will not go away . . . a problem that has now alienated him from the two people he cares most about in the world. Hundreds of hours of therapy have not helped; at 34 he is still at the mercy of an event that traumatized him when he was six, an event that is now etched into his very psyche, beyond erasing, beyond forgetting. As he picks out the notes of the hymn, a disheartening conclusion forces its way into consciousness, "There's no escape; I'm doomed to do the same thing over and over again. No matter how hard I try, I cannot hide from the shadow of the past." He drops his hands into his lap, then looks out the window. "The only answer is to avoid getting close to people . . . just accept the fact that I am better off going it alone. No one will get hurt that way . . . neither me nor anyone else." In the ensuing silence, Kwatz, sensing that something is amiss, comes out from under the piano and jumps into his lap. The purring starts immediately.

Back in Boston, Tashi starts a new life without Richard; that means a life without the anticipation of cello/piano duets, canoe trips on the lake or Saturday night dinners over candlelight. Most painfully, it is a life without an object for her precocious capacity for love. From now on, it's back to the way things used to be before she knocked on his door three summers ago. There is one exception, however; to her friends, she is now Tashi, despite the fact that her parents continue to call her Eleanor.

While she flirts with depression, the demands of school work keep her from collapsing into the abyss of hopelessness. As a senior she is confronted with the consuming task of applying to college. Besides writing essays justifying her worthiness and explaining why she wants to go to a particular college, she has to show up for interviews. While tedious and draining, the whole process serves as a welcome distraction from her ongoing grief.

Asadour and Esther are particularly pleased when she accepts an invitation to go dancing with a classmate. Their hope that the infatuation with Richard is over and she is now receptive to boys her own age is dashed when she comes home in tears, insisting that her dancing partner tried to mount her in the car. Beneath the apparent return to normalcy, the depression lingers. The loss, so devastating to one who has never loved so deeply, is simply too great to digest in a matter of months. Sometimes she wakes from a dream with an overwhelming desire to call him, to ask him why he didn't show up at the hearing. The questions continue to haunt her: "Do you still love me? Did you ever love me? Was your loyalty to Raul stronger than your love for me? Couldn't you have told the judge about Raul's lack of self-control while still pleading for leniency? Why did you stay away? Are you aware how much you hurt me?"

Her grades suffer, but she still gets accepted at Harvard. As the year winds down, she withdraws increasingly into books and music. To all but the most casual observers her pallid cheeks tell of a grief that remains unresolved. In December her seventeenth birthday comes and goes, evoking memories of the previous year when Richard gave her the Beethoven sonatas. Against her will she plays the CD's over and over in her bedroom, weeping at the associations they bring to mind.

As the months pass, it is e-mails to Bapu that provide the sole outlet for her feelings. She holds back nothing, neither the grief nor the disappointment. Her posts are filled with questions for which she has no answers. Despite hours, even days of anguished pondering, Richard's absence at the hearing remains a mystery. What does it say about his feelings; what does it say about his capacity for love?

Bapu's response is surprisingly critical of Richard, especially in light of his previous plea for patience and understanding. Where before he saw wariness and distrust on the composer's part, he now sees weakness and an unwillingness to deal with difficult situations. Raul is the center of his concern. In one e-mail he argues that while Richard understandably wanted to avoid saying things that would get Raul transferred to a higher security prison, he could have recommended keeping him here with stricter safeguards while stressing his potential for a productive life as composer. Later in the e-mail he asks, "Did he stay away because he was afraid of disappointing you and your parents or was he mainly concerned about the boys at the Center?" In conclusion he writes, "He was obviously caught between the two sides . . . but it is strange that he resolved the dilemma by staying home and saying nothing. To me this suggests weakness . . . even cowardice . . . which is confusing because he seemed to be stronger than that when I met him." At the end he adds, "Sorry I'm not being of much help here."

In his next e-mail, he takes an entirely different tack. "How about a trip to Europe next summer . . . a graduation present . . . with all expenses paid? We can visit London, Paris, Berlin, Rome . . . wherever you want to go."

Tashi writes back: "That's a wonderful idea . . . I would love it . . . but Daddy is already talking about a trip to the Middle East to visit some ancestral family sites in Palestine and Jordan. Can I take a rain check . . . perhaps for the following summer? Your European trip sounds much more exciting than the Middle East."

During the summer following high school graduation she travels to Palestine with her parents. As expected . . . and feared . . . the trip turns into a long, unrelenting lecture from her father . . . some of it interesting (like a visit to the town where he grew up) . . . but most of it tedious. She is relieved to be home when they return to Boston in late August.

In the fall Tashi enters college and decides to major in music . . . specializing in either performance or composition. With Bapu's encouragement she adds courses in fine arts, literature, psychology and world history. Her exposure to new fields helps to keep thoughts about Richard in the background although certain kinds of music rekindle painful memories, piano-cello duets in particular.

Throughout her freshman year she stays in touch with Bapu through e-mails and phone calls. Finally, June arrives and with it the promised European trip. Their first stop is in London where they start with the museums; later they visit Elgar's home and attend an all-English concert in Prince Albert Hall where they are treated to a performance of the Enigma Variations plus works by Vaughan Williams. With music still ringing in their ears, they drive out to the Lake district to see where Wordsworth lived and wrote. At every step along the way . . . whether looking at paintings or listening to music in London or thrilling to nature's beauties in England's unspoiled back country, they are reminded how compatible they are. For Tashi who has spent so much of the year alone, wrapped in a cloud of lingering grief, this is a welcome blessing. Although he is less open about it, Bapu is equally grateful for the company.

From Britain it is on to Paris and Rome with a two day stop-over in Florence where they divide their time between the Uffizi and a sampling of cafes along the Arno. A rented convertible takes them all the way south to Sicily. Toward the end of the trip, they drive up through Venice and into Switzerland and Germany, stopping finally in Stuttgart where Bapu spots a poster advertising a concert scheduled for that very evening. "It looks like the Stuttgart Philharmonic is playing mostly American works . . . all conducted by the new sensation, Gretchen Rudolf. Sounds interesting. You want to go?" Tashi's nods her enthusiastic agreement. After a dinner of sauerbraten, brat kartoffeln and a local Riesling, they head for the concert hall and an evening of classical music.

Once in their seats, Tashi opens the program to see if she is familiar with any of the works to be played. She runs her fingers down the list . . . "Bernstein, Rochberg, Copland and . . . Oh my God," she shouts, drawing scowls from the couple to her left, "It's Richard . . . (*pause*) . . . I can't believe it . . . they're going to play his Iglesia de los Dolores . . . the piece based on a hymn he heard in Mexico."

Bapu picks up his own program and scans the list. "Yes, I see it. Richard Dunwoody . . . that's your Richard, right?"

Tashi: "Well, I wouldn't exactly call him *my* Richard after what happened in Saranac. But yes, he's the one I played duets with at the restaurant."

Bapu: "The one you used to be so enamored of."

Tashi *(softly)*: "Yes."

The lights dim as the conductor enters to widespread applause. Ms. Rudolf is one of the few female conductors to be given a permanent assignment to a large, well-known orchestra like this one. Her stride to the podium suggests a combination of confidence and grace; when she turns to bow, her beauty is apparent even from the mezzanine seats. Bernstein's Candide is the first number to be played. Bapu is about to whisper something when he realizes Tashi is not listening. He pulls his head back, not wanting to intrude on whatever memories or fantasies might be swirling around inside of her.

For Tashi, what is happening on stage cannot compete with the drama unfolding internally. The first two pieces slip by unnoticed as she relives the scene at Richard's cottage when he first played the Oaxaca hymn for her. That was the afternoon when he massaged her shoulder, the one she hurt playing field hockey at school. When she closes her eyes, she can feel his strong hand on her neck. In the privacy of her imagination, she reaches up and pulls it down to her chest, then onto her breast. He is shy, reticent about touching her so intimately. His shyness excites her . . . perhaps it is his innocence . . . a reserve that gains her trust and makes it safe for her to be bold. She turns her head, offering her lips, her eyes begging for a kiss.

Her reverie is broken by thunderous applause. She looks up to see Ms. Rudolf bowing to the audience. Bapu is clapping, but says nothing. As the applause fades, Tashi turns and asks, "Which piece was that?" "Copland's Appalachian Spring," he answers with a twinkle, adding "May I ask where you've been?" "No, you may not" comes the immediate response. She glances again at the program . . . then rubs her eyes open when she sees that Iglesia de los Dolores is next.

The part she is familiar with . . . the Oaxaca hymn . . . does not appear until the third movement. Well before that time, however, Richard's style is recognizable in the way he builds the orchestra to a climax only to stop short of a final resolution. As the piece unfolds, she begins to feel some of the same uneasiness she felt on the very first day they met at his cottage. Like the piece he played for her that day, this one seems to toy with the listener's emotions . . . stirring up long-hidden desires and fears without offering any kind of release. By the time the symphony reaches the third movement, the one with the hymn, the tension is palpable. She senses it not only in herself, but in the faces of people in the row just ahead of her. It is as if the music were undecided what to do with all the feelings it has aroused and in its confusion, retreats from the brink, withdrawing into quietude. "What is the music saying," she murmurs, "What is it *really* saying?"

She leans forward now, elbows on her thighs, determined to penetrate its mystery. To concentrate better on the sound, she closes her eyes. Note by note she follows the hymn, first carried by the violins, now picked up and varied by the clarinets and oboes. Trumpets, trombones and French horns follow, offering a theme separate from either the strings or woodwinds. The back-and-forth counterpoint is complex and hard to follow . . . but dramatic in the tension it creates. Skillfully the composer alternates the themes, letting one dominate, then the other. Surely, he will bring them together before the movement ends; it will be maddening if he fails to do so. The hymn is repeated over and over, each time in a different form. Sometimes the key is changed, at other times it is the rhythm; even the harmony undergoes its own transformations.

As the orchestra builds toward a climax, Tashi opens her eyes to watch Ms. Rudolf. She sees her arms outstretched, her hands pleading for more sound. The conductor grips her baton with a new urgency. She knows the score; she has practiced this piece before; the intensity of her movements is a clear sign that a climax is coming. By now everyone in the concert hall is prepared for it. For measure after measure, they have listened to the torturous build-up of tension as the two main themes . . . one in the strings and woodwinds, the other in the brass . . . battle for supremacy. Now they crave release. Nothing less than a final, transcendent catharsis in which one of the themes is allowed to win or the two are woven into a single, unified voice will satisfy.

But no. As it approaches the summit . . . the point where all tensions beg to be discharged in a final explosion of sound . . . the music pulls back. The violins, clarinets and oboes grow soft; the trumpets and horns stop playing altogether. The conductor raises her arms, as if reaching for notes that are not there . . . then lets them fall in reluctant acceptance of what the composer has written. A soft, barely audible moan fills the concert hall.

Tashi grabs Bapu by the wrist and squeezes. "Oh my God," she gasps. "Of course, of course."

"Of course what?" Bapu asks, as the movement fades into silence.

Tashi: "Why he didn't come to the hearing. The answer is in his music. Don't you see?"

Bapu: "Enlighten me, please."

Tashi (*turning to face Bapu*): "What did you think of that ending . . . the ending to the third movement?

Bapu: "A bit disappointing I would say."

Tashi: "Just a bit?"

Bapu: "Well, O.K. *Very* disappointing . . . but the rest of the piece was gorgeous."

The fourth movement begins with a flourish from the cellos and basses. Tashi waits until the music grows louder before turning to Bapu.

Tashi (*whispering*): "Disappointing in what way?"

Bapu: "Well, the piece seemed to be heading for some kind of resolution, then backed down . . . leaving us all hanging. The long build-up was quite dramatic, but I don't understand why he didn't carry through with it . . . you know, to some kind of conclusion. It felt a little like I was being teased."

Tashi: "My reaction was pretty much the same . . . although I don't think I felt teased. It felt more like . . . I'm not quite sure how to put it . . . frustrated definitely . . . maybe even a little angry"

Bapu: "Angry?"

Tashi: "Well, angry and disappointed . . . disappointed that he couldn't decide what to do with the different themes he had introduced. Those were the first feelings to come up. But after a while something new emerged. A new kind of feeling."

Bapu (*smiling*): "You started to feel sorry for him."

Tashi (*softly*): "Yes. But it's more than that. I think I began to understand why he couldn't testify at the hearing. There's something blocking him from making a decision. I know this sounds a bit crazy . . . but composers express their personalities in what they write, don't they? Here in the music, it's not a matter of deciding . . . more like choosing . . . choosing between the themes that he was playing with . . . letting one rise to the top at the end of the movement. But he couldn't do it. He backed down at the last minute and left the audience hanging, just as you said."

Bapu: "So, you're saying that he's got a problem making up his mind."

Tashi (quickly): "Yes. That's one way of putting it. He can't choose. When confronted with a choice, he gets frozen. It shows up in his music just like it does in the rest of his life. The two are connected. He's got this mental block and it keeps him from making choices when the situation demands one. What we just heard in that last movement is similar to what happened back in Saranac."

Bapu (*wryly*): "Which means what . . . that we should excuse him for not testifying because . . . because he has an emotional problem?"

Tashi: "Something like that. It must be really painful. Just think what he must have gone through when he was working on this piece. After presenting the original hymn, then developing it in all kinds of skillful ways, he comes to the place where some kind of climax is called for and . . . what happens? . . . he stops, freezes, then pulls back. For us listeners, it's really frustrating . . . all that interweaving of conflicting themes . . . all that build-up of tension and then no resolution. Well, if we find it frustrating, don't you think it's true for him too?"

Bapu: "Perhaps. I don't know. Right now, I'm more interested in what's happening to you. It certainly sounds like this insight of yours is bringing back some of your old feelings toward Richard. For one thing, you seem much more sympathetic than you were before . . . sympathetic and forgiving. So, . . . what are you going to do?"

Tashi *(shaking her head)*: "I don't know. It's too early to tell. Maybe nothing . . . but I might write to him . . . let him know that I understand why he never showed up at the hearing. I should think that would ease some of his pain, don't you?"

Bapu: "Well, yes, assuming that he feels guilty about not coming."

Tashi: "From what I know about Richard, my guess is that he's feeling a lot of guilt . . . (*pause*) . . . and there's no one he can talk to about it."

Bapu: "I sense a letter coming."

Tashi: "Perhaps."

The fourth and final movement comes to an end. It's only intermission, but Tashi's silence suggests a lack of interest in staying for the second half of the concert. Bapu asks, "Do you want to leave now? We can grab a pastry and tea at the café across the street . . . and then head for our hotel. Our flight back to London is an early one . . . so a little extra sleep might help."

Tashi: "That sounds good to me. Let's go."

Back in Cambridge it is with some relief that she returns to her studies. Her sophomore year brings further discoveries . . . first poetry then philosophy. At her roommate's suggestion she takes a course in the philosophy of aesthetics; despite voluminous readings in Aristotle,

Nietzsche, James and Dewey, she finishes the course without any clear idea of what constitutes beauty, but still enjoys all the theorizing about it. Thanks to a year-long course on the history of music from medieval chants to the atonal compositions of Schoenberg and his followers, her love for the classics deepens. There is no doubt now that in one form or another, music is to be the center of her life. In addition to weekly lessons, she starts playing in small ensembles with her fellow students, sometimes as part of a string quartet, sometimes as the cellist in a piano/cello duet. As her technical skills improve, she finds herself wishing she could show Richard how much she has learned. "He is a trained musician himself," she reflects, "and would appreciate how much progress I have made." Such thoughts serve to remind her that he is far from forgotten . . . not that she needs any reminders. In some part of her psyche, she is aware that her love is very much alive and eager to be reignited, but temporarily suppressed by concern over his failure to testify at the hearing. The thought of writing to him . . . to talk about the Stuttgart concert in particular . . . is never far from awareness, but is pushed aside in the rush to read new books, to master new courses, to ponder new ideas.

All that is changed by a phone call on her birthday. "Hello," she says, expecting to hear her mother's voice. There is no response. Silence. She tries again, "Hello," she repeats, this time with greater urgency. There is a sound . . . undecipherable at first . . . certainly not a human voice . . . more like . . . yes . . . a cat purring. Her breathing stops as the words form on her lips, "Richard . . . is it you?" Before she can speak, there is a click and the phone goes dead. Convinced that it was indeed Richard, eager to hear her voice, but not ready to talk, she puts her books aside and pulls out pen and paper. As she sits at her desk mulling over what she wants to say, a brilliant idea arises.

Dear Richard,

I thought a lot about you last summer when my grandfather and I heard your Church of Sorrows piece performed in Stuttgart (actually I've never stopped thinking about you). You could tell from the loud clapping afterwards that everyone in the audience found it beautiful. I know I did. You really captured the suffering of the Mexican people, especially in the third movement, the one based on the Oaxacan hymn.

It was that same movement that opened my eyes as to why you couldn't show up at the judge's hearing several summers ago. You didn't want to hurt Raul and you didn't want to hurt me . . . so you stayed away. I could hear the same ambivalence in your music . . . two themes weaving contrapuntally . . . both treated with loving care . . . but neither one allowed to predominate. So, instead of a rousing conclusion where one theme triumphs over the other, you pull back . . . stay away so to speak . . . with the result that the piece has no real ending. I don't mean to be critical Richard . . . the piece as a whole is lovely . . . I'm just trying to say that I heard something in your music that sounded familiar. It has helped me to understand your behavior . . . and to forgive you for it. I'm not angry like I used to be . . . not even disappointed. More than anything, I am aware how painful the whole hearing episode must have been for you. I just wish I had figured this out earlier and been more supportive.

Enough of my psychologizing.

I have an idea. Next year I'm supposed to give a junior recital . . . it's required of all music performance majors. Do you remember my earlier suggestion that some of your cello/piano duets might be turned into a cello concerto? You said at the time that it would take months to make that happen . . . months you couldn't afford to take away from your other work. Well, perhaps you have the time now. If you do, I can provide the orchestra . . . the Harvard-Radcliffe Orchestra . . . and of course the cello soloist . . . namely, yours truly. So, do you have any interest in writing such a concerto and letting me play it for my recital next year?

Love,

Tashi

P.S. I will be coming to Saranac in June and would love to resume our duets at the restaurant. My parents will no doubt frown on this, but I am old enough now (19 going on 20) to make up my own mind.

Richard's response comes quickly.

Dear Tashi,

Thanks for the kind words about my Church of Sorrows piece. You're quite right about the ending . . . seems like I run into the same problem whatever I do. I've given it a lot of thought over the years . . . but still don't know how to resolve it. As you surmised, my not going to the hearing caused everybody a lot of grief. What hurt me most was letting you down. The boys at the Center were pretty disappointed too . . . especially Raul who got transferred to the medium-security facility in Utica. I guess nobody won.

It would have been quite a surprise if I had been at the Stuttgart concert and seen you there. It almost happened. The orchestra invited me to come over for the performance (all expenses paid), but I had too much work going on back here.

About the concerto, I would be very happy to give it a try. Just tell me when the first rehearsal is going to be and I'll plan accordingly. May I assume that you're playing is even better than it used to be . . . so I can put in some fast, virtuosic passages suitable for a real concerto?

By the way, I called you in December to wish you a happy birthday, but hung up instead when I couldn't decide what to say. Don't know if you could hear Kwatz purring . . . he was in my lap when I called.

Love, Richard

To Tashi, Richard's willingness to write the proposed cello concerto is almost as pleasing as the way he signs his letter. He has never closed his note that way before, suggesting at the very least that he misses her, perhaps even more. Together with the phone call on her birthday, his letter points to a new opening on his part, brought on presumably by the long separation.

She is quick to respond.

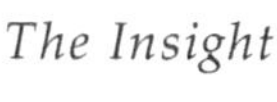

Dear Richard,

I'm so happy to hear that you're willing to write the concerto. From all that I know about your music, I have no doubt that it will be a tremendous success. Perhaps we can work on it together this summer when I come to Saranac. That idea pleases me very much.

I thought it was you calling on my birthday . . . Kwatz's purring gave you away. That was really thoughtful of you . . . I had been thinking of you a lot anyway . . . just wish you had been willing to talk . . . but I understand.

You mentioned in your e-mail that Raul is still at the medium-security prison in Utica. I'm relieved that he hasn't been transferred to Attica, but it bothers me to think that he may be going there soon. From what I read in the papers, young boys don't do well there. He may not even survive . . . unless some older, stronger inmate takes him under his wing . . . and that probably means becoming the other man's sexual toy. So, what can we do to keep all that from happening?

Love, Tashi

Dear Tashi,

I failed to mention in my last note that I have been out to Utica to see Raul twice now . . . and he is doing fine. The Saranac judge, who turned out to be a lot more understanding than I realized, stipulated in the transfer order that Raul be allowed to serve the rest of his time in Utica . . . including the three years that they added to his sentence for what he did to you. If he gets into any kind of trouble there, then it's Attica. If he behaves, he could get out on probation two years from now. So, he still has a chance.

Aside from his mother I'm apparently the only one who has visited him, a fact that has increased his trust in me to the point where he has really opened up . . . all the way . . . telling me things about his past that I never knew before. And what a past it is, Tash, sordid beyond belief . . . involving sexual liaisons with his mother's best friend and, if you can believe this, with his mother herself. I've come away with a much better understanding of why he's had so much trouble controlling his sex drive . . . as evidenced by the way he acted toward the girl he calls Hippo and then later toward you. I've already had one chat with his counselor, a uniquely compassionate man, in which we discussed ways to get him the kind of therapy he needs. We're agreed that there's still time to turn his life around before he gets thrown to the wolves in Attica. If I hear any more, I'll keep you posted.

Love, Richard

The e-mail has a riveting effect on Tashi. In the past two years her feelings toward Raul have changed significantly. Rage toward her youthful attacker has long since given way to concern over what will happen to him as he approaches adulthood and faces the prospect of transfer to an adult prison. While Richard's latest letter brings renewed anxiety, it also helps to crystallize her thinking. Within days, she replies.

Dear Richard,

That is so reassuring to learn that Raul can stay in Utica for the rest of his sentence . . . as long as he behaves. I think it's up to us now to give him reason to behave himself and get out early. Tell me what you think of this idea: I can write to that judge you mentioned and tell him that I not only forgive Raul for what he did to me, but make a case for letting him out early so he can attend music school. Do you think that would help? I'm also thinking that maybe the Berklee School of Music in Boston could start training him even when he's in prison . . . you know, online or through the mail? I would be happy to inquire at their front office if you want me to.

So nice to be talking to you again, Richard

Love, Tashi

Dear Tashi,

I like your idea . . . about Berklee's offering some kind of course to Raul while he's still in Utica. Fortunately, they do have a small music studio there in the prison . . . much nicer than what we had at the Correctional Center . . . so he does have an opportunity to work on his composing. And I have offered to critique any pieces he sends me . . . so, you can tell the people at Berklee that he is getting some help now but could use a lot more. And remind them that I am willing to pick up the tab for any of his expenses not covered by scholarship.

I admire you for your willingness to forgive Raul for what he did . . . makes you even more lovable . . . if that's possible. I think a letter to the judge explaining not only that you forgive your attacker, but telling him why you think Raul should be given a chance to prove himself could be very convincing. If I add my own letter . . . detailing what I know about Raul's past (without divulging too many confidences), the judge might see his way to reducing his sentence . . . or even transferring him to a minimum security facility near Boston where he could attend music classes at Berklee.

Missing you, Richard

20   The Revelation

Tashi arrives at the restaurant in her own car, a used Plymouth convertible given to her by Bapu on her last birthday. From the door, Richard watches with a mixture of curiosity and apprehension. While his discomfort at Thursday's practice session disappeared quickly in a flurry of hugs and kisses, he is still not sure how he feels toward her. More mysterious still, after three years of separation, is how she feels toward him.

His confidence starts to return as they take up their customary places at the bandstand. As in the past, he opens the evening with a piano solo, this time a Bach partita carefully chosen to display his technical virtuosity while avoiding the suggestion of anything romantic. The applause is polite, at best.

Sisyphus, the very first duet they ever played together, is scheduled next. When Tashi rises to announce the piece, she is greeted with thunderous applause. A few of the patrons, those who come to dine every Saturday night, remember hearing her play five years ago when she was only fourteen and in middle school. For them, her return after a long absence is an unanticipated gift. As manager, Tim has gone out of his way to advertise the event, thereby guaranteeing a full house for the evening.

Richard places the Sisyphus score in front of him, but having played it so many times in the past, rarely looks up. While his fingers find their way instinctively up and down the keyboard, his eyes remain fixed on the young woman at his side. With her attention focused on the notes in front of her, he feels free to study her every feature. The black, wavy hair that frames her pale face and graces her slender neck is still there, but she is taller now, her shoulders broader and more alluring in their nakedness. When she lifts her bow, leaning back to pause between phrases, her breasts heave in synchrony with her breathing. They are no longer the newly-awakened protuberances of youth . . . but the ripe, life-giving fruit of an adult woman. Her arms, hips and legs, once scrawny extensions of a frame favoring bone over flesh, radiate a voluptuousness graced by the black, strapless gown that falls to just below her knees.

Even without looking, she can feel his eyes upon her.

When she turns to smile at him, it is a delicious smile made sweeter by the knowledge that he is stunned by how beautiful she has become since they last saw each other. "Three years is a long time," he comments between pieces, eager to be talking. His voice is diffident, nervous . . . unable to mask the unease he feels as he faces her. At the root of his discomfort is the intersection of two disparate feelings . . . lingering guilt for failing to support her at the hearing and awe at her new attractiveness. Under ordinary circumstances either one alone would be enough to tie his tongue; together they threaten to bring him to his knees. He is saved only when she leans over to say how pleased she is to be back in the restaurant playing for an enthusiastic audience. He responds quickly by praising her new skills: "Your articulation is so much cleaner now Tash; you're better at bringing out the beauty of each note. I can tell that you've had some good teachers at Harvard."

Tashi: "Thanks. What's helped the most is not the individual lessons I got, but the skills I picked up in my ensemble playing. I'm not sure if you can tell, but when I play in a small group, I'm a lot more aware now of what the other instruments are doing. I can see it happening tonight too. In the past when we've played together, I've concentrated almost exclusively on my own playing . . . with the expectation that you'll somehow blend your part into mine. In the piece we just played it was different. I heard every one of your notes and adjusted my playing accordingly. I'm not sure the audience can hear the difference but it's much more of a duet now . . . rather than a cello solo with piano accompaniment."

Richard: "I heard the difference and you're right. We just played a real duet . . . and my guess is that a few people out there in the audience picked up on it. For my part, it makes this little gig of ours even more pleasurable than it used to be . . . (*pause*) . . . By the way, I have some sketches for your cello concerto at my place . . . at least for the first two movements. You might want to stop by later in the week and tell me what you think."

His words touch her deeply . . . not so much by their content as by their sound. It is his reticence, his gentleness, the pain so obvious behind his show of support that moves her. She has all she can do to refrain from taking him in her arms and whispering, "It's alright darling. I understand." By the end of the evening all misgivings of the past three years have dropped away, revealing a familiar but never-fully-expressed need for closeness . . . a longing for intimacy brought to maturity now by the forces of time, age, grief and disappointment.

"I can do it any day that's good for you, Richard. Perhaps we can combine it with a walk to the meadow, the one just above your cottage. I haven't forgotten our last visit there . . . (*softly*) . . . have you?"

Richard: "You mean the time a bug bit my leg and I jolted you onto the grass?"

Tashi (*laughing*): I prefer to think of it as the place where I lay in your lap as you combed my hair with your fingers."

Richard (*blushing*): "Shall we bring our lunch? There's a shady spot under that old hickory . . . you know, where the meadow drops off into the valley. That might make a nice place to sit and eat."

Tashi: "I would love it."

Richard: "And on the way back, we can stop at my place to look over sketches for the cello concerto."

Tashi: "So when is a good day for you?"

Richard: "Let's make it Thursday . . . around noon?"

Tashi: "That's fine. I'll bring a little something for dessert."

Richard: "Nice. See you in the meadow."

Thursday morning turns out to be cloudy with a threat of rain. Undeterred, Tashi goes about preparing her lunch as soon as the breakfast dishes are cleaned and put away. To her sandwich, chips and peach she adds two sections from a raspberry tart baked last night. At the side of each portion, she places a small piece of chocolate, reminiscent of a dessert from the 23 course Tibetan dinner she prepared years ago. To be on the safe side, she decides to take a small umbrella in case the forecasters are right.

Richard delays his preparations until the last minute. Tashi's recent comments about his music . . . particularly what she said in her letter about the Stuttgart piece . . . leave him confused. As the morning draws to a close, he sits at the piano pondering her opinion that the work, particularly the third movement, never resolves the conflicts it so meticulously explores. Is she right . . . that instead of carrying the listener to a climax where all the emotion is released in a final burst of sound, the music falls back into a quietude which leaves everyone hanging? This is not the first time he has gotten such feedback. After all, Tashi reacted similarly to the piece he played for her on the very first day they met. A few of the diners at the restaurant have also said things that suggest a similar kind of disappointment in the way his pieces end.

He holds the score in his hand now, trying to grasp what this feedback means. "How does one go about ending a piece decisively? Why can't I see it?" Turning to the end of the third movement, he summarizes what he sees, "There are two separate themes at work here and the struggle between them is what gives the movement its power. This much is clear. Yet one of these themes is supposed to prevail at the end. Is this what she is saying? Or is she saying that I should bring them together . . . to somehow fuse them into a single voice that captures the essence of each?" Frustrated by his inability to come up with a solution, he rises and goes into the kitchen where he throws together two pieces of cold pizza, a pickle and a bottle of soda. Slinging the backpack over his shoulder, he heads out the door and up the trail to the meadow.

As he comes out of the woods into the meadow, he spots Tashi over on the other side sitting under the hickory tree. From fifty yards away he can see that she is dressed in tan shorts and a white blouse . . . with a Red Sox baseball cap holding her hair in place. She has a book in her hands and is munching on something.

Richard: "So, what are you reading?" he asks as he approaches.

Tashi (*turning and smiling*): "Hi . . . it's an old book . . . well, I mean it was written a long time ago . . . Moll Flanders. Ever read it?"

Richard (*sitting down next to her*): "Nope. Missed that one. What's it about?"

Tashi: "It's a sad tale about a woman who loses husband after husband and is forced to survive as a single woman in male-dominated 17th C. London."

Richard (*smiling*): "And how does she do it?"

Tashi: "She becomes a thief . . . a very accomplished one."

Richard (*chuckling*): "I guess things have improved over the years. It's much easier for single women to survive today . . . right?"

Tashi: "Of course. You can be single now if you want to . . . but you'll still miss a lot if you decide to go it alone."

Richard (*smiling*): "You're referring to the advantages of filing a joint tax return?"

Tashi (*laughing*): "Something like that."

The banter continues as the sun reaches its noon-day peak. With the summer solstice coming soon, the meadow lies bathed in life-giving light. Forget-me-nots and wild lupine luxuriate in its warmth while blue flox gather their energy for the blooming ahead. From high in the tree, a raven calls to its mate in the woods, then spreads it massive wings and leaps from an overhead branch with a raucous cry . . . AWWK!

It is at this point that the conversation turns serious.

Richard: "I don't think I've ever apologized to you for not showing up at the evidentiary hearing. It was unforgivable I know. I agonized over it for months afterwards. What hurt most was knowing how much I had let you down. You must have been surprised and terribly disappointed when you heard that I hadn't come . . . (*pause*) . . . after being such good friends for two years. What amazes me is that you still want to get together . . . for duets at the restaurant . . . and now here for a picnic lunch. It's all a mystery to me."

Tashi: "Yes, I was hurt and disappointed at first . . . before I put the whole episode into perspective. I think I understand you better now. At least that's my hope . . . (*pause*) . . . but thank you for the apology."

Richard takes off his backpack and spreads its meager contents onto the grass. He is aware of a new warmth in his chest . . . a warmth mixed with an unknown fear. Tashi picks up on it immediately.

Tashi: "The music didn't go well this morning?"

Richard: "True. I found myself going over and over your comments about the Iglesia piece. For the life of me I . . . "

Tashi: "Oh, I' m sorry . . . I didn't . . . "

Richard: "No . . . I think you're absolutely right. It's just that I can't figure out how to fix the problem."

Tashi: "Do you think it's a technical problem . . . something strictly musical . . . or part of something bigger?"

Richard: "You mean like a psychological problem?"

Tashi: "Yes. That would be my guess. At least that's what occurred to me in Stuttgart as I was listening to the Church of Sorrows . . . (*pause*) . . . I think it all goes together . . . your difficulty in ending a piece of music and the trouble you have choosing between alternatives, like at the hearing . . . (*pause*) . . . but what do you think, Richard?"

Richard: "I don't know what to think. All I'm sure of is that I've had the same problem all my life . . . unable to make up my mind, unable to act decisively at critical times . . . and now, you're saying that you can hear it in my music as well. Whew! I'm beginning to feel like a basket case . . . (*pause*) . . . Next thing you know someone is going to say he can see it in my face or in the way I walk or in the way I brush my teeth."

Tashi: "I *can* see it in your face, Richard. And it makes me sad."

Richard: "Really? What do you see?"

Tashi: "Come closer (*taking his face between her hands*). It's a kind face, a handsome face. It is also the face of a little boy startled by what he sees, unable to make sense of something. Your eyes have a questioning look. They seem bewildered, drawn inward . . . reluctant to confront what stands before you . . . (*shaking her head*) . . . I don't know whether that makes any sense."

Richard: "It does . . . more than you realize (*sighing*). I'm amazed that after so many years that look is still there. I have my therapist, Dr. Sachar, to thank for helping me to remember how it all started. When I was six years old, I woke up one night to find my parents, both of whom I adored, fighting in the living room. It wasn't any old argument . . . but, as I remember it, a lethal, screaming fight to the finish involving fireplace pokers and glass ashtrays. Both ended up in the hospital with wounds that took weeks to heal. Watching from my bedroom, I was paralyzed with fear . . . unable to speak, even to cry. Apparently, that experience was etched indelibly into my brain and triggered a whole series of responses over the years where I found myself similarly unable to act, leading eventually to the event that changed my life forever."

Tashi (*softly*): "Your children?"

Richard: "Yes." At this point he gets up and walks over to the end of meadow . . . head down, visibly stooped by the memories bubbling up inside of him. Tashi turns to watch him, fearful that she has driven him away with her question. At that point, where the grass gives way to the forest, he turns and heads back to her. As he approaches, she pats the place to her left, inviting him to sit close. She says nothing, communicating only with her hands and eyes.

Richard: "We were hiking in the Rockies . . . Margot and I with both kids . . . when . . . (*biting his lips*) . . ."

Tashi reaches over and places her hand on top of his. He stops for a moment then takes a deep breath.

Richard: ". . . when we came to this stream. It was June and the water was flowing pretty fast . . . maybe too fast . . . but we had to cross the stream to reach the trail on the other side. The water was up to my knees . . . which meant it was up to the kids' waists. I picked up Jolie, the five-year old, and put her on my shoulders. Bruce, who was six and a half and a little taller, insisted that he could manage by himself. When Jolie saw me allow Bruce to cross on his own, she began crying that she could do it too. After consulting with Margot who was already in the water, I put her down and let both of them wade into the stream. The four of us now formed a line with Margot in front, the two kids in the middle and me bringing up the rear."

Tashi continues looking into his eyes and massaging his hand.

Richard: "Out of nowhere this big, fallen log came shooting around the bend to our immediate left. The bark on it was dark making it impossible to see until it was right on us. At the last minute I saw it and yelled to Margot as I braced myself for contact. The log hit me at the knees, knocking me over before I could sidestep it. By the time I managed to stand up again, the kids were gone. Margot was screaming from the middle of the stream, pointing to the kids who were already 30 feet downstream. Jolie had drifted to the left while Bruce was being swept to the right. Both were floundering as they fought to keep their heads above water."

Tashi: "They couldn't swim?"

Richard: "No . . . although both had started lessons at the YMCA back home. I figured I had time to save one but not both."

Tashi (*shuddering*): "Where was Margot?"

Richard: "She had stumbled on a rock and was now too far from either child to be of any help . . . (*pause*) . . . As Margot screamed for me to do something, I looked at one, then the other . . . then froze. I couldn't move. It was if my feet were set in concrete. A primitive cry formed in my throat as I watched the water carry them further and further out of reach . . . but the cry died stillborn on my lips. I couldn't even yell. By the time I felt my legs moving, both children were out of sight. I climbed out onto the bank and raced toward where I had last seen them bobbing in the water . . . but it was too late. When I finally found them further down the stream, they had been pushed together against a large rock. Both were blue in the face, dead."

At this, Tashi begins sobbing, then screaming. "Oh no, oh no. That is so terrible, Richard. I don't want to believe it." In the ensuing silence Richard struggles to breathe. He chokes repeatedly . . . then turns his back to heave. His whole body shakes with dry convulsions . . . the spasms ending only when Tashi puts her arms around him and pulls him to her chest. As they cling to each other, still trembling with the horror of Richard's story, their mutual cries burst from their lungs, fill the air, then ripple across the meadow like the searing wail of a doe forced to witness a bear devouring her newborn fawn.

Tashi waits until her heart stops pounding before speaking. Leaning against him, her lips almost touching his ear, she says the only thing she can think of, "I love you, Richard. I love you." Over and over she repeats the words . . . until he finally turns his head and presses his lips to hers. They remain kissing, their lips frozen in time, even as the sun begins its descent to the horizon. To anyone entering the meadow at that time, the two figures, locked in unmoving embrace, might easily be mistaken for a statue, a sculpture in marble or stone dedicated to the enduring joy of love.

Tashi is the first to move as she pulls away and falls back onto the grass, her arms outstretched in welcome. Still breathing heavily, Richard kneels at her side, then wipes the tears from his eyes lest they fall onto her face. His mouth hangs open in speechless adoration. When he shakes his head in disbelief, she smiles, then reaches up and pulls him to her. Leaning over, he takes her head between his hands and brushes his lips against her forehead, then her nose. When she sticks her tongue out ever so slightly, he grasps it with his lips and draws it into his mouth. She giggles coyly, then wriggles free, pushing his head down onto her chest.

As he runs his lips up and down her neck, she reaches over with her left hand and undoes the top button on her blouse. Still kneeling, he slides his lips onto the bare flesh now accessible to him. "You taste salty," he whispers. "Does it make you want more of me," she teases. Before he can say yes, she reaches up and undoes the second button; the lack of a bra is now quite evident. As the folds of her blouse open, he runs his lips into her cleavage, mesmerized by the smell and taste of her bare flesh. Inch by delicious inch he makes his way down between her breasts, kissing and licking, until he feels her undoing the last of the three buttons. His heart begins to race. Freed of all thinking, he lets his animal instincts guide him. With eyes closed, he follows the movements of her hands as she pulls her blouse to the sides, offering him unfettered access to both breasts. Like an underground mole seeking the nourishment of unseen roots he moves his lips one way then the other, feeling, smelling, tasting . . . until at last he comes upon his prize. With his tongue he circles her areola, then, in mindless bliss, fastens his lips on her nipple. His breathing slows; he stops trembling. Slowly, all the day's torments with their images of water, children, panic and death yield to the quiet joy of sucking. Through it all Tashi purrs softly with the contentment of a cat nursing her newborn kittens.

As the heat of day gives way to the cool of evening, he remains by her side, drawing from her teats the milk of forgiveness he could never give himself. She brushes back his hair and matches his slow breathing with her own as together they drink their fill of that peace granted only to the innocent of heart. When he has satisfied himself of her mercies, he slumps to the grass beside her, still holding her in his arms. "Tashi, sweetheart," he whispers. "I have not known this kind of joy since I was a little boy."

Dusk now hurries toward nightfall; a hermit thrush deep in the forest echoes the pair's joy with a song of its own. Tashi listens, looks up into the darkening sky and pulls Richard tight. Out of sight, the fox and rabbit, enemies by day, retire to their separate burrows and the comfort of a mate's warming embrace. A lonely owl hoots at the ascending moon. Across the meadow forget-me-nots and lupines close their blossoms, girding themselves against the coming cold. All is still.

21   **The Concert**

Throughout July and August Richard and Tashi continue meeting at the restaurant for their concerts and taking occasional walks to the meadow. The cello concerto that Richard is working on provides further opportunities for interaction, much to the consternation of Tashi's parents who continue to see Richard as an inappropriate mate for their daughter. Her new show of independence poses particular problems for Asadour who has always taken her obedience for granted. With each act of rebellion, he experiences a shrinking of power. On a morning midway through August, his frustration finally erupts. With breakfast over and Tashi upstairs in her bedroom, he turns to his wife, "What are we supposed to do now? The girl who never questioned my authority is now thumbing her nose at me whenever she wants to. I don't like it one damn bit."

Esther: "She's growing up, Asi. When they get that age, kids . . . "

Asadour (*interrupting*): "She's only 19 for Christ's sake. She's still in school . . . and I'm paying \$40,000 a year for it. I hope she realizes that I could cut her off at any moment . . . and that would be the end of Harvard."

Esther (*squinting*): "You wouldn't do that, would you, Asi? Think of how much a Harvard degree will mean to her career."

Asadour: "Well, why isn't she thinking that way? If she's willing to take my money, why isn't she willing to take my advice? Doesn't she realize that I've been around for a lot more years than she has . . . that I know what the hell I'm talking about? Why doesn't . . . ?"

Esther (*interrupting*): "Please Asi, she might hear you."

Asadour (*shouting*): "I don't care if she does. Maybe she needs to be reminded that I'm her father and that I deserve some respect."

Esther: "Of course she respects you. She's always turned to you for advice."

Asadour: "Then why is she turning against me now? Is she saying that she knows more about people than I do? Why the hell is she insisting on seeing this guy Richard when I've made it clear that he's a dangerous character? Did something happen to convince her that she knows better than I do? . . . (*pause*) . . . I told her to stop seeing him and she's doing it anyway . . . in direct contradiction to my orders. I see that as a slap in the face, don't you?"

Esther: "Maybe college is changing her. She's in with a lot of kids her own age and . . . "

Asadour (*interrupting*): "Don't be silly. I didn't stop obeying my parents when I got to college . . . did you?"

Esther: "Well, I was never very strong . . . not like Eleanor."

While she can't make out her father's precise words from her bedroom, Tashi can tell from the shouting that he is angry . . . and that probably means he's mad at her. She cringes at the thought, then quietly slips down the stairs and out the back door. Ten minutes later she is knocking on Richard's cottage door. Once inside the door she holds her arms open for a welcoming hug. He rises from the piano bench and comes toward her, smiling. For the first time . . . ever . . . he greets her not with a hug but a kiss. She is startled but responds by wrapping her arms around his neck. As the morning wears on, it is clear that much has changed. His response suggests a new buoyancy, a greater freedom in both actions and words. He seems eager to touch her . . . even kisses her on the neck when they stand next to each other. The term 'darling' passes between them often. He's clearly no longer avoiding attachment, but may not be ready for the intimacies of love-making, even though she repeatedly signals her willingness to take that step. Having waited this long, she is hesitant to push the issue and risk reigniting his fears.

When they go over his preliminary sketches for the cello concerto, she can see a difference in his music as well. "I love what you've done so far, Richard. It's quite bold, especially in the first movement. I don't see any evidence of that old problem . . . you know, the trouble you've had bringing pieces to a conclusion. At least in the first movement, you seem quite decisive . . . a great build-up followed by an unmistakable climax. I think audiences will love it."

Richard: "Thanks. It feels different even to me. I'm not sure why, but it's coming more easily now. Before I always held back . . . as if it were a sin to resolve the tension. Sounds crazy, doesn't it? What could possibly be sinful about bringing matters to a close?"

Tashi: "You still don't know?"

Richard: "No, It's a mystery to me. Why, do you think *you* know?"

Tashi: "What I know . . . or think I know . . . is not important. It's what you know about yourself that counts."

The issue is left hanging as they go over the score in greater detail. Tashi offers many suggestions for making the cello part more playable . . . but remains consistently supportive of Richard's efforts. For his part, Richard cannot help comparing Tashi's enthusiastic encouragement with Margot's refusal to grant approval even when she knew it was warranted. The comparison of the two women triggers a string of thoughts. Perhaps it's Tashi's affection that's making the difference in his music. After all, she continues to be loving despite what she knows about his past. He's not sure. Music aside, it's clear that she has a lot to do with the fact that he no longer despises himself for his past failures. He is aware, of course, that the old doubts and self-loathing could still come back. It's too early to know for sure.

When the summer ends, Tashi returns to Harvard for her junior year. Not long after she gets there, she sends Richard an e-mail saying that the cello concerto is scheduled to be performed in late December. That means that all parts must be ready by sometime in October . . . copied, engraved, and checked for mistakes. Two rehearsals have been scheduled and Richard, as composer, is expected to attend both.

Richard writes back thanking her for the information. As a postscript he adds that talks with the judge about Raul are going well . . . and that Tashi's letter about forgiving the boy for what he did has made an impression.

He goes on to ask what she has heard from Berklee about possibilities for some online instruction.

In her next e-mail Tashi acknowledges her letter to the judge and shares details about what she has learned at Berklee. She goes on to say that she still likes the idea of playing a CD of Raul's music during intermissions at the restaurant. Her tone is consistently upbeat, leaving no doubt of her steadfast conviction that what happened in the forest three years ago must not stand in the way of the boy's future.

In the same e-mail she adds that Gretchen Rudolf, the woman who conducted his Iglesia piece in Stuttgart, will be conducting the Boston Symphony earlier in December and has graciously consented to make a guest appearance with the Harvard-Radcliffe orchestra (she is an alumna herself). If she is to conduct the cello concerto score, she needs to see the score at least a month in advance.

For the next two months Richard works furiously to finish in time. Throughout it all he receives a steady stream of encouragement from Tashi's e-mails and phone calls. Well before he has finished the whole score, he sends her a copy of the cello part and a piano reduction of the orchestral score so she can start practicing with the other students.

At the first rehearsal in December, Gretchen introduces herself to Richard. His fears of her rumored haughtiness are quickly dissipated when she greets him warmly and invites him to stand next to her at the podium. Throughout the piece, she stops often to ask his advice, particularly regarding dynamics and tempo. Richard, who is accustomed to working alone in his mountain studio, is made nervous with all the attention, including nods from Tashi who as soloist is positioned in front of the orchestra to the left, and inquiries from the conductor whose smiles, even to one as innocent as Richard, are beginning to suggest more than a professional interest.

At the end of the rehearsal Gretchen invites Richard to have lunch at the faculty club. Over tomato bisque soup and salad, she lavishes praise on the composer for his Iglesia de los Dolores, the piece she conducted in Stuttgart. "I just wish you had been there, Richard, so you could have heard all the applause. *(Shaking her head)* Why didn't you come? We were willing to pay all your expenses . . . *(pause)* . . . and besides, you and I could have gotten to know each other a little." As Richard searches for a response, she assures him that as conductor of the Stuttgart Symphony, she is in a position to further his career by performing his works all over Europe. To an aspiring but still unknown composer, the offer is magnanimous enough to hint of divine intervention.

Half way through his soup, he begins to awaken not only to her words but to her beauty. With his hopes rising, he lets his eyes roam casually around her face and shoulders. When she stoops to pick up a fallen napkin, he studies her breasts as well. Her size alone suggests a figure from Wagner's ring cycle . . . tall, voluptuous, statuesque, a woman whose commanding presence makes it clear that she is not to be trifled with. She leans forward now, quite aware of his interest, and whispers, "Would you like to come to Germany next year and spend some time with me in Stuttgart?" It is a generous offer, an almost guaranteed ticket to world-wide acceptance as a composer; it also comes with obvious romantic overtones. He hesitates . . . then offers a non-committal response. "That's really kind of you Gretchen; let me sleep on it."

The concert itself is held in Sander's Theater, a small, intimate auditorium inside Memorial Hall, that colorful but, to some, grotesque structure built to honor Harvard men who gave their lives in the Civil War. In the audience, half-way back, Asadour, Esther, and Bapu sit nervously awaiting the arrival on stage of Tashi and Ms. Rudolf. Richard has a seat off to the right, closer to the orchestra, where he scrutinizes the program, checking among other things to see what they say about Tashi. After so many years of calling her Tashi, he is more than a little startled to see the cello soloist referred to as Eleanor Said, Harvard '10. In the back of the program, he checks to see what they say about the composer. The biographical information is all there . . . plus a few quotes from reviewers, the primary one from a newspaper in Stuttgart. He is pleased to see himself referred to as "one of America's most promising young composers," but rather less excited to read, "He has still not learned how to finish a piece convincingly." Closing the program, he looks around, hoping to see someone he knows. Eventually his eyes fall on Tashi's parents and grandfather over in the middle section; he waves and smiles. Esther is about to wave back when Asadour pulls her arm down, whispering, "Don't do anything to encourage him." Bapu notices the exchange and stands to wave enthusiastically. Richard rises to return the greeting.

The lights dim. When the principal violinist emerges to tune the orchestra, there is a scattering of polite applause. The audience grows more enthusiastic when the conductor strides to the podium, turns and then bows. The concert opens with Wagner's Overture to Lohengrin. Gretchen's love for her childhood idol is quickly apparent in the rich, lush sound she manages to pull from the all-student orchestra. From the soft, atmospheric notes of the opening to the hushed, fade-away of the ending, the audience listens in awe as she draws everyone into the music's other-worldly spell. It is over all too soon . . . followed by a few seconds of breathless silence . . . then a deluge of hysterical applause after which the conductor leaves the stage. From his seat in the audience Richard grows concerned that the Wagner overture will prove too tough an act to follow.

He doesn't have long to wait. The applause starts the moment the stage door opens and grows to a deafening roar as Tashi emerges in a Chinese-red strapless gown with the tuxedoed Ms. Rudolf just behind her. At the podium the contrast in figures is striking . . . with the slender, comely, black-haired youth bowing alongside the tall, blonde, full-figured Fuehrerin. To an opera lover, it is as if Puccini's Mimi, delicate of health and demure in posture were standing shoulder to shoulder with Wagner's Brunnhilde, fearless daughter of Wotan, defiant even unto immolation.

From the outset Tashi's nervousness can be seen in the way she bites her lips; her anxiety becomes obvious even to the most casual listener when she trips over the cadenza in the first movement. Gretchen grimaces but smiles when Tashi recovers quickly and finishes the movement with a sixteenth-note flourish ending in a dramatic double stop fortissimo. The cello doesn't really come into its own, however, until the slow, second movement where Richard's genius for melody, until now obscured by the demands of virtuosic display, is allowed to soar without restraint. To those who took time to read the program notes, it is clear from the way Tashi plays, with eyes closed, her head swaying in mindless ecstasy, that the composer penned these transcendent phrases with her in mind. Each sound, warm and unbridled in its passion, leaps from her instrument as if she were testifying to a secret, undying love between composer and soloist. Not a cough or whisper can be heard throughout the auditorium. When the movement ends, many listeners, although fully conscious of concert etiquette, throw off restraint and burst into tearful applause. A few stand as they clap; others sit daubing their cheeks with tissues.

The magic continues throughout the third movement. As the music approaches its final climax, Gretchen opens her arms, begging the players for more volume. Against a sustained major chord in the strings and brass, the timpanist starts his drum roll . . . softly at first, then slowly growing louder until its thunder matches the sound of the whole orchestra. No one in the audience can breathe; many inch forward in their seats. All eyes are on the cellist as she works her way feverishly up the scale, following Gretchen's lead every note of the way, her bow whipping back and forth in a fury of 32nd notes until it gives way to a single, searing, high G. At this point strings, woodwinds, brass and percussion all come together in a triumphant frenzy of sound. The final note lingers high in the air, mushrooming louder until the orchestra has filled the hall with an ear-splitting G major chord. As the timpanist brings his mallet down for the final note, Gretchen clenches her fist in victory, then collapses to her knees, still clinging to her baton.

The applause is electric. Not a listener remains sitting as Tashi and Gretchen are called back for bow after bow. After returning for the third time, Gretchen looks out into the audience, locates Richard, and blows him a kiss. With a sweep of her hand, she beckons him up on stage. With Tashi on one side and Gretchen on the other, Richard bows to the cheering throng, then turns around to applaud the orchestra. Once the ritual is concluded, everyone files out into the foyer for intermission.

That evening at the hotel reception in Harvard Square Tashi joins Bapu and her parents at a reserved table. Several of Tashi's college friends join them. The talk is animated, much of it about the soloist, some about the composer . . . all of it about music. Asadour's bass voice can be heard above all others. After a mini-lecture on how he helped nurture Eleanor's love for music, punctuated by occasional nods for confirmation from his wife, he sits down. As others go on to share their own musical experiences, he closes his eyes and falls asleep. From his seat across the table, Bapu elbows Esther and points. "Too much to eat at lunch?"

"No," she replies, "We both had a small sandwich."

"Really? Perhaps you stayed up too late last night," he continues.

"We were in bed by 10:00," she answers (*looking over at her dozing husband*) "I don't know what's wrong. Perhaps it's the heat; it's rather warm in here, don't you think?"

Bapu persists. "Maybe, but not so warm that anyone else has fallen asleep . . . (*pause*) . . . I can think of another, less generous explanation . . . (*pause*) . . . Could it be that Asi loves to talk, but gets bored when he's no longer the center of attention, so bored in fact that he actually falls asleep even with other people at the table . . . (*pause*) . . . Have you ever seen it happen before?"

Esther (*shaking her head*): "I've seen him look out the window and close his eyes . . . but never actually fall asleep."

An hour later Richard makes his appearance. After scanning the large reception room, he spots Tashi sitting against the wall, drink in hand, talking with family and a host of well-wishers. Richard waves a greeting, but is immediately taken by the arm by Gretchen who has entered just behind him. The glow on her handsome face is accentuated by a low-cut saffron gown featuring tanned shoulders and tantalizing cleavage. As they stand, looking for a table, she begins talking about the differences she sees between Iglesia and the concerto just performed . . . much bolder, she says, greater command of materials, and a more satisfying ending. He smiles a thank you and compliments her in turn on her conducting.

She places her hand on his shoulder and whispers into his ear, "Let's get a table so we can talk." He stops in his tracks . . . trembling . . . then looks over at Tashi who smiles back at him. His heart begins pounding. In his mind's eye he sees a six-year-old boy . . . frozen with fear as he stands at his bedroom door watching his father and mother fling themselves at each other in a frenzied attempt to maim or even kill. Still rooted to the spot, he fails to hear Gretchen say, "Together, my friends and I can help you become famous." What he hears instead is Tashi's voice, the voice in the meadow saying, "I love you Richard; I love you" as she wraps her arms around his neck. Above the din of party noises, he hears that voice more clearly than ever now as she says it over and over, the words growing louder with each iteration until the fearsome image of his parents begins to fade. With eyes half-closed, he watches as her words perform their magic, sliding back and forth now like an eraser on a blackboard, rubbing out one memory after another, effacing faces, irons, ashtrays, blood and screams until the gruesome tableau disappears altogether. As his breathing returns to normal, he rubs his eyes and looks around. Gradually, the room and all its guests come back into focus. Outwardly everything looks the same as before . . . but something has changed inside. He is conscious of a new clarity, a lighter, more spacious feeling. When he gropes for the image that has haunted him since childhood, he can't find it. Gone are the ghosts of the past; gone are the icy tongs of fear that for years have held his will in thrall. In their place he senses a new openness, a new freedom to move, to decide, to choose according to his own lights. He lowers his head in silent gratitude. No longer trembling, he reaches out to shake Gretchen's hand . . . then makes his apologies and heads for Tashi's table.

Bapu is the first to greet him. "Well done sir . . . I enjoyed every note."

Tashi: "Yeah, but how about that B flat in the first movement cadenza, the one that should have been an A?"

Bapu: "Well, O.K. Every note but one."

Richard *(laughing)*: "Hmm. And that was my favorite note."

Asadour dozes with eyes closed as the banter continues. Unable to stand the tension, Esther says, "Richard, please sit down (*pointing to the empty chair next to Bapu*)."

Tashi: "I want him next to me . . . if he is willing."

Richard: "How could I resist such an attractive offer?" (*sitting down next to her*).

Tashi (*nuzzling against Richard*): "I saw you standing there with Gretchen. Did she offer you the moon if you would sleep with her?"

Richard: "Just an asteroid or two. Nothing I can't do without."

Tashi (*purring*): "I'm glad to hear that."

Bapu: "So Richard, how did you like the way Ms. Rudolf conducted your piece?"

Richard: "I thought she squeezed every bit of emotion from the score that she could. She definitely has a flair for the dramatic . . . (*pause*) . . . Did it come across as too romantic?"

Bapu: "Not at all . . . at least for my taste . . . (*pause)* . . . I think your sidekick (*pointing to Tashi*) kept it from becoming maudlin. I thought her technique was marvelous, especially in the second movement."

Asadour (*abruptly opening his eyes*) "What do you mean, sidekick? She was the star of the show; the audience showed that by giving her most of the applause. Let's face it . . . anybody can write a piece of music . . . I'm sure I could do it myself . . . but without a performer to bring it to life, it's just notes on a page. Eleanor made that piece work. So please . . . let's not refer to her as a sidekick. It's demeaning."

Tashi (*shaking her head*): "I disagree. Yes, Richard put notes on a page, notes that have to be interpreted by someone else before they take on meaning . . . but they were not just any old notes. They came out of the composer's imagination. If it weren't for Richard's inspiration, the soloist, no matter how good, would have nothing to play. I personally was moved by what he wrote. If you liked what came out of my instrument, you should thank Richard for telling me what to play."

Richard (*nodding*): "Those are kind words, Tash, but let's remember that I didn't really *create* the sounds you played. They came to me out of the blue. As every composer knows, no matter how hard you try, you can't force the notes to come. They have a life of their own; when they come, arising spontaneously from the depths of your psyche, they come as gifts. When that happens, the only feeling that makes sense to me is gratitude."

Asadour (*reddening*): "I don't believe that for a minute. People who argue that way are just trying to escape responsibility for what they create. When I finish writing a book, for example, what I feel is not gratitude but pride. I see it as a product of all the reports and studies I have read plus the countless hours I've spent thinking about the material. Without my skill and a lot of hard work the book would never have made it into the world. So, I feel justified in crowing about it a little."

Bapu: "Just a little?"

Tashi (*turning to Richard*): "I think it's time to go. Do you want me to go back to the hotel with you? I'm ready for a more private celebration."

Richard (*rising*): "Yes. I'm a bit tired myself."

Tashi (*coyly*): "That's not exactly what I had in mind."

Esther (*nervously*): "Are you going to be alright Eleanor . . . . I mean . . . after all this excitement?"

Tashi: "Mom, I'm grown up now. I can take care of myself."

At the hotel they go immediately to Richard's room, not stopping for either drinks or dinner. Once inside, Tashi heads for the bathroom, emerging minutes later wrapped in a towel.

"What happened to your clothes?" Richard asks, feigning innocence.

Tashi (*turning to face him*): "Who needs clothes at a time like this, darling?" With a wave of her arm, she jumps into bed, tossing the towel onto the floor. As he bends to kiss her, she grabs him by the shoulders and pulls him onto the bed. Together they remove his socks, shirt, pants, and underwear. Finally, they are both naked.

Tashi: "I like you better this way. For once, I get to know all of you." At that point she reaches over to the bedside table and turns off the lamp.

Richard: "How can you see me if the room is dark?"

Tashi (*giggling*): "What I can't see, I can feel."

Richard (*smiling*): "Do you think we know each other well enough to be doing this?"

Tashi: "It's been almost six years. We're not exactly strangers."

Richard (*boldly*): "That's true . . . (*pause*) . . . Maybe we should think about getting married" (*brushing his lips against hers*).

Tashi (*nodding*): "Interesting idea."

Richard (*cupping her breasts*): "Is that all you can say? I'm telling you I want to get married."

Tashi: "I'm glad to hear that . . . really (*smiling*)."

Richard: "Well?" (*rubbing her nipple between thumb and finger*).

Tashi: "Well what (*mischievous grin*)?"

Richard: "Will you stop teasing. I'm being serious."

Tashi (*lifting her head from the pillow*): "What do you want me to say, darling?"

Richard (*voice rising*): "Just give me your answer."

Tashi: "I haven't heard a question yet. Have I missed something?" (*eyes sparkling*).

Richard (*forehead wrinkled*): "I've told you I want us to be husband and wife . . . to live together as a married couple. How can I be any clearer?"

Tashi: "Yes, I heard that's what *you* want. Don't you want to know what *I* want? (*eyebrows lifted*) All you have to do is ask."

Richard: "Oh Jesus. So that's it . . . (*pause*) . . . I'm sorry . . . O.K . . . .(*softly, with extreme tenderness*) Tashi, will you marry me?"

Tashi: "Oh Richard (*tears running down her cheek*). Do you know how long I have waited to hear you say that? My darling . . . of course I will marry you. There is nothing in life that means more to me than to be your wife. I've wanted to be your mate ever since we met six years ago."

Richard: "But you were only 14 back then. How could you have known?"

Tashi: "There are things that only we females know . . . and you don't have to be grown up to know them. Remember the day we met at your house . . . and I said that an 18-year difference in age wasn't all that much between husband and wife. You thought I was being silly . . . (*pause*) . . . I was serious. I already knew that we belonged together."

Richard: "I wish I had known as well. I'm sorry Tash . . . sorry that it has taken me so long to wake up to what I feel. It's part of the same old problem I guess . . . not being able to make up my mind . . . which is strange since it is so clear to me now . . . (*pause*) . . . Is there some way I can make it up to you?"

Tashi: "Yes (*reaching up and pulling him down on top of her*). Come into me darling. Let me feel you inside me. Treat me like your wife, the person you love above all else in the world. Possess me. Make me yours."

Richard (*squinting*): "I thought women, at least modern women, didn't like being possessed. It sounds old-fashioned . . . like I own you."

Tashi: "I want to belong to you . . . and you to me. I want the whole world to know that we belong to each other. And that's why getting married is so important. Even if we can't live together until I finish school, once we are married, everyone will know that we are a couple. It's not enough that you and I know it. I want all our friends and family, people we haven't even met yet, to know that there is a bond between us that surpasses all other relationships we might have."

With eyes fixed on hers, he moistens his manhood with the cream glistening on her puffy lips, then slowly slides into the soft darkness within. She yields, throws her head back on the pillow and closes her eyes.

Tashi (*breathless*): "Tell me again that you love me Richard. Tell me."

Richard *(grinning)*: "Hmmm. Let me think about it."

Tashi: "You devil (*raising her head and wrapping her legs around his*). Tell me or I'll squeeze you to death."

Richard: "O.K., O.K. You win. I love you."

Tashi: "But how much? (*tightening her grip*)?"

Richard (*with breath accelerating as he plunges deeper into her pelvis*): "This much Tashi, this much my love . . . I love you . . . I adore you . . . oh God . . . you are everything in the world to me (*collapsing onto her breasts as his body jerks and spasms into her*)." Seconds later her moans fill the room, echoing his ecstasy.

Silence follows as words give way to the peace of physical union.

She holds him tight, brushing back the curls hanging over his forehead, then adding in a whisper: "Now sir, do you take this woman to be your lawfully wedded wife . . . to love and cherish, to make breakfast for her every morning, to make love to her every night?" (*laughing*).

Richard (*with mock seriousness*): "Does that include weekends? I may need a break."

Tashi: "24/7 . . . 52 weeks a year."

Richard: "You drive a hard bargain. We may need Kwatz's consent. He doesn't like to sleep alone."

Tashi: "He can sleep at the end of the bed. I want your butt next to mine every night of the year."

Richard (*lips moving back and forth across hers*): "Is it O.K if I turn over during the night. My back might need it."

Tashi: "As long as you let me hug you."

Richard: "I think I can handle it."

Tashi (*teasing*): "Kiss me again . . . pretend that you mean it this time."

Gripping her head with both hands, he locks his lips on hers, letting his warm breath flow into her lungs. Their tongues play a caressing game, first in one mouth, then the other. Who is kissing whom it is impossible to say. As the night unfolds, neither pulls away, not wanting this dream of oneness to end. They are still there when the morning sun calls them from their sleep, welcoming them to a new day.

www.ingramcontent.com/pod-product-compliance
Lightning Source LLC
Chambersburg PA
CBHW060917190726
48286CB00002B/535